"AN EXCELL...
FOCUSING ON C...... ....D
PUZZLES, HORROR, TERROR AND
SPOOKINESS AT CHRISTMAS."
Booklist

"AND AT CHRISTMAS-TIME, TOO"

Whenever some despicable thing is done during the month of December, the general reaction is a disapproving "and at Christmas-time, too," as though it would be less despicable if done at any other time.

This, you may be sure, has not escaped the attention of crime writers. Consequently, we bring you a dozen fictional transgressions and misdeeds that are associated with Christmas. If by any chance you feel a bit cloyed at that time of year and need a salutary counterweight to the saccharinity of the season (and which of us does not, now and then) here is the book for you.

So stretch out beside the Christmas tree and read.

—From the Introduction by Isaac Asimov

"IT'S TIME TO TRIM THE TREE, STRETCH OUT BESIDE IT AND WATCH AS A DOZEN MASTERS OF MALEVOLENCE BURY THE BODIES."

Chicago Tribune

Avon Books are available at special quantity discounts for bulk purchases for sales promotions, premiums, fund raising or educational use. Special books, or book excerpts, can also be created to fit specific needs.

For details write or telephone the office of the Director of Special Markets, Avon Books, Dept. FP, 105 Madison Avenue, New York, New York 10016, 212-481-5653.

THE TWELVE CRIMES OF CHRISTMAS

EDITED BY CAROL-LYNN RÖSSEL WAUGH,
MARTIN HARRY GREENBERG AND
ISAAC ASIMOV

AVON BOOKS ◆ NEW YORK

THE TWELVE CRIMES OF CHRISTMAS is an original
publication of Avon Books. This work has never before appeared in
book form.

AVON BOOKS
A division of
The Hearst Corporation
105 Madison Avenue
New York, New York 10016

First Avon Books Printing: November 1981

AVON TRADEMARK REG. U.S. PAT. OFF. AND IN OTHER COUNTRIES, MARCA
REGISTRADA, HECHO EN CANADA

Printed in Canada

UNV   10   9   8   7   6   5   4   5   4

To Charles Gordon Waugh

C-L. R. W.,
M. H. G. and
I. A.

CONTENTS

CONTENTS

ACKNOWLEDGMENTS

"The Thirteenth Day of Christmas," by Isaac Asimov. Copyright © 1977 by Isaac Asimov. First published in *Ellery Queen's Mystery Magazine.* Reprinted by permission of the author.

"Blind Man's Hood," by John Dickson Carr. From *The Department of Queer Complaints,* by Carter Dickson. Copyright © 1940 by William Morrow and Company; renewed 1968 by John Dickson Carr. Reprinted by permission of the publishers.

"The Adventure of the Unique Dickensians," by August Derleth. Copyright © 1968 by Arkham House Publishers, Inc. Reprinted by permission of Arkham House Publishers, Inc., Sauk City, Wisconsin.

"Death on Christmas Eve," by Stanley Ellin. Copyright © 1950, 1978 by Stanley Ellin. First published in *Ellery Queen's Mystery Magazine.* Reprinted by permission of Curtis Brown, Ltd.

"The Problem of the Christmas Steeple," by Edward D. Hoch. Copyright © 1976 by Edward D. Hoch. First published in *Ellery Queen's Mystery Magazine.* Reprinted by permission of Larry Sternig Literary Agency.

"By the Chimney with Care," by Nick O'Donohoe. Copyright © 1978 by Renown Publications, Inc. First published in *Mike Shayne's Mystery Magazine.* Reprinted by permission of Hintz Literary Agency.

Introduction: NOEL, NOEL!

by Isaac Asimov

Throughout the North Temperate zone (in which western civilization arose and matured), there is always a reminder in the sky that things will not last.

All through the summer and fall, when the world is smiling and green things are growing and harvests are collected and stored, the Sun marks out a path in the sky that each day is lower toward the southern horizon than on the day before. The lower the sun is, the less intense is its warmth and the shorter the days get, so that the less-intense warmth has ever less time to do its job.

This is a sobering reminder in the very midst of prosperity that winter is coming, a time of dreary cold and of the apparent death of the plant world.

Yet the decline of the Sun slows and finally there comes a time when the Sun halts its southward drop altogether and then begins to mark out a higher and higher path each day than the day before. The weather continues cold for months after the Sun starts its rise, but that rise is a portent and a promise in the midst of decay that the winter will not last forever and that spring is coming, and with it a renewal of warmth and life and happiness.

We know exactly what causes this. We know about the Earth's tipped axis and how it affects the Sun's apparent path in the sky in the course of the Earth's annual revolution about its luminary.

Primitive man did not know this, however, nor did he have any concept of the Sun being kept on course by the inexorability of celestial mechanics. He felt the fall and rise of the Sun to be the work of all-powerful gods, who acted out of obscure motives of their own, either in whimsical benevolence or petulant anger.

In short, primitive man could never be sure that the Sun would not, on *this* occasion, continue its weary decline until it disappeared forever beyond the southern horizon, leaving Earth to eternal winter and death.

Consequently, on or about the time when the Sun halts in its southern flight and begins its climb back to warmth and life (this turning point—the "winter solstice"—comes on December 21, by our calendar), there is a vast outpouring of relief. It is natural that the time be celebrated with grand festivals and merrymaking.

To the Romans, Saturn was the god of the spring planting and was eventually viewed as being in charge of agriculture generally. When the Sun made its turn, therefore, and there was the promise of successful spring planting to come, the Romans considered it the result of Saturn's benevolent care in setting a limit to the Solar decline. Their winter solstice festival was thus in his honor and was called the "Saturnalia."

It was the happiest and most popular of all the Roman festivals and it was eventually extended to seven days in length, running from December 17 to December 24. It was a time of unrestrained gaiety and feasting; public offices, businesses, schools were all closed in its honor; servants and slaves were allowed a period of relative freedom in which they might mingle with their masters in mutual bonhomie; gifts were exchanged. Such was the all-round benevolence of the time that a little sexual license was winked at. (It was this last that incurred the wrath of moralists and has caused "saturnalian" to refer to anything marked by orgies of drink and sex.)

By the third century of our era, however, the Roman gods were moribund, and eastern religions more and more swayed the hearts and minds of Roman citizens. Yet one aspect of the old religion remained untouchable, and that was the Saturnalia. Whatever else of their old ways the peoples of the Roman Empire were willing to give up, the Saturnalia had to remain.

The most prominent of the new religions was, for a time, Mithraism, which was a form of Sun worship. Mithraists saw in the fall and rise of the Sun the promise that after man's death there would come a glorious resurrection. The Saturnalia suited them, therefore, and they added to it a climactic day of their own. On December 25, the day after the conclusion of the Saturnalia, the Mithraists celebrated the birth of Mithra, the symbolic representation of the light of the Sun. This great "day of the invincible Sun" was the most popular aspect of Mithraism.

The Mithraists made the major mistake, however, of excluding women from their religious rituals. The rival religion of Christianity wisely included women, which insured that while many fathers were Mithraists, many mothers were Christians, and the children were far more apt to follow their mothers' early teachings than their fathers' later ones.

Even so, Mithraism remained hard to defeat while it celebrated the Saturnalia and the day of the invincible Sun. Some time after A.D. 300, therefore, the Christians invented Christmas. It became proper for Christians to enjoy December 25 and all the saturnalian happiness associated with it, provided they called it a celebration of the birth of Jesus the Son and not Mithra the Sun. (There is, of course, no Biblical warrant for December 25 as the day of the birth of Jesus.)

The Saturnalia is, in any case, the victor, and the Christmas we now celebrate is only formally Jesus' birthday. For many, that aspect of it is quickly disposed of with minimum fuss. It is the Saturnalia on which our attention is fixed—the gift-giving, the holiday cheer, the time of good feeling, the eating, drinking, celebrating.

In fact, in the modern United States we have a much bigger and better Saturnalia than ever the Romans did. From the moment Thanksgiving is over, all the traditional Christmas decorations begin to blossom forth in businesses, homes and streets, and we all enjoy (or sometimes suffer) an intense four-week celebration. Even the permitted sexual license survives—in attenuated form— in the tradition of kissing under the mistletoe. What we celebrate is a purely pagan festival presided over by Santa Claus—a comparatively modern invention, frozen into his present form in 1822, with the publication of "A Visit from St. Nicholas," by Clement C. Moore.

Another modern myth that has grown up around Christmas is that it is a time of universal benevolence in which even the hardest heart will soften, a theme im-

mortalized forever in Charles Dickens's "A Christmas
Carol," first published in 1843.

As a result, whenever some despicable thing is done
during the month of December, the general reaction is a
disapproving "and at Christmastime, too," as though it
would be less despicable if done at any other time.

This, you may be sure, has not escaped the attention
of crime writers. In their search for graphic wrongdoing,
they need not stress violence or sex if they do not wish to;
they need only place the deed in the month of December
and draw attention to Christmas.

Consequently, we bring you a dozen fictional transgressions and misdeeds that are somehow associated with
Christmas. If by any chance you feel a bit cloyed at that
time of year and need a salutary counterweight to the
saccharinity of the season (and which of us does not, now
and then), here is the book for you.

So stretch out beside the Christmas tree and read.

CHRISTMAS PARTY

by Rex Stout

America's best-known fictional detective is most likely Rex Stout's corpulent creation, Nero Wolfe. His New York brownstone, its inhabitants, his lifestyle and idiosyncracies are nearly as familiar to the reader as are Holmes's digs at 221B Baker Street.

Stout was in love with the English language and a stickler (as is Nero Wolfe) for its correct usage. He used it gracefully, ingeniously and with good humor.

I

"I'm sorry, sir," I said. I tried to sound sorry. "But I told you two days ago, Monday, that I had a date for Friday afternoon, and you said all right. So I'll drive you to Long Island Saturday or Sunday."

Nero Wolfe shook his head. "That won't do. Mr. Thompson's ship docks Friday morning, and he will be at Mr. Hewitt's place only until Saturday noon, when he leaves for New Orleans. As you know, he is the best hybridizer in England, and I am grateful to Mr. Hewitt for inviting me to spend a few hours with him. As I remember, the drive takes about an hour and a half, so we should leave at twelve-thirty."

I decided to count ten, and swiveled my chair, facing my desk, so as to have privacy for it. As usual when we have no important case going, we had been getting on each other's nerves for a week, and I admit I was a little touchy, but his taking it for granted like that was a lit-

tle too much. When I had finished the count I turned my
head, to where he was perched on his throne behind his
desk, and darned if he hadn't gone back to his book,
making it plain that he regarded it as settled. That was
much too much. I swiveled my chair to confront him.

"I really am sorry," I said, not trying to sound sorry,
"but I have to keep that date Friday afternoon. It's a
Christmas party at the office of Kurt Bottweill—you remember him, we did a job for him a few months ago, the
stolen tapestries. You may not remember a member of
his staff named Margot Dickey, but I do. I have been
seeing her some, and I promised her I'd go to the party.
We never have a Christmas office party here. As for going
to Long Island, your idea that a car is a death trap if I'm
not driving it is unsound. You can take a taxi, or hire a
Baxter man, or get Saul Panzer to drive you."

Wolfe had lowered his book. "I hope to get some useful
information from Mr. Thompson, and you will take
notes."

"Not if I'm not there. Hewitt's secretary knows orchid
terms as well as I do. So do you."

I admit those last three words were a bit strong, but he
shouldn't have gone back to his book. His lips tightened.
"Archie. How many times in the past year have I asked
you to drive me somewhere?"

"If you call it asking, maybe eighteen or twenty."

"Not excessive, surely. If my feeling that you alone are
to be trusted at the wheel of a car is an aberration, I have
it. We will leave for Mr. Hewitt's place Friday at twelve-
thirty."

So there we were. I took a breath, but I didn't need to
count ten again. If he was to be taught a lesson, and he
certainly needed one, luckily I had in my possession a
document that would make it good. Reaching to my inside breast pocket, I took out a folded sheet of paper.

"I didn't intend," I told him, "to spring this on you until tomorrow, or maybe even later, but I guess it will have
to be now. Just as well, I suppose."

I left my chair, unfolded the paper, and handed it to
him. He put his book down to take it, gave it a look,
shot a glance at me, looked at the paper again, and let it
drop on his desk.

He snorted. "Pfui. What flummery is this?"

"No flummery. As you see, it's a marriage license for

Archie Goodwin and Margot Dickey. It cost me two bucks. I could be mushy about it, but I won't. I will only say that if I am hooked at last, it took an expert. She intends to spread the tidings at the Christmas office party, and of course I have to be there. When you announce you have caught a fish it helps to have the fish present in person. Frankly, I would prefer to drive you to Long Island, but it can't be done."

The effect was all I could have asked. He gazed at me through narrowed eyes long enough to count eleven, then picked up the document and gazed at it. He flicked it from him to the edge of the desk as if it were crawling with germs, and focused on me again.

"You are deranged," he said evenly and distinctly. "Sit down."

I nodded. "I suppose," I agreed, remaining upright, "it's a form of madness, but so what if I've got it? Like what Margot was reading to me the other night—some poet, I think it was some Greek—'O love, resistless in thy might, thou triumphest even—' "

"Shut up and sit down!"

"Yes, sir." I didn't move. "But we're not rushing it. We haven't set the date, and there'll be plenty of time to decide on adjustments. You may not want me here any more, but that's up to you. As far as I'm concerned, I would like to stay. My long association with you has had its flaws, but I would hate to end it. The pay is okay, especially if I get a raise the first of the year, which is a week from Monday. I have grown to regard this old brownstone as my home, although you own it and although there are two creaky boards in the floor of my room. I appreciate working for the greatest private detective in the free world, no matter how eccentric he is. I appreciate being able to go up to the plant rooms whenever I feel like it and look at ten thousand orchids, especially the odontoglossums. I fully appreciate—"

"Sit down!"

"I'm too worked up to sit. I fully appreciate Fritz's cooking. I like the billiard table in the basement. I like West Thirty-fifth Street. I like the one-way glass panel in the front door. I like this rug I'm standing on. I like your favorite color, yellow. I have told Margot all this, and more, including the fact that you are allergic to women. We have discussed it, and we think it may be worth trying, say for a month, when we get back from the honeymoon. My room could be our bedroom, and the other room on that floor could be our living room. There are plenty of closets. We could eat with you, as I have been, or we could eat up there, as you prefer. If the trial works out, new furniture or redecorating would be up to us. She will keep her job with Kurt Bottweill, so she wouldn't be here during the day, and since he's an interior decorator we would get things wholesale. Of course we merely suggest this for your consideration. It's your house."

I picked up my marriage license, folded it, and returned it to my pocket.

His eyes had stayed narrow and his lips tight. "I don't believe it," he growled. "What about Miss Rowan?"

"We won't drag Miss Rowan into this," I said stiffly.

"What about the thousands of others you dally with?"

"Not thousands. Not even a thousand. I'll have to look up 'dally.' They'll get theirs, as Margot has got hers. As you see, I'm deranged only up to a point. I realize—"

"Sit down."

"No, sir. I know this will have to be discussed, but right now you're stirred up and it would be better to wait for a day or two, or maybe more. By Saturday the idea of a woman in the house may have you boiling even worse than you are now, or it may have cooled you down to a simmer. If the former, no discussion will be needed. If the latter, you may decide it's worth a try. I hope you do."

I turned and walked out.

In the hall I hesitated. I could have gone up to my room and phoned from there, but in his present state it was quite possible he would listen in from his desk, and the call I wanted to make was personal. So I got my hat and coat from the rack, let myself out, descended the stoop steps, walked to the drugstore on Ninth Avenue, found the booth unoccupied, and dialed a number. In a moment a musical little voice—more a chirp than a voice —was in my ear.

"Kurt Bottweill's studio, good morning."

"This is Archie Goodwin, Cherry. May I speak to Margot?"

"Why, certainly. Just a moment."

It was a fairly long moment. Then another voice. "Archie, darling!"

"Yes, my own. I've got it."

"I knew you could!"

"Sure, I can do anything. Not only that, you said up to a hundred bucks, and I thought I would have to part with twenty at least, but it only took five. And not only that, but it's on me, because I've already had my money's worth of fun out of it, and more. I'll tell you about it when I see you. Shall I send it up by messenger?"

"No, I don't think—I'd better come and get it. Where are you?"

"In a phone booth. I'd just as soon not go back to the office right now because Mr. Wolfe wants to be alone to boil, so how about the Tulip Bar at the Churchill in twenty minutes? I feel like buying you a drink."

"I feel like buying *you* a drink!"

She should, since I was treating her to a marriage license.

II

When, at three o'clock Friday afternoon, I wriggled out of the taxi at the curb in front of the four-story building in the East Sixties, it was snowing. If it kept up, New York might have an off-white Christmas.

During the two days that had passed since I got my money's worth from the marriage license, the atmosphere around Wolfe's place had not been very seasonable. If we had had a case going, frequent and sustained communication would have been unavoidable, but without one there was nothing that absolutely had to be said, and we said it. Our handling of that trying period showed our true natures. At table, for instance, I was polite and reserved, and spoke, when speaking seemed necessary, in low and cultured tones. When Wolfe spoke he either snapped or barked. Neither of us mentioned the state of bliss I was headed for, or the adjustments that would have to be made, or my Friday date with my fiancée, or his trip to Long Island. But he arranged it somehow, for precisely at twelve-thirty on Friday a black limousine drew up in front of the house, and Wolfe, with the brim of his old black hat turned down and the collar of his new gray overcoat turned up for the snow, descended the stoop, stood massively, the mountain of him, on the bottom step until the uniformed chauffeur had opened the

door, and crossed the sidewalk and climbed in. I watched
it from above, from a window of my room.

I admit I was relieved and felt better. He had unques-
tionably needed a lesson and I didn't regret giving him
one, but if he had passed up a chance for an orchid
powwow with the best hybridizer in England I would
never have heard the last of it. I went down to the kitchen
and ate lunch with Fritz, who was so upset by the atmosphere that he forgot to put the lemon juice in the soufflé.
I wanted to console him by telling him that everything
would be rosy by Christmas, only three days off, but of
course that wouldn't do.

I had a notion to toss a coin to decide whether I would
have a look at the new exhibit of dinosaurs at the Natural History Museum or go to the Bottweill party, but I
was curious to know how Margot was making out with the
license, and also how the other Bottweill personnel were
making out with each other. It was surprising that they
were still making out at all. Cherry Quon's position in the
setup was apparently minor, since she functioned chiefly
as a receptionist and phone-answerer, but I had seen her
black eyes dart daggers at Margot Dickey, who should
have been clear out of her reach. I had gathered that it
was Margot who was mainly relied upon to wrangle
prospective customers into the corral, that Bottweill himself put them under the spell, and that Alfred Kiernan's
part was to make sure that before the spell wore off an
order got signed on the dotted line.

Of course that wasn't all. The order had to be filled,
and that was handled, under Bottweill's supervision, by
Emil Hatch in the workshop. Also funds were required to
buy the ingredients, and they were furnished by a speci-
men named Mrs. Perry Porter Jerome. Margot had told
me that Mrs. Jerome would be at the party and would
bring her son Leo, whom I had never met. According to
Margot, Leo, who had no connection with the Bottweill
business or any other business, devoted his time to two
important activities: getting enough cash from his mother
to keep going as a junior playboy, and stopping the flow
of cash to Bottweill, or at least slowing it down.

It was quite a tangle, an interesting exhibit of bipeds
alive and kicking, and, deciding it promised more entertainment than the dead dinosaurs, I took a taxi to the
East Sixties.

The ground floor of the four-story building, formerly
a deluxe double-width residence, was now a beauty shop.
The second floor was a real-estate office. The third floor
was Kurt Bottweill's workshop, and on top was his studio.
From the vestibule I took the do-it-yourself elevator to
the top, opened the door, and stepped out into the glossy
gold-leaf elegance I had first seen some months back,
when Bottweill had hired Wolfe to find out who had
swiped some tapestries. On that first visit I had decided
that the only big difference between chrome modern and
Bottweill gold-leaf modern was the color, and I still
thought so. Not even skin deep; just a two-hundred-
thousandth of an inch deep. But on the panels and racks
and furniture frames it gave the big skylighted studio
quite a tone, and the rugs and drapes and pictures, all
modern, joined in. It would have been a fine den for a
blind millionaire.

"Archie!" a voice called. "Come and help us sample!"

It was Margot Dickey. In a far corner was a gold-leaf
bar, some eight feet long, and she was at it on a gold-leaf
stool. Cherry Quon and Alfred Kiernan were with her,
also on stools, and behind the bar was Santa Claus, pouring from a champagne bottle. It was certainly a modern
touch to have Santa Claus tend bar, but there was nothing
modern about his costume. He was strictly traditional,
cut, color, size, mask, and all, except that the hand grasping the champagne bottle wore a white glove. I assumed,
crossing to them over the thick rugs, that that was a touch
of Bottweill elegance, and didn't learn until later how
wrong I was.

They gave me the season's greetings and Santa Claus
poured a glass of bubbles for me. No gold leaf on the
glass. I was glad I had come. To drink champagne with a
blonde at one elbow and a brunette at the other gives a
man a sense of well-being, and those two were fine specimens—the tall, slender Margot relaxed, all curves, on
the stool, and little slant-eyed black-eyed Cherry Quon,
who came only up to my collar when standing, sitting
with her spine as straight as a plumb line yet not stiff. I
thought Cherry worthy of notice not only as a statuette,
though she was highly decorative, but as a possible source
of new light on human relations. Margot had told me
that her father was half Chinese and half Indian—not
American Indian—and her mother was Dutch.

I said that apparently I had come too early, but Alfred Kiernan said no, the others were around and would be in shortly. He added that it was a pleasant surprise to see me, as it was just a little family gathering and he hadn't known others had been invited. Kiernan, whose title was business manager, had not liked a certain step I had taken when I was hunting the tapestries, and he still didn't, but an Irishman at a Christmas party likes everybody. My impression was that he really was pleased, so I was too. Margot said she had invited me, and Kiernan patted her on the arm and said that if she hadn't he would. About my age and fully as handsome, he was the kind who can pat the arm of a queen or a president's wife without making eyebrows go up.

He said we needed another sample and turned to the bartender. "Mr. Claus, we'll try the Veuve Clicquot." To us: "Just like Kurt to provide different brands. No monotony for Kurt." To the bartender: "May I call you by your first name, Santy?"

"Certainly, sir," Santa Claus told him from behind the mask in a thin falsetto that didn't match in size. As he stooped and came up with a bottle, a door at the left opened and two men entered. One of them, Emil Hatch, I had met before. When briefing Wolfe on the tapestries and telling us about his staff, Bottweill had called Margot Dickey his contact woman, Cherry Quon his handy girl, and Emil Hatch his pet wizard, and when I met Hatch I found that he both looked the part and acted it. He wasn't much taller than Cherry Quon, and skinny, and something had either pushed his left shoulder down or his right shoulder up, making him lopsided, and he had a sour face, sour voice, and a sour taste.

When the stranger was named to me as Leo Jerome, that placed him. I was acquainted with his mother, Mrs. Perry Porter Jerome. She was a widow and an angel—that is, Kurt Bottweill's angel. During the investigation she had talked as if the tapestries belonged to her, but that might have only been her manners, of which she had plenty. I could have made guesses about her personal relations with Bottweill, but hadn't bothered. I have enough to do to handle my own personal relations without wasting my brain power on other people's. As for her son Leo, he must have got his physique from his father—tall, bony, big-eared and long-armed. He was probably approaching thirty, below Kiernan but above Margot and Cherry.

When he shoved in between Cherry and me, giving me his back, and Emil Hatch had something to tell Kiernan —sour, no doubt—I touched Margot's elbow and she slid off the stool and let herself be steered across to a divan which had been covered with designs by Euclid in six or seven colors. We stood looking down at it.

"Mighty pretty," I said, "but nothing like as pretty as you. If only that license were real! I can get a real one for two dollars. What do you say?"

"*You!*" she said scornfully. "You wouldn't marry Miss Universe if she came on her knees with a billion dollars."

"I dare her to try it. Did it work?"

"Perfect. Simply perfect."

"Then you're ditching me?"

"Yes, Archie darling. But I'll be a sister to you."

"I've got a sister. I want the license back for a souvenir, and anyway I don't want it kicking around. I could be hooked for forgery. You can mail it to me, once my own."

"No, I can't. He tore it up."

"The hell he did. Where are the pieces?"

"Gone. He put them in his wastebasket. Will you come to the wedding?"

"What wastebasket where?"

"The gold one by his desk in his office. Last evening after dinner. Will you come to the wedding?"

"I will not. My heart is bleeding. So will Mr. Wolfe's— and by the way, I'd better get out of here. I'm not going to stand around and sulk."

"You won't have to. He won't know I've told you, and anyway, you wouldn't be expected— Here he comes!"

She darted off to the bar and I headed that way. Through the door on the left appeared Mrs. Perry Porter Jerome, all of her, plump and plushy, with folds of mink trying to keep up as she breezed in. As she approached, those on stools left them and got onto their feet, but that courtesy could have been as much for her companion as for her. She was the angel, but Kurt Bottweill was the boss. He stopped five paces short of the bar, extended his arms as far as they would go, and sang out, "Merry Christmas, all my blessings! Merry merry merry!"

I still hadn't labeled him. My first impression, months

ago, had been that he was one of them, but that had
been wrong. He was a man, all right, but the question
was, what kind. About average in height, round but not
pudgy, maybe forty-two or -three, his fine black hair
slicked back so that he looked balder than he was, he was
nothing great to look at, but he had something, not only
for women but for men too. Wolfe had once invited him
to stay for dinner, and they had talked about the scrolls
from the Dead Sea. I had seen him twice at baseball
games. His label would have to wait.

As I joined them at the bar, where Santa Claus was
pouring Mumms Cordon Rouge, Bottweill squinted at
me a moment and then grinned. "Goodwin! You here?
Good! Edith, your pet sleuth!"

Mrs. Perry Porter Jerome, reaching for a glass, stopped
her hand to look at me. "Who asked you?" she demanded, then went on, with no room for a reply,
"Cherry, I suppose. Cherry *is* a blessing. Leo, quit tug-
ging at me. Very well, take it. It's warm in here." She let
her son pull her coat off, then reached for a glass. By the
time Leo got back from depositing the mink on the divan,
we all had glasses, and when he had his we raised them,
and our eyes went to Bottweill.

His eyes flashed around. "There are times," he said,
"when love takes over. There are times—"

"Wait a minute," Alfred Kiernan cut in. "You enjoy it
too. You don't like this stuff."

"I can stand a sip, Al."

"But you won't enjoy it. Wait." Kiernan put his glass
on the bar and marched to the door on the left and on
out. In five seconds he was back, with a bottle in his
hand, and as he rejoined us and asked Santa Claus for a
glass I saw the Pernod label. He pulled the cork, which
had been pulled before, filled the glass halfway, and held
it out to Bottweill. "There," he said. "That will make it
unanimous."

"Thanks, Al." Bottweill took it. "My secret public
vice." He raised the glass. "I repeat, there are times when
love takes over. (Santa Claus, where is yours? But I
suppose you can't drink through that mask.) There are
times when all the little demons disappear down their
ratholes, and ugliness itself takes on the shape of beauty;
when the darkest corner is touched by light; when the
coldest heart feels the glow of warmth; when the trumpet

call of good will and good cheer drowns out all the Babel of mean little noise. This is such a time. Merry Christmas! Merry merry merry!"

I was ready to touch glasses, but both the angel and the boss steered theirs to their lips, so I and the others followed suit. I thought Bottweill's eloquence deserved more than a sip, so I took a healthy gulp, and from the corner of my eye I saw that he was doing likewise with the Pernod. As I lowered the glass my eyes went to Mrs. Jerome, as she spoke.

"That was lovely," she declared. "Simply lovely. I must write it down and have it printed. That part about the trumpet call—*Kurt!* What is it? *Kurt!*"

He had dropped the glass and was clutching his throat with both hands. As I moved he turned loose of his throat, thrust his arms out, and let out a yell. I think he yelled *"Merry!"* but I wasn't really listening. Others started for him too, but my reflexes were better trained for emergencies than any of theirs, so I got him first. As I got my arms around him he started choking and gurgling, and a spasm went over him from head to foot that nearly loosened my grip. They were making noises, but no screams, and someone was clawing at my arm. As I was telling them to get back and give me room, he was suddenly a dead weight, and I almost went down with him and might have if Kiernan hadn't grabbed his arm.

I called, "Get a doctor!" and Cherry ran to a table where there was a gold-leaf phone. Kiernan and I let Bottweill down on the rug. He was out, breathing fast and hard, but as I was straightening his head his breathing slowed down and foam showed on his lips. Mrs. Jerome was commanding us, "Do something, do something!"

There was nothing to do, and I knew it. While I was holding onto him I had got a whiff of his breath, and now, kneeling, I leaned over to get my nose an inch from his, and I knew that smell, and it takes a big dose to hit that quick and hard. Kiernan was loosening Bottweill's tie and collar. Cherry Quon called to us that she had tried a doctor and couldn't get him and was trying another. Margot was squatting at Bottweill's feet, taking his shoes off, and I could have told her she might as well let him die with his boots on but didn't. I had two fingers on his wrist and my other hand inside his shirt, and could feel him going. When I could feel nothing I abandoned the chest and wrist, took his hand, which was a fist, straightened the middle finger, and pressed its nail with my thumbtip until it was white. When I removed my thumb the nail stayed white. Dropping the hand, I yanked a little cluster of fibers from the rug, told Kiernan not to move, placed the fibers against Bottweill's nostrils, fastened my eyes on them, and held my breath for thirty seconds. The fibers didn't move.

I stood up and spoke. "His heart has stopped and he's not breathing. If a doctor came within three minutes and washed out his stomach with chemicals he wouldn't have with him, there might be one chance in a thousand. As it is—"

"Can't you *do* something?" Mrs. Jerome squawked.

"Not for him, no. I'm not an officer of the law, but I'm a licensed detective, and I'm supposed to know how to act in these circumstances, and I'll get it if I don't follow the rules. Of course—"

"*Do something!*" Mrs. Jerome squawked.

Kiernan's voice came from behind me. "He's dead."

I didn't turn to ask what test he had used. "Of course," I told them, "his drink was poisoned. Until the police come no one will touch anything, especially the bottle of Pernod, and no one will leave this room. You will—"

I stopped dead. Then I demanded, "Where is Santa Claus?"

Their heads turned to look at the bar. No bartender. On the chance that it had been too much for him, I pushed between Leo Jerome and Emil Hatch to step to the end of the bar, but he wasn't on the floor either.

I wheeled. "Did anyone see him go?"

They hadn't. Hatch said, "He didn't take the elevator. I'm sure he didn't. He must have—" He started off.

I blocked him. "You stay here. I'll take a look. Kiernan, phone the police. Spring seven-three-one-hundred."

I made for the door on the left and passed through, pulling it shut as I went, and was in Bottweill's office, which I had seen before. It was one-fourth the size of the studio, and much more subdued, but was by no means squalid. I crossed to the far end, saw through the glass panel that Bottweill's private elevator wasn't there, and pressed the button. A clank and a whirr came from inside the shaft, and it was coming. When it was up and had jolted to a stop I opened the door, and there on the floor was Santa Claus, but only the outside of him. He had molted. Jacket, breeches, mask, wig . . . I didn't check to see if it was all there, because I had another errand and not much time for it.

Propping the elevator door open with a chair, I went and circled around Bottweill's big gold-leaf desk to his gold-leaf wastebasket. It was one-third full. Bending, I started to paw, decided that was inefficient, picked it up and dumped it, and began tossing things back in one by one. Some of the items were torn pieces of paper, but none of them came from a marriage license. When I had finished I stayed down a moment, squatting, wondering if I had hurried too much and possibly missed it, and I might have gone through it again if I hadn't heard a faint noise from the studio that sounded like the elevator door opening. I went to the door to the studio and opened it, and as I crossed the sill two uniformed cops were deciding whether to give their first glance to the dead or the living.

III

Three hours later we were seated, more or less in a group, and my old friend and foe, Sergeant Purley Stebbins of Homicide, stood surveyiing us, his square jaw jutting and his big burly frame erect.

He spoke. "Mr. Kiernan and Mr. Hatch will be taken to the District Attorney's office for further questioning. The rest of you can go for the present, but you will keep yourselves available at the addresses you have given. Before you go I want to ask you again, here together, about the man who was here as Santa Claus. You have all claimed you know nothing about him. Do you still claim that?"

It was twenty minutes to seven. Some two dozen city employees—medical examiner, photographer, finger-printers, meat-basket bearers, the whole kaboodle—had finished the on-the-scene routine, including private interviews with the eyewitnesses. I had made the highest score, having had sessions with Stebbins, a precinct man, and Inspector Cramer, who had departed around five o'clock to organize the hunt for Santa Claus.

"I'm not objecting," Kiernan told Stebbins, "to going to the District Attorney's office. I'm not objecting to anything. But we've told you all we can, I know I have. It seems to me your job is to find him."

"Do you mean to say," Mrs. Jerome demanded, "that no one knows anything at all about him?"

"So they say," Purley told her. "No one even knew there was going to be a Santa Claus, so they say. He was brought to this room by Bottweill, about a quarter to three, from his office. The idea is that Bottweill himself had arranged for him, and he came up in the private elevator and put on the costume in Bottweill's office. You may as well know there is some corroboration of that. We have found out where the costume came from—Burleson's, on Forty-sixth Street. Bottweill phoned them yesterday afternoon and ordered it sent here, marked personal. Miss Quon admits receiving the package and taking it to Bottweill in his office."

For a cop, you never just state a fact, or report it or declare it or say it. You admit it.

"We are also," Purley admitted, "covering agencies which might have supplied a man to act Santa Claus, but that's a big order. If Bottweill got a man through an agency there's no telling what he got. If it was a man with a record, when he saw trouble coming he beat it. With everybody's attention on Bottweill, he sneaked out, got his clothes, whatever he had taken off, in Bottweill's office, and went down in the elevator he had come up in. He shed the costume on the way down and after he was down, and left it in the elevator. If that was it, if he was just a man Bottweill hired, he wouldn't have had any reason to kill him—and besides, he wouldn't have known that Bottweill's only drink was Pernod, and he wouldn't have known where the poison was."

"Also," Emil Hatch said, sourer than ever, "if he was just hired for the job he was a damn fool to sneak out. He might have known he'd be found. So he wasn't just hired. He was someone who knew Bottweill, and knew about the Pernod and the poison, and had some good reason for wanting to kill him. You're wasting your time on the agencies."

Stebbins lifted his heavy broad shoulders and dropped them. "We waste most of our time, Mr. Hatch. Maybe he was too scared to think. I just want you to understand that if we find him and that's how Bottweill got him, it's going to be hard to believe that he put poison in that bottle, but somebody did. I want you to understand that so you'll understand why you are all to be available at the addresses you have given. Don't make any mistake about that."

"Do you mean," Mrs. Jerome demanded, "that we are under suspicion? That *I* and *my son* are under suspicion?"

Purley opened his mouth and shut it again. With that kind he always had trouble with his impulses. He wanted to say, "You're goddam right you are." He did say, "I mean we're going to find that Santa Claus, and when we do we'll see. If we can't see him for it we'll have to look further, and we'll expect all of you to help us. I'm taking it for granted you'll all want to help. Don't you want to, Mrs. Jerome?"

"I would help if I could, but I know nothing about it. I only know that my very dear friend is dead, and I don't intend to be abused and threatened. What about the poison?"

"You know about it. You have been questioned about it."

"I know I have, but what about it?"

"It must have been apparent from the questions. The medical examiner thinks it was cyanide and expects the autopsy to verify it. Emil Hatch uses potassium cyanide in his work with metals and plating, and there is a large jar of it on a cupboard shelf in the workshop one floor below, and there is a stair from Bottweill's office to the workroom. Anyone who knew that, and who also knew that Bottweill kept a case of Pernod in a cabinet in his office and an open bottle of it in a drawer of his desk, couldn't have asked for a better setup. Four of you have admitted knowing both of those things. Three of you— Mrs. Jerome, Leo Jerome, and Archie Goodwin—admit they knew about the Pernod but deny they knew about the potassium cyanide. That will—"

"That's not true! She did know about it!"

Mrs. Perry Porter Jerome's hand shot out across her son's knees and slapped Cherry Quon's cheek or mouth or both. Her son grabbed her arm. Alfred Kiernan sprang to his feet, and for a second I thought he was going to sock Mrs. Jerome, and he did too, and possibly he would have if Margot Dickey hadn't jerked at his coattail. Cherry put her hand to her face but, except for that, didn't move.

"Sit down," Stebbins told Kiernan. "Take it easy. Miss

Quon, you say Mrs. Jerome knew about the potassium cyanide?"

"Of course she did." Cherry's chirp was pitched lower than normal, but it was still a chirp. "In the workshop one day I heard Mr. Hatch telling her how he used it and how careful he had to be."

"Mr. Hatch? Do you verify—"

"Nonsense," Mrs. Jerome snapped. "What if he did? Perhaps he did. I had forgotten all about it. I told you I won't tolerate this abuse!"

Purley eyed her. "Look here, Mrs. Jerome. When we find that Santa Claus, if it was someone who knew Bott- weill and had a motive, that may settle it. If not, it won't help anyone to talk about abuse, and that includes you. So far as I know now, only one of you has told us a lie. You. That's on the record. I'm telling you, and all of you, lies only make it harder for you, but sometimes they make it easier for us. I'll leave it at that for now. Mr. Kiernan and Mr. Hatch, these men"—he aimed a thumb over his shoulder at two dicks standing back of him— "will take you downtown. The rest of you can go, but re- member what I said. Goodwin, I want to see you."

He had already seen me, but I wouldn't make a point of it. Kiernan, however, had a point to make, and made it: he had to leave last so he could lock up. It was so ar- ranged. The three women, Leo Jerome, and Stebbins and I took the elevator down, leaving the two dicks with Kier- nan and Hatch. Down on the sidewalk, as they headed in different directions, I could see no sign of tails taking af- ter them. It was still snowing, a fine prospect for Christmas and the street cleaners. There were two police cars at the curb, and Purley went to one and opened the door and motioned to me to get in.

I objected. "If I'm invited downtown too I'm willing to oblige, but I'm going to eat first. I damn near starved to death there once."

"You're not wanted downtown, not right now. Get in out of the snow."

I did so, and slid across under the wheel to make room for him. He needs room. He joined me and pulled the door shut.

"If we're going to sit here," I suggested, "we might as well be rolling. Don't bother to cross town, just drop me at Thirty-fifth."

He objected. "I don't like to drive and talk. Or listen. What were you doing there today?"

"I've told you. Having fun. Three kinds of champagne. Miss Dickey invited me."

"I'm giving you another chance. You were the only outsider there. Why? You're nothing special to Miss Dickey. She was going to marry Bottweill. Why?"

"Ask her."

"We have asked her. She says there was no particular reason, she knew Bottweill liked you, and they've regarded you as one of them since you found some tapestries for them. She stuttered around about it. What I say, any time I find you anywhere near a murder, I want to know. I'm giving you another chance."

So she hadn't mentioned the marriage license. Good for her. I would rather have eaten all the snow that had fallen since noon than explain that damn license to Sergeant Stebbins or Inspector Cramer. That was why I had gone through the wastebasket. "Thanks for the chance," I told him, "but I can't use it. I've told you everything I saw and heard there today." That put me in a class with Mrs. Jerome, since I had left out my little talk with Margot. "I've told you all I know about those people. Lay off and go find your murderer."

"I know you, Goodwin."

"Yeah, you've even called me Archie. I treasure that memory."

"I know you." His head was turned on his bull neck, and our eyes were meeting. "Do you expect me to believe that guy got out of that room and away without you knowing it?"

"Nuts. I was kneeling on the floor, watching a man die, and they were around us. Anyway, you're just talking to hear yourself. You don't think I was accessory to the murder or to the murderer's escape."

"I didn't say I did. Even if he was wearing gloves—and what for if not to leave no prints?—I don't say he was the murderer. But if you knew who he was and didn't want him involved in it, and let him get away, and if you let us wear out our ankles looking for him, what about that?"

"That would be bad. If I asked my advice I would be against it."

"Goddam it," he barked, "do you know who he is?"

"No."

"Did you or Wolfe have anything to do with getting him there?"

"No."

"All right, pile out. They'll be wanting you downtown."

"I hope not tonight. I'm tired." I opened the door. "You have my address." I stepped out into the snow, and he started the engine and rolled off.

It should have been a good hour for an empty taxi, but in a Christmas-season snowstorm it took me ten minutes to find one. When it pulled up in front of the old brownstone on West Thirty-fifth Street it was eight minutes to eight.

As usual in my absence, the chain-bolt was on, and I had to ring for Fritz to let me in. I asked him if Wolfe was back, and he said yes, he was at dinner. As I put my hat on the shelf and my coat on a hanger I asked if there was any left for me, and he said plenty, and moved aside for me to precede him down the hall to the door of the dining room. Fritz has fine manners.

Wolfe, in his oversized chair at the end of the table, told me good evening, not snapping or barking. I returned it, got seated at my place, picked up my napkin, and apologized for being late. Fritz came, from the kitchen, with a warm plate, a platter of braised boned ducklings, and a dish of potatoes baked with mushrooms and cheese. I took enough. Wolfe asked if it was still snowing and I said yes. After a good mouthful had been disposed of, I spoke.

"As you know, I approve of your rule not to discuss business during a meal, but I've got something on my chest and it's not business. It's personal."

He grunted. "The death of Mr. Bottweill was reported on the radio at seven o'clock. You were there."

"Yeah. I was there. I was kneeling by him while he died." I replenished my mouth. Damn the radio. I hadn't intended to mention the murder until I had dealt with the main issue from my standpoint. When there was room enough for my tongue to work I went on, "I'll report on that in full if you want it, but I doubt if there's a job in it. Mrs. Perry Porter Jerome is the only suspect with enough jack to pay your fee, and she has already notified Purley Stebbins that she won't be abused. Besides, when they find Santa Claus that may settle it. What I want to

report on happened before Bottweill died. That marriage
license I showed you is for the birds. Miss Dickey has
called it off. I am out two bucks. She told me she had decided to marry Bottweill."

He was sopping a crust in the sauce on his plate. "Indeed," he said.

"Yes, sir. It was a jolt, but I would have recovered, in
time. Then ten minutes later Bottweill was dead. Where
does that leave me? Sitting around up there through the
routine, I considered it. Perhaps I could get her back now,
but no thank you. That license has been destroyed. I get
another one, another two bucks, and then she tells me
she has decided to marry Joe Doakes. I'm going to forget
her. I'm going to blot her out."

I resumed on the duckling. Wolfe was busy chewing.
When he could he said, "For me, of course, this is satisfactory."

"I know it is. Do you want to hear about Bottweill?"

"After dinner."

"Okay. How did you make out with Thompson?"

But that didn't appeal to him as a dinner topic either.
In fact, nothing did. Usually he likes table talk, about
anything from refrigerators to Republicans, but apparently the trip to Long Island and back, with all its dan-
gers, had tired him out. It suited me all right, since I had
had a noisy afternoon too and could stand a little silence.
When we had both done well with the duckling and potatoes and salad and baked pears and cheese and coffee,
he pushed back his chair.

"There's a book," he said, "that I want to look at. It's
up in your room—*Here and Now*, by Herbert Block. Will
you bring it down, please?"

Though it meant climbing two flights with a full stomach, I was glad to oblige, out of appreciation for his calm
acceptance of my announcement of my shattered hopes.
He could have been very vocal. So I mounted the stairs
cheerfully, went to my room, and crossed to the shelves
where I keep a few books. There were only a couple of
dozen of them, and I knew where each one was, but *Here
and Now* wasn't there. Where it should have been was a
gap. I looked around, saw a book on the dresser, and
stepped to it. It was *Here and Now*, and lying on top of it
was a pair of white cotton gloves.

I gawked.

IV

I would like to say that I caught on immediately, the second I spotted them, but I didn't. I had picked them up and looked them over, and put one of them on and taken it off again, before I fully realized that there was only one possible explanation. Having realized it, instantly there was a traffic jam inside my skull, horns blowing, brakes squealing, head-on collisions. To deal with it I went to a chair and sat. It took me maybe a minute to reach my first clear conclusion.

He had taken this method of telling me he was Santa Claus, instead of just telling me, because he wanted me to think it over on my own before we talked it over together.

Why did he want me to think it over on my own? That took a little longer, but with the traffic under control I found my way through to the only acceptable answer. He had decided to give up his trip to see Thompson, and instead to arrange with Bottweill to attend the Christmas party disguised as Santa Claus, because the idea of a woman living in his house—or of the only alternative, my leaving—had made him absolutely desperate, and he had to see for himself. He had to see Margot and me together, and to talk with her if possible. If he found out that the marriage license was a hoax he would have me by the tail; he could tell me he would be delighted to welcome my bride and watch me wriggle out. If he found that I really meant it he would know what he was up against and go on from there. The point was this, that he had shown what he really thought of me. He had shown that rather than lose me he would do something that he wouldn't have done for any fee anybody could name. He would rather have gone without beer for a week than admit it, but now he was a fugitive from justice in a murder case and needed me. So he had to let me know, but he wanted it understood that that aspect of the matter was not to be mentioned. The assumption would be that he had gone to Bottweill's instead of Long Island because he loved to dress up like Santa Claus and tend bar.

A cell in my brain tried to get the right of way for the question, considering this development, how big a raise should I get after New Year's? but I waved it to the curb.

I thought over other aspects. He had worn the gloves so I couldn't recognize his hands. Where did he get them? What time had he got to Bottweill's and who had seen him? Did Fritz know where he was going? How had he got back home? But after a little of that I realized that he hadn't sent me up to my room to ask myself questions he could answer, so I went back to considering whether there was anything else he wanted me to think over alone. Deciding there wasn't, after chewing it thoroughly, I got *Here and Now* and the gloves from the dresser, went to the stairs and descended, and entered the office.

From behind his desk, he glared at me as I crossed over.

"Here it is," I said, and handed him the book. "And much obliged for the gloves." I held them up, one in each hand, dangling them from thumb and fingertip.

"It is no occasion for clowning," he growled.

"It sure isn't." I dropped the gloves on my desk, whirled my chair, and sat. "Where do we start? Do you want to know what happened after you left?"

"The details can wait. First where we stand. Was Mr. Cramer there?"

"Yes. Certainly."

"Did he get anywhere?"

"No. He probably won't until he finds Santa Claus. Until they find Santa Claus they won't dig very hard at the others. The longer it takes to find him the surer they'll be he's it. Three things about him: nobody knows who he was, he beat it, and he wore gloves. A thousand men are looking for him. You were right to wear the gloves, I would have recognized your hands, but where did you get them?"

"At a store on Ninth Avenue. Confound it, I didn't know a man was going to be murdered!"

"I know you didn't. May I ask some questions?"

He scowled. I took it for yes. "When did you phone Bottweill to arrange it?"

"At two-thirty yesterday afternoon. You had gone to the bank."

"Have you any reason to think he told anyone about it?"

"No. He said he wouldn't."

"I know he got the costume, so that's okay. When you left here today at twelve-thirty did you go straight to Bottweill's?"

"No. I left at that hour because you and Fritz expected me to. I stopped to buy the gloves, and met him at Rusterman's, and we had lunch. From there we took a cab to his place, arriving shortly after two o'clock, and took his private elevator up to his office. Immediately upon entering his office, he got a bottle of Pernod from a drawer of his desk, said he always had a little after lunch, and invited me to join him. I declined. He poured a liberal portion in a glass, about two ounces, drank it in two gulps, and returned the bottle to the drawer."

"My God." I whistled. "The cops would like to know *that*."

"No doubt. The costume was there in a box. There is a dressing room at the rear of his office, with a bathroom—"

"I know. I've used it."

"I took the costume there and put it on. He had ordered the largest size, but it was a squeeze and it took a while. I was in there half an hour or more. When I re-entered the office it was empty, but soon Bottweill came, up the stairs from the workshop, and helped me with the mask and wig. They had barely been adjusted when Emil Hatch and Mrs. Jerome and her son appeared, also coming up the stairs from the workshop. I left, going to the studio, and found Miss Quon and Miss Dickey and Mr. Kiernan there."

"And before long I was there. Then no one saw you unmasked. When did you put the gloves on?"

"The last thing. Just before I entered the studio."

"Then you may have left prints. I know, you didn't know there was going to be a murder. You left your clothes in the dressing room? Are you sure you got everything when you left?"

"Yes. I am not a complete ass."

I let that by. "Why didn't you leave the gloves in the elevator, with the costume?"

"Because they hadn't come with it, and I thought it better to take them."

"That private elevator is at the rear of the hall downstairs. Did anyone see you leaving it or passing through the hall?"

"No. The hall was empty."

"How did you get home? Taxi?"

"No. Fritz didn't expect me until six or later. I walked to the public library, spent some two hours there, and then took a cab."

I pursed my lips and shook my head to indicate sympathy. That was his longest and hardest tramp since Montenegro. Over a mile. Fighting his way through the blizzard, in terror of the law on his tail. But all the return I got for my look of sympathy was a scowl, so I let loose. I laughed. I put my head back and let it come. I had wanted to ever since I had learned he was Santa Claus, but had been too busy thinking. It was bottled up in me, and I let it out, good. I was about to taper off to a cackle, when he exploded.

"Confound it," he bellowed, "marry and be damned!"

That was dangerous. That attitude could easily get us onto the aspect he had sent me up to my room to think over alone, and if we got started on that anything could happen. It called for tact.

"I beg your pardon," I said. "Something caught in my throat. Do you want to describe the situation, or do you want me to?"

"I would like to hear you try," he said grimly.

"Yes, sir. I suspect that the only thing to do is to phone Inspector Cramer right now and invite him to come and have a chat, and when he comes open the bag. That will—"

"No. I will not do that."

"Then, next best, I go to him and spill it there. Of course—"

"No." He meant every word of it.

"Okay, I'll describe it. They'll mark time on the others until they find Santa Claus. They've got to find him. If he left any prints they'll compare them with every file they've got, and sooner or later they'll get to yours. They'll cover all the stores for sales of white cotton gloves to men. They'll trace Bottweill's movements and learn that he lunched with you at Rusterman's, and you left together, and they'll trace you to Bottweill's place. Of course your going there won't prove you were Santa Claus, you might talk your way out of that, and it will account for your prints if they find some, but what about the gloves? They'll trace that sale if you give them time, and with a description of the buyer they'll find Santa Claus. You're sunk."

I had never seen his face blacker.

"If you sit tight till they find him," I argued, "it will be quite a nuisance. Cramer has been itching for years to lock you up, and any judge would commit you as a material witness who had run out. Whereas if you call Cramer now, and I mean now, and invite him to come and have some beer, while it will still be a nuisance, it will be bearable. Of course he'll want to know why you went there and played Santa Claus, but you can tell him anything you please. Tell him you bet me a hundred bucks, or what the hell, make it a grand, that you could be in a room with me for ten minutes and I wouldn't recognize you. I'll be glad to cooperate."

I leaned foward. "Another thing. If you wait till they find you, you won't dare tell them that Bottweill took a drink from that bottle shortly after two o'clock and it didn't hurt him. If you told about that after they dug you up, they could book you for withholding evidence, and they probably would, and make it stick. If you get Cramer here now and tell him, he'll appreciate it, though naturally he won't say so. He's probably at his office. Shall I ring him?"

"No. I will not confess that performance to Mr. Cramer. I will not unfold the morning paper to a disclosure of that outlandish masquerade."

"Then you're going to sit and read *Here and Now* until they come with a warrant?"

"No. That would be fatuous." He took in air through his mouth, as far down as it would go, and let it out through his nose, "I'm going to find the murderer and present him to Mr. Cramer. There's nothing else."

"Oh. You are."

"Yes.'

"You might have said so and saved my breath, instead of letting me spout."

"I wanted to see if your appraisal of the situation agreed with mine. It does."

"That's fine. Then you also know that we may have two weeks and we may have two minutes. At this very second some expert may be phoning Homicide to say that he has found fingerprints that match on the card of Wolfe, Nero—"

The phone rang, and I jerked around as if someone had stuck a needle in me. Maybe we wouldn't have even two minutes. My hand wasn't trembling as I lifted the receiver, I hope. Wolfe seldom lifts his until I have found out who it is, but that time he did.

"Nero Wolfe's office, Archie Goodwin speaking."

"This is the District Attorney's office, Mr. Goodwin. Regarding the murder of Kurt Bottweill. We would like you to be here at ten o'clock tomorrow morning."

"All right. Sure."

"At ten o'clock sharp, please."

"I'll be there."

We hung up. Wolfe sighed. I sighed.

"Well," I said, "I've already told them six times that I know absolutely nothing about Santa Claus, so they may not ask me again. If they do, it will be interesting to compare my voice when I'm lying with when I'm telling the truth."

He grunted. "Now. I want a complete report of what happened there after I left, but first I want background. In your intimate association with Miss Dickey you must have learned things about those people. What?"

"Not much." I cleared my throat. "I guess I'll have to explain something. My association with Miss Dickey was not intimate." I stopped. It wasn't easy.

"Choose your own adjective. I meant no innuendo."

"It's not a question of adjectives. Miss Dickey is a good dancer, exceptionally good, and for the past couple of months I have been taking her here and there, some six or eight times altogether. Monday evening at the Flamingo Club she asked me to do her a favor. She said Bottweill was giving her a runaround, that he had been going to marry her for a year but kept stalling, and she wanted to do something. She said Cherry Quon was making a play for him, and she didn't intend to let Cherry take the rail. She asked me to get a marriage-license blank and fill it out for her and me and give it to her. She would show it to Bottweill and tell him now or never. It struck me as a good deed with no risk involved, and, as I say, she is a good dancer. Tuesday afternoon I got a blank, no matter how, and that evening, up in my room, I filled it in, including a fancy signature."

Wolfe made a noise.

"That's all," I said, "except that I want to make it clear

that I had no intention of showing it to you. I did that on the spur of the moment when you picked up your book. Your memory is as good as mine. Also, to close it up, no doubt you noticed that today just before Bottweill and Mrs. Jerome joined the party Margot and I stepped aside for a little chat. She told me the license did the trick. Her words were, 'Perfect, simply perfect.' She said that last evening, in his office, he tore the license up and put the pieces in his wastebasket. That's okay, the cops didn't find them. I looked before they came, and the pieces weren't there."

His mouth was working, but he didn't open it. He didn't dare. He would have liked to tear into me, to tell me that my insufferable flummery had got him into this awful mess, but if he did so, he would be dragging in the aspect he didn't want mentioned. He saw that in time, and saw that I saw it. His mouth worked, but that was all. Finally he spoke.

"Then you are not on intimate terms with Miss Dickey."

"No, sir."

"Even so, she must have spoken of that establishment and those people."

"Some, yes."

"And one of them killed Bottweill. The poison was put in the bottle between two-ten, when I saw him take a drink, and three-thirty, when Kiernan went and got the bottle. No one came up in the private elevator during the half-hour or more I was in the dressing room. I was getting into that costume and gave no heed to footsteps or other sounds in the office, but the elevator shaft adjoins the dressing room, and I would have heard it. It is a strong probability that the opportunity was even narrower, that the poison was put in the bottle while I was in the dressing room, since three of them were in the office with Bottweill when I left. It must be assumed that one of those three, or one of the three in the studio, had grasped an earlier opportunity. What about them?"

"Not much. Mostly from Monday evening, when Margot was talking about Bottweill. So it's all hearsay, from her. Mrs. Jerome has put half a million in the business— probably you should divide that by two at least—and thinks she owns him. Or thought. She was jealous of Margot and Cherry. As for Leo, if his mother was dish-ing out the dough he expected to inherit to a guy who was trying to corner the world's supply of gold leaf, and possibly might also marry him, and if he knew about the jar of poison in the workshop, he might have been tempted. Kiernan, I don't know, but from a remark Margot made and from the way he looked at Cherry this afternoon, I suspect he would like to mix some Irish with her Chinese and Indian and Dutch, and if he thought Bottweill had him stymied he might have been tempted to. So much for hearsay."

"Mr. Hatch?"

"Nothing on him fom Margot, but, dealing with him during the tapestry job, I wouldn't have been surprised if he had wiped out the whole bunch on general principles. His heart pumps acid instead of blood. He's a creative artist, he told me so. He practically told me that he was responsible for the success of that enterprise but got no credit. He didn't tell me that he regarded Bottweill as a phony and a fourflusher, but he did. You may remember that I told you he had a persecution complex and you told me to stop using other people's jargon."

"That's four of them. Miss Dickey?"

I raised my brows. "I got her a license to marry, not to kill. If she was lying when she said it worked, she's almost as good a liar as she is a dancer. Maybe she is. If it didn't work she might have been tempted too."

"And Miss Quon?"

'She's half Oriental. I'm not up on Orientals, but I understand they slant their eyes to keep you guessing. That's what makes them inscrutable. If I had to be poisoned by one of that bunch I would want it to be her. Except for what Margot told me—"

The doorbell rang. That was worse than the phone. If they had hit on Santa Claus's trail and it led to Nero Wolfe, Cramer was much more apt to come then to call. Wolfe and I exchanged glances. Looking at my wristwatch and seeing 10:08, I arose, went to the hall and flipped the switch for the stoop light, and took a look through the one-way glass panel of the front door. I have good eyes, but the figure was muffled in a heavy coat with a hood, so I stepped halfway to the door to make sure. Then I returned to the office and told Wolfe, "Cherry Quon. Alone."

He frowned. "I wanted—" He cut it off. "Very well. Bring her in."

V

As I have said, Cherry was highly decorative, and she went fine with the red leather chair at the end of Wolfe's desk. It would heve held three of her. She had let me take her coat in the hall and still had on the neat little woolen number she had worn at the party. It wasn't exactly yellow, but there was yellow in it. I would have called it off-gold, and it and the red chair and the tea tint of her smooth little carved face would have made a very nice kodachrome.

She sat on the edge, her spine straight and her hands together in her lap. "I was afraid to telephone," she said, "because you might tell me not to come. So I just came. Will you forgive me?"

Wolfe grunted. No commitment. She smiled at him, a friendly smile, or so I thought. After all, she was half Oriental.

"I must get myself together." she chirped. "I'm nervous because it's so exciting to be here." She turned her head. "There's the globe, and the bookshelves, and the safe, and the couch, and of course Archie Goodwin. And you. You behind your desk in your enormous chair! Oh, I know this place! I have read about you so much—everything there is, I think. It's exciting to be here, actually here in this chair, and see you. Of course I saw you this afternoon, but that wasn't the same thing, you could have been anybody in that silly Santa Claus costume. I wanted to pull your whiskers."

She laughed, a friendly little tinkle like a bell.

I think I looked bewildered. That was my idea, after it had got through my ears to the switchboard inside and been routed. I was too busy handling my face to look at Wolfe, but he was probably even busier, since she was looking straight at him. I moved my eyes to him when he spoke.

"If I understand you, Miss Quon, I'm at a loss. If you think you saw me this afternoon in a Santa Claus costume, you're mistaken."

"Oh, I'm sorry!" she exclaimed. "Then you haven't told them?"

"My dear madam." His voice sharpened. "If you must talk in riddles, talk to Mr. Goodwin. He enjoys them."

"But I *am* sorry, Mr. Wolfe. I should have explained first how I know. This morning at breakfast Kurt told me you had phoned him and arranged to appear at the party as Santa Claus, and this afternoon I asked him if you had come and he said you had and you were putting on the costume. That's how I know. But you haven't told the police? Then it's a good thing I haven't told them either, isn't it?"

"This is interesting," Wolfe said coldly. "What do you expect to accomplish by this fantastic folderol?"

She shook her pretty little head. "You, with so much sense. You must see that it's no use. If I tell them, even if they don't like to believe me they will invesitgate. I know they can't investigate as well as you can, but surely they will find something."

He shut his eyes, tightened his lips, and leaned back in his chair. I kept mine open, on her. She weighed about a hundred and two. I could carry her under one arm with my other hand clamped on her mouth. Putting her in the spare room upstairs wouldn't do, since she could open a window and scream, but there was a cubbyhole in the basement, next to Fritz's room, with an old couch in it. Or, as an alternative, I could get a gun from my desk drawer and shoot her. Probably no one knew she had come here.

Wolfe opened his eyes and straightened up. "Very well. It is still fantastic, but I concede that you could create an unpleasant situation by taking that yarn to the police. I don't suppose you came here merely to tell me that you intend to. What do you intend?"

"I think we understand each other," she chirped.

"I understand only that you want something. What?"

"You are so direct," she complained. "So very abrupt, that I must have said something wrong. But I do want something. You see, since the police think it was the man who acted Santa Claus and ran away, they may not get on the right track until it's too late. You wouldn't want that, would you?"

No reply.

"I wouldn't want it," she said, and her hands on her

lap curled into little fists. "I wouldn't want whoever killed Kurt to get away, no matter who it was, but you see, I know who killed him. I have told the police, but they won't listen until they find Santa Claus, or if they listen they think I'm just a jealous cat, and besides, I'm an Oriental and their ideas of Orientals are very primitive. I was going to make them listen by telling them who Santa Claus was, but I know how they feel about you from what I've read, and I was afraid they would try to prove it was you who killed Kurt, and of course it could have been you, and you did run away, and they still wouldn't listen to me when I told them who did kill him."

She stopped for breath. Wolfe inquired. "Who did?"

She nodded. "I'll tell you. Margot Dickey and Kurt were having an affair. A few months ago Kurt began on me, and it was hard for me because I—I—" She frowned for a word, and found one. "I had a feeling for him. I had a strong feeling. But you see, I am a virgin, and I wouldn't give in to him. I don't know what I would have done if I hadn't known he was having an affair with Margot, but I did know, and I told him the first man I slept with would be my husband. He said he was willing to give up Margot, but even if he did he couldn't marry me on account of Mrs. Jerome, because she would stop backing him with her money. I don't know what he was to Mrs. Jerome, but I know what she was to him."

Her hands opened and closed again to be fists. "That went on and on, but Kurt had a feeling for me too. Last night late, it was after midnight, he phoned me that he had broken with Margot for good and he wanted to marry me. He wanted to come and see me, but I told him I was in bed and we would see each other in the morning. He said that would be at the studio with other people there, so finally I said I would go to his apartment for breakfast, and I did, this morning. But I am still a virgin, Mr. Wolfe."

He was focused on her with half-closed eyes. "That is your privilege, madam."

"Oh," she said. "Is it a privilege? It was there, at breakfast, that he told me about you, your arranging to be Santa Claus. When I got to the studio I was surprised to see Margot there, and how friendly she was. That was part of her plan, to be friendly and cheerful with everyone. She has told the police that Kurt was going to marry

her, that they decided last night to get married next week.
Christmas week. I am a Christian."

Wolfe stirred in his chair. "Have we reached the
point? Did Miss Dickey kill Mr. Bottweill?"

"Yes. Of course she did."

"Have you told the police that?"

"Yes. I didn't tell them all I have told you, but
enough."

"With evidence?"

"No. I have no evidence."

"Then you're vulnerable to an action for slander."

She opened her fists and turned her palms up. "Does
that matter? When I know I'm right? When I *know* it?
But she was so clever, the way she did it, that there can't
be any evidence. Everybody there today knew about the
poison, and they all had a chance to put it in the bottle.
They can never prove she did it. They can't even prove
she is lying when she says Kurt was going to marry her,
because he is dead. She acted today the way she would
have acted if that had been true. But it has got to be
proved somehow. There has got to be evidence to prove
it."

"And you want me to get it?"

She let that pass. "What I was thinking, Mr. Wolfe,
you are vulnerable too. There will always be the danger
that the police will find out who Santa Claus was, and if
they find it was you and you didn't tell them—"

"I haven't conceded that," Wolfe snapped.

"Then we'll just say there will always be the danger
that I'll tell them what Kurt told me, and you did concede that that would be unpleasant. So it would be better
if the evidence proved who killed Kurt and also proved
who Santa Claus was. Wouldn't it?"

"Go on."

"So I thought how easy it would be for you to get the
evidence. You have men who do things for you, who
would do anything for you, and one of them can say that
you asked him to go there and be Santa Claus, and he
did. Of course it couldn't be Mr. Goodwin, since he was
at the party, and it would have to be a man they couldn't
prove was somewhere else. He can say that while he was
in the dressing room putting on the costume he heard
someone in the office and peeked out to see who it was,
and he saw Margot Dickey get the bottle from the desk

drawer and put something in it and put the bottle back in the drawer, and go out. That must have been when she did it, because Kurt always took a drink of Pernod when he came back from lunch."

Wolfe was rubbing his lip with a fingertip. "I see," he muttered.

She wasn't through. "He can say," she went on, "that he ran away because he was frightened and wanted to tell you about it first. I don't think they would do anything to him if he went to them tomorrow morning and told them all about it, would they? Just like me. I don't think they would do anything to me if I went to them tomorrow morning and told them I had remembered that Kurt told me that you were going to be Santa Claus, and this afternoon he told me you were in the dressing room putting on the costume. That would be the same kind of thing, wouldn't it?"

Her little carved mouth thinned and widened with a smile. "That's what I want," she chirped. "Did I say it so you understand it?"

"You did indeed," Wolfe assured her. "You put it admirably."

"Would it be better, instead of him going to tell them, for you to have Inspector Cramer come here, and you tell him? You could have the man here. You see, I know how you do things, from all I have read."

"That might be better," he allowed. His tone was dry but not hostile. I could see a muscle twitching beneath his right ear, but she couldn't. "I suppose, Miss Quon, it is futile to advance the possibility that one of the others killed him, and if so it would be a pity—"

"Excuse me, I interrupt." The chirp was still a chirp, but it had hard steel in it. "I know she killed him."

"I don't. And even if I bow to your conviction, before I could undertake the stratagem you propose I would have to make sure there are no facts that would scuttle it. It won't take me long. You'll hear from me tomorrow. I'll want—"

She interrupted again. "I can't wait longer than tomorrow morning to tell what Kurt told me."

"Pfui. You can and will. The moment you disclose that, you no longer have a whip to dangle at me. You will hear from me tomorrow. Now I want to think. Archie?"

I left my chair. She looked up at me and back at Wolfe.

For some seconds she sat, considering, inscrutable of course, then stood up.

"It was very exciting to be here," she said, the steel gone, "to see you here. You must forgive me for not phoning. I hope you will be early tomorrow." She turned and headed for the door, and I followed.

After I had helped her on with her hooded coat, and let her out, and watched her picking her way down the seven steps, I shut the door, put the chain bolt on, returned to the office, and told Wolfe, "It has stopped snowing. Who do you think will be best for it, Saul or Fred or Orrie or Bill?"

"Sit down," he growled. "You see through women. Well?"

"Not that one. I pass. I wouldn't bet a dime on her one way or the other. Would you?"

"No. She is probably a liar and possibly a murderer. Sit down. I must have everything that happened there today after I left. Every word and gesture."

I sat and gave it to him. Including the question period, it took an hour and thirty-five minutes. It was after one o'clock when he pushed his chair back, levered his bulk upright, told me good night, and went up to bed.

VI

At half past two the following afternoon, Saturday, I sat in a room in a building on Leonard Street, the room where I had once swiped an assitant district attorney's lunch. There would be no need for me to repeat the performance, since I had just come back from Ost's restaurant, where I had put away a plateful of pig's knuckles and sauerkraut.

As far as I knew, there had not only been no steps to frame Margot for murder; there had been no steps at all. Since Wolfe is up in the plant rooms every morning from nine to eleven, and since he breakfasts from a tray up in his room, and since I was expected downtown at ten o'clock, I had buzzed him on the house phone a little before nine to ask for instructions and had been told that he had none. Downtown Assistant DA Farrell, after letting me wait in the anteroom for a hour, had spent two hours with me, together with a stenographer and a dick

who had been on the scene Friday afternoon, going back
and forth and zigzag, not only over what I had already
reported, but also over my previous association with the
Bottweill personnel. He only asked me once if I knew
anything about Santa Claus, so I only had to lie once, if
you don't count my omitting any mention of the marriage
license. When he called a recess and told me to come
back at two-thirty, on my way to Ost's for the pig's
knuckles I phoned Wolfe to tell him I didn't know when
I would be home, and again he had no instructions. I said
I doubted if Cherry Quon would wait until after New
Year's to spill the beans, and he said he did too and hung
up.

When I was ushered back into Farrell's office at two-
thirty he was alone—no stenographer and no dick. He
asked me if I had had a good lunch, and even waited
for me to answer, handed me some typewritten sheets,
and leaned back in his chair.

"Read it over," he said, "and see if you want to sign
it."

His tone seemed to imply that I might not, so I went
over it carefully, five full pages. Finding no editorial re-
visions to object to, I pulled my chair forward to a corner
of his desk, put the statement on the desk top, and got
my pen from my pocket.

"Wait a minute," Farrell said. "You're not a bad guy
even if you are cocky, and why not give you a break?
That says specifically that you have reported everything
you did there yesterday afternoon."

"Yeah, I've read it. So?"

"So who put your fingerprints on some of the pieces of
paper in Bottweill's wastebasket?"

"I'll be damned," I said. "I forgot to put gloves on."

"All right, you're cocky. I already know that." His eyes
were pinning me. "You must have gone through that
wastebasket, every item, when you went to Bottweill's
office ostensibly to look for Santa Claus, and you hadn't
just forgotten it. You don't forget things. So you have
deliberately left it out. I want to know why, and I want
to know what you took from that wastebasket and what
you did with it."

I grinned at him. "I am also damned because I thought
I knew how thorough they are and apparently I didn't. I
wouldn't have supposed they went so far as to dust the

contents of a wastebasket when there was nothing to connect them, but I see I was wrong, and I hate to be wrong." I shrugged. "Well, we learn something new every day." I screwed the statement around to position, signed it at the bottom of the last page, slid it across to him, and folded the carbon copy and put it in my pocket.

"I'll write it in if you insist," I told him, "but I doubt if it's worth the trouble. Santa Claus had run, Kiernan was calling the police, and I guess I was a little rattled. I must have looked around for something that might give me a line on Santa Claus, and my eye lit on the wastebasket, and I went through it. I haven't mentioned it because it wasn't very bright, and I like people to think I'm bright, especially cops. There's your why. As for what I took, the answer is nothing. I dumped the wastebasket, put everything back in, and took nothing. Do you want me to write that in?"

"No. I want to discuss it. I know you *are* bright. And you weren't rattled. You don't rattle. I want to know the real reason you went through the wastebasket, what you were after, whether you got it, and what you did with it."

It cost me more than an hour, twenty minutes of which were spent in the office of the District Attorney himself, with Farrell and another assistant present. At one point it looked as if they were going to hold me as a material witness, but that takes a warrant, the Christmas weekend had started, and there was nothing to show that I had monkeyed with anything that could be evidence, so finally they shooed me out, after I had handwritten an insert in my statement. It was too bad keeping such important public servants sitting there while I copied the insert on my carbon, but I like to do things right.

By the time I got home it was ten minutes past four, and of course Wolfe wasn't in the office, since his afternoon session up in the plant rooms is from four to six. There was no note on my desk from him, so apparently there were still no instructions, but there was information on it. My desk ashtray, which is mostly for decoration since I seldom smoke—a gift, not to Wolfe but to me, from a former client—is a jade bowl six inches across. It was there in its place, and in it were three stubs from Pharaoh cigarettes.

Saul Panzer smokes Pharaohs, Egyptians. I suppose a few other people do too, but the chance that one of

them had been sitting at my desk while I was gone was
too slim to bother with. And not only had Saul been
there, but Wolfe wanted me to know it, since one of the
eight million things he will not tolerate in the office is ash-
trays with remains. He will actually walk clear to the
bathroom himself to empty one.

So steps were being taken, after all. What steps? Saul,
a free lance and the best operative anywhere around,
asks and gets sixty bucks a day, and is worth twice that.
Wolfe had not called him in for any routine errand, and
of course the idea that he had undertaken to sell him on
doubling for Santa Claus never entered my head. Framing someone for murder, even a woman who might be
guilty, was not in his bag of tricks. I got at the house
phone and buzzed the plant rooms, and after a wait had
Wolfe's voice in my ear.

"Yes, Fritz?"

"Not Fritz. Me. I'm back. Nothing urgent to report.
They found my prints on stuff in the wastebasket, but I
escaped without loss of blood. Is it all right for me to
empty my ashtray?"

"Yes. Please do so."

"Then what do I do?"

"I'll tell you at six o'clock. Possibly earlier."

He hung up. I went to the safe and looked in the cash
drawer to see if Saul had been supplied with gen-
erous funds, but the cash was as I had last seen it and
there was no entry in the book. I emptied the ashtry. I
went to the kitchen, where I found Fritz pouring a mixture into a bowl of fresh pork tenderloin, and said I hoped
Saul had enjoyed his lunch, and Fritz said he hadn't
stayed for lunch. So steps must have been begun right after I left in the morning. I went back to the office, read
over the carbon copy of my statement before filing it, and
passed the time by thinking up eight different steps that
Saul might have been assigned, but none of them struck
me as promising. A little after five the phone rang and I
answered. It was Saul. He said he was glad to know I was
back home safe, and I said I was too.

"Just a message for Mr. Wolfe," he said. "Tell him
everything is set, no snags."

"That's all?"

"Right. I'll be seeing you."

I cradled the receiver, sat a moment to consider

whether to go up to the plant rooms or use the house phone, decided the latter would do, and pulled it to me and pushed the button. When Wolfe's voice came it was peevish; he hates to be disturbed up there.

"Yes?"

"Saul called and said to tell you everything is set, no snags. Congratulations. Am I in the way?"

"Oddly enough, no. Have chairs in place for visitors; ten should be enough. Four or five will come shortly after six o'clock; I hope not more. Others will come later."

"Refreshments?"

"Liquids, of course. Nothing else."

"Anything else for me?"

"No."

He was gone. Before going to the front room for chairs, and to the kitchen for supplies, I took time out to ask myself whether I had the slightest notion what kind of charade he was cooking up this time. I hadn't.

VII

It was four. They all arrived between six-fifteen and six-twenty—first Mrs. Perry Porter Jerome and her son Leo, then Cherry Quon, and last Emil Hatch. Mrs. Jerome copped the red leather chair, but I moved her, mink and all, to one of the yellow ones when Cherry came. I was willing to concede that Cherry might be headed for a very different kind of chair, wired for power, but even so I thought she rated that background and Mrs. Jerome didn't. By six-thirty, when I left them to cross the hall to the dining room, not a word had passed among them.

In the dining room Wolfe had just finished a bottle of beer. "Okay," I told him, "it's six-thirty-one. Only four. Kiernan and Margot Dickey haven't shown."

"Satisfactory." He arose. "Have they demanded information?"

"Two of them have, Hatch and Mrs. Jerome. I told them it will come from you, as instructed. That was easy, since I have none."

He headed for the office, and I followed. Though they didn't know, except Cherry, that he had poured champagne for them the day before, introductions weren't necessary because they had all met him during the tap-

estry hunt. After circling around Cherry in the red leather
chair, he stood behind his desk to ask them how they did,
then sat.

"I don't thank you for coming," he said, "because you
came in your own interest, not mine. I sent—"

"I came," Hatch cut in, sourer than ever, "to find out
what you're up to."

"You will," Wolfe assured him. "I sent each of you an
identical message, saying that Mr. Goodwin has certain
information which he feels he must give the police not
later than tonight, but I have persuaded him to let me
discuss it with you first. Before I—"

"I didn't know others would be here," Mrs. Jerome
blurted, glaring at Cherry.

"Neither did I," Hatch said, glaring at Mrs. Jerome.

Wolfe ignored it. "The message I sent Miss Quon was
somewhat different, but that need not concern you. Before I tell you what Mr. Goodwin's information is, I need
a few facts from you. For instance, I understand that any
of you—including Miss Dickey and Mr. Kiernan, who will
probably join us later—could have found an opportunity
to put the poison in the bottle. Do any of you challenge
that?"

Cherry, Mrs. Jerome, and Leo all spoke at once. Hatch
merely looked sour.

Wolfe showed them a palm. "If you please. I point no
finger of accusation at any of you. I merely say that none
of you, including Miss Dickey and Mr. Kiernan, can
prove that you had no opportunity. Can you?"

"Nuts." Leo Jerome was disgusted. "It was that guy
playing Santa Claus. Of course it was. I was with Bottweill
and my mother all the time, first in the workshop and
then in his office. I can prove *that*."

"But Bottweill is dead," Wolfe reminded him, "and
your mother is your mother. Did you go up to the office a
little before them, or did your mother go up a little before
you and Bottweill did? Is there acceptable proof that you
didn't? The others have the same problem. Miss Quon?"

There was no danger of Cherry's spoiling it. Wolfe had
told me what he had told her on the phone: that he had
made a plan which he thought she would find satisfactory,
and if she came at a quarter past six she would see it
work. She had kept her eyes fixed on him ever since he

entered. Now she chirped, "If you mean I can't prove I wasn't in the office alone yesterday, no, I can't."

"Mr. Hatch?"

"I didn't come here to prove anything. I told you what I came for. What information has Goodwin got?"

"We'll get to that. A few more facts first. Mrs. Jerome, when did you learn that Bottweill had decided to marry Miss Quon?"

Leo shouted, "No!" but his mother was too busy staring at Wolfe to hear him. "What?" she croaked. Then she found her voice. "Kurt marry *her*? That little strumpet?"

Cherry didn't move a muscle, her eyes still on Wolfe.

"This is wonderful!" Leo said. "This is marvelous!"

"Not so damn wonderful," Emil Hatch declared. "I get the idea, Wolfe. Goodwin hasn't got any information, and neither have you. Why you wanted to get us together and start us clawing at each other, I don't see that, I don't know why you're interested, but maybe I'll find out if I give you a hand. This crowd has produced as fine a collection of venom as you could find. Maybe we all put poison in the bottle and that's why it was such a big dose. If it's true that Kurt had decided to marry Cherry, and Al Kiernan knew it, that would have done it. Al would have killed a hundred Kurts if it would get him Cherry. If Mrs. Jerome knew it, I would think she would have gone for Cherry instead of Kurt, but maybe she figured there would soon be another one and she might as well settle it for good. As for Leo, I think he rather liked Kurt, but what can you expect? Kurt was milking mamma of the pile Leo hoped to get some day, and I suspect that the pile is not all it's supposed to be. Actually—"

He stopped, and I left my chair. Leo was on his way up, obviously with the intention of plugging the creative artist. I moved to head him off, and at the same instant I gave him a shove and his mother jerked at his coattail. That not only halted him but nearly upset him, and with my other hand I steered him back onto his chair and then stood beside him.

Hatch inquired, "Shall I go on?"

"By all means," Wolfe said.

"Actually, though, Cherry would seem to be the most likely. She has the best brain of the lot and by far the strongest will. But I understand that while she says Kurt was going to marry her, Margot claims that he was going to marry *her*. Of course that complicates it, and anyway Margot would be my second choice. Margot has more than her share of the kind of pride that is only skin deep and therefore can't stand a scratch. If Kurt did decide to marry Cherry and told Margot so, he was even a bigger imbecile than I thought he was. Which brings us to me. I am in a class by myself. I despise all of them. If I had decided to take to poison I would have put it in the champagne as well as the Pernod, and I would have drunk vodka, which I prefer—and by the way, on that table is a bottle with the Korbeloff vodka label. I haven't had a taste of Korbeloff for fifteen years. Is it real?"

"It is. Archie?"

Serving liquid refreshment to a group of invited guests can be a pleasant chore, but it wasn't that time. When I asked Mrs. Jerome to name it she only glowered at me, but by the time I had filled Cherry's order for scotch and soda, and supplied Hatch with a liberal dose of Korbeloff, no dilution, and Leo had said he would take bourbon and water, his mother muttered that she would have that too. As I was pouring the bourbon I wondered where we would go from there. It looked as if the time had come for Wolfe to pass on the information which I felt I must give the police without delay, which made it difficult because I didn't have any. That had been fine for a bait to get them there, but what now? I suppose Wolfe would have held them somehow, but he didn't have to. He had rung for beer, and Fritz had brought it and was putting the tray on his desk when the doorbell rang. I handed Leo his bourbon and water and went to the hall. Out on the stoop, with his big round face nearly touching the glass, was Inspector Cramer of Homicide.

Wolfe had told me enough, before the company came, to give me a general idea of the program, so the sight of Cramer, just Cramer, was a letdown. But as I went down the hall other figures appeared, none of them strangers, and that looked better. In fact it looked fine. I swung the door wide and in they came—Cramer, then Saul Panzer, then Margot Dickey, then Alfred Kiernan, and, bringing up the rear, Sergeant Purley Stebbins. By the time I had the door closed and bolted they had their coats off, including Cramer, and it was also fine to see that he expected to stay a while. Ordinarily, once in, he marches down the hall and into the office without ceremony, but that time he waved the others ahead, including me, and he and Stebbins came last, herding us in. Crossing the sill, I stepped aside for the pleasure of seeing his face when his eyes lit on those already there and the empty chairs waiting. Undoubtedly he had expected to find Wolfe alone, reading a book. He came in two paces, glared around, fastened the glare on Wolfe, and barked, "What's all this?"

"I was expecting you," Wolfe said politely. "Miss Quon, if you don't mind moving, Mr. Cramer likes that chair. Good evening, Miss Dickey. Mr. Kiernan, Mr. Stebbins. If you will all be seated—"

"Panzer!" Cramer barked. Saul, who had started for a chair in the rear, stopped and turned.

"I'm running this," Cramer declared. "Panzer, you're under arrest and you'll stay with Stebbins and keep your mouth shut. I don't want—"

"No," Wolfe said sharply. "If he's under arrest take him out of here. You are not running this, not in my house. If you have warrants for anyone present, or have taken them by lawful police power, take them and leave these premises. Would you bulldoze me, Mr. Cramer? You should know better."

That was the point, Cramer did know him. There was the stage, all set. There were Mrs. Jerome and Leo and Cherry and Emil Hatch, and the empty chairs, and above all, there was the fact that he had been expected. He wouldn't have taken Wolfe's word for that; he wouldn't have taken Wolfe's word for anything; but whenever he appeared on our stoop *not* expected I always left the chain-bolt on until he had stated his business and I had reported to Wolfe. And if he had been expected there was no telling what Wolfe had ready to spring. So Cramer gave up the bark and merely growled, "I want to talk with you."

"Certainly." Wolfe indicated the red leather chair, which Cherry had vacated. "Be seated."

"Not here. Alone."

Wolfe shook his head. "It would be a waste of time. This way is better and quicker. You know quite well, sir, it was a mistake to barge in here and roar at me that you are running my house. Either go, with whomever you can lawfully take, or sit down while I tell you who killed Kurt Bottweill." Wolfe wiggled a finger. "Your chair."

Cramer's round red face had been redder than normal from the outside cold, and now was redder still. He glanced around, compressed his lips until he didn't have any, and went to the red leather chair and sat.

VIII

Wolfe sent his eyes around as I circled to my desk. Saul had got to a chair in the rear after all, but Stebbins had too and was at his elbow. Margot had passed in front of the Jeromes and Emil Hatch to get to the chair at the end nearest me, and Cherry and Al Kiernan were at the other end, a little back of the others. Hatch had finished his Korbeloff and put the glass on the floor, but Cherry and the Jeromes were hanging on to their tall ones.

Wolfe's eyes came to rest on Cramer and he spoke. "I must confess that I stretched it a little. I can't tell you, at the moment, who killed Bottweill; I have only a supposition; but soon I can, and will. First some facts for you. I assume you know that for the past two months Mr. Goodwin has been seeing something of Miss Dickey. He says she dances well."

"Yeah." Cramer's voice came over sandpaper of the roughest grit. "You can save that for later. I want to know if you sent Panzer to meet—"

Wolfe cut him off. "You will. I'm headed for that. But you may prefer this firsthand. Archie, if you please. What Miss Dickey asked you to do last Monday evening, and what happened."

I cleared my throat. "We were dancing at the Flamingo Club. She said Bottweill had been telling her for a year that he would marry her next week, but next week never came, and she was going to have a showdown with him. She asked me to get a blank marriage license and fill it out for her and me and give it to her, and she would show it to Bottweill and tell him now or never. I got the blank on Tuesday, and filled it in, and Wednesday I gave it to her."

I stopped. Wolfe prompted me. "And yesterday afternoon?"

"She told me that the license trick had worked perfectly. That was about a minute before Bottweill entered the studio. I said in my statement to the District Attorney that she told me Bottweill was going to marry her, but I didn't mention the license. It was immaterial."

"Did she tell you what happened to the license?"

So we were emptying the bag. I nodded. "She said Bottweill had torn it up and put the pieces in the waste-basket by the desk in his office. The night before. Thursday evening."

"And what did you do when you went to the office after Bottweill had died?"

"I dumped the wastebasket and put the stuff back in it, piece by piece. No part of the license was there."

"You made sure of that?"

"Yes."

Wolfe left me and asked Cramer, "Any questions?"

"No. He lied in his statement. I'll attend to that later. What I want—"

Margot Dickey blurted, "Then Cherry took it!" She craned her neck to see across the others. "You took it, you slut!"

"I did not." The steel was in Cherry's chirp again. Her eyes didn't leave Wolfe, and she told him, "I'm not going to wait any longer—"

"Miss Quon!" he snapped. "I'm doing this." He returned to Cramer. "Now another fact. Yesterday I had a luncheon appointment with Mr. Bottweill at Rusterman's restaurant. He had once dined at my table and wished to reciprocate. Shortly before I left to keep the appointment he phoned to ask me to do him a favor. He said he was extremely busy and might be a few minutes late, and he needed a pair of white cotton gloves, medium size, for a man, and would I stop at some shop on the way and get them. It struck me as a peculiar request, but he was a peculiar man. Since Mr. Goodwin had chores to do, and I will not ride in taxicabs if there is any alternative, I had engaged a car at Baxter's, and the chauffeur recommended a shop on Eighth Avenue between Thirty-ninth and Fortieth Streets. We stopped there and I bought the gloves."

Cramer's eyes were such narrow slits that none of the blue-gray showed. He wasn't buying any part of it, which was unjustified, since some of it was true.

Wolfe went on. "At the lunch table I gave the gloves to Mr. Bottweill, and he explained, somewhat vaguely, what he wanted them for. I gathered that he had taken pity on some vagabond he had seen on a park bench, and had hired him to serve refreshments at his office party, costumed as Santa Claus, and had decided that the only way to make his hands presentable was to have him wear gloves. You shake your head, Mr. Cramer?"

"You're damn right I do. You would have reported that. No reason on earth not to. Go ahead and finish."

"I'll finish this first. I didn't report it because I thought you would find the murderer without it. It was practically certain that the vagabond had merely skedaddled out of fright, since he couldn't possibly have known of the jar of poison in the workshop, not to mention other considerations. And as you know, I have a strong aversion to involvement in matters where I have no concern or interest. You can of course check this—with the staff at Rusterman's, my presence there with Mr. Bottweill, and with the chauffeur, my conferring with him about the gloves and our stopping at the shop to buy them."

"You're reporting it now."

"I am indeed." Wolfe was unruffled. "Because I understood from Mr. Goodwin that you were extending and intensifying your search for the man who was there as Santa Claus, and with your army and your resources it probably wouldn't take you long when the holiday had ended to learn where the gloves were bought and get a description of the man who bought them. My physique is not unique, but it is—uncommon, and the only question was how long it would take you to get to me, and then I would be under inquisition. Obviously I had to report the episode to you and suffer your rebuke for not reporting it earlier, but I wanted to make it as tolerable as possible. I had one big advantage: I knew that the man who acted Santa Claus was almost certainly not the murderer, and I decided to use it. I needed first to have a talk with one of those people, and I did so, with Miss Quon, who came here last evening."

"Why Miss Quon?"

Wolfe turned a hand over. "When I have finished you can decide whether such details are important. With her I discussed her associates at that place and their relationships, and I became satisfied that Bottweill had in fact decided to marry her. That was all. You can also decide later whether it is worthwhile to ask her to corroborate that, and I have no doubt she will."

He was looking at Cherry, of course, for any sign of

danger. She started to blurt it out once, and might again. But, meeting his gaze, she didn't move a muscle.

Wolfe returned to Cramer. "This morning I acted. Mr. Goodwin was absent, at the District Attorney's office, so I called in Mr. Panzer. After spending an hour with me here he went to do some errands. The first one was to learn whether Bottweill's wastebasket had been emptied since his conversation with Miss Dickey in his office Thursday evening. As you know, Mr. Panzer is highly competent. Through Miss Quon he got the name and address of the cleaning woman, found her and talked with her, and was told that the wastebasket had been emptied at about six o'clock Thursday afternoon and not since then. Meanwhile I—"

"Cherry took it—the pieces," Margot said.

Wolfe ignored her. "Meanwhile I was phoning everyone concerned—Mrs. Jerome and her son, Miss Dickey, Miss Quon, Mr. Hatch, and Mr. Kiernan—and inviting them to come here for a conference at six-fifteen. I told them that Mr. Goodwin had information which he intended to give the police, which was not true, and that I thought it best to discuss it first with them."

"I told you so," Hatch muttered.

Wolfe ignored him too. "Mr. Panzer's second errand, or series of errands, was the delivery of some messages. He had written them in longhand, at my dictation here this morning, on plain sheets of paper, and had addressed plain envelopes. They were identical and ran as follows:

"When I was there yesterday putting on my costume I saw you through a crack in the door and I saw what you did. Do you want me to tell the cops? Be at Grand Central information booth upper level at 6:30 today. I'll come up to you and say 'Saint Nick.'"

"By God," Cramer said, "you admit it."

Wolfe nodded. "I proclaim it. The messages were signed 'Santa Claus.' Mr. Panzer accompanied the messenger who took them to the persons I have named, and made sure they were delivered. They were not so much shots at random as they may appear. If one of those people had killed Bottweill it was extremely likely that the poison had been put in the bottle while the vagabond was

donning the Santa Claus costume; Miss Quon had told
me, as no doubt she has told you, that Bottweill invariably took a drink of Pernod when he returned from lunch;
and, since the appearance of Santa Claus at the party
had been a surprise to all of them, and none of them
knew who he was, it was highly probable that the murderer would believe he had been observed and would be
irresistibly impelled to meet the writer of the message.
So it was a reasonable assumption that one of the shots
would reach its target. The question was, which one?"

Wolfe stopped to pour beer. He did pour it, but I suspected that what he really stopped for was to offer an
opening for comment or protest. No one had any, not
even Cramer. They all just sat and gazed at him. I was
thinking that he had neatly skipped one detail: that the
message from Santa Claus had not gone to Cherry Quon.
She knew too much about him.

Wolfe put the bottle down and turned to go on to
Cramer. "There was the possibility, of course, that more
than one of them would go to you with the message, but
even if you decided, because it had been sent to more
than one, that it was some hoax, you would want to know
who perpetrated it, and you would send one of them to
the rendezvous under surveillance. Any one or more,
excepting the murderer, might go to you, or none might;
and surely only the murderer would go to the rendezvous without first consulting you. So if one of those six
people was guilty, and if it had been possible for Santa
Claus to observe him, disclosure seemed next to certain.
Saul, you may now report. What happened? You were
in the vicinity of the information booth shortly before
six-thirty?"

Necks were twisted for a view of Saul Panzer. He
nodded. "Yes, sir. At six-twenty. Within three minutes I
had recognized three Homicide men scattered around in
different spots. I don't know if they recognized me or not.
At six twenty-eight I saw Alfred Kiernan walk up near
the booth and stand there, about ten feet away from it. I
was just about to go and speak to him when I saw Margot Dickey coming up from the Forty-second Street side.
She approached to within thirty feet of the booth and
stood looking around. Following your instructions in case
more than one of them appeared and Miss Dickey was
one of them, I went to her and said, 'Saint Nick.' She

said, 'Who are you and what do you want?' I said, 'Excuse me, I'll be right back,' and went over to Alfred Kiernan and said to him, 'Saint Nick.' As soon as I said that he raised a hand to his ear, and then here they came, the three I had recognized and two more, and then Inspector Cramer and Sergeant Stebbins. I was afraid Miss Dickey would run, and she did start to, but they had seen me speak to her, and two of them stopped her and had her."

Saul halted because of an interruption. Purley Stebbins, seated next to him, got up and stepped over to Margot Dickey and stood there behind her chair. To me it seemed unnecessary, since I was sitting not much more than arm's length from her and might have been trusted to grab her if she tried to start anything, but Purley is never very considerate of other people's feelings, especially mine.

Saul resumed, "Naturally it was Miss Dickey I was interested in, since they had moved in on a signal from Kiernan. But they had her, so that was okay. They took us to a room back of the parcel room and started in on me, and I followed your instructions. I told them I would answer no questions, would say nothing whatever, except in the presence of Nero Wolfe, because I was acting under your orders. When they saw I meant it they took us out to two police cars and brought us here. Anything else?"

"No," Wolfe told him. "Satisfactory." He turned to Cramer. "I assume Mr. Panzer is correct in concluding that Mr. Kiernan gave your men a signal. So Mr. Kiernan had gone to you with the message?"

"Yes." Cramer had taken a cigar from his pocket and was squeezing it in his hand. He does that sometimes when he would like to squeeze Wolfe's throat instead. "So had three of the others—Mrs. Jerome, her son, and Hatch."

"But Miss Dickey hadn't?"

"No. Neither had Miss Quon."

"Miss Quon was probably reluctant, understandably. She told me last evening that the police's ideas of Orientals are very primitive. As for Miss Dickey, I may say that I am not surprised. For a reason that does not concern you, I am even a little gratified. I have told you that she told Mr. Goodwin that Bottweill had torn up the mar-

riage license and put the pieces in his wastebasket, and
they weren't there when Mr. Goodwin looked for them,
and the wastebasket hadn't been emptied since early
Thursday evening. It was difficult to conceive a reason
for anyone to fish around in the wastebasket to remove
those pieces, so presumably Miss Dickey lied; and if she
lied about the license, the rest of what she told Mr.
Goodwin was under suspicion."

Wolfe upturned a palm. "Why would she tell him that
Bottweill was going to marry her if it wasn't true? Surely
a stupid thing to do, since he would inevitably learn the
truth. But it wasn't so stupid if she knew that Bottweill
would soon die; indeed it was far from stupid if she had
already put the poison in the bottle; it would purge her of
motive, or at least help. It was a fair surmise that at their
meeting in his office Thursday evening Bottweill had told
her, not that he would marry her, but that he had decided to marry Miss Quon, and she decided to kill him
and proceeded to do so. And it must be admitted that she
would probably never have been exposed but for the
complications injected by Santa Claus and my resulting
intervention. Have you any comment, Miss Dickey?"

Cramer left his chair, commanding her, "Don't answer! I'm running this now," but she spoke.

"Cherry took those pieces from the wastebasket! She
did it! She killed him!" She started up, but Purley had
her arm and Cramer told her, moving for her, "She didn't
go there to meet a blackmailer, and you did. Look in her
bag, Purley. I'll watch her."

IX

Cherry Quon was back in the red leather chair. The
others had gone, and she and Wolfe and I were alone.
They hadn't put cuffs on Margot Dickey, but Purley had
kept hold of her arm as they crossed the threshold, with
Cramer right behind. Saul Panzer, no longer in custody,
had gone along by request. Mrs. Jerome and Leo had
been the first to leave. Kiernan had asked Cherry if he
could take her home, but Wolfe had said no, he wanted
to speak with her privately, and Kiernan and Hatch had
left together, which showed a fine Christmas spirit, since

Hatch had made no exceptions when he said he despised all of them.

Cherry was on the edge of the chair, spine straight, hands together in her lap. "You didn't do it the way I said," she chirped, without steel.

"No," Wolfe agreed, "but I did it." He was curt. "You ignored one complication, the possibility that you killed Bottweill yourself. I didn't, I assure you. I couldn't very well send you one of the notes from Santa Claus, under the circumstances; but if those notes had flushed no prey, if none of them had gone to the rendezvous without first notifying the police, I would have assumed that you were guilty and would have proceeded to expose you. How, I don't know; I let that wait on the event; and now that Miss Dickey has taken the bait and betrayed herself it doesn't matter."

Her eyes had widened. "You really thought I might have killed Kurt?"

"Certainly. A woman capable of trying to blackmail me to manufacture evidence of murder would be capable of anything. And, speaking of evidence, while there can be no certainty about a jury's decision when a personable young woman is on trial for murder, now that Miss Dickey is manifestly guilty you may be sure that Mr. Cramer will dig up all he can get, and there should be enough. That brings me to the point I wanted to speak about. In the quest for evidence you will all be questioned exhaustively and repeatedly. It will—"

"We wouldn't," Cherry put in, "if you had done it the way I said. That would have been proof."

"I preferred my way." Wolfe, having a point to make, was controlling himself. "It will be an ordeal for you. They will question you at length about your talk with Bottweill yesterday morning at breakfast, wanting to know all that he said about his meeting with Miss Dickey in his office Thursday evening, and under the pressure of inquisition you might inadvertently let something slip regarding what he told you about Santa Claus. If you do they will certainly follow it up. I strongly advise you to avoid making such a slip. Even if they believe you, the identity of Santa Claus is no longer important, since they have the murderer, and if they come to me with such a tale I'll have no great difficulty dealing with it."

He turned a hand over. "And in the end they probably

won't believe you. They'll think you invented it for some
cunning and obscure purpose—as you say, you are an
Oriental—and all you would get for it would be more
questions. They might even suspect that you were somehow involved in the murder itself. They are quite capable
of unreasonable suspicions. So I suggest these considerations as much on your behalf as on mine. I think you will
be wise to forget about Santa Claus."

She was eying him, straight and steady. "I like to be
wise," she said.

"I'm sure you do, Miss Quon."

"I still think you should have done it my way, but it's
done now. Is that all?"

He nodded. "That's all."

She looked at me, and it took a second for me to realize
that she was smiling at me. I thought it wouldn't hurt to
smile back, and did. She left the chair and came to me,
extending a hand, and I arose and took it. She looked up
at me.

"I would like to shake hands with Mr. Wolfe, but I
know he doesn't like to shake hands. You know, Mr.
Goodwin, it must be a very great pleasure to work for a
man as clever as Mr. Wolfe. So extremely clever. It has
been very exciting to be here. Now I say good-by."

She turned and went.

DO YOUR CHRISTMAS SHOPLIFTING EARLY

by Robert Somerlott

Robert Somerlott is a versatile writer who has published numerous novels and short stories under his own name and under several pen names, including two novels that were alternate selections of the Book-of-the-Month Club. His shorter fiction has appeared in The Best American Short Stories, *several college textbooks and in both the mystery-genre and "slick" magazines. Novels published under his own name include* The Flamingos, The Inquisitor's House, *and most recently,* Blaze.

Shortly after Mrs. Whistler retired from the stage, she discovered her true genius for escapades bordering on crime. But with modesty astounding in an actress, she has always managed to stay in the background. No one—except her son, Johnny Creighton—has ever suspected that Mrs. Whistler was the secret force behind several headline events that startled the country in the last few years.

For instance, millions of newspaper readers are aware that 267 animals staged a mass breakout from the St. Louis pound on Thanksgiving Day, 1959. Only Johnny Creighton knows that Mrs. Whistler engineered the escape. (The incident, headlined by newspapers as "Dog Days in Missouri," triggered pound reform laws in that state.)

Johnny was also the only one to know every detail of how Mrs. Whistler brought the powerful MacTavish De-

partment Store of Los Angeles to its knees in less than 24
hours. There exists no court transcript, and the only me-
mento of this case is an unflattering mug shot of Mrs.
Whistler taken at the Los Angeles jail. Despite the atro-
cious lighting, Mrs. Whistler looks exactly as she did in
her farewell performance on Broadway as the artist's
mother in *Arrangement in Gray,* a role she became so
identified with that she legally adopted the name of the
character. In the photo she wears a dark dress; her white
round collar is visible, but her lace cuffs are not. Her
sweet expression of sublime patience was not marred by
the ordeal she was suffering—an ordeal for which others
would soon pay heavily.

Mrs. Whistler had no intention of getting involved in
"The Affair of the Capricorn Brooch." When she de-
scended, unannounced, from the smoggy skies of Southern
California on Friday, December 18, it was for the inno-
cent purpose of spending the Christmas holiday with
Johnny.

Still, the moment he heard the voice on the phone he
had a premonition of trouble. Oddly enough, he was
thinking about his mother when her call came through.
He had been sitting in his two-by-four law office, day-
dreaming of pretty Joyce Gifford, who had almost, but not
quite, agreed to marry him. How, he wondered, could he
explain his mother to Joyce? Just then the phone rang.

"Johnny, dear," said a gentle voice. "Surprise! It's
Mother."

"Mother?" His first reaction was panic. "Where are
you? What have you done?"

"I'm at the airport. I've come for Christmas."

"Don't make a move till I get there. And, Mother," he
pleaded, "don't *do* anything!"

"Whatever do you mean, dear?" Mrs. Whistler was
faintly reproachful.

As he battled through the freeway traffic, Johnny could
not rid himself of the suspicion that his mother was up to
something. But at the airport, and later in his apartment,
her manner was so subdued that Johnny was totally un-
prepared for the events that followed. She's getting old, he
thought, she's settling down at last. The idea brought relief—and a little sadness.

At 6:30 Joyce Gifford, her usually calm face white with
anger, knocked at Johnny's door.

Johnny greeted her with a quick hug. "Hi, darling. Merry Christmas!" He lowered his voice. "I want you to meet my mother. She just arrived from New York."

In the living room an elderly lady was seated on the couch. Vainly, Joyce tried to remember where she'd seen her before—there was something hauntingly familiar about the black dress, the folded hands, the sad-sweet face.

"How do you do?" said the old lady. "I'm Mrs. Whistler." Joyce nearly dropped her purse. "You're upset, my dear," she said. "I could tell the moment you came in."

"Does it show that much? I've—I've had a horrible day!"

"Good Lord," said Johnny, "what's the matter?"

"Tomorrow I'm quitting my job at MacTavish's. Mr. Schlag can find himself a secretary—if anybody alive can stand him! It was the most terrible scene! All over this poor pathetic woman they caught shoplifting."

"Shoplifting?" Mrs. Whistler leaned forward. "Isn't that interesting!"

Johnny saw the intent expression on his mother's face. A danger signal flashed through him and he tried to interrupt. But it was too late.

"I just can't tell you how horrible the whole thing was," said Joyce.

"Try, my dear," said Mrs. Whistler gently. "Try."

During the first thirty-three years of its existence, MacTavish's ("A Wee Penny Saved Is a Big Penny Earned") had dealt with petty shoplifters in a routine way: first offenders were usually dismissed with threats of embarrassment. Otherwise respectable kleptomaniacs were delivered to their humiliated relatives. Suspected professionals were prosecuted relentlessly.

Then Dudley P. Schlag, nephew of a large stockholder, become manager, and things changed.

"Once a thief, always a thief!" he declared, beating his bony little fist on the desk top. He assumed personal charge of store security and would neglect any other duty for the pleasure of watching a terrified teen-ager squirm under his merciless, watery eye.

"There are *no* extenuating circumstances at MacTavish's!" By political influence and exaggerated statistics he induced several local judges to cooperate in his crusade, and after each arrest Schlag called the newspapers to make sure the suspect was well publicized.

"He's inhuman!" said Joyce Gifford, close to tears. "Of course, thieves should go to jail. But two weeks ago there was a teen-age girl—really a nice kid—who took a little piece of costume jewelry on a high-school dare. Mr. Schlag went to Juvenile Court himself and swore he'd seen her around the store several times—that this wasn't really her first theft. And I'm sure that wasn't true! A month ago they caught this old woman, a doctor's wife. She's been taking little things for years, and her husband always pays for them. She's really pathetic. And Mr. Schlag had her taken to jail!"

Mrs. Whistler clucked sympathetically. "The quality of mercy is not strained," she said.

"Today Miss Vought—she's the meanest store detective—dragged in a woman who tried to take a cotton sweater from Infants' Wear. Her name is Mrs. Blainey. She has an invalid husband, and she's trying to support him and four children by doing domestic work. I just know she'd never stolen anything before. When Miss Vought searched her purse it was enough to make you cry. She had exactly forty-three cents. There was an unpaid gas bill and a notice that a mortgage payment on their house was overdue."

"What happened to her?" asked Mrs. Whistler.

"Mr. Schlag told her that if she'd sign a confession the store wouldn't prosecute. Well, she signed it, crying. Then he called the police. She's in jail right now—at Christmastime! Her case comes up Monday—"

"And they'll throw the book at her," said Johnny slowly.

Joyce nodded. "Oh, that Mr. Schlag! There just isn't anything bad enough that could happen to him!"

Mrs. Whistler smiled slightly. "Oh, I'm sure there is, my dear!"

Joyce turned to Johnny. "You're a lawyer. What can be done about it?"

"Nothing."

"But, Johnny," she protested, "surely you can do *something!*"

"I don't see what. I suppose I could appear in court for her on Monday. But it wouldn't do any good. The sentencing is going to be routine. You'd just better forget the whole thing, Joyce."

"Forget it? I can't forget it!"

"Someone," said Mrs. Whistler, "should take action."

"They certainly should," agreed Joyce.

Johnny was suddenly aware that both women were staring at him expectantly. There was a dreadful silence in the room. He had never seen Joyce so angry or so determined.

"Hold on, you two! What can I do about it? I'm just a guy who draws wills and sets up escrows. There just isn't any use in getting mixed up in something that can't—" Johnny's voice trailed off when he saw the expression on Joyce's face.

Mrs. Whistler glanced at the tiny watch pinned to her dress. "My goodness! If you young people will excuse me—" She took a step toward the guest room.

Johnny saw the gleam in her eye. He was on his feet in an instant. "Mother! You're planning something!"

Mrs. Whistler smiled at Joyce. "Johnny's always so worried about me. Isn't that sweet? Good night, dears." Mrs. Whistler closed her door behind her.

Johnny turned to Joyce accusingly. "You've set her off! I can tell by the look in her eye!"

"What on earth do you mean?"

"You don't know her!" Johnny paced the floor. "Last year she took on Mr. Moses and the whole New York Park Department—singlehanded! Six months ago it was Internal Revenue!"

"Johnny Creighton, stop shouting at me! It isn't my fault."

"Oh, yes, it is! You got her started with this Mrs. Blainey story. It's made to order for her—invalid husband, four kids, even an overdue mortgage payment! It's right out of Charles Dickens. And tomorrow, you can bet, she'll try to *do* something to MacTavish's!"

Joyce stood up quickly. "Well, I'm glad somebody in your family has a little spunk! If she can teach MacTavish's a lesson, more power to her!" Joyce looked at him coldly. "Johnny Creighton, you're a stick-in-the-mud! So cautious it's plain dull! You're supposed to be an attorney, but—"

"What do you want? Perry Mason?"

Joyce gave him her coolest secretarial smile. "Perry Mason is a very attractive guy. Good night, Johnny!"

"Stick-in-the-mud!" he repeated softly. Slowly a grim expression came over Johnny's pleasant face. "Mother," he called. "Are you awake?"

Mrs. Whistler's door opened instantly. "Yes, dear."

Johnny's voice was stiff with determination. "We've got some planning to do."

"Planning?" Mrs. Whistler blinked at him. "Oh, darling, I've already done *that*."

At six o'clock Saturday morning Mrs. Whistler bounced out of bed. Three times she stretched, bent, pressed her palms flat on the floor. Thirty minutes later she stood over the stove, dreamily preparing scrambled eggs for Johnny while she examined a full page ad that pictured items on sale at MacTavish's. Her son, still in pajamas, sat at the breakfast bar, his face a mask of stony heroism. He was convinced his mother's fantastic scheme would fail, but he was determined to go down fighting.

Mrs. Whistler pointed to a small item in the MacTavish ad. "One of these would do nicely," she said. Johnny looked doubtful but nodded bravely. "If we can only think of some way to handle the last part!" Suddenly Mrs. Whistler smiled happily. "Santa Claus!" she exclaimed. "You'll be Santa Claus!"

"Mother! No!"

"Johnny, dear." Mrs. Whistler's tone was stern. "Please don't be stubborn."

"I'll go along with the rest of it, but I won't be Santa Claus!"

Mrs. Whistler sighed. "Very well, darling." She stirred the eggs thoughtfully. "Now, we'll rent a nice red suit, and with whiskers no one will recognize you, and—"

Johnny groaned and surrendered.

At 8:15, as Joyce Gifford was leaving for her last day at MacTavish's, her telephone rang.

"Good morning, Joyce, dear. This is Mrs. Whistler."

"Why, good morning."

"Joyce, I have a dreadful premonition that disaster is about to overtake poor Mr. Schlag. If you happen to see me later today—and you will—please don't recognize me."

"I don't understand."

"Don't try, dear. Just don't recognize me. Or Johnny, either."

"Johnny? You don't mean that Johnny's actually going to—"

Mrs. Whistler chuckled. "Still waters run deep. Goodbye, my dear. See you later."

At the height of the noon rush hour, Traffic Officer "Spud" Battersby trembled in the middle of a terrifying intersection, blowing a whistle, waving his arms, and narrowly avoiding death at every second. Suddenly Officer Battersby's whistle nearly fell out of his mouth. A prim elderly lady carrying a straw shopping bag was calmly coming toward him, oblivious of the screaming brakes and blaring horns.

"My God!" he shouted. "Get back! You'll be run over!"

A truck screeched to a halt six inches from the old lady. "Officer," she said, "I want to report a crime."

Battersby snatched her from the path of an oncoming cab. They huddled in the middle of the street. "You want to be killed?"

"Killed? Oh, no. No one's been killed. But my purse was snatched not ten minutes ago."

"Get out of here! Call the police station!" A red light changed and a wheeled onslaught avalanched by.

"My," said the old lady, "you are busy, aren't you?" She gave him a slip of paper. "If my purse is found, here's my name and phone number."

"Lady, please . . . Look out for that truck!"

"Merry Christmas, Officer!" Battersby shoved the paper into his pocket and managed to halt a hundred racing vehicles while the old lady made her unhurried way to the curb.

"Another nut!" he said. "A one-hundred-percent Los Angeles nut!"

At 12:45 Mrs. Whistler hesitated at the costume jewelry counter in MacTavish's, smiling at Miss Hefron, the harassed and yule-weary salesgirl. "Everything's lovely! I simply have to see every piece!"

Dear Lord, no! Miss Hefron thought. "Our pleasure, Ma'am," she said brightly.

"Look at all these pretty things!" A velvet-lined tray stood open on the counter.

"They're horoscope brooches, Ma'am. An advertised special. We still have Virgo and Capricorn and—"

"Capricorn? Of course! I bought one of those for—"

Mrs. Whistler stopped speaking. Her eyes rolled wildly as she grasped the counter for support. With a crash the tray of costume jewelry fell to the floor, and Mrs. Whistler collapsed on top of it. Before Miss Hefron could reach the stricken customer, Mrs. Whistler had miraculously recovered. Struggling to her feet, she replaced the tray awkwardly.

Mrs. Whistler's eyelids fluttered. "I've just been on my feet too long—a little dizzy spell. No more shopping today!"

Slowly Mrs. Whistler made her way toward the doors of the store, clutching her straw shopping bag firmly. For a dreadful moment she believed nothing was going to happen to her; then her spirits soared as a strong hand gripped her elbow. An ash-blond woman with a flashing gold tooth was beside her.

"Let's just step right up to the mezzanine office, honey."

Mrs. Whistler seemed bewildered. "Pardon? I can't look at anything else today."

The steely grip of the woman's talons tightened. "Step along, honey, d'ya hear? We'll straighten this out and everything will be hunky-dory."

Mrs. Whistler felt herself propelled toward a service elevator, whisked upstairs, and forcibly ushered into an austere office.

"Sit down, honey," said the woman. "I'm Miss Vought, Store Security. I didn't catch your name."

"No," said Mrs. Whistler. "You didn't."

Miss Vought flipped the switch of an intercom. "Miss Gifford, this is Vought. Tell Mr. Schlag I've landed a real pro."

Miss Vought rested her thin hips on the edge of the desk and inserted a cigarette between her raspberry lips. "Relax, honey. You'll sign a little statement and breeze out of here in no time."

"I don't understand."

Miss Vought laughed unpleasantly. "You're fabulous,

honey. Just fabulous. That get-up you're wearing would fool anybody."

Dudley P. Schlag, drawn up to his full five feet one, strutted into the office, his pointed lapels bristling. Joyce Gifford, notebook in hand, followed. He did not see the astonished look that flashed across his secretary's face.

"We got the cool goods," Miss Vought told him. She rummaged in Mrs. Whistler's shopping bag and brought forth a Capricorn brooch set with tiny rhinestones. "Counter Eighteen. Pulled the old fainting act, glammed this. I had my eye on her for twenty minutes. She cased perfume first, then checked out novelties, finally wound up in jewelry."

"Kindly put down my brooch, young lady." said Mrs. Whistler, sweetly but firmly. "You might drop it."

"You're fabulous, honey," said Miss Vought, "fabulous."

"Name and address?" said Mr. Schlag.

"I live in New York. I'm Mrs. Whistler."

"Occupation?"

"I," said Mrs. Whistler, "am a Senior Citizen."

"All right, Grandma," said Schlag. "What about the brooch?"

"I bought it this morning. I don't remember the name of the store. I don't know your city very well."

"Where's the sales slip?"

"Of course!" Mrs. Whistler smiled brightly. "The name will be on the sales slip, and I'm careful about saving them." Then her face clouded. She seemed near tears. "But it was in my purse. And someone stole my purse just an hour or so ago."

"Tragic," said Schlag.

"I reported it to the police, of course."

Mr. Schlag spoke into the intercom. "Mrs. Luden, call police headquarters and ask if a stolen purse was reported by a . . . *Mrs. Whistler.*" He smiled thinly.

"It won't wash, honey," said Miss Vought. "There were six Capricorn brooches when you staged your tumble at Counter Eighteen. But only five when you left."

"You double-checked?" asked Schlag.

"Sure. While she was ankling for the door."

Thoughtfully Schlag cracked his knuckles, then spun violently on Mrs. Whistler. "Those brooches were a plant,

Grandma," he said. "That's why they were on the open counter."

"Gracious," said Mrs. Whistler. "You mean you were deliberately tempting people? Why, that's *wicked!*"

"My secretary will type out a little statement," he said, "saying you admit taking the brooch. You'll sign it, and then you can leave."

"Dear me," said Mrs. Whistler. "I almost believe you are accusing me of *stealing*. Why, I can't sign anything. It would be a lie." She stood up abruptly, snatching the brooch from Miss Vought. "Good afternoon," said Mrs. Whistler, taking a step toward the door.

Miss Vought and Schlag swooped like hawks, seizing her. "No, you don't, sister!" Miss Vought pried the brooch from Mrs. Whistler's fingers. "That's evidence!"

"You're under arrest!" shouted Schlag, then howled in pain as Mrs. Whistler's teeth sank into his hand.

Joyce Gifford sat in paralyzed shock, unable to move.

"The cooler for you, honey!" cried Miss Vought, restraining Mrs. Whistler with a hammerlock. "We've got the goods to fry you, and we'll see that they throw away the key!"

In less than an hour Mrs. Whistler had been booked, mugged, and fingerprinted.

At 2:15 P.M. a nervous, bedraggled Santa Claus elbowed through the crowded first floor aisles of MacTavish's. Like the Pied Piper, he acquired pursuing children at every step. "A bike!" "A beach ball!" "A 'rector set!"

For a moment he leaned against Counter 18, warding off his tormentors. "Oh, Lord," he whispered hoarsely to Miss Hefron. "What a hell of a way to make a living!"

"Aren't you on the fourth floor?" she asked.

"Coffee break," Santa groaned. His closed hand rested near the tray of horoscope brooches. A customer called to Miss Hefron and she turned away. Only for a moment—

At 4:25 P.M. Mr. Schlag glared across his desk at a resolute young man who returned his hostile look unflinchingly. "I, sir, am John R. Creighton, attorney-at-law." A business card was slammed onto the desk. "You, sir, are being sued for five hundred thousand dollars!"

"I beg your pardon?" The young attorney's piercing eyes were utterly unnerving. Mr. Schlag's mouth felt dry.

"My client," continued John Creighton, "a distinguished American actress, is suffering torment in the Los Angeles jail on trumped-up charges of shoplifting. You, sir, are responsible for this malicious accusation." The attorney's voice grew hollow. "May the Lord pity you, Mr. Schlag, for the courts never will!"

Schlag's confidence returned. He spoke quickly into the intercom. "Send Miss Vought up, please. And come in yourself, Miss Gifford—with your notebook." He turned back to the lawyer. "You're wasting your time, Mr. Creighton. This is clear-cut theft, and we'll prosecute to the fullest."

"Take notes, Miss Gifford," snapped Schlag.

"Yes, sir." Joyce glanced at Johnny without batting an eyelash.

Five minutes later Schlag was summing up the evidence. "The brooches were counted. Only five remained. Then your client, this Mrs. Whistler—" he smirked at the name "—told a preposterous tale about a stolen purse with a sales slip from some imaginery store. We checked with the police and caught her flat-footed in her lie."

"I see," said Johnny slowly. "Who would have believed it?"

Joyce looked anxiously at Johnny. He looked humble and defeated as her eyes pleaded with him to do something.

At last he spoke. "Maybe we could check the brooches one more time?"

"Certainly." The four marched downstairs to Counter 18, Joyce tagging behind in despair. "Miss Hefron," said Schlag, "has the number of brooches on this tray changed since our incident with the *thief?*"

Johnny Creighton stared at the glittering jewelry. "The tray was knocked over," he said softly. "I wonder . . . Would you please pick up the tray? There's just a chance . . ."

Joyce lifted the tray from the counter. A Capricorn brooch, its clasp open, fell to the floor with a twinkle of light. "Under the tray!" exclaimed Johnny. "Who would have believed it!"

Miss Hefron was wide-eyed. "When they spilled! One got caught in the velvet underneath!"

Johnny's tone was ominous. "I count six brooches, Mr. Schlag. Shall we return to your office?"

On the mezzanine steps Schlag hesitated, then raced on toward the door marked Manager. A moment later he was shouting into the phone. "You've already gone to press? But I only gave you that shoplifter story a couple of hours ago! You can't kill it?"

He hung up quickly as Johnny entered the office, followed by a smiling Joyce Gifford and a tense Miss Vought.

Taking the phone, Johnny dialed a number. "Police Headquarters? Missing Property, please . . . Yes, I'm calling about a black leather purse with identification for a Mrs. Whistler . . . Oh, it's been turned in? Fine!"

Johnny smiled at the store manager. "It was turned in an hour ago. By a child—a mere street urchin. A touching development, I think."

"Lemme talk to them!" Schlag snatched the phone. "That purse—is there a store sales slip in it?" During the moment's pause the receiver trembled against Schlag's ash-colored ear. "Yes? From Teague's? For $8.85?" His voice sank to a hopeless whisper. "Officer, at the bottom of that slip has a special tax been added . . . like for jewelery."

Fifteen seconds later the phone was in its cradle and Dudley P. Schlag had collapsed in his swivel chair.

Johnny Creighton spoke softly but menacingly. "No doubt you'll soon learn that Mrs. Whistler reported the theft of her purse. Perhaps the officers didn't report to headquarters immediately. And I'm sure a clerk at Teague's will remember Mrs. Whistler's buying a brooch this morning. We are charging you with false arrest and imprisonment, slander, physical assault—"

"Assault? No one touched her!"

"You're lying!" Joyce Gifford slammed her notebook shut. "You both attacked her! I saw the whole brutal thing. You twisted her arm until she screamed and Mr. Schlag tried to kick her. It's a wonder the poor old lady isn't dead!" She stepped close to Johnny. "And I'll swear to that, Mr. . . . . is it Leighton?"

At 6:10 four people sat in Schlag's office. Joyce Gifford was not present. She had left MacTavish's, never to return. Next to the store manager was Walter Matson, legal counsel for MacTavish's. Johnny Creighton was seated beside Mrs. Whistler, whose hands were folded in her lap. A faraway look on her sweet face revealed signs of recent suffering.

Johnny was concluding his remarks. "On Monday we will sue for five hundred thousand dollars. Mrs. Whistler will be an appealing plaintiff, don't you think?"

"Five hundred thousand!" Attorney Matson's face was faintly purple. "You're out of your mind!"

"I agree." Mrs. Whistler put a gentle hand on Johnny's arm. "Let's end this unpleasantness without a lot of fuss. I'll drop this whole thing in exchange for two little favors. I've been through a shocking experience. And I hate to say it, but it's entirely your fault, Mr. Schlag. So I expect MacTavish's to pay me six thousand four hundred and eight dollars and eighty-five cents. Also, I met a charming woman today—in jail, of all places. Her name is Mrs. Blainey, and—"

"A shoplifter!" Schlag interrupted. "We've got a confession."

"You could drop the charges," said Mrs. Whistler. "I just couldn't be happy knowing she was in prison." Mrs. Whistler smiled brightly. "And when I'm unhappy, only one thing consoles me. Money—lots of it. Five hundred thousand dollars of it."

"Relax, Dudley," said the lawyer. "You've had it."

Joyce met them at the door of the apartment. She threw her arms first around Mrs. Whistler, then around Johnny. "You were just wonderful," she said. "Johnny, I never saw you like that before!"

Johnny blushed modestly. "Routine," he said.

They celebrated in a small candlelit restaurant. Johnny raised his glass. "Merry Christmas for the Blainey family! Sixty-four hundred will pay off the mortgage on their house."

Mrs. Whistler nodded. "And I'm getting back the eight eighty-five I spent for that dreadful brooch this morning." She frowned. "Oh, dear! I forgot about the rent for the Santa costume."

"What Santa costume?" Joyce asked. But Johnny quickly changed the subject.

THE NECKLACE OF PEARLS

by Dorothy L. Sayers

Dorothy Leigh Sayers was perhaps the best English mystery writer of the 1920s. She invented a sort of crossbreed between the novel and the detective story. Lord Peter Wimsey had his debut in 1923, in Whose Body. *His popularity was firmly established by Sayers's second book (1926),* Clouds of Witness.

A long list of Wimsey stories, two non-Wimsey mysteries and three excellent anthologies are evidence that Miss Sayers was an expert in the field of crime literature. She never thought much, however, of her mystery career, preferring to pursue her real interest, religious (Church-of-England) literature. In 1947 she announced that she would write no more detective stories.

Sir Septimus Shale was accustomed to assert his authority once in the year, and once only. He allowed his young and fashionable wife to fill his house with diagrammatic furniture made of steel, to collect advanced artists and antigrammatical poets, to believe in cocktails and relativity and to dress as extravagantly as she pleased; but he did insist on an old-fashioned Christmas. He was a simple-hearted man who really liked plum pudding and cracker mottoes, and he could not get it out of his head that other people, "at bottom," enjoyed these things also. At Christmas, therefore, he firmly retired to his country house in Essex, called in the servants to hang holly and mistletoe upon the cubist electric fittings, loaded the steel sideboard with delicacies from Fortnum & Mason, hung up stockings at the heads of the polished walnut bedsteads, and even, on this occasion only, had the electric radiators removed from the modernist grates and installed wood fires and a Yule log. He then gathered his family and friends about him, filled them with as much Dickensian good fare as he could persuade them to swallow, and, after their Christmas dinner, set them down to play "Charades" and "Clumps" and "Animal, Vegetable, and Mineral" in the drawing-room, concluding these diversions by "Hide-and-Seek" in the dark all over the house. Because Sir Septimus was a very rich man, his guests fell in with this invariable program, and if they were bored, they did not tell him so.

Another charming and traditonal custom which he followed was that of presenting to his daughter Margharita, a pearl on each successive birthday—this anniversary happening to coincide with Christmas Eve. The pearls now numbered twenty, and the collection was beginning to enjoy a certain celebrity and had been photographed in the Society papers. Though not sensationally large— each one being about the size of a marrow-fat pea—the pearls were of very great value. They were of exquisite color and perfect shape and matched to a hair's-weight. On this particular Christmas Eve, the presentation of the twenty-first pearl had been the occasion of a very special ceremony. There was a dance and there were speeches. On the Christmas night, following, the more restricted family party took place, with the turkey and the Victorian games. There were eleven guests in addition to Sir Septimus and Lady Shale and their daughter, nearly all related or connected to them in some way: John Shale, a brother with his wife and their son and daughter, Henry and Betty; Betty's fiancé, Oswald Truegood a young man with parliamentary ambitions; George Comphrey, a cousin of Lady Shale's, aged about thirty and known as a man about town; Lavinia Prescott, asked on George's account; Joyce Trivett, asked on Henry Shale's account; Richard and Beryl Dennison, distant relations of Lady Shale, who lived a gay and expensive life in town on nobody precisely knew what resources; and Lord Peter Wimsey, asked, in a touching spirit of unreasonable hope, on Margharita's account. There were also, of course, William Norgate, secretary to Sir Septimus, and Miss Tomkins, secretary to Lady Shale, who had to be there because, with-

out their calm efficiency, the Christmas arrangements
could not have been carried through.

Dinner was over—a seemingly endless succession of
soup, fish, turkey, roast beef, plum pudding, mince pies,
crystallized fruit, nuts, and five kinds of wine, presided
over by Sir Septimus, all smiles, by Lady Shale, all mock-
ing deprecation, and by Margharita, pretty and bored,
with the necklace of twenty-one pearls gleaming softly
on her slender throat. Gorged and dyspeptic and longing
only for the horizontal position, the company had been
shepherded into the drawing room and set to play "Musical Chairs" (Miss Tomkins at the piano), "Hunt the Slipper" (slipper provided by Miss Tomkins), and "Dumb
Crambo" (costumes by Miss Tomkins and Mr. William
Norgate). The back drawing room (for Sir Septimus clung
to these old-fashioned names) provided an admirable
dressing room, being screened by folding doors from the
large drawing room, in which the audience sat on alumi-
num chairs, scrabbling uneasy toes on a floor of black
glass under the tremendous illumination of electricity reflected from a brass ceiling.

It was William Norgate who, after taking the temper-
ature of the meeting, suggested to Lady Shale that they
should play at something less athletic. Lady Shale agreed
and, as usual, suggested bridge. Sir Septimus, as usual,
blew the suggestion aside.

"Bridge? Nonsense! Nonsense! Play bridge every day
of your lives. This is Christmastime. Something we can
all play together. How about 'Animal, Vegetable, and
Mineral'?"

This intellectual pastime was a favorite with Sir
Septimus; he was rather good at putting pregnant questions. After a brief discussion, it became evident that
this game was an inevitable part of the program. The
party settled down to it, Sir Septimus undertaking to "go
out" first and set the thing going.

Presently they had guessed, among other things, Miss
Tomkin's mother's photograph, a gramophone record of
"I want to be happy" (much scientific research into the
exact composition of records, settled by William Norgate
out of the *Encyclopaedia Britannica*), the smallest stick-
leback in the stream at the bottom of the garden, the new
planet, Pluto, the scarf worn by Mrs. Dennison (very
confusing, because it was not silk, which would be ani-

mal, or artifical silk, which would be vegetable, but made of spun glass—mineral, a very clever choice of subject), and had failed to guess the Prime Minister's wireless speech—which was voted not fair, since nobody could decide whether it was animal by nature or a kind of gas. It was decided that they should do one more word and then go on to "Hide-and-Seek." Oswald Truegood had retired into the back room and shut the door behind him while the party discussed the next subject of examination, when suddenly Sir Septimus broke in on the argument by calling to his daughter:

"Hullo, Margy! What have you done with your necklace?"

"I took it off, Dad, because I thought it might get broken in 'Dumb Crambo.' It's over here on this table. No, it isn't. Did you take it, mother?"

"No, I didn't. If I'd seen it, I should have. You are a careless child."

"I believe you've got it yourself, Dad. You're teasing."

Sir Septimus denied the accusation with some energy. Everybody got up and began to hunt about. There were not many places in that bare and polished room where a necklace could be hidden. After ten minutes' fruitless investigation, Richard Dennison, who had been seated next to the table where the pearls had been placed, began to look rather uncomfortable.

"Awkward, you know," he remarked to Wimsey.

At this moment, Oswald Truegood put his head through the folding doors and asked whether they hadn't settled on something by now, because he was getting the fidgets.

This directed the attention of the searchers to the inner room. Margharita must have been mistaken. She had taken it in there, and it had got mixed up with the dressing-up clothes somehow. The room was ransacked. Everything was lifted up and shaken. The thing began to look serious. After half an hour of desperate energy it became apparent that the pearls were nowhere to be found.

"They must be somewhere in these two rooms, you know," said Wimsey. "The back drawing room has no door, and nobody could have gone out of the front drawing room without being seen. Unless the windows—"

No. The windows were all guarded on the outside by heavy shutters which it needed two footmen to take down and replace. The pearls had not gone out that way. In fact, the mere suggestion that they had left the drawing room at all was disagreeable. Because—because—

It was William Norgate, efficient as ever, who coldly and boldly faced the issue.

"I think, Sir Septimus, it would be a relief to the minds of everybody present if we could all be searched."

Sir Septimus was horrified, but the guests, having found a leader, backed up Norgate. The door was locked, and the search was conducted—the ladies in the inner room and the men in the outer.

Nothing resulted from it except some very interesting information about the belongings habitually carried about by the average man and woman. It was natural that Lord Peter Wimsey should possess a pair of forceps, a pocket lens, and a small folding foot rule—was he not a Sherlock Holmes in high life? But that Oswald Truegood should have two liver pills in a screw of paper and Henry Shale a pocket edition of *The Odes of Horace* was unexpected. Why did John Shale distend the pockets of his dress suit with a stump of red sealing wax, an ugly little mascot, and a five-shilling piece? George Comphrey had a pair of folding scissors and three wrapped lumps of sugar, of the sort served in restaurants and dining cars—evidence of a not uncommon form of kleptomania; but that the tidy and exact Norgate should burden himself with a reel of white cotton, three separate lengths of string, and twelve safety pins on a card seemed really remarkable till one remembered that he had superintended all the Christmas decorations. Richard Dennison, amid some confusion and laughter, was found to cherish a lady's garter, a powder compact, and half a potato; the last-named, he said, was a prophylactic against rheumatism (to which he was subject), while the other objects belonged to his wife. On the ladies' side, the more striking exhibits were a little book on palmistry, three invisible hairpins, and a baby's photograph (Miss Tomkins); a Chinese trick cigarette-case with a secret compartment (Beryl Dennison); a *very* private letter and an outfit for mending stocking runs (Lavinia Prescott); and a pair of eyebrow tweezers and a small packet of white powder, said to be for headaches (Betty Shale). An agitating moment followed the production from Joyce Trivett's handbag of a small string of pearls—but it was promptly remembered that these had come out of one of the crackers at dinner time, and they were, in fact, synthetic. In short, the search was unproductive of anything beyond a general shamefacedness and the discomfort always produced by undressing and redressing in a hurry at the wrong time of the day.

It was then that somebody, very grudgingly and haltingly, mentioned the horrid word "Police." Sir Septimus, naturally, was appalled by the idea. It was disgusting. He would not allow it. The pearls must be somewhere. They must search the rooms again. Could not Lord Peter Wimsey, with his experience of—er—mysterious happenings, do something to assist them?

"Eh?" said his lordship. "Oh, by Jove, yes—by all means, certainly. That is to say, provided nobody supposes—eh, what? I mean to say, you don't know that I'm not a suspicious character, do you, what?"

Lady Shale interposed with authority.

"We don't think *anybody* ought to be suspected," she said, "but, if we did, we'd know it couldn't be you. You know *far* too much about crimes to want to commit one."

"All right," said Wimsey. "But after the way the place has been gone over . . ." He shrugged his shoulders.

"Yes, I'm afraid you won't be able to find any footprints," said Margharita. "But we may have overlooked something."

Wimsey nodded.

"I'll try. Do you all mind sitting down on your chairs in the outer room and staying there? All except one of you—I'd better have a witness to anything I do or find. Sir Septimus—you'd be the best person, I think."

He shepherded them to their places and began a slow circuit of the two rooms, exploring every surface, gazing up to the polished brazen ceiling and crawling on hands and knees in the approved fashion across the black and shining desert of the floors. Sir Septimus followed, staring when Wimsey stared, bending with his hands upon his knees when Wimsey crawled, and puffing at intervals with astonishment and chagrin. Their progress rather resembled that of a man taking out a very inquisitive puppy for a very leisurely constitutional. Fortunately, Lady Shale's taste in furnishing made investigation easier; there were scarcely any nooks or corners where anything could be concealed.

They reached the inner drawing room, and here the

dressing-up clothes were again minutely examined, but without result. Finally, Wimsey lay down flat on his stomach to squint under a steel cabinet which was one of the very few pieces of furniture which possessed short legs. Something about it seemed to catch his attention. He rolled up his sleeve and plunged his arm into the cavity, kicked convulsively in the effort to reach farther than was humanly possible, pulled out from his pocket and extended his folding foot rule, fished with it under the cabinet, and eventually succeeded in extracting what he sought.

It was a very minute object—in fact, a pin. Not an ordinary pin, but one resembling those used by entomologists to impale extremely small moths on the setting board. It was about three-quarters of an inch in length, as fine as a very fine needle, with a sharp point and a particularly small head.

"Bless my soul!" said Sir Septimus. "What's that?"

"Does anybody here happen to collect moths or beetles or anything?" asked Wimsey, squatting on his haunches and examining the pin.

"I'm pretty sure they don't," replied Sir Septimus. "I'll ask them."

"Don't do that." Wimsey bent his head and stared at the floor, from which his own face stared meditatively back at him.

"I see," said Wimsey presently. "That's how it was done. All right, Sir Septimus. I know where the pearls are, but I don't know who took them. Perhaps it would be as well—for everybody's satisfaction—just to find out. In the meantime they are perfectly safe. Don't tell anyone that we've found this pin or that we've discovered anything. Send all these people to bed. Lock the drawing-room door and keep the key, and we'll get our man—or woman—by breakfast-time."

"God bless my soul," said Sir Septimus, very much puzzled.

Lord Peter Wimsey kept careful watch that night upon the drawing-room door. Nobody, however, came near it. Either the thief suspected a trap or he felt confident that any time would do to recover the pearls. Wimsey, however, did not feel that he was wasting his time. He was making a list of people who had been left alone in the back drawing room during the playing of "Animal, Vegetable, and Mineral." The list ran as follows:

Sir Septimus Shale
Lavinia Prescott
William Norgate
Joyce Trivett and Henry Shale (together, because they
   had claimed to be incapable of guessing anything un-
   aided)
Mrs. Dennison
Betty Shale
George Comphrey
Richard Dennison
Miss Tomkins
Oswald Truegood

He also made out a list of the persons to whom pearls might be useful or desirable. Unfortunately, this list agreed in almost all respects with the first (always excepting Sir Septimus) and so was not very helpful. The two secretaries had both come well recommended, but that was exactly what they would have done had they come with ulterior designs; the Dennisons were notorious livers from hand to mouth; Betty Shale carried mysterious white powders in her handbag and was known to be in with a rather rapid set in town; Henry was a harmless dilettante, but Joyce Trivett could twist him round her little finger and was what Jane Austen liked to call "expensive and dissipated"; Comphrey speculated; Oswald Truegood was rather frequently present at Epsom and Newmarket—the search for motives was only too fatally easy.

When the second housemaid and the under-footman appeared in the passage with household implements, Wimsey abandoned his vigil, but he was down early to breakfast. Sir Septimus, with his wife and daughter, was down before him, and a certain air of tension made itself felt. Wimsey, standing on the hearth before the fire, made conversation about the weather and politics.

The party assembled gradually, but, as though by common consent, nothing was said about pearls until after breakfast, when Oswald Truegood took the bull by the horns.

"Well, now!" said he. "How's the detective getting along? Got your man, Wimsey?"

"Not yet," said Wimsey easily.

Sir Septimus, looking at Wimsey as though for his cue, cleared his throat and dashed into speech.

"All very tiresome," he said, "all very unpleasant. Hr'rm. Nothing for it but the police, I'm afraid. Just at Christmas, too. Hr'rm. Spoiled the party. Can't stand seeing all this stuff about the place." He waved his hand towards the festoons of evergreens and colored paper that adorned the walls. "Take it all down, eh, what? No heart in it. Hr'rm. Burn the lot."

"What a pity, when we worked so hard over it," said Joyce.

"Oh, leave it, Uncle," said Henry Shale. "You're bothering too much about the pearls. They're sure to turn up."

"Shall I ring for James?" suggested William Norgate.

"No," interrupted Comphrey, "let's do it ourselves. It'll give us something to do and take our minds off our troubles."

"That's right," said Sir Septimus. "Start right away. Hate the sight of it."

He savagely hauled a great branch of holly down from the mantelpiece and flung it, crackling, into the fire.

"That's the stuff," said Richard Dennison. "Make a good old blaze!" He leaped up from the table and snatched the mistletoe from the chandelier. "Here goes! One more kiss for somebody before it's too late."

"Isn't it unlucky to take it down before the New Year?" suggested Miss Tomkins.

"Unlucky be hanged. We'll have it all down. Off the stairs and out of the drawing room too. Somebody go and collect it."

"Isn't the drawing room locked?" asked Oswald.

"No. Lord Peter says the pearls aren't there, wherever else they are, so it's unlocked. That's right, isn't it, Wimsey?"

"Quite right. The pearls were taken out of these rooms. I can't tell yet how, but I'm positive of it. In fact, I'll pledge my reputation that wherever they are, they're not up there."

"Oh, well," said Comphrey, "in that case, have at it! Come along, Lavinia—you and Dennison do the drawing room, and I'll do the back room. We'll save a race."

"But if the police are coming in," said Dennison, "oughtn't everything to be left just as it is?"

"Damn the police!" shouted Sir Septimus. "They don't want evergreens."

"Oswald and Margharita were already pulling the holly and ivy from the staircase, amid peals of laughter. The party dispersed. Wimsey went quietly upstairs and into the drawing room, where the work of demolition was taking place at a great rate, George having bet the other two ten shillings to a tanner that they would not finish their part of the job before he finished his.

"You mustn't help," said Lavinia, laughing to Wimsey. "It wouldn't be fair."

Wimsey said nothing, but waited till the room was clear. Then he followed them down again to the hall, spluttering, suggestive of Guy Fawkes night. He whispered to Sir Septimus, who went forward and touched George Comphrey on the shoulder.

"Lord Peter wants to say something to you, my boy," he said.

Comphrey started and went with him a little reluctantly, as it seemed. He was not looking very well.

"Mr. Comphrey," said Wimsey, "I fancy these are some of your property." He held out the palm of his hand, in which rested twenty-two fine, small-headed pins.

"Ingenious," said Wimsey, "but something less ingenious would have served his turn better. It was very unlucky, Sir Septimus, that you should have mentioned the pearls when you did. Of course, he hoped that the loss wouldn't be discovered till we'd chucked guessing games and taken to 'Hide-and-Seek.' The pearls might have been anywhere in the house, we wouldn't have locked the drawing-room door, and he could have recovered them at his leisure. He had had this possibility in his mind when he came here, obviously, and that was why he brought the pins, and Miss Shale's taking off the necklace to play 'Dumb Crambo' gave him his opportunity.

"He had spent Christmas here before, and knew perfectly well that 'Animal, Vegetable, and Mineral' would form part of the entertainment. He had only to gather up the necklace from the table when it came to his turn to retire, and he knew he could count on at least five minutes by himself while we were all arguing about the choice of a word. He had only to snip the pearls from the string with his pocket scissors, burn the string in the grate, fasten the pearls to the mistletoe with the fine pins. The mistletoe was hung on the chandelier, pretty high—it's a lofty room—but he could easily reach it by standing on the glass table, which wouldn't show footmarks, and it was almost certain that nobody would think of examining the mistletoe for extra berries. I shouldn't have thought of it myself if I hadn't found that pin which he had dropped. That gave me the idea that the pearls had been separated, and the rest was easy. I took the pearls off the mistletoe last night—the clasp was there, too, pinned among the holly leaves. Here they are. Comphrey must have got a nasty shock this morning. I knew he was our man when he suggested that the guests should tackle the decorations themselves and that he should do the back drawing room —but I wish I had seen his face when he came to the mistletoe and found the pearls gone."

"And you worked it all out when you found the pin?" said Sir Septimus.

"Yes; I knew then where the pearls had gone to."

"But you never even looked at the mistletoe."

"I saw it reflected in the black glass floor, and it struck me then how much the mistletoe berries looked like pearls."

FATHER CRUMLISH
CELEBRATES CHRISTMAS

by Alice Scanlan Reach

Alice Scanlan Reach is well known in the mystery field for her charming and frequently exciting stories about Father Crumlish. For evidence of her skills, just read on.

"Eat that and you'll be up all night with one of your stomach gas attacks." Emma Catt's voice boomed out from the doorway of what she considered to be her personal sanctuary—the kitchen of St. Brigid's rectory.

Caught in the act of his surreptitious mission, Father Francis Xavier Crumlish hastily withdrew the arthritic fingers of his right hand, which had been poised to enfold one of several dozen cookies cooling on the wide, old-fashioned table.

"I—I was just thinking to myself that a crumb or two would do no harm," he murmured, conscious of the guilty flush seeping into the seams, tucks, and gussets of his face.

"It would seem to me that a man of the cloth would be the first to put temptation behind him," Emma observed tartly as she strode across the worn linoleum flooring. "Particularly a man of your age," she added, giving him a meaningful look.

The pastor swallowed a heavy sigh. After Emma had arrived to take charge of St. Brigid's household chores some twenty-two years ago, he had soon learned to his sorrow that her culinary feats were largely confined to bland puddings, poached prunes, and a concoction which she called "Irish Stew" and which was no more than a feeble attempt to disguise the past week's leftovers.

So he was most agreeably surprised one day when Emma miraculously produced a batch of cookies of such flavorful taste and texture that the priest mentally forgave her all her venial sins. And since it was Father Crumlish's nature to share his few simple pleasures with others, he promptly issued instructions that, once a year, Emma should bake as many of the cookies as the parish's meager budget would allow. As a result, although St. Brigid's pastor and his housekeeper were on extra-short rations from Thanksgiving until Christmas Eve, many a parishioner's otherwise cheerless Christmas Day was brightened by a bag of the sugar-and-spice delicacies.

Now, today, as the priest quickly left the kitchen area to avoid any further allusions to his ailments and his advancing years, the ringing of the telephone was entirely welcome. He hurried down the hallway to his office and picked up the receiver.

"St. Brigid's."

"It's Tom, Father."

Father Crumlish recognized the voice of Lieutenant Thomas Patrick "Big Tom" Madigan of Lake City's police force and realized, from the urgency in the policeman's tone, that his call was not a social one.

"I'm at the Liberty Office Building," Madigan said in a rush. "A guy's sitting on a ledge outside the top-story window. Says he's going to jump. If I send a car for you—"

"I'll be waiting at the curb, Tom," Father interrupted and hung up the phone.

"Big Tom" Madigan was waiting outside the elderly office building when Father Crumlish arrived some minutes later. Quickly he ushered the priest through the emergency police and fire details and the crowd of curious onlookers who were gazing in awe at the scarecrow figure perched on a ledge high above the street.

"Do you know the man, Tom?" Father asked. He followed the broad-shouldered policeman into the building lobby, and together they entered a self-service elevator.

"And so do you, Father," Madigan said as he pressed the elevator button. "He's one of your people. Charley Abbott."

"God bless us!" the pastor exclaimed. "What do you suppose set Charley off this time?" He sighed. "The poor lad's been in and out of sanitariums half a dozen times in his thirty years. But this is the first time he's ever tried to do away with himself."

"This may not be just one of Abbott's loony notions," Madigan replied grimly. "Maybe he's got a good reason for wanting to jump off that ledge."

"What do you mean, Tom?"

"Last week a man named John Everett was found murdered in his old farmhouse out in Lake City Heights. He was a bachelor, lived alone, no relatives—"

"I read about it," Father interrupted impatiently. "What's that got to do—"

"We haven't been able to come up with a single clue," Madigan broke in, "until half an hour ago. One of my detectives, Dennis Casey, took an anonymous phone call from a man who said that if we wanted to nab Everett's murderer we should pick up the daytime porter at the Liberty Office Building."

"That's Charley." Father nodded, frowning. "I myself put in a good word for him for the job."

"Casey came over here on a routine check," Madigan went on as the elevator came to a halt and he and the priest stepped out into the corridor. "He showed Abbott his badge, said he was investigating Everett's murder, and wanted to ask a few questions. Abbott turned pale—looked as if he was going to faint, Casey says. Then he made a dash for the elevator, rode it up to the top floor, and climbed out the corridor window onto the ledge."

"But surely, now, Tom," Father protested, "you can't be imagining that Charley Abbott had a hand in that killing? Why, you know as well as I that, for all his peculiar ways, Charley's gentle as a lamb."

"All I know," Madigan replied harshly, "is that when we tried to ask him a few questions, he bolted." He ran a hand over his crisp, curly brown hair. "And I know that innocent men don't run."

"Innocent or guilty," Father Crumlish said, "the man's in trouble. Take me to him, Tom."

When Father Crumlish entered the priesthood more than forty years before, he never imagined that he was destined to spend most of those years in St. Brigid's parish —that weary bedraggled section of Lake City's waterfront where destitution and despair, avarice and evil, walked hand in hand. And although, on the occasions when he

lost a battle with the Devil, he too sometimes teetered on
the brink of despair, he unfailingly rearmed himself with
his intimate, hard-won knowledge of his people.

But now, as the old priest leaned out the window and
caught sight of the man seated on the building's ledge, his
confidence was momentarily shaken. Charley Abbott had
the appearance and demeanor of a stranger. The man's
usually slumped, flaccid shoulders were rigid with purpose; his slack mouth and chin were set in taut, hard lines;
and in place of his normal attitude of wavering indecision, there was an aura about him of implacable determination.

There was not a doubt in Father Crumlish's mind that
Abbott intended to take the fatal plunge into eternity. The
priest took a deep breath and silently said a prayer.

"Charley," he then called out mildly, "it's Father Crumlish. I'm right here close to you, lad. At the window."

Abbott gave no indication that he'd heard his pastor's
voice.

"Can you hear me, Charley?"

No response.

"I came up here to remind you that we have been
through a lot of bad times together," Father continued
conversationally. "And together we'll get through whatever it is that's troubling you now."

The priest waited for a moment, hoping to elicit some
indication that Abbott was aware of his presence. But the
man remained silent and motionless, staring into space.
Father decided to try another approach.

"I've always been proud of you, Charley," Father said.
"And never more so than when you were just a tyke and
ran in the fifty-yard dash at our Annual Field Day Festival." He sighed audibly. "Ah, but that's so many years
ago, and my memory plays leprechaun's tricks. I can't recall for the life of me, lad—did you come in second or
third?"

Again Father waited, holding his breath. Actually he
remembered the occasion clearly. The outcome had been
a major triumph in his attempts to bring a small spark of
reality into his young parishioner's dreamy, listless life.

Suddenly Abbott's long legs, which were dangling aim-
lessly over the perilous ledge, stiffened, twitched. Slowly
he turned his head and focused his bleak eyes on the
priest.

"I—I won!" he said, in the reproachful, defensive voice of a small child.

"I can't hear you, Charley," Father said untruthfully, striving to keep the tremor of relief from his voice. "Could you speak a little louder? Or come a bit closer?"

To Father Crumlish it seemed an eternity before Abbott's shoulders relaxed a trifle, before his deathlike grip on the narrow slab of concrete and steel diminished, before slowly, ever so slowly, the man began to inch his way along the ledge until he came within an arm's reach of the window and the priest. Then he paused and leaned tiredly against the building's brick wall.

"I won," he repeated, this time in a louder and firmer tone.

"I remember now," Father said, never taking his dark blue eyes from his parishioner's pale, distraught face. "So can you tell me why a fellow like yourself, with a fine pair of racing legs, would be hanging them out there in the breeze?"

The knuckles of Charley's hands grasping the ledge whitened. "The cops are going to say I murdered Mr. Everett—" He broke off in agitation.

"Go on, Charley."

"They're going to arrest me. Put me away." Abbott's voice rose hysterically. "And this time it'll be forever. I can't stand that, Father." Abruptly he turned his head away from the priest and made a move as if to rise to his feet. "I'll kill myself first."

"Stay where you are!" Father Crumlish commanded. "You'll not take your life in the sight of God, with me standing by to have it on my conscience that I wasn't able to save you."

Cowed by Father's forcefulness, Abbott subsided and once more turned his stricken gaze on the pastor's face.

"I want you to look me straight in the eye, Charley," Father said, "and answer my question: as God is your Judge, did you kill the man?"

"No, Father. No!" The man's slight form swayed dangerously. "But nobody will believe me."

Father Crumlish stared fixedly into Abbott's pale blue eyes, which were dazed now and dark with desperation. But the pastor also saw in them his parishioner's inherent bewilderment, fear—and his childlike innocence. Poor lad, he thought compassionately. Poor befuddled lad.

"*I* believe you, Charley," he said in a strong voice. "And I give you my word that you'll not be punished for a crime you didn't commit." With an effort the priest leaned further out the window and extended his hand. "Now come with me."

Hesitatingly Abbott glanced down at the priest's outstretched, gnarled fingers.

"My word, Charley."

Abbott sat motionless, doubt and indecision etched on his thin face.

"Give me your hand, lad," Father said gently.

Once again the man raised his eyes until they met the priest's.

"Give me your hand!"

It was a long excruciating moment before Charley released his grip on the ledge, extended a nail-bitten, trembling hand, and permitted the pastor's firm warm clasp to lead him to safety.

It was Father Crumlish's custom to read the *Lake City Times* sports page while consuming his usual breakfast of coddled egg, dry toast, and tea. But this morning he delayed learning how his beloved Giants, and in particular Willie Mays, were faring until he'd read every word of the running story on John Everett's murder.

Considerable space had been devoted to the newest angle on the case—Charley Abbott's threatened suicide after the police had received an anonymous telephone tip and had sought to question him. Abbott, according to the story, had been taken to Lake City Hospital for observation. Meanwhile, the police were continuing their investigation, based on the few facts at their disposal.

To date, John Everett still remained a "mystery man." With the exception of his lawyer, banker, and the representative of a large real-estate management concern—and his dealings with all three had been largely conducted by mail or telephone—apparently only a handful of people in Lake City were even aware of the man's existence. As a result, his murder might not have come to light for some time, had it not been for two youngsters playing in the wooded area which surrounded Everett's isolated farmhouse. Prankishly peering in a window, they saw his body sprawled on the sparsely furnished living-room floor and notified the police. According to the Medical Examiner,

Everett had been dead less than twenty-four hours. Death was the result of a bullet wound from a .25 automatic.

Although from all appearances Everett was a man of modest means, the story continued, investigation showed that in fact he was extremely wealthy—the "hidden owner" of an impressive amount of real estate in Lake City. Included in his holdings was the Liberty Office Building where Charley Abbott had almost committed suicide.

Frowning, Father Crumlish put down the newspaper and was about to pour himself another cup of tea when the telephone rang. Once again it was Big Tom Madigan —and Father was not surprised. It was a rare day when Madigan failed to "check in" with his pastor—a habit formed years ago, when he'd been one of the worst hooligans in the parish and the priest had intervened to save him from reform school. And in circumstances like the present, where one of St. Brigid's parishioners was involved in a crime, the policeman always made sure that Father Crumlish was acquainted with the latest developments.

"I've got bad news, Father," Madigan said, his voice heavy with fatigue.

The priest braced himself.

"Seems Everett decided to demolish quite a few old buildings that he owned. Turn the properties into parking lots. I've got a list of the ones that were going to be torn down and the Liberty is on it." Madigan paused a moment. "In other words, Charley Abbott was going to lose his job. Not for some months, of course, but—"

"Are you trying to tell me that any man would commit murder just because he was going to lose his job?" Father was incredulous.

"Not *any* man. *Charley*. You know that he didn't think his porter's job was menial. To him it was a 'position,' a Big Deal, the most important thing that ever happened to him."

Father Crumlish silently accepted the truth of what Big Tom had said. And yet . . . "But I still can't believe that Charley is capable of murder," he said firmly. "There's something more to all this, Tom."

"You're right, Father, there is," Madigan said. "Abbott lived in the rooming house run by his sister and brother-in-law, Annie and Steve Swanson."

"That I know."

"Casey—the detective who tried to question Charley yesterday—went over to the house to do a routine check on Charley's room. Hidden under the carpet, beneath the radiator, he found a recently fired .25 automatic."

The priest caught his breath.

"Casey also found a man's wallet. Empty—except for a driver's license issued to John Everett."

"What will happen to poor Charley now, Tom?" Father finally managed to ask.

"In view of the evidence I'll have to book him on suspicion of murder."

After hanging up the phone, the priest sat, disconsolate and staring into space, until Emma Catt burst into the room, interrupting his troubled thoughts.

"I just went over to church to put some fresh greens on the roof of the crib," Emma reported. "Some of the statuettes have been stolen again."

Wincing at her choice of the word, the pastor brushed at his still-thick, snow-white hair, leaned back in his desk chair, and closed his eyes.

In observance of the Christmas season St. Brigid's church traditionally displayed a miniature crib, or manger, simulating the scene of the Nativity. Statuettes representing the participants in the momentous event were grouped strategically in the stable. And to enhance the setting, boughs of fir, pine, and holly were placed around the simple structure.

So while Father Crumlish was pleased by Emma's attention to the crib's appearance, he also understood the full meaning of her report. It was sad but true that each year, on more than one occasion, some of the statuettes would be missing. But, unlike Emma, Father refused to think of the deed as "stealing." From past experience (sometimes from a sobbing whisper in the Confessional), he knew that some curious child had knelt in front of the crib, stretched out an eager hand, perhaps to caress the Infant, and then . . .

"What's missing this time?" the priest asked tiredly.

"The Infant, the First Wise Man, and a lamb."

"Well, no harm done. I'll step around to Herbie's and buy some more."

"It would be cheaper if you preached a sermon on stealing."

" 'They know not what they do,' " the old priest mur-mured as he adjusted his collar and his bifocals, shrugged himself into his shabby overcoat, quietly closed the rec-tory door behind him, and walked out into the gently falling snow.

Minutes later he opened the door of Herbie's Doll House, a toy and novelty store which had occupied the street floor of an aged three-story frame building on Broad Street as long as the pastor could remember. As usual at this time of the year, the store was alive with the shrill voices of excited youngsters as they examined trains, wag-ons, flaxen-haired dolls, and every imaginable type of Christmas decoration. Presiding over the din was the pro-prietor, Herbie Morris, a shy, slight man in his late sixties.

Father Crumlish began to wend his way through the crowd, reflecting sadly that most of his young parishioners would be doomed to disappointment on Christmas Day. But in a moment Herbie Morris caught sight of the priest, quickly elbowed a path to his side, and eagerly shook Fa-ther's outstretched hand.

"I can see that the Christmas spirit has caught hold of you again this year," Father Crumlish said with a chuckle. "You're a changed man." It was quite true. Herbie Mor-ris' normally pale cheeks were rosy with excitement, and his usually dull eyes were shining.

"I know you and all the storekeepers in the parish think I'm a fool to let the kids take over in here like this every Christmas," Herbie said sheepishly but smiling broadly. "You think they rob me blind." He sighed. "You're right. But it's worth it just to see them enjoying themselves—" He broke off, and a momentary shadow crossed his face. "When you have no one—no real home to go to—it gets lonely—" His voice faltered. "Especially at Christmas."

Father Crumlish put an arm around the man's thin shoulder. "It's time you had a paying customer," he said heartily. "I need a few replacements for the crib."

Nodding, Morris drew him aside to a counter filled with statuettes for the manger, and Father quickly made his selections. The priest was about to leave, when Herbie clasped his arm.

"Father," he said, "I've been hearing a lot about Char-ley Abbott's trouble. I room with the Swansons."

"I know you do," Father said, "I'm on my way now to
see Annie and Steve."

"George says Charley had been acting funny lately."

"George?"

"George Floss. He rooms there too."

"The same fellow who's the superintendent of the Liberty Office Building?" Father was surprised.

"That's him. Charley's boss."

Thoughtfully the priest tucked the box of statuettes under his arm and departed. Although his destination was
only a few minutes' walk, it was all of half an hour before
he arrived. He'd been detained on the way in order to
halt a fistfight or two, admire a new engagement ring,
console a recently bereaved widow, and steer homeward a
parishioner who'd been trying to drain dry the beer tap in
McCaffery's Tavern. But finally he mounted the steps of
a battered house with a sign on the door reading: *Rooms.*

He had little relish for his task. Annie and Steve were
a disagreeable, quarrelsome pair, and the pastor knew
very well that they considered his interest in Charley's
welfare all through the years as "meddling." Therefore
he wasn't surprised at the look of annoyance of Steve's
face when he opened the door.

"Oh, it's you, Father," Steve said ungraciously. "C'mon
in. Annie's in the kitchen."

Silently Father followed the short, barrel-chested man,
who was clad in winter underwear and a pair of soiled
trousers, down a musty hallway. Annie was seated at the
kitchen table, peeling potatoes. She was a scrawny, pallid-
complexioned woman who, Father knew, was only in her
mid-forties. But stringy gray hair and deep lines of discontent crisscrossing her face made her appear to be much
older. Now, seeing her visitor, she started to wipe her
hands on her stained apron and get to her feet. A word
from the pastor deterred her.

"I suppose you've come about Charley," she said sulk-
ily.

"Ain't nothing you can do for him this time, Father,"
Steve said with a smirk. "This time they got him for good
—and good riddance."

"Shut up," Annie snapped, shooting her husband a
baleful glance.

"First time the crazy fool ever had a decent-paying
job," Steve continued, ignoring her. "And what does he

do?" He cocked his thumb and forefinger. "Gets a gun and—"

"Shut up, I said!" Annie's face flamed angrily.

"Hiya, Father," a jovial voice interrupted from the doorway. "You here to referee?"

Father turned and saw that the tall burly man entering the kitchen was one of the stray lambs in his flock— George Floss. Murmuring a greeting, the priest noticed that Floss was attired in a bathrobe and slippers.

"It's my day off," George volunteered, aware of Father's scrutiny. He yawned widely before his heavy-jowled face settled into a grin. "So I went out on the town last night."

"That explains your high color," Father remarked dryly. He turned back to the table, where Annie and Steve sat glowering at each other. "Now, if you can spare a moment from your bickering," he suggested, "maybe you can tell me what happened to set Charley off again."

Steve pointed a finger at Floss. "He'll tell you."

"Charley was doing fine," George said as he poured a cup of coffee from a pot on the stove. "Didn't even seem to take it too hard—at least, not at first—when I told him he was going to be out of a job."

"*You* told him?" the priest said sharply.

"Why, sure," Floss replied with an important air. "I'm the super at the Liberty Building. Soon as I knew the old dump was going to be torn down, I told everybody on the maintenance crew that they'd be getting the ax. Me too." He scowled and his face darkened. "A stinking break. There aren't too many good super jobs around town."

He gulped some coffee and then brightened. "Of course it won't be for some time yet. That's what I kept telling Charley. But I guess it didn't sink in. He started worrying and acting funny—" He broke off with a shrug.

"You haven't heard the latest, George," Steve said. "That cop—Casey—was here nosing around Charley's room. Found a gun and the Everett guy's wallet."

"No kidding!" Floss's eyes widened in surprise. He shook his head and whistled.

"Gun, wallet, no matter what that cop found," Annie shrilled, waving the paring knife in her hand for emphasis, "I don't believe it. Charley may be a little feeble-minded, but he's no murderer—"

The air was suddenly pierced by a loud and penetrating wail. In an upstairs bedroom a child was crying.

"Now see what you've done," Steve said disgustedly. "Started the brat bawling."

Annie gave a potato a vicious stab with her knife. "Go on up and quiet her."

"Not me," Steve retorted with a defiant shake of his balding head. "That's your job."

"I've got enough jobs, cooking and cleaning around here. It won't kill you to take care of the kid once in a while."

Father Crumlish had stood in shocked silence during the stormy scene. But now he found his tongue.

"It's ashamed you should be," he said harshly, turning his indignant dark blue eyes first on Annie, then on Steve. "When I baptized our little Mary Ann, four years ago, I told both of you that you were blessed to have a child at your age and after so many years. Is this disgraceful behavior the way you give thanks to the good Lord? And is this home life the best you can offer the poor innocent babe?"

He took a deep breath to cool his temper. Annie and Steve sat sullen and wordless. The only sound in the silence was the child's crying.

"I'll go and see what's eating her," George offered, obviously glad to escape from the scene.

"I've an errand to do," Father told the Swansons. "But mind you—he held up a warning finger—"I'll be back before long to have another word or two with you."

Turning on his heel, he crossed the kitchen floor, walked down the hallway, and let himself out the door. But before he was halfway down the steps to the street, he heard Annie's and Steve's strident voices raised in anger again. And above the din he was painfully aware of the plaintive, persistent sound of the crying child.

Lieutenant Madigan was seated at his desk, engrossed in a sheaf of papers, when Father Crumlish walked into headquarters.

"Sit down, Father," Big Tom said sympathetically. "You look tired. And worried."

Irritated, the pastor clicked his tongue against his upper plate. He disliked being told that he looked tired and worried; he knew very well that he *was* tired and wor-

ried, and that was trouble enough. He considered remaining on his feet, stating his business succinctly, and
then being on his way. But the chair next to Madigan's
desk looked too inviting. He eased himself into it, sup-
pressing a sigh of relief.

"I know all this is rough on you, Father," Madigan
continued in a kind tone. "But facts are facts." He
paused, extracted one of the papers in front of him, and
handed it to the priest.

Father Crumlish read it slowly. It was a report on the
bullet which had killed John Everett; the bullet definitely
had been fired from the gun found in Charley Abbott's
room. Silently the pastor placed the report on Big Tom's
desk.

"This is one of those cases that are cut and dried," the
policeman said. "One obvious suspect, one obvious motive." He shifted his gaze away from the bleak look on
Father's face. "But you know that with his mental record
Charley will never go to prison."

Abruptly Father Crumlish got to his feet.

"Can you tell me where I'll find Detective Dennis
Casey?" he asked.

Madigan stared in astonishment. "Third door down the
hall. But why—?"

Father Crumlish had already slipped out the door,
closed it behind him, and a moment later he was seated
beside Detective Casey's desk. Then, in response to the
priest's request, Casey selected a manila folder from his
files.

"Here's my report on the anonymous phone call, Father," he said obligingly. "Not much to it, as you can
see."

A glance at the typed form confirmed that the report
contained little information that Father didn't already
have.

"I was hoping there might be more," the pastor said
disappointedly. "I know you've been on this case since
the beginning and I thought to myself that maybe there
was something that might have struck you about the
phone call. Something odd in the man's words, perhaps."
Father paused and sighed. "Well, then, maybe you can
tell me about your talk with Charley. Exactly what you
said to him—"

"Wait a minute, Father," Casey interrupted. He ran a

hand through his carrot-hued hair. "Now that you mention it, I *do* remember something odd about that call. I remember hearing a funny sound. Just before the guy hung up."

"Yes?" Father waited hopefully for the detective to continue.

Casey's brows drew together as he tried to recall.

"It was a sort of whining. A cry, maybe." Suddenly his eyes lit up. "Yeah, that's it! It sounded like a baby—a kid—crying."

As Father Crumlish wearily started up the steps to the rectory door, his left foot brushed against a small patch of ice buried beneath the new-fallen snow. He felt himself slipping, sliding, and he stretched out a hand to grasp the old wrought-iron railing and steady himself. As he did, the package of statuettes, which he'd been carrying all these long hours, fell from under his arm and tumbled to the sidewalk.

"Hellfire!"

Gingerly Father bent down to retrieve the package. At that moment St. Brigid's chimes ran out. Six o'clock! Only two hours before Evening Devotions, the priest realized in dismay as he straightened and stood erect. And in even less time his parishioners would be arriving at church to kneel down at the crib, light their candles, and say their prayers.

Well, Father thought, he would have to see to it that they wouldn't be disappointed, that there would be nothing amiss in the scene of the Nativity. Moments later he stood in front of the crib and unwrapped the package. To his chagrin he discovered that the tumble to the sidewalk had caused one of the lambs to lose its head and one leg. But Herbie Morris could easily repair it, Father told himself as he stuffed the broken lamb into his pocket and proceeded to put his replacements in position. First, in the center of the crib, the Infant. Next, to the left, the First Wise Man. And then, close to the Babe, another unbroken lamb that he'd purchased.

Satisfied with his handiwork, Father knelt down and gazed at the peaceful tableau before him. Ordinarily the scene would have evoked a sense of serenity. But the priest's heart was heavy. He couldn't help but think that it was going to be a sad Christmas for Charley Abbott. And that the man's prospects for the future were even worse. Moreover, Father couldn't erase the memory of what he'd seen and heard at the Swansons—the anger, bitterness, selfishness, and, yes, even the cruelty.

Hoping to dispel his disquieting thoughts, the pastor started to close his eyes. But a slight movement in the crib distracted him. He stared in astonishment as he saw that a drop of moisture had appeared on the face of the Infant and had begun to trickle slowly down the pink waxen cheeks.

Even as he watched, fascinated, another drop appeared—and then the priest quickly understood the reason for the seeming phenomenon. The greens that Emma had placed on the roof of the stable had begun to lose their resilience in the steam heat of the church. The fir, pine, and holly boughs were drooping, shedding moisture on the face of the Child. . . .

In the flickering rosy glow of the nearby vigil lights it struck the priest that the scene seemed almost real—as if the Child were alive and crying. As if He were weeping for all the people in the world. All the poor, lonely, homeless—

Father Crumlish stiffened. A startled expression swept over his face. For some time he knelt, alert and deep in thought, while his expression changed from astonishment to realization and, finally, to sadness. Then he rose from his knees, made his way to the rectory office, and dialed police headquarters.

"Could you read me that list you have of the buildings that John Everett was going to have torn down?" Father said when Madigan's voice came on the wire. The policeman complied.

"That's enough, Tom," the priest interrupted after a moment. "Now tell me, lad, will you be coming to Devotions tonight? I've a call to make and I thought, with this snow, you might give me a lift."

"Glad to, Father." Suspicion crept into Madigan's voice. "But if you're up to something—"

The pastor brought the conversation to an abrupt end by hanging up.

Herbie Morris was on the verge of locking up The Doll House when Father Crumlish and Big Tom walked in.

"Can you give this a bit of glue, Herbie?" Father asked as he handed the storekeeper the broken lamb.

"Forget it, Father," Herbie said, shrugging. "Help yourself to a new one."

"No need. I'm sure you can fix this one and it'll do fine."

Then, as Herbie began to administer to the statuette, the pastor walked over to a display of flaxen-haired dolls and leaned across the counter to select one. But the doll eluded his grasp and toppled over. The motion caused it to close its eyes, open its mouth, and emit the realistic sound of a child crying.

"I see your telephone is close by," Father said, pointing to the instrument on a counter across the aisle. "So it's little wonder that Detective Casey thought he heard a real child crying while you were on the phone with him at headquarters. One of these dolls must have fallen over just as you were telling him to arrest Charley Abbott for John Everett's murder."

The priest was aware of Madigan's startled exclamation and the sound of something splintering. Herbie stood staring down at his hands, which had convulsively gripped the lamb he'd been holding, and broken it beyond repair.

"I know that you were notified that this building is going to be torn down, Herbie," Father said, "and I know these four walls are your whole life. But were you so bitter that you were driven to commit murder to get revenge?"

"I didn't want revenge," Herbie burst out passionately. "I just wanted to keep my store. That's all!" He wrung his hands despairingly. "I pleaded with Everett for two months, but he wouldn't listen. Said he wanted this land for a parking lot." Morris's shoulders sagged and he began to weep.

Madigan moved to the man's side. "Go on," he said in a hard voice.

"When I went to his house that night, I took the gun just to frighten him. But he still wouldn't change his mind. I went crazy, I guess, and—" He halted and looked pleadingly at the priest. "I didn't really mean to kill him, Father. Honest!"

"What about his wallet?" Madigan prodded him.

"It fell out of his pocket. There was a lot of money in it—almost a thousand dollars. I—I just took it."

"And then hid it, along with the gun, in the room of a poor innocent man," Father Crumlish said, trying to contain his anger. "And to make sure that Charley would be charged with your crime, you called the police."

"But the police would have come after *me*," Herbie protested, as if to justify his actions. "I read in the papers that they were checking Everett's properties and all his tenants. I was afraid—" The look on Father's face caused Herbie's voice to trail away.

"Not half as afraid as Charley when you kept warning him that the police would accuse him because of his mental record, because he worked in the Liberty Building and was going to lose his job. That's what you did, didn't you?" Father asked in a voice like thunder. "You deliberately put fear into his befuddled mind, told him he'd be put away—"

The priest halted and gazed at the little storekeeper's bald bowed head. There were many more harsh words on the tip of his tongue that he might have said. But, as a priest, he knew that he must forego the saying of them.

Instead he murmured, "God have mercy on you."

Then he turned and walked out into the night. It had begun to snow again—soft, gentle flakes. They fell on Father Crumlish's cheeks and mingled with a few drops of moisture that were already there.

It was almost midnight before Big Tom Madigan rang St. Brigid's doorbell. Under the circumstances Father wasn't surprised by the policeman's late visit.

"How did you know, Father?" Madigan asked as he sank into a chair.

Wearily Father related the incident at the crib. "After what I heard at the Swansons and what Casey told me, a crying child was on my mind. And then, when I saw what looked like tears on the Infant's face, I got to thinking about all the homeless—" He paused for a long moment.

"Only a few hours before, Herbie had told me how hard it was, particularly at Christmas, to be lonely and without a real home. Charley was suspected of murder because he was going to lose his job. But wasn't it more reasonable to suspect a man who was going to lose his life's work? His whole world?" Father sighed. "I knew Herbie never could have opened another store in a new location. He would have had to pay much higher rent, and he was barely making ends meet where he was."

It was some moments before Father spoke again.

"Tom," he said brightly, sitting upright in his chair. "I happen to know that the kitchen table is loaded down with Christmas cookies."

The policeman chuckled. "And I happen to know that Emma Catt counts every one of 'em. So don't think you can sneak a few."

"Follow me, lad," Father said confidently as he got to his feet. "You're on the list for a dozen for Christmas. Is there any law against my giving you your present now?"

"Not that I know of, Father," Madigan replied, grinning.

"And in the true Christmas spirit, Tom"—Father Crumlish's eyes twinkled merrily—"I'm sure you'll want to share and share alike."

Father Crumlish's Christmas Cookies

RECIPE:
  3 tablespoons butter
  1/2 cup sugar
  1/2 cup heavy cream
  1/3 cup sifted flour
  1 1/4 cups very finely chopped blanched almonds
  3/4 cup very finely chopped candied fruit and peels
  1/4 teaspoon ground cloves
  1/4 teaspoon ground nutmeg
  1/4 teaspoon ground cinnamon

(1) Preheat oven to 350 degrees.
(2) Combine butter, sugar, and cream in a saucepan and bring to a boil. Remove from the heat.
(3) Stir in other ingredients to form a batter.
(4) Drop batter by spoonfuls onto a greased baking sheet, spacing them about three inches apart.
(5) Bake ten minutes or until cookies begin to brown around the edges. Cool and then remove to a flat surface. If desired, while cookies are still warm, drizzle melted chocolate over tops.

YIELD: About 24 cookies

—*Courtesy of the author*

THE CHRISTMAS MASQUE

by S. S. Rafferty

Born in New England in 1930, "S. S. Rafferty" worked as a newspaperman and free-lance writer, and was a Marine Corps news correspondent during the Korean conflict. Following military service, he went into the advertising business in Boston and later New York, where he served as vice president of a major agency.

In 1977 he decided to write full time and has now published over sixty short stories in the mystery genre. He is perhaps best known for three series detectives: Captain Jeremy Cork, an eighteenth-century American colonial "fact finder"; Dr. Amos Phipps, a nineteenth-century New York criminologist known as "The Hawk"; and Chick Kelly, a modern-day stand-up comic who delightfully mixes detection with schtick. The Captain Cork stories were collected under the title Fatal Flourishes, *and the other two richly deserve to be.*

As much as I prefer the steady ways of New England, I have to agree with Captain Jeremy Cork that the Puritans certainly know how to avoid a good time. They just ignore it. That's why every twenty-third of December we come to the New York colony from our home base in Connecticut to celebrate the midwinter holidays.

I am often critical of my employer's inattention to his many business enterprises and his preoccupation with the solution of crime—but I give him credit for the way he keeps Christmas. That is, as long as I can stop him from keeping it clear into February.

In our travels about these colonies, I have witnessed
many merry parties, from the lush gentility of the Caroli-
nas to the roughshod ribaldry of the New Hampshire
tree line; but nothing can match the excitement of the
Port of New York. The place teems with prosperous men
who ply their fortunes in furs, potash, naval timber, and
other prime goods. And the populace is drawn from
everywhere: Sephardim from Brazil, Huguenots from
France, visitors from London, expatriates from Naples,
Irishmen running to or from something. I once counted
eighteen different languages being spoken here.

And so it was in the Christmas week of 1754 that we
took our usual rooms at Marshall's, in John Street, a few
steps from the Histrionic Academy, and let the yuletide
roll over us. Cork's celebrity opens many doors to us, and
there was the expected flood of invitations for one frivol-
ity after another.

I was seated at a small work table in our rooms on
December twenty-third, attempting to arrange our social
obligations into a reasonable program. My primary task
was to sort out those invitations which begged our presence on Christmas Eve itself, for that would be our high
point. Little did I realize that a knock on our door would
not only decide the issue, but plunge us into one of the
most bizarre of those damnable social puzzles Cork so
thoroughly enjoys.

The messenger was a small lad, no more than seven or
eight, and he was bundled against the elements from head
to toe. Before I could open the envelope to see if an immediate reply was required, the child was gone.

I was opening the message when Cork walked in from
the inner bedchamber. Marshall's is one of the few places
on earth with doorways high enough to accommodate his
six-foot-six frame.

"I take the liberty," I said. "It's addressed to us both."

"On fine French linen paper, I see."

"Well, well," I said, reading fine handscript. "This is
quite an honor."

"From the quality of the paper and the fact that you
are 'honored' just to read the message, I assume the
reader is rich, money being the primer for your respect,
Oaks."

That is not absolutely true. I find nothing wrong with
poverty; however, it is a condition I do not wish to ex-

perience. In fact, as Cork's financial yeoman, it is my sworn duty to keep it from our doorsill. The invitation was from none other than Dame Ilsa van Schooner, asking us to take part in her famous Christmas Eve Masque at her great house on the Broad Way. Considering that we had already been invited to such questionable activites as a cockfight, a party at a doss house, a drinking duel at Cosgrove's, and an evening of sport at the Gentlemen's Club, I was indeed honored to hear from a leader of New York quality.

Cork was glancing at the invitation when I discovered a smaller piece of paper still in the envelope.

"This is odd," I said, reading it:

van Schooner Haus
22 December
Dear Sirs:
    I implore you to accept the enclosed, for I need you very much to investigate a situation of some calamity for us. I shall make myself known at the Masque.

It was unsigned. I passed it to the captain, who studied it for a moment and then picked up the invitation again.

"I'm afraid your being honored is misplaced, my old son," he said. "The invitation was written by a skilled hand, possibly an Ephrata penman, hired for such work. But our names have been fitted in by a less skilled writer. The author of the note has by some means invited us without the hostess's knowledge. Our *sub rosa* bidder must be in some dire difficulty, for she does not dare risk discovery by signing her name."

"Her?"

"No doubt about it. The hand is feminine, and written in haste. I thought it odd that a mere boy should deliver this. It is usually the task of a footman, who would wait for a reply. This is truly intriguing—an impending calamity stalking the wealthy home in which she lives."

"How can you be sure of that, sir?"

"I can only surmise. She had access to the invitations and she says 'calamity for us,' which implies her family. Hello." He looked up suddenly as the door opened and a serving girl entered with a tray, followed by a man in royal red. "Sweet Jerusalem!" Cork got to his feet. "Major Tell in the flesh! Sally, my girl, you had better have Marshall send up extra Apple Knock and oysters. Tell, it is prophetic that you should appear just as a new puzzle emerges."

Prophetic indeed. Major Philip Tell is a King's agent-at-large, and he invariably embroiled us in some case of skulduggery whenever he was in our purlieu. But I bode him no ill this time, for he had nothing to do with the affair. In fact, his vast knowledge of the colonial scene might prove helpful.

"Well, lads," Tell said, taking off his *rogueloure* and tossing his heavy cloak onto a chair. "I knew Christmas would bring you to New York. You look fit, Captain, and I see Oaks is still at his account books."

When Cork told him of our invitation and the curious accompanying note, the officer gave a low whistle. "The van Schooners, no less! Well, we shall share the festivities, for I am also a guest at the affair. The note is a little disturbing, however. Dame Ilsa is the mistress of a large fortune and extensive land holdings, which could be the spark for foul play."

"You think she sent the note?" I asked.

"Nonsense," Cork interjected. "She would not have had to purloin her own invitation. What can you tell us of the household, Major?"

I don't know if Tell's fund of knowledge is part of his duties or his general nosiness, but he certainly keeps his ear to the ground. No gossip-monger could hold a candle to him.

"The family fortune was founded by her grandfather, Nils van der Malin—patroon holdings up the Hudson, pearl potash, naval stores, that sort of old money. Under Charles the Second's Duke of York grant, Nils was rewarded for his support with a baronetcy. The title fell in the distaff side to Dame Ilsa's mother, old Gretchen van der Malin. She was a terror of a woman, who wore men's riding clothes and ran her estates with an iron fist and a riding crop. She had a young man of the Orange peerage brought over as consort, and they produced Ilsa. The current Dame is more genteel than her mother was, but just as stern and autocratic. She, in turn, married a van Schooner—Gustave, I believe, a soldier of some distinction in the Lowland campaigns. He died of drink after fathering two daughters, Gretchen and her younger sister, Wilda.

"The line is certainly Amazonite and breeds true," Cork said with a chuckle. "Not a climate I would relish, although strong women have their fascination."

"Breeds true is correct, Captain. The husbands were little more than sire stallions; good blood but ruined by idleness."

This last, about being "ruined by idleness," was ignored by Cork, but I marked it, as well he knew.

"Young Gretchen," Tell went on, "is also true to her namesake. A beauty, but cold as a steel blade, and as well honed. They say she is a dead shot and an adept horsewoman."

"You have obviously been to the van Schooner Haus, as our correspondent calls it."

"Oh, yes, on several occasions. It is truly a place to behold."

"No doubt, Major." Cork poured a glass of Apple Knock. "Who else lives there besides the servants?"

"The younger daughter, Wilda, of course, and the Dame's spinster sister, Hetta van der Malin, and an ancient older brother of the dead husband—the brother is named Kaarl. I have only seen him once, but I am told he was quite the wastrel in his day, and suffers from the afflictions of such a life."

"Mmm," Cork murmured, offering the glass to Tell. "I change my original Amazonite observation to that of Queen Bee. Well, someone in that house feels in need of help, but we shall have to wait until tomorrow night to find out why."

"Or who," I said.

"That," Cork said, "is the heart of the mystery."

The snow started falling soon after dinner that night and kept falling into the dawn. By noon of the twenty-fourth, the wind had drifted nature's white blanket into knee-high banks. When it finally stopped in the late afternoon, New York was well covered under a blotchy sky. The inclemency, however, did not deter attendance at the van Schooner Ball.

I had seen the van Schooner home from the road many times, and always marveled at its striking architecture, which is in the Palladio style. The main section is a three-story structure, and it is flanked by one-story wings at both sides.

The lights and music emanating from the north wing clearly marked it a ballroom of immese size. The front entrance to the main house had a large raised enclosure which people in these parts call a stoop. The interior was as rich and well appointed as any manse I have ever seen. The main hall was a gallery of statuary of the Greek and Roman cast, collected, I assumed, when the family took the mandatory Grand Tour.

Our outer clothes were taken at the main door, and we were escorted through a sculptured archway across a large salon towards the ballroom proper. We had purposely come late to avoid the reception line and any possible discovery by Dame van Schooner. We need not have bothered. There were more than two-hundred people there, making individual acquaintance impossible. Not that some of the guests were without celebrity. The Royal Governor was in attendance, and I saw General Seaton and Solomon deSilva, the fur king, talking with Reeves, the shipping giant.

It was difficult to determine the identity of the majority of the people, for most wore masks, although not all, including Cork and myself. Tell fluttered off on his social duties, and Cork fell to conversation with a man named Downs, who had recently returned from Spanish America and shared common friends there with the Captain.

I helped myself to some hot punch and leaned back to take in the spectacle. It would be hard to say whether the men or the women were the more lushly bedizened. The males were adorned in the latest fashion with those large and, to my mind, cumbersome rolled coat cuffs. The materials of their plumage were a dazzling mixture of gold and silver stuffs, bold brocades, and gaudy flowered velvets. The women, not to be outdone by their peacocks, were visions in fan-hooped gowns of silks and satins and fine damask. Each woman's *tête-de-mouton* back curls swung gaily as her partner spun her around the dance floor to madcap tunes such as "Roger de Coverly," played with spirit by a seven-piece ensemble. To the right of the ballroom entrance was a long table with three different punch bowls dispensing cheer.

The table was laden with all manner of great hams, glistening roast goose, assorted tidbit meats and sweets of unimaginable variety. Frothy syllabub was cupped up for the ladies by liveried footmen, while the gentlemen had their choice of Madeira, rum, champagne, or Holland gin, the last served in small crystal thimbles which were embedded and cooled in a silver bowl mounded with snow.

"This is most lavish'" I said to Cork when he disengaged himself from conversation with Downs. "It's a good example of what diligent attention to industry can produce."

"Whose industry, Oaks? Wealth has nothing more to do with industry than privilege has with merit. Our hostess, over there, does not appear to have ever perspired in her life."

He was true to the mark in his observation, for Dame van Schooner, who stood chatting with the Governor near the buffet, was indeed as cold as fine-cut crystal. Her well formed face was sternly beautiful, almost arrogantly defying any one to marvel at its handsomeness and still maintain normal breathing.

"She *is* a fine figure of a woman, Captain, and, I might add, a widow."

He gave me a bored look and said, "A man would die of frostbite in her bedchamber. Ah, Major Tell, congratulations! You are a master at the jig!"

"It's a fantastical do, but good for the liver, I'm told. Has the mysterious sender of your invitation made herself known to you?"

"Not as yet. Is that young lady now talking with the Dame one of her daughters?"

"Both of them are daughters. The one lifting her mask is Gretchen, and I might add, the catch of the year. I am told she has been elected Queen of the Ball, and will be crowned this evening."

The girl was the image of her mother. Her sister, however, must have followed the paternal line.

"The younger one is Wilda," Tell went on, "a dark pigeon in her own right, but Gretchen is the catch."

"Catch, you say." I winked at Cork. "Perhaps *her* bedchamber would be warmer?"

"You'll find no purchase there, gentlemen," Tell told us. "Along with being crowned Queen, her betrothal to Brock van Loon will probably be announced this evening."

"Hand-picked by her mother, no doubt?" Cord asked.

"Everything is hand-picked by the Dame. Van Loon is

a stout fellow, although a bit of a tailor's dummy. Family is well landed, across the river, in Brueckelen. Say, they're playing 'The Green Cockade,' Captain. Let me introduce you to Miss Borden, one of our finest steppers."

I watched them walk over to a comely piece of frippery, and then Cork and the young lady stepped onto the dance floor. "The Green Cockade" is one of Cork's favorite tunes, and he dances it with gusto.

I drifted over to the serving table and took another cup of punch, watching all the time for some sign from our mysterious "hostess," whoever she was. I mused that the calamity mentioned in the note might well have been pure hyperbole, for I could not see how any misfortune could befall this wealthy, joyous home.

With Cork off on the dance floor, Tell returned to my side and offered to find a dance partner for me. I declined, not being the most nimble of men, but did accept his bid to introduce me to a lovely young woman named Lydia Daws-Smith. The surname declared her to be the offspring of a very prominent family in the fur trade, and her breeding showed through a delightfully pretty face and pert figure. We were discussing the weather when I noticed four footmen carrying what appeared to be a closed sedan chair into the hall and through a door at the rear.

"My word, is a sultan among the assemblage?" I asked my companion.

"The sedan chair?" She giggled from behind her fan. "No, Mr. Oaks, no sultan. It's our Queen's throne. Gretchen will be transported into the hall at the stroke of midnight, and the Governor will proclaim her our New Year's Sovereign." She stopped for a moment, the smile gone. "Then she will step forward to our acclaim, and of course, mandatory idolatry."

"I take it you do not like Gretchen very much, Miss Daws-Smith."

"On the contrary, sir. She is one of my best friends. Now you will have to excuse me, for I see Gretchen is getting ready for the crowning, and I must help her."

I watched the young girl as she followed Gretchen to the rear of the hall, where they entered a portal and closed the door behind them. Seconds later, Lydia Daws-Smith came back into the main hall and spoke with the Dame, who then went through the rear door.

Cork had finished his dance and rejoined me. "This exercise may be good for the liver," he said, "but it plays hell with my thirst. Shall we get some refills?"

We walked back to the buffet table to slake his thirst, if that were ever possible. From the corner of my eye I caught sight of the Dame reentering the hall from the rear door. She crossed over to the Governor and was about to speak to him, when the orchestra struck up another tune. She seemed angry at the intrusion into what was obviously to have been the beginning of the coronation. But the Dame was ladylike and self-contained until the dancing was over. She then took a deep breath and nervously adjusted the neckline of her dress, which was shamefully bare from the bodice to the neck.

"Looks like the coronation is about to begin," Major Tell said, coming up to us. "I'll need a cup for the toast."

We were joking at the far end of the table when a tremendous crash sounded. We turned to see a distraught Wilda van Schooner looking down at the punch bowl she had just dropped. The punch had splashed down her beautiful velvet dress, leaving her drenched and mortified.

"Oh-Oh," Tell said under his breath. "Now we'll hear some fireworks from Dame van Schooner."

True to his prediction, the Dame sailed across the floor and gave biting instructions to the footmen to bring mops and pails. A woman, who Tell told me in a whisper was Hetta van der Malin, the Dame's sister, came out of the crowd of tittering guests to cover her niece's embarrassment.

"She was only trying to help, Ilsa," the aunt said as she dabbed the girl's dress with a handkerchief.

The Dame glared at them. "You'd better help her change, Hetta, if she is going to attend the coronation."

The aunt and niece quickly left the ballroom, and the Dame whirled her skirts and returned to the Governor's side. I overheard her say her apologies to him, and then she added, "My children don't seem to know what servants are for. Well, shall we begin?"

At a wave of her hand, the orchestra struck up the "Grenadier's March," and six young stalwarts lined up in two ranks before the Governor. At his command, the lads did a left turn and marched off towards the rear portal in the distinctive long step of the regiment whose music they had borrowed for the occasion.

They disappeared into the room where Gretchen waited for transport, and within seconds they returned bearing the ornate screened sedan chair. "Aah's" filled the room over the beauty and pageantry of the piece. I shot a glance at Dame van Schooner and noted that she was beaming proudly at the impeccably executed production.

When the sedan chair had been placed before the Governor, he stepped forward, took the curtain drawstrings, and said, "Ladies and gentlemen, I give you our New Year's Queen."

The curtains were pulled open, and there she sat in majesty. More "aah's" from the ladies until there was a screech and then another and, suddenly, pandemonium. Gretchen van Schooner sat on her portable throne, still beautiful, but horribly dead, with a French bayonet through her chest.

"My Lord!" Major Tell gasped and started forward toward the sedan chair. Cork touched his arm.

"You can do no good there. The rear room, man, that's where the answer lies. Come, Oaks." He moved quickly through the crowd, and I followed like a setter's tail on point. When we reached the door, Cork turned to Tell.

"Major, used your authority to guard this door. Let no one enter." He motioned me inside and closed the door behind us.

It was a small room, furnished in a masculine manner. Game trophies and the heads of local beasts protruded from the walls and were surrounded by a symmetrical display of weaponry such as daggers, blunderbusses, and swords.

"Our killer had not far to look for his instrument of death," Cork said, pointing to an empty spot on the wall about three feet from the fireplace and six feet up from the floor. "Move with care, Oaks, lest we disturb some piece of evidence."

I quickly looked around the rest of the chamber. There was a door in the south wall and a small window some ten feet to the left of it.

"The window!" I cried. "The killer must have come in—"

"I'm afraid not, Oaks," Cork said, after examining it.

"The snow on the sill and panes is undisturbed. Besides, the floor in here is dry. Come, let's open the other door."

He drew it open to reveal a short narrow passage that was dimly lit with one sconced candle and had another door at its end. I started toward it and found my way blocked by Cork's outthrust arm.

"Have a care, Oaks," he said. "Don't confound a trail with your own spore. Fetch a candelabrum from the table for more light."

I did so, and to my amazement he got down on his hands and knees and inched forward along the passageway. I, too, assumed this stance and we crept along like a brace of hounds.

The polished planked floor proved dry and bare of dust until we were in front of the outer door. There, just inside the portal, was a pool of liquid.

"My Lord, it is blood!" I said.

"Mostly water from melted snow."

"But, Captain, there is a red stain to it."

"Yes," he said. "Bloody snow, and yet the bayonet in that woman's breast was driven with such force that no blood escaped from her body."

Cork got to his feet and lifted the door latch, opening the passageway to pale white moonlight which reflected off the granules of snow. He carefully looked at the doorstoop and then out into the yard.

"Damnation," he muttered, "it looks as if an army tramped through here."

Before us, the snow was a mass of furrows and upheavals with no one set of footprints discernible.

"Probably the servants coming and going from the wood yard down by the gate," I said, as we stepped out into the cold. At the opposite end of the house, in the left wing, was another door, obviously leading to the kitchen, for a clatter of plates and pots could be heard within the snug and frosty windowpanes. I turned to Cork and found myself alone. He was at the end of the yard, opening a slatted gate in the rear garden wall.

"What ho, Captain," I called ahead, as I went to meet him.

"The place abounds in footprints," he snarled in frustration.

"Then the killer has escaped us," I muttered. "Now

we have the whole population of this teeming port to consider."

He turned slowly, the moonlight glistening off his
barba, his eyes taking on a sardonic glint. "For the moment, Oaks, for the moment. Besides, footprints are like
empty boots. In the long run we would have had to fill
them."

I started to answer, when a voice called from our
backs, at the passage doorway. It was Major Tell.

"Hello, is that you there, Cork? Have you caught the
dastard?"

"Some gall," I said to the captain. "As if we could pull
the murderer out of our sleeves like a magician."

"Not yet, Major," Cork shouted and then turned to
me. "Your powers of simile are improving, Oaks."

"Well," I said, with a bit of a splutter. "Do you think
magic is involved?"

"No, you ass. Sleight of hand! The quick flick that the
eye does not see nor the mind inscribe. We'll have to use
our intincts on this one."

He strode off towards the house, and I followed. I have
seen him rely on instinct over hard evidence only two
times in our years together, and in both cases, although
he was successful, the things he uncovered were too gruesome to imagine.

The shock that had descended on the van Schooner
manse at midnight still lingered three hours later, when
the fires in the great fireplaces were reduced to embers,
the shocked guests had been questioned, and all but the
key witnesses had been sent homeward. Cork, after consultation with the Royal Governor, had been given a
free hand in the investigation, with Major Tell stirred in
to keep the manner of things official.

Much to my surprise, the captain didn't embark on a
flurry of questions of all concerned, but rather drew up a
large baronial chair to the ballroom hearth and brooded
into its sinking glow.

"Two squads of cavalry are in the neighbourhood,"
Major Tell said. "If any stranger were in the vicinity, he
must have been seen."

"You can discount a stranger, Major," Cork said, still
gazing into the embers.

"How so?"

"Merely a surmise, but with stout legs to it. If a stranger came to kill, he would have brought a weapon with him. No, the murderer knew the contents of the den's walls. He also seems to have known the coronation schedule."

"The window," I interjected. "He could have spied the bayonet, and when the coast was clear, entered and struck."

"Except for the singular fact that the snow on the ground in front of the window is undisturbed."

"Well, obviously someone entered by the back passage," Tell said. "We have the pool of water and the blood."

"Then where are the wet footprints into the den, Major?"

"Boots!" I shouted louder than I meant to. "He took off his boots and then donned them again on leaving."

"Good thinking, Oaks," Tell complimented me. "And in the process, his bloody hands left a trace in the puddle."

"And what, pray, was the motive?" Cork asked. "Nothing of value was taken that we can determine. No, we will look within this house for an answer."

Tell was appalled. "Captain Cork, I must remind you that this is the home of a powerful woman, and she was hostess tonight to the cream of New York society. Have a care how you cast aspersions."

"The killer had best have a care, Major. For a moment, let us consider some *facts*. Mistress Gretchen went into the den to prepare for her coronation with the aid of —ah—"

"Lydia Daws-Smith," I supplied.

"So we have one person who saw her before she died. Then these six society bucks who were to transport her entered, and among their company was Brock van Loon, her affianced. Seven people involved between the time we all saw her enter the den and the time she was carried out dead."

"Eight," I said, and then could have bit my tongue.

"Who else?" Cork demanded.

"The Dame herself. I saw her enter after Miss Daws-Smith came out."

"That is highly irresponsible, Oaks," Tell admonished.

"And interesting," Cork said. "Thank you, Oaks, you have put some yeast into it with your observation."

"You're not suggesting that the Dame killed her own daughter!"

"Major," Cork said, "she-animals have been known to eat their young when they are endangered. But enough of this conjecture. Let us get down to rocks and hard places. We will have to take it step by step. First, let us have a go at the footmen who carried the chair into the den before Gretchen entered."

They were summoned, and the senior man, a portly fellow named Trask, spoke for the lot.

"No, sir," he answered Cork's question. "I am sure no one was lurking in the room when we entered. There is no place to hide."

"And the passage to the back door?"

"Empty, sir. You see, the door leading to the passage was open, and I went over to close it against any drafts coming into the den. There was no one in the den, sir, I can swear to it."

"Is the outside door normally kept locked?"

"Oh, yes, sir. Leastways, it's supposed to be. It was locked earlier this afternoon when I made my rounds, preparing for the festivities."

"Tell me, Trask," Cork asked, "do you consider yourself a good servant, loyal to your mistress's household?"

The man's chubby face looked almost silly with its beaming pride. "Twenty-two years in the house, sir, from kitchen boy to head footman, and every day of it in the Dame's service."

"Very commendable, Trask, but you are most extravagant with tapers."

"Sir?" Trask looked surprised.

"If the back-yard door was locked, why did you leave a candle burning in the passageway? Since no one could come in from the outside, no light would be needed as a guide. Certainly any one entering from the den would carry his own."

"But Captain," the footman protested, "I left no light in the passageway. When I was closing the inner door, I held a candelabrum in my hand, and could see clear to the other end. There was no candle lit."

"My apologies, Trask. Thank you, that will be all."

When the footmen had left, I said, "Yet we found a lit

candle out there right after the murder. The killer must have left it, in his haste."

Cork merely shrugged. Then he said, "So we got a little further. Major, I would like to see Miss Daws-Smith next."

Despite the circumstances, I was looking forward to seeing the comely Miss Daws-Smith once more. However, she was not alone when she entered, and her escort made it clear by his protective manner that her beauty was his property alone. She sat down in a straight-backed chair opposite Cork, nervously fingering the fan in her lap. Brock van Loon took a stance behind her.

"I prefer to speak to this young lady alone," Cork said.

"I am aware of your reputation, Captain Cork," van Loon said defensively, "and I do not intend to have Lydia drawn into this."

"Young man, she *is* in it, and from your obvious concern for her, I'd say you are, too."

"It is more than concern, sir. I love Lydia and she loves me."

"Brock," the girl said, turning to him.

"I don't care, Lydia. I don't care what my father says and I don't care what the Dame thinks."

"That's a rather anticlimactic statement, young man. Since your betrothed is dead, you are free of that commitment."

"You see, Brock? Now he suspects that we had something to do with Gretchen's death. I swear, Captain, we had no hand in it."

"Possibly not as cohorts. Was Gretchen in love with this fellow?"

"No. I doubt Gretchen could love any man. She was like her mother, and was doing her bidding as far as a marriage went. The van Schooner women devour males. Brock knows what would have become of him. He saw what happened to Gretchen's father."

"Her father?"

"Gustave van Schooner," Brock said, "died a worthless drunkard, locked away on one of the family estates up the Hudson. He had been a valiant soldier, I am told, and yet, once married to the Dame, he was reduced to a captured stallion."

"Quite poetic," Cork said. "Now, my dear, can you tell

me what happened when you and Gretchen entered the den this evening?"

The girl stopped toying with the fan and sent her left hand to her shoulder, where Brock had placed his. "There's nothing to tell, really. We went into the den together and I asked her if she wanted a cup of syllabub. She said no."

"What was her demeanor? Was she excited?"

"About being the Queen? Mercy, no. She saw that as her due. Gretchen was not one to show emotion." She stopped suddenly in thought and then said, "But now that I think back, she was fidgety. She walked over to the fireplace and tapped on the mantel with her fingers. Then she turned and said, 'Tell the Dame I'm ready,' which was strange, because she never called her mother that."

"Was she being sarcastic?"

"No, Captain, more a poutiness. I went and gave Dame van Schooner the message. That was the last I saw of Gretchen." Her eyes started to moisten. "The shock is just wearing off, I suppose. She was spoiled and autocratic, but Gretchen was a good friend."

"Hardly, Miss Daws-Smith. She had appropriated your lover."

"No. She knew nothing of how I felt towards Brock. We were all children together, you see—Gretchen, Wilda, Brock, and I. When you grow up that way, you don't always know childish affection from romantic love. I admit that when plans were being made for the betrothal, love for Brock burned in me, but I hid it, Captain. I hid it well. Then, earlier this evening, Brock told me how he felt, and I was both elated and miserable. I decided that both Brock and I would go the Dame tomorrow. Gretchen knew nothing of our love."

"And you, sir," Cork said to Brock, "you made no mention of your change of heart to Gretchen?"

The fellow bowed his head. "Not in so many words. This has been coming on me for weeks, this feeling I have for Lydia. Just now, as you were talking to her, I wondered—God, how terrible—if Gretchen could have committed suicide out of despair."

"Oh, Brock!" Lydia was aghast at his words.

"Come," Cork commanded sharply, "this affair is burdensome enough without the added baggage of melodrama. Use your obvious good sense, Miss Daws-Smith.

Is it likely that this spoiled and haughty woman would take her own life? Over a man?"

Lydia raised her head and looked straight at Cork. "No. No, of course not. It's ridiculous."

"Now, Mr. van Loon, when you entered the den with the others in the escort party to bring in the sedan chair, were the curtains pulled shut?"

"Yes, they were."

"And no one spoke to its occupant?"

"No, we didn't."

"Strange, isn't it? Such a festive occasion, and yet no one spoke?"

"We were in a hurry to get her out to where the Governor was waiting. Wait, someone did say, 'Hang on, Gretchen' when we lifted the chair. I don't remember who said it, though."

"You heard no sound from inside the chair? No groan or murmur?"

"No, sir, not a sound."

"Well, thank you for your candor. Oh, yes, Miss Daws-Smith, when you left Gretchen, was she still standing by the fire?"

"Yes, Captain."

"Was her mask on or off?"

She frowned. "Why, she had it on. What a queer question!"

"It's a queer case, young lady."

The great clock in the center hall had just tolled three when Cork finished talking with the other five young men who had carried the murdered girl in the sedan chair. They all corroborated Brock's version. All were ignorant of any expression of love between Brock and Lydia, and they were unanimous in their relief that Brock, and not one of them, had been Gretchen's intended. As one young man named Langley put it, "At least Brock has an inheritance of his own, and would not have been dependent on his wife and mother-in-law."

"Dependent?" Cork queried. "Would he not assume her estate under law?"

"No, sir, not in this house," Langley explained. "I am told it's a kind of morganatic arrangement and a tradition with the old van der Malin line. I have little income, so

Gretchen would have been no bargain for me. Not that I am up to the Dame's standards."

When Langley had left, Trask, the footman, entered to tell us that rooms had been prepared for us at the major's request. Cork thanked him and said, "I know the hour is late, but is your mistress available?"

He told us he would see, and showed us to a small sitting room off the main upstairs hall. It was a tight and cozy chamber with a newly-stirred hearth and the accoutrements of womankind—a small velvet couch with tiny pillows, a secretaire in the corner, buckbaskets of knitting and mending.

Unusual, however, was the portrait of the Dame herself that hung on a wall over the secretaire. It was certainly not the work of a local limner, for the controlled hand of a master painter showed through. Each line was carefully laid down, each color blended one with the other, to produce a perfect likeness of the Dame. She was dressed in a gown almost as beautiful as the one she had worn this evening. At her throat was a remarkable diamond necklace which, despite the two dimensions of the portrait, was lifelike in its cool, blue-white lustre.

Cork was drawn to the portrait and even lifted a candle to study it more closely. I joined him and was about to tell him to be careful of the flame when a voice from behind startled me.

"There are additional candles if you need more light."

We both turned to find Wilda van Schooner standing in the doorway. She looked twice her seventeen years, with the obvious woe she carried inside her. Her puffed eyes betrayed the tears of grief that had recently welled there.

"Forgive my curiosity, Miss van Schooner," Cork said, turning back to the portrait. "Inquisitiveness and a passion for details are my afflictions. This work was done in Europe, of course?"

"No, sir, here in New York, although Jan der Trogue is from the continent. He is—was—to have painted all of us eventually." She broke off into thought and then rejoined us. "My mother is with my sister, gentlemen, and is not available. She insists on seeing to Gretchen herself."

"That is most admirable." Cork bid her to seat herself, and she did so. She did not have her sister's or her mother's coloring, nor their chiseled beauty, but there was something strangely attractive about this tall, dark-haired girl.

"I understand, Captain, that you are here to help us discover the fiend who did this thing, but you will have to bear with my mother's grief."

"To be sure. And what can you tell me, Miss Wilda?"

"I wish I could offer some clue, but my sister and I were not close—we did not exchange confidences."

"Was she in love with Brock van Loon?"

"Love!" she cried, and then did a strange thing. She giggled almost uncontrollably for a few seconds. "That's no word to use in this house, Captain."

"Wilda, my dear," a female voice said from the open door. "I think you are too upset to make much sense to-night. Perhaps in the morning, gentlemen?"

The speaker was the girl's aunt, Hetta van der Malin, and we rose as she entered.

"Forgive our intrusion into your sitting room, ma'am," Cork said with a bow. "Perhaps you are right. Miss Wilda looks exhausted."

"I agree, Captain Cork," the aunt said, and she put her arm around the girl and ushered her out the door.

"Pray," Cork interrupted, "could *you* spare us some time in your niece's stead?"

Her smile went faint, but it was a smile all the same. "How did you know this was *my* room, Captain? Oh, of course. Trask must have—"

"On the contrary, my eyes told me. Your older sister does not fit the image of a woman surrounded by knitting and mending and pert pillowcases."

"No, she doesn't. The den is Ilsa's sitting room. Our mother raised her that way. She is quite a capable person, you know."

"So it would seem. Miss Hetta, may I ask why you invited us here this evening?"

I was as caught off guard as she was.

"Whatever put that notion into your head? My sister dispatched the invitations herself."

"Precisely! That's why you had to purloin one and fill in our names yourself. Come, dear woman, the sample of your hand on the letters on your secretaire matches the hand that penned the unsigned note I received."

"You have looked through my things!"

"I snoop when forced to. Pretence will fail you, ma'am,

for the young lad who delivered this invitation will undoubtedly be found and will identify you. Come, now,
you wrote to invite me here and now you deny it. I will
have an answer."

"Captain Cork," I cautioned him, for the woman was
quivering.

"Yes, I sent it." Her voice was tiny and hollow. "But it
had nothing to do with this horrible murder. It was trivial
compared to it, and it is senseless to bring it up now.
Please believe me, Captain. It was foolish of me."

"You said 'calamity' in your note, and now we have a
murder done. Is that not the extreme of calamity?"

"Yes, of course it is. I used too strong a word in my
note. I would gladly have told you about it after the coronation. But now it would just muddle things. I can't."

"Then, my dear woman, I must dig it out. Must I play
the ferret while you play the mute?" His voice was getting sterner. I know how good an actor he is, but was he
acting?

"Do you know what a colligation is, Madam?"
She shook her head.

"It is the orderly bringing together of isolated facts.
Yet you blunt my efforts; half facts can lead to half
truths. Do you want a half truth?" He paused and then
spat it out. "Your sister may have killed her older daughter!"

"That is unbearable!" she cried.

"A surmise based on a half truth. She was the last person to see Gretchen alive, if the Daws-Smith girl is to be
believed. And why not believe her? If Lydia had killed
Gretchen, would she then send the mother into the room
to her corpse? Take the honor guards who were to carry
the sedan chair: if Gretchen were alive when her mother
left her, could one of those young men have killed her in
the presence of five witnesses?"

"Anyone could have come in from the outside." Miss
Hetta's voice was frantic.

"Nonsense. The evidence is against it."

"Why would Ilsa want to kill her own flesh and blood?
It is unthinkable!"

"And yet people will think it, rest assured. The whole
ugly affair can be whitewashed and pinned to some mysterious assailant who stalked in the night season, but people will think it just the same, Madam."

She remained silent now, and I could feel Cork's mind turning from one tactic to another, searching for leverage. He got to his feet and walked over to the portrait.

"So in the face of silence, I must turn the ferret loose in my mind. Take, for example, the question of this necklace."

"The van der Malin Chain," she said, looking up at the portrait. "What about it?"

"If the painter was accurate, it seems of great worth, both in pounds sterling and family prestige. It's very name proclaims it an heirloom."

"It is. It has been in our family for generations."

"Do you wear it at times?"

"No, of course not. It is my sister's property."

"Your estates are not commingled?"

"Our family holds with primogeniture."

"I do not. Exclusive rights to a first born make a fetish of nature's caprice. But that is philosophy, and beyond a ferret. Where is the necklace, Madam?"

"Why, in my sister's strong box, I assume. This is most confusing, Captain Cork."

I could have added my vote to that. I have seen Cork search for answers with hopscratch questions, but this display seemed futile.

"It is I who am confused, Madam. I am muddled by many things in this case. Why, for instance, didn't your sister wear this necklace to the year's most important social function? She thought enough of it to have it painted in a portrait for posterity."

"Our minds sometimes work that way, Captain. Perhaps it didn't suit her costume."

Cork turned from the picture as if he had had enough of it. "I am told there is a Uncle Kaarl in the household, yet he was not in attendance at the ball tonight. Did he not suit the occasion?"

"You are most rude, sir. Kaarl is an ill man, confined to his bed for several years." She got to her feet. "I am very tired, gentlemen."

"I, too, grow weary, Madam. One last question. Your late neice was irritable this evening, I am told. Did something particular happen recently to cause that demeanor?"

"No. What would she have to sulk about? She was the

center of attraction. I really must retire now. Good night."

When the rustle of her skirts had faded down the silent hallway, I said, "Well, Captain, we've certainly had a turn around the mulberry bush."

He gave me that smirk-a-mouth of his. "Some day, Oaks, you will learn to read between the lines where women are concerned. I am sure you thought me a bully for mistreating her, but it was necessary, and it worked."

"Worked?"

"To a fair degree. I started on her with several assumptions. Some have more weight now, others are discounted. Don't look so perplexed. I am sure that Hetta's note to us did not concern Gretchen directly. She did not fear for the girl's life in this calamity she now chooses to keep secret."

"How is that?"

"Use your common sense, man. If she had suspected an attempt on her niece's life, would she stand mute? No, she would screech her accusations to the sky. Her seeking outside aid from us must have been for another problem. Yes, Trask?"

I hadn't seen the footman in the shadows, nor had I any idea how long he had been there.

"Beg pardon, Captain Cork, but Major Tell has retired to his room and would like to see you when you have a moment."

"Thank you, Trask. Is your mistress available to us now?"

"Her maid tells me she is abed, sir."

"A shame. Maybe you can help me, Trask. My friend and I were wondering why the Dame's picture hangs in this small room. I say it was executed in such a large size to hang in a larger room. Mr. Oaks, however, says it was meant for Miss Hetta's room as an expression of love between the two sisters."

"Well, there is an affection between them, sirs, but the fact is that the portrait hung in the Grand Salon until the Dame ordered it destroyed."

"When was this, Trask?"

"Two days ago. 'Trask,' she said to me, 'take that abomination out and burn it.' Strange, she did like it originally, then, just like that, she hated it. Of course, Miss

Hetta wouldn't let me burn it, so we spirited it in here, where the Dame never comes."

"Ha, you see I was right, Oaks. Thanks for settling the argument, Trask. Where is Major Tell's room?"

"Right next to yours, if you'll follow me, gentlemen."

Tell's chamber was at the back of the house, where we found him sitting in the unlighted room, looking out at the moonlit yard.

"Nothing yet, Major?" Cork asked, walking to the window to join him.

"Not a sign or a shadow. I have men hiding at the front and down there near the garden gate and over to the left by the stable. Do you really expect him to make a move?"

"Conjecture coasts us nothing, although I have more information now."

Although the room was bathed in moonlight, as usual I was in the dark. "Would either of you gentlemen mind telling me what this is all about? *Who* is coming?"

"Going would be more like it," the major said.

"Going—ah, I see! The killer hid himself in the house somewhere and you expect him to make a break for it when everyone is bedded down. But where could he have hidden? Your men searched the den and passageway for secret panels, did they not?"

"Ask your employer," Tell said. "I am only following his orders—hold on, Cork, look down by the passage door."

I looked over Cork's shoulder to catch a glimpse of a cloaked figure in a cockade, moving among the shadows towards the stable.

"Our mounts are ready, Major?" Tell nodded. "Excellent. Let us be off.'

As I followed them downstairs, I remarked on my own puzzlement. "Why are we going to *follow* this scoundrel? Why not stop him and unmask him?"

"Because I know who our mysterious figure is, Oaks. It is the destination that is the heart of the matter," Cork said as we hurried into the ballroom and back to the den door.

Once inside, I saw that Tell had placed our greatcoats in readiness, and we bustled into them. Cork walked over to the weapon wall and looked at two empty hooks.

"A brace of pistols are gone. Our shadow is armed, as expected," he said.

"I'll take this one," I said, reaching for a ball-shot handgun.

"No need, Oaks," Cork said. "We are not the targets. Come, fellows, we want to be mounted and ready."

The night was cold as we waited behind a small knoll twenty yards down from the stable yard. Suddenly the doors of the stable burst open and a black stallion charged into the moonlight, bearing its rider to the south. "Now, keep a small distance but do not lose sight for a second," Cork commanded, and spurred his horse forward.

We followed through the drifts for ten minutes and saw our quarry turn into a small alley. When we reached the spot, we found the lathered mount tied to a stairway which went up the side of the building to a door on the second-story landing. With Cork in the lead, we went up the cold stairs and assembled ourselves in front of the door. "Now!" Cork whispered, and we butted our shoulders against the wood paneling and fell into the room.

Our cloaked figure had a terrified man at gunpoint. The victim was a man in his forties, coiled into a corner. I was about to rush the person with the pistols, when the tricornered hat turned to reveal the chiseled face and cold blue eyes of Dame Ilsa van Schooner.

"Drop the pistols, Madam; you are only compounding your problem," Cork said firmly.

"He murdered my child!"

"I swear, Dame Ilsa!" The man groveled before her. His voice was foreign in inflection. "Please, you must hear me out. Yes, I am scum, but I am not a murderer."

Cork walked forward and put his hands over the pistol barrels. For a split second, the Dame looked up at him and her stern face went soft. "He's going to pay," she said.

"Yes, but not for your daughter's death."

"But only he could have—" She caught herself up in a flash of thought. Her lips quivered, and she released the pistol butts into Cork's control. He took her by the arm and guided her to a chair.

The tension was broken, and I took my first look about. It was a large and comfortable bachelor's room. Then I saw the work area at the far end—with an easel, palettes, and paint pots.

"The painter! He's Jan der Trogue, the one who painted the portrait."

"You know about the painting?" the Dame said with surprise.

I started to tell her about seeing it in her sister's sitting room, but never got it out. Der Trogue had grabbed the pistol that Cork had stupidly left on the table and pointed it at us as he edged towards the open door. "Stay where you are," he warned. "I owe you my life, sir." He bowed to Cork. "But it is not fitting to die at a woman's hands."

"Nor a hangman's," Cork said. "For you will surely go to the gallows for your other crime."

"Not this man, my fine fellow. Now, stay where you are, and no one will get hurt." He whirled out onto the landing and started to race down the stairs. Cork walked to the door. To my surprise, he had the other pistol in his hand. He stepped out onto the snowy landing.

"Defend yourself!" Cork cried. Then, after a tense moment, Cork took careful aim and fired. I grimaced as I heard der Trogue's body tumbling down the rest of the stairs.

Cork came back into the room with the smoking pistol in his hand. "Be sure your report says 'fleeing arrest,' Major," he said, shutting the door.

"Escape from what? You said he didn't kill the girl! This is most confusing and, to say the least, irregular!"

"Precisely put, Major. Confusing from the start and irregular for a finish. But first to the irregularity. What we say, see, and do here tonight stays with us alone." He turned to the Dame. "We will have to search the room. Will you help, since you have been here before?"

"Yes." She got up and started to open drawers and cupboards. She turned to us and held out a black felt bag which Cork opened.

"Gentlemen, I give you the van der Malin Chain, and quite exquisite it is."

"So he did steal it," I said.

"In a manner of speaking, Oaks, yes. But, Madam, should we not also find what you were so willing to pay a king's ransom for?"

"Perhaps it is on the easel. I only saw the miniature."

Cork took the drape from the easel and revealed a portrait of a nude woman reposing on a couch.

"It's Gretchen!" I gasped. "Was that der Trogue's game? Blackmail?"

"Yes, Mr. Oaks, it was," the Dame said. "I knew it was not an artist's trick of painting one head on another's body. That strawberry mark on the thigh was Gretchen's. How did you know of its existence, Captain? I told no one, not even my sister."

"Your actions helped tell me. You ordered your own portrait burned two days ago, the same day your sister sent me a note and an invitation to the Masque."

"A note?"

"Portending calamity," I added.

"Oh, the fool. She must have learned about my failure to raise enough cash to meet that fiend's demands."

"Your sudden disdain for a fine portrait betrayed your disgust with the artist, not with the art. Then Wilda told us that you had planned to have your daughters painted by the same man, and, considering the time elapsed since your portrait was finished, I assumed that Gretchen's had been started."

"It was, and he seduced her. She confessed it to me after I saw the miniature he brought to me."

"Why did you not demand its delivery when you gave him the necklace tonight?"

"I never said I gave it to him to-night."

"But you did. You went into the den, not to see your daughter, but to meet der Trogue at the outside passage door. You lit a taper there, and he examined his booty at the entryway and then left, probably promising to turn over that scandalous painting when he had verified that the necklace was not an imitation."

"Captain, you sound as if you were there."

"The clues were. In the puddle just inside the door, there was a red substance. Oaks believed it was blood. It was a natural assumption, but when the question of your anger with a painter came to light, I considered what my eyes now confirm. Painters are sloppy fellows; look at this floor. Besides, blood is rarely magenta. It was paint, red paint, from his boot soles. Then, Madam, your part of the bargain completed, you returned to the den. Your daughter was still by the fire."

"Yes."

"And you returned to the ballroom."

"Yes, leaving my soiled child to be murdered! He came back and killed her!"

"No, Dame van Schooner, he did not, although that is the way it will be recorded officially. The report will show that you entered the den and presented the van der Malın Chain to your daughter to wear on her night of triumph. My observation of the paint in the puddle will stand as the deduction that led us to der Trogue. We will say he gained entry into the house, killed your daughter, and took the necklace. And was later killed resisting capture."

"But he *did* kill her!" the Dame insisted. "He had to be the one! She was alive when I left her. No one else entered the room until the honor guard went for her."

Cork took both her hands.

"Dame van Schooner, I have twisted truth beyond reason for your sake tonight, but now you must face the hard truth. Der Trogue was a scoundrel, but he had no reason to kill Gretchen. What would he gain? And how could he get back in without leaving snow tracks? Gretchen's executioner was in the den all the time—when Lydia was there, when you were. I think in your heart you know the answer—if you have the courage to face it."

To watch her face was to see ice melt. Her eyes, her cold, diamond-blue eyes watered. "I can. But must it be said—here?"

"Yes."

"Wilda. Oh, my God, Wilda."

"Yes, Wilda. You have a great burden to bear, my dear lady."

Her tears came freely now. "The curse of the van Schooners," she cried. "Her father was insane, and his brother, Kaarl, lives in his lunatic's attic. My mother thought she was infusing quality by our union."

"Thus your stern exterior and addiction to purifying the bloodline with good stock."

"Yes, I have been the man in our family far too long. I have had to be hard. I thank you for your consideration, Captain. Wilda will have to be put away, of course. Poor child, I saw the van Schooner blood curse in her years ago, but I never thought it would come to this." The last was a sob. Then she took a deep breath. "I think I am needed at home." She rose. "Thank you again, Captain. Will you destroy that?" She pointed to the portrait.

"Rest assured."

As he opened the door for her, she turned back, with the breaking dawn framing her. "I wish it was I who had invited you to the ball. I saw you dancing and wondered who you were. You are quite tall."

"Not too tall to bow, Madam," Cork said, and all six-foot-six of him bent down and kissed her cheek. She left us with an escort from the detachment of soldiers that had followed our trail.

The room was quiet for a moment before Major Tell exploded. "Confound it, Cork, what the deuce is this? I am to falsify records to show der Trogue was a thief and a murderer and yet you say it was Wilda who killed her sister. What's your proof, man?"

Cork walked over to the painting and smashed it on a chair back. "You deserve particulars, both of you. I said that Wilda was in the den all the time. Your natural query is, how did she get there unseen? Well, we all saw her. She was carried in—in the curtained sedan chair. In her twisted mind, she hated her sister, who would inherit everything, by her mother's design. One does not put a great fortune into a madwoman's hands."

"Very well," Tell said, "I can see her entry. How the deuce did she get out?"

"Incipient madness sometimes makes the mind clever, Major. She stayed in the sedan chair until her mother had left, then presented herself to Gretchen."

"And killed her," I interjected. "But she was back in the ballroom before the honor guard went in to get her sister."

"There is the nub of it, Oaks. She left the den by the back passage, crossed the yard, and re-entered the house by the kitchen, in the far wing. Who would take any notice of a daughter of the house in a room filled with bustling cooks and servants coming and going with vittles for the buffet?"

"But she would have gotten her skirts wet in the snow," I started to object. "Of course! The spilled punch bowl! It drenched her!"

Cork smiled broadly. "Yes, my lad. She entered the kitchen, scooped up the punch bowl, carried it into the ballroom, and then deliberately dropped it."

"Well," Tell grumped, "she may be sprung in the mind, but she understands the theory of tactical diversion."

"Self-preservation is the last instinct to go, Major."

"Yes, I believe you are right, Cork, but how are we to explain all this and still shield the Dame's secret?"

Cork looked dead at me. "You, Oaks, have given us the answer."

"I? Oh, when I said the killer took off his boots to avoid tracks in the den? You rejected that out of hand when I mentioned it."

"I rejected it as a probability, not a possibility. Anything is possible, but not everything is probable. Is it probable that a killer bent on not leaving tracks would take off his boots *inside* the entry, where they would leave a puddle? No, I couldn't accept it, but I'm sure the general public will."

The major looked disturbed. "I can appreciate your desire to protect the Dame," he said, "but to *suppress* evidence—"

"Calm yourself, Major, we are just balancing the books of human nature. I have saved the Crown the time and expense of trying and executing an extortionist. God knows how many victims he has fleeced by his artistic trickery over the years. And we have prevented the Dame from the commission of a homicide that any jury, I think, would have found justifiable. Let it stand as it is, Major; it is a neater package. The Dame has had enough tragedy in her life."

The last of his words were soft and low-toned, and I watched as he stared into the flames. By jing, could it possibly be that this gallivanting, sunburnt American had fallen in love? But I quickly dismissed the thought. We are fated to our roles, we two—he, the unbroken stallion frolicking from pasture to pasture, and I, the frantic ostler following with an empty halter, hoping some day to put the beast to work. I persist.

THE DAUPHIN'S DOLL

by Ellery Queen

"Ellery Queen" has a split personality. It is the pseudonym of Brooklyn-born cousins Frederic Dannay and Manfred Lee, whose contrasting personalities gave a keen edge to their many years of mystery collaboration. Together they wrote a long list of novels, novelettes and short stories featuring their namesake detective, Ellery Queen. They edited over seventy anthologies and founded and edited Ellery Queen's Mystery Magazine. Seven Edgars and a Raven attest to Ellery's popularity.

However, Ellery Queen was more knowledgeable about crime than he was about plangonology, as the following story demonstrates. Attitudes have drastically changed since the 1940s. What contemporary collector wouldn't give her eyeteeth to find the dolls in this story under her Christmas tree?

There is a law among storytellers, originally passed by Editors at the cries (they say) of their constituents, which states that stories about Christmas shall have Children in them. This Christmas story is no exception; indeed, misopedists will complain that we have overdone it. And we confess in advance that this is also a story about Dolls, and that Santa Claus comes into it, and even a Thief; though as to this last, whoever he was—and that was one of the questions—he was certainly not Barabbas, even parabolically.

Another section of the statute governing Christmas stories provides that they shall incline toward Sweetness and Light. The first arises, of course, from the orphans and the never-souring savor of the annual Miracle; as for Light, it will be provided at the end, as usual, by that luminous prodigy, Ellery Queen. The reader of gloomier temper will also find a large measure of Darkness, in the person and works of one who, at least in Inspector Queen's harassed view, was surely the winged Prince of that region. His name, by the way, was not Satan, it was Comus; and this is paradox enow, since the original Comus, as everyone knows, was the god of festive joy and mirth, emotions not commonly associated with the Underworld. As Ellery struggled to embrace his phantom foe, he puzzled over this *non sequitur* in vain; in vain, that is, until Nikki Porter, no scorner of the obvious, suggested that he *might* seek the answer where any ordinary mortal would go at once. And there, to the great man's mortification it was indeed to be found: On page 262b of Volume 6, *Coleb to Damasci*, of the 175th Anniversary edition of the *Encyclopedia Britannica*. A French conjuror of that name, performing in London in the year 1789, caused his wife to vanish from the top of a table—the very first time, it appeared, that this feat, uxorial or otherwise, had been accomplished without the aid of mirrors. To track his dark adversary's *nom de nuit* to its historic lair gave Ellery his only glint of satisfaction until that blessed moment when light burst all around him and exorcised the darkness, Prince and all.

But this is chaos.

Our story properly begins not with our invisible character but with our dead one.

Miss Ypson had not always been dead; *au contraire*. She had lived for seventy-eight years, for most of them breathing hard. As her father used to remark, "She was a very active little verb." Miss Ypson's father was a professor of Greek at a small Midwestern university. He had conjugated his daughter with the rather bewildered assistance of one of his brawnier students, an Iowa poultry heiress.

Professor Ypson was a man of distinction. Unlike most professors of Greek, he was a Greek professor of Greek, having been born Gerasymos Aghamos Ypsilonomon in Polykhnitos, on the island of Mytilini, "where," he was fond of recalling on certain occasions, "burning Sappho loved and sung"—a quotation he found unfailingly useful in his extracurricular activities; and, the Hellenic ideal notwithstanding, Professor Ypson believed wholeheartedly in immoderation in all things. This hereditary and cultural background explains the professor's interest in fatherhood —to his wife's chagrin, for Mr. Ypson's own breeding prowess was confined almost exclusively to the barnyards on which her income was based; he held their daughter to be nothing less than a biological miracle.

The professor's mental processes also tended to confuse Mrs. Ypson. She never ceased to wonder why, instead of shortening his name to Ypson, her husband had not sensibly changed it to Jones. "My dear," the professor once replied, "you are an Iowa snob." "But nobody," Mrs. Ypson cried, "can spell it or pronounce it!" "This is a cross," murmured Professor Ypson, "which we must bear with ypsilanti." "Oh," said Mrs. Ypson.

There was invariably something Sibylline about his conversation. His favorite adjective for his wife was "ypsiliform," a term, he explained, which referred to the germinal spot at one of the fecundation states in a ripening egg and which was, therefore, exquisitely à propos. Mrs. Ypson continued to look bewildered; she died at an early age.

And the professor ran off with a Kansas City variety girl of considerable talent, leaving his baptized chick to be reared by an eggish relative of her mother, named Jukes.

The only time Miss Ypson heard from her father— except when he wrote charming and erudite little notes requesting, as he termed it, *lucrum*—was in the fourth decade of his Odyssey, when he sent her a handsome addition to her collection, a terra-cotta play doll of Greek origin over three thousand years old which, unhappily, Miss Ypson felt duty-bound to return to the Brooklyn museum from which it had unaccountably vanished. The note accompanying her father's gift had said, whimsically: *"Timeo Danaos et dona ferentes."*

There was poetry behind Miss Ypson's dolls. At her birth the professor, ever harmonious, signalized his devotion to fecundity by naming her Cytherea. This proved the Olympian irony. For, it turned out, her father's philoprogenitiveness throbbed frustrate in her mother's stony womb: even though Miss Ypson interred five husbands of quite adequate vigor, she remained infertile to the end of her days. Hence it is classically tragic to find her, when all passion was spent, a sweet little old lady with a vague if

eager smile who, under the name of her father, pattered
about a vast and echoing New York apartment, playing
enthusiastically with dolls.

In the beginning they were dolls of common clay: a
Billiken, a kewpie, a Kathe Kruse, a Patsy, a Foxy
Grandpa, and so forth. But then, as her need increased,
Miss Ypson began her fierce sack of the past.

Down into the land of Pharaoh she went for two pieces
of thin desiccated board, carved and painted and with
hair of strung beads, and legless—so that they might not
run away—which any connoisseur will tell you are the
most superb specimens of ancient Egyptian paddle doll
extant, far superior to those in the British Museum, although this fact will be denied in certain quarters.

Miss Ypson unearthed a foremother of "Letitia Penn,"
until her discovery held to be the oldest doll in America,
having been brought to Philadelphia from England in
1699 by William Penn as a gift for a playmate of his small
daughter's. Miss Ypson's find was a wooden-hearted "little lady" in brocade and velvet which had been sent by
Sir Walter Raleigh to the first English child born in the
New World. Since Virginia Dare had been born in 1587,
not even the Smithsonian dared impugn Miss Ypson's
triumph.

On the old lady's racks, in her plate-glass cases, might
be seen the wealth of a thousand childhoods, and some
riches—for such is the genetics of dolls—possessed by
children grown. Here could be found "fashion babies"
from fourteenth-century France, sacred dolls of the
Orange Free State Fingo tribe, Satsuma paper dolls and
court dolls from old Japan, beady-eyed "Kalifa" dolls of
the Egyptian Sudan, Swedish birch-bark dolls, "Katcina"
dolls of the Hopis, mammoth-tooth dolls of the Eskimos,
feather dolls of the Chippewa, tumble dolls of the ancient
Chinese, Coptic bone dolls, Roman dolls dedicated to
Diana, *pantin* dolls which had been the street toys of
Parisian exquisites before Madame Guillotine swept the
boulevards, early Christian dolls in their *crèches* representing the Holy Family—to specify the merest handful
of Miss Ypson's Briarean collection. She possessed dolls
of pasteboard, dolls of animal skin, spool dolls, crab-claw
dolls, eggshell dolls, cornhusk dolls, rag dolls, pine-cone
dolls with moss hair, stocking dolls, dolls of *bisque*, dolls
of palm leaf, dolls of *papier-mâché*, even dolls made of

seed pods. There were dolls forty inches tall, and there were dolls so little Miss Ypson could hide them in her gold thimble.

Cytherea Ypson's collection bestrode the centuries and took tribute of history. There was no greater—not the fabled playthings of Montezuma, or Victoria's, or Eugene Field's; not the collection at the Metropolitan, or the South Kensington, or the royal palace in old Bucharest, or anywhere outside the enchantment of little girls' dreams.

It was made of Iowan eggs and the Attic shore, corn-fed and myrtle-clothed; and it brings us at last to Attorney John Somerset Bondling and his visit to the Queen residence one December twenty-third not so very long ago.

DECEMBER THE TWENTY-THIRD is ordinarily not a good time to seek the Queens. Inspector Richard Queen likes his Christmas old-fashioned; his turkey stuffing, for instance, calls for twenty-two hours of overall preparation, and some of its ingredients are not readily found at the corner grocer's. And Ellery is a frustrated gift-wrapper. For a month before Christmas he turns his sleuthing genius to tracking down unusual wrapping papers, fine ribbons, and artistic stickers; and he spends the last two days creating beauty.

So it was that when Attorney John S. Bondling called, Inspector Queen was in his kitchen, swathed in a barbecue apron, up to his elbows in *fines herbes,* while Ellery, behind the locked door of his study, composed a secret symphony in glittering fuchsia metallic paper, forest-green moiré ribbon, and pine cones.

"It's almost useless," shrugged Nikki, studying Attorney Bondling's card, which was as crackly-looking as Attorney Bondling. "You say you know the Inspector, Mr. Bondling?"

"Just tell him Bondling the estate lawyer," said Bondling neurotically. "Park Row. He'll know."

"Don't blame me," said Nikki, "if you wind up in his stuffing. Goodness knows he's used everything else." And she went for Inspector Queen.

While she was gone, the study door opened noiselessly for one inch. A suspicious eye reconnoitered from the crack.

"Don't be alarmed," said the owner of the eyes, slipping through the crack and locking the door hastily behind him. "Can't trust them, you know. Children, just children."

"Children!" Attorney Bondling snarled. "You're Ellery Queen, aren't you?"

"Yes."

"Interested in youth? Christmas? Orphans, dolls, that sort of thing?" Mr. Bondling went on in a remarkably nasty way.

"I suppose so."

"The more fool you. Ah, here's your father. Inspector Queen—"

"Oh, that Bondling," said the old gentleman absently, shaking his visitor's hand. "My office called to say someone was coming up. Here, use my handkerchief; that's a bit of turkey liver. Know my son? His secretary, Miss Porter? What's on your mind, Mr. Bondling?"

"Inspector, I'm handling the Cytherea Ypson estate, and—"

"Cytherea Ypson," frowned the Inspector. "Oh, yes. She died only recently."

"Leaving me with the headache," said Mr. Bondling bitterly, "of disposing of her Dollection."

"Her what?" asked Ellery.

"Dolls—collection. Dollection. She coined the word." Ellery strolled over to his armchair.

"Do I take this down?" sighed Nikki.

"Dollection," said Ellery.

"Spent about thirty years at it. Dolls!"

"Yes, Nikki, take it down."

"Well, well, Mr. Bondling," said Inspector Queen. "What's the problem? Christmas comes but once a year, you know."

"Will provides the Dollection be sold at auction," grated the attorney, "and the proceeds used to set up a fund for orphan children. I'm holding the public sale right after New Year's."

"Dolls and orphans, eh?" said the Inspector, thinking of Javanese black pepper and Country Gentleman Seasoning Salt.

"That's *nice*," beamed Nikki.

"Oh, is it?" said Mr. Bondling softly. "Apparently, young woman, you've never tried to satisfy a Surrogate. I've administered estates for nineteen years without a whisper against me, but let an estate involve the interests of just one little fatherless child, and you'd think from the Surrogate's attitude I was Bill Sykes himself!"

"My stuffing," began the inspector.

"I've had those dolls catalogued. The result is ominous! Did you know there's no set market for the damnable things? And aside from a few personal possessions, the Dollection constitutes the old lady's entire estate. Sank every nickel she had in it."

"But it should be worth a fortune," remarked Ellery.

"To whom, Mr. Queen? Museums always want such things as free and unencumbered gifts. I tell you, except for one item, those hypothetical orphans won't realize enough from that sale to keep them in—in bubble gum for two days!"

"Which item would that be, Mr. Bondling?"

"Number Six-seventy-four," the lawyer snapped. "This one."

"Number Six-seventy-four," read Inspector Queen from the fat catalogue Bondling had fished out of a large great-coat pocket. "The Dauphin's Doll. Unique. Ivory figure of a boy Prince eight inches tall, clad in court dress, genuine ermine, brocade, velvet. Court sword in gold strapped to waist. Gold circlet crown surmounted by single blue brilliant diamond of finest water, weight approximately 49 carats—"

"How many carats?" exclaimed Nikki.

"Larger than the *Hope* and the *Star of South Africa*," said Ellery, with a certain excitement.

"—appraised," continued his father, "at one hundred and ten thousand dollars."

"Expensive dollie."

"Indecent!" said Nikki.

"This indecent—I mean exquisite, royal doll," the inspector read on, "was a birthday gift from King Louis XVI of France to Louis Charles, his second son, who became dauphin at the death of his elder brother, in 1789. The little dauphin was proclaimed Louis XVII by the royalists during the French Revolution while in custody of the *sans-culottes*. His fate is shrouded in mystery. Romantic, historic item."

"*Le prince perdu*. I'll say," muttered Ellery. "Mr. Bondling, is this on the level?"

"I'm an attorney, not an antiquarian," snapped their

visitor. "There are documents attached, one of them a sworn statement—holograph—by Lady Charlotte Atkyns, the English actress-friend of the Capet family—she was in France during the Revolution—on purporting to be in Lady Atkyns's hand. It doesn't matter, Mr. Queen. Even if the history is bad, the diamond's good!"

"I take it this hundred-and-ten-thousand-dollar dollie consitutes the bone, as it were, or that therein lies the rub?"

"You said it!" cried Mr. Bondling, cracking his knuckles in a sort of agony. "For my money the Dauphin's Doll is the only negotiable asset of that collection. And what's the old lady do? She provided by will that on the day preceding Christmas the Cytherea Ypson Dollection is to be publicly displayed . . . on the main floor of Nash's Department Store! *The day before Christmas, gentlemen!* Think of it!"

"But why?" asked Nikki, puzzled.

"Why? Who knows why? For the entertainment of New York's army of little beggers, I suppose! Have you any notion how many peasants pass through Nash's on the day before Christmas? My cook tells me—she's a very religious woman—it's like Armageddon."

"Day before Christmas," frowned Ellery. "That's to-morrow."

"It does sound chancy," said Nikki anxiously. Then she brightened. "Oh, well, maybe Nash's won't cooperate, Mr. Bondling."

"Oh, won't they!" howled Mr. Bondling. "Why, old lady Ypson had this stunt cooked up with that gang of peasant-purveyors for years! They've been snapping at my heels ever since the day she was put away!"

"It'll draw every crook in New York," said the inspector, his gaze on the kitchen door.

"Orphans," said Nikki. "The orphans' interests *must* be protected." She looked at her employer accusingly.

"Special measures, Dad," he said.

"Sure, sure," said the inspector, rising. "Don't you worry about this, Mr. Bondling. Now, if you'll be kind enough to excu—"

"Inspector Queen," hissed Mr. Bondling, leaning forward tensely, "that is not all."

"Ah," said Ellery briskly, lighting a cigarette. "There's

a specfic villain in this piece, Mr. Bondling, and you know
who he is."

"I do," said the lawyer hollowly, "and then again I
don't. I mean, it's Comus."

"Comus!" the inspector screamed.

"Comus?" said Ellery slowly.

"Comus?" said Nikki. "Who dat?"

"Comus," nodded Mr. Bondling. "First thing this morning. Marched right into my office, bold as day—must
have followed me, I hadn't got my coat off, my secretary
wasn't even in. Marched in and tossed this card on my
desk."

Ellery seized it. "The usual, Dad."

"His trademark," growled the inspector, his lips working.

"But the card just says 'Comus,'" complained Nikki.
"Who—?"

"Go on, Mr. Bondling!" thundered the inspector.

"And he calmly announced to me," said Bondling,
blotting his cheeks with an exhausted handkerchief, "that
he's going to steal the Dauphin's Doll tomorrow, in
Nash's."

"Oh, a maniac," said Nikki.

"Mr. Bondling," said the old gentleman in a terrible
voice, "just what did this fellow look like?"

"Foreigner—black beard—spoke with a European accent of some sort. To tell you the truth, I was so thunder-
struck I didn't notice details. Didn't even chase him till it
was too late."

The Queens shrugged at each other, Gallically.

"The old story," said the inspector; the corners of his
nostrils were greenish. "The brass of the colonel's mon-
key, and when he does show himself nobody remembers
anything but beards and foreign accents. Well, Mr. Bondling, with Comus in the game it's serious business.
Where's the collection right now?"

"In the vaults of the Life Bank & Trust, Forty-third
Street branch."

"What time are you to move it over to Nash's?"

"They wanted it this evening. I said nothing doing.
I've made special arrangements with the bank, and the
collection's to be moved at seven-thirty tomorrow morning."

"Won't be much time to set up," said Ellery thoughtfully, "before the store opens its doors." He glanced at his father.

"You leave Operation Dollie to us, Mr. Bondling," said the inspector grimly. "Better give me a buzz this afternoon."

"I can't tell you, Inspector, how relieved I am——'"

"Are you?" said the old gentleman sourly. "What makes you think he won't get it?"

WHEN ATTORNEY BONDLING had left, the Queens put their heads together, Ellery doing most of the talking, as usual. Finally, the inspector went into the bedroom for a session with his direct line to headquarters.

"Anybody would think," sniffed Nikki, "you two were planning the defense of the Bastille. Who is this Comus, anyway?"

"We don't know, Nikki," said Ellery slowly. "Might be anybody. Began his criminal career about five years ago. He's in the grand tradition of Lupin—a saucy, highly intelligent rascal who's made stealing an art. He seems to take a special delight in stealing valuble things under virtually impossible conditions. Master of make-up—he's appeared in a dozen different disguises. And he's an uncanny mimic. Never been caught, photographed, or fingerprinted. Imaginative, daring—I'd say he's the most dangerous thief operating in the United States."

"If he's never been caught," said Nikki skeptically, "how do you know he commits these crimes?"

"You mean, and not someone else?" Ellery smiled pallidly. "The techniques mark the thefts as his work. And then, like Arsène, he leaves a card—with the name 'Comus' on it—on the scene of each visit."

"Does he usually announce in advance that he's going to swipe the crown jewels?"

"No." Ellery frowned. "To my knowledge, this is the first such instance. Since he's never done anything without a reason, that visit to Bondling's office this morning must be part of his greater plan. I wonder if——"

The telephone in the living room rang clear and loud.

Nikki looked at Ellery. Ellery looked at the telephone.

"Do you suppose——?" began Nikki. But then she said, "Oh, it's too absurd."

"Where Comus is involved," said Ellery wildly, "nothing is too absurd!" and he leaped for the phone. "Hello!"

"A call from an old friend," announced a deep and hollowish male voice. "Comus."

"Well," said Ellery. "Hello again."

"Did Mr. Bondling," asked the voice jovially, "persuade you to 'prevent' me from stealing the Dauphin's Doll in Nash's tomorrow?"

"So you know Bondling's been here."

"No miracle involved, Queen. I followed him. Are you taking the case?"

"See here, Comus," said Ellery. "Under ordinary circumstances I'd welcome the sporting chance to put you where you belong. But these circumstances are not ordinary. That doll represents the major asset of a future fund for orphaned children. I'd rather we didn't play catch with it. Comus, what do you say we call this one off?"

"Shall we say," asked the voice gently, "Nash's Department Store—tomorrow?"

THUS THE EARLY morning of December twenty-fourth finds Messrs. Queen and Bondling, and Nikki Porter, huddled on the iron sidewalk of Forty-third Street, before the holly-decked windows of the Life Bank & Trust Company, just outside a double line of armed guards. The guards form a channel between the bank entrance and an armored truck, down which Cytherea Ypson's Dollection flows swiftly. And all about gapes New York, stamping callously on the aged, icy face of the street, against the uncharitable Christmas wind.

Now is the winter of his discontent, and Mr. Queen curses.

"I don't know what you're beefing about," moans Miss Porter. "You and Mr. Bondling are bundled up like Yukon prospectors. Look at *me*."

"It's that rat-hearted public relations tripe from Nash's," says Mr. Queen murderously. "They all swore themselves to secrecy, Brother Rat included. Honor! Spirit of Christmas!"

"It was all over the radio last night," whimpers Mr. Bondling. "And in this morning's papers."

"I'll cut his creep's heart out. Here! Velie, keep those people away!"

Sergeant Velie says good-naturedly from the doorway of the bank, "You jerks stand back." Little does the Sergeant know the fate in store for him.

"Armored trucks," says Miss Porter bluishly. "Shot-guns."

"Nikki, Comus made a point of informing us in advance that he meant to steal the Dauphin's Doll in Nash's Department Store. It would be just like him to have said that in order to make it easier to steal the doll en route."

"Why don't they hurry?" shivers Mr. Bondling. "Ah!" Inspector Queen appears suddenly in the doorway. His hands clasp treasure.

"Oh!" cries Nikki.

New York whistles.

It is magnificence, an affront to democracy. But street mobs, like children, are royalists at heart.

New York whistles, and Sergeant Thomas Velie steps menacingly before Inspector Queen, Police Positive drawn, and Inspector Queen dashes across the sidewalk, between the bristling lines of guards.

Queen the Younger vanishes, to materialize an instant later at the door of the armored truck.

"It's just immorally, hideously beautiful, Mr. Bond-ling," breathes Miss Porter, sparkly-eyed.

Mr. Bondling cranes, thinly.

ENTER *Santa Claus, with bell.*

Santa. Oyez, oyez. Peace, good will. Is that the dollie the radio's been yappin' about, folks?

Mr. B. Scram.

Miss P. Why, Mr. Bondling.

Mr. B. Well, he's got no business here. Stand back, er, Santa. Back!

Santa. What eateth you, my lean and angry friend? Have you no compassion at this season of the year?

Mr. B. Oh . . . Here! *(Clink.)* Now will you *kindly* . . . ?

Santa. Mighty pretty dollie. Where they takin' it, girlie?

Miss P. Over to Nash's, Santa.

Mr. B. You asked for it. Officer!!!

Santa. (Hurriedly) Little present for you, girlie. Compliments of old Santy. Merry, merry.

Miss P. For *me*?? (EXIT *Santa, rapidly, with bell.*) Really, Mr. Bondling, was it necessary to . . . ?

Mr. B. Opium for the masses! What did that flatulent faker hand you, Miss Porter? What's in that unmentionable envelope?

Miss P. I'm sure I don't know, but isn't it the most touch-

ing idea? Why, it's addressed to *Ellery*. Oh! El-
leryyyyyy!

Mr. B. (Exit *excitedly*) Where is he? You—! Officer!
Where did that baby-deceiver disappear to? A Santa
Claus . . . !

Mr. Q. (*Entering on the run*) Yes? Nikki, what is it?
What's happened?

Miss P. A man dressed as Santa Claus just handed me
this envelope. It's addressed to you.

Mr. Q. Note? *(He snatches it, withdraws a miserable
slice of paper from it on which is block-lettered in pen-
cil a message which he reads aloud with considerable
expression.)* "Dear Ellery, Don't you trust me? I said
I'd steal the Dauphin in Nash's emporium today, and
that's exactly where I'm going to do it. Yours—"
Signed . . .

Miss P. (*Craning*) "Comus." That Santa?

Mr. Q. (*Sets his manly lips. An icy wind blows*)

Even the master had to acknowledge that their defenses
against Comus were ingenious.

From the Display Department of Nash's they had re-
quisitioned four miter-jointed counters of uniform length.
These they had fitted together, and in the center of the
hollow square thus formed they had erected a platform
six feet high. On the counters, in plastic tiers, stretched
the long lines of Miss Ypson's babies. Atop the platform,
dominant, stood a great chair of handcarved oak, filched
from the Swedish Modern section of the Fine Furniture
Department; and on this Valhalla-like throne, a huge and
rosy rotundity, sat Sergeant Thomas Velie, of police headquarters, morosely grateful for the anonymity endowed by
the scarlet suit and the jolly mask and whiskers of his appointed role.

Nor was this all. At a distance of six feet outside the
counters shimmered a surrounding rampart of plate glass,
borrowed in its various elements from *The Glass Home
of the Future* display on the sixth-floor rear, and assembled to shape an eight-foot wall quoined with chrome, its
glistening surfaces flawless except at one point, where a
thick glass door had been installed. But the edges fitted
intimately, and there was a formidable lock in the door,
the key to which lay buried in Mr. Queen's right trouser
pocket.

It was 8:54 A.M. The Queens, Nikki Porter, and Attorney Bondling stood among store officials and an army of plainclothesmen on Nash's main floor, surveying the product of their labors.

"I think that about does it," muttered Inspector Queen at last. "Men! Positions around the glass partition."

Twenty-four assorted gendarmes in mufti jostled one another. They took marked places about the wall, facing it and grinning up at Sergeant Velie. Sergeant Velie, from his throne, glared back.

"Hagstrom and Piggott—the door."

Two detectives detached themselves from a group of reserves. As they marched to the glass door, Mr. Bondling plucked at the inspector's overcoat sleeve. "Can all these men be trusted, Inspector Queen?" he whispered. "I mean, this fellow Comus—"

"Mr. Bondling," replied the old gentleman coldly, "you do your job and let me do mine."

"But—"

"Picked men, Mr. Bondling! I picked 'em myself."

"Yes, yes, Inspector. I merely thought I'd—"

"Lieutenant Farber."

A little man with watery eyes stepped forward.

"Mr. Bondling, this is Lieutenant Geronimo Farber, headquarters jewelry expert. Ellery?"

Ellery took the Dauphin's Doll from his greatcoat pocket, but he said, "If you don't mind, Dad, I'll keep holding on to it."

Somebody said, "Wow," and then there was silence.

"Lieutenant, this doll in my son's hand is the famous Dauphin's Doll with the diamond crown that—"

"Don't touch it, Lieutenant, please," said Ellery. "I'd rather nobody touched it."

"The doll," continued the inspector, "has just been brought here from a bank vault which it ought never to have left, and Mr. Bondling, who's handling the Ypson estate, claims it's the genuine article. Lieutenant, examine the diamond and give us your opinion."

Lieutenant Farber produced a loupe. Ellery held the dauphin securely, and Farber did not touch it.

Finally, the expert said: "I can't pass an opinion about the doll itself, of course, but the diamond's a beauty. Easily worth a hundred thousand dollars at the present state of the market—maybe more. Looks like a very strong setting, by the way."

"Thanks, Lieutenant. Okay, son," said the inspector. "Go into your waltz."

Clutching the dauphin, Ellery strode over to the glass gate and unlocked it.

"This fellow Farber," whispered Attorney Bondling in the inspector's hairy ear. "Inspector, are you absolutely sure he's—?"

"He's really Lieutenant Farber?" The inspector controlled himself. "Mr. Bondling, I've known Gerry Farber for eighteen years. Calm yourself."

Ellery was crawling perilously over the nearest counter. Then, bearing the dauphin aloft, he hurried across the floor of the enclosure to the platform.

Sergeant Velie whined, "Maestro, how in hell am I going to sit here all day without washin' my hands?"

But Mr. Queen merely stooped and lifted from the floor a heavy little structure faced with black velvet consisting of a floor and a backdrop, with a two-armed chromium support. This object he placed on the platform directly between Sergeant Velie's massive legs.

Carefully, he stood the Dauphin's Doll in the velvet niche. Then he clambered back across the counter, went through the glass door, locked it with the key, and turned to examine his handiwork.

Proudly the prince's plaything stood, the jewel in his little golden crown darting "on pale electric streams" under the concentrated tide of a dozen of the most powerful floodlights in the possession of the great store.

"Velie," said Inspector Queen, "you're not to touch that doll. Don't lay a finger on it."

The Sergeant said, "Gaaaaa."

"You men on duty. Don't worry about the crowds. Your job is to keep watching that doll. You're not to take your eyes off it all day. Mr. Bondling, are you satisfied?" Mr. Bondling seemed about to say something, but then he hastily nodded. "Ellery?"

The great man smiled. "The only way he can get that bawbie," he said, "is by spells and incantations. Raise the portcullis!"

THEN BEGAN THE interminable day, *dies irae,* the last shopping day before Christmas. This is traditionally the day of the inert, the procrastinating, the undecided, and the forgetful, sucked at last into the mercantile machine by the perpetual pump of Time. If there is peace upon earth, it descends only afterward; and at no time, on the part of anyone embroiled, is there good will toward men. As Miss Porter expresses it, a cat fight in a bird cage would be more Christian.

But on this December twenty-fourth, in Nash's, the normal bedlam was augmented by the vast shrilling of thousands of Children. It may be, as the Psalmist insists, that happy is the man that hath his quiver full of them; but no bowmen surrounded Miss Ypson's darlings this day, only detectives carrying revolvers, not a few of whom forbore to use same only by the most heroic self-discipline. In the black floods of humanity overflowing the main floor, little folks darted about like electrically charged minnows, pursued by exasperated maternal shrieks and the imprecations of those whose shins and rumps and toes were at the mercy of hot, happy little limbs; indeed, nothing was sacred, and Attorney Bondling was seen to quail and wrap his greatcoat defensively about him against the savage innocence of childhood. But the guardians of the law, having been ordered to simulate store employees, possessed no such armor; and many a man earned his citation that day for unique cause. They stood in the very millrace of the tide; it churned about them, shouting, "Dollies! *Dollies!*" until the very word lost its familiar meaning and became the insensate scream of a thousand Loreleis beckoning strong men to destruction below the eye-level of their diamond Light.

But they stood fast.

And Comus was thwarted. Oh, he tried. At 11:18 A.M. a tottering old man holding fast to the hand of a small boy tried to wheedle Detective Hagstrom into unlocking the glass door "so my grandson, here—he's terrible nearsighted—can get a closer look at the pretty dollies." Detective Hagstrom roared, "Rube!" and the old gentleman dropped the little boy's hand violently and with remarkable agility lost himself in the crowd. A spot investigation revealed that, coming upon the boy, who had been crying for his mommy, the old gentleman had promised to find her. The little boy, whose name—he said—was Lance Morganstern, was removed to the Lost and Found Department; and everyone was satisfied that the great

thief had finally launched his attack. Everyone, that
is, but Ellery Queen. He seemed puzzled. When Nikki
asked him why, he merely said: "Stupidity, Nikki. It's not
in character."

At 1:46 P.M., Sergeant Velie sent up a distress signal.
Inspector Queen read the message aright and signaled
back: "O.K. Fifteen minutes." Sergeant Santa C. Velie
scrambled off his perch, clawed his way over the counter,
and pounded urgently on the inner side of the glass door.
Ellery let him out, relocking the door immediately,
and the Sergeant's redclad figure disappeared on the
double in the general direction of the main-floor gentlemen's relief station, leaving the dauphin in solitary possession of the dais.

During the sergeant's recess Inspector Queen circulated
among his men, repeating the order of the day.

The episode of Velie's response to the summons of
Nature caused a temporary crisis. For at the end of the
specified fifteen minutes he had not returned. Nor was
there a sign of him at the end of a half hour. An aide
dispatched to the relief station reported back that the sergeant was not there. Fears of foul play were voiced at
an emergency staff conference held then and there, and
counter-measures were being planned even as, at 2:35
P.M., the familiar Santa-clad bulk of the sergeant was
observed battling through the lines, pawing at his mask.

"Velie," snarled Inspector Queen, "where have you
been?"

"Eating my lunch," growled the Sergeant's voice, defensively. "I been taking my punishment like a gook soldier all day, Inspector, but I draw the line at starvin' to
death, even in line of duty."

"Velie—!" choked the inspector; but then he waved his
hand feebly and said, "Ellery, let him back in there."

And that was very nearly all. The only other incident
of note occurred at 4:22 P.M. A well-upholstered woman
with a red face yelled, "Stop! Thief! He grabbed my
pocketbook! Police!" about fifty feet from the Ypson exhibit. Ellery instantly shouted, *"It's a trick! Men, don't
take your eyes off that doll!"*

"It's Comus disguised as a woman," exclaimed Attorney Bondling, as Inspector Queen and Detective Hesse
wrestled the female figure through the mob. She was now
a wonderful shade of magenta. "What are you *doing?"*

she screamed. "Don't arrest *me!*—catch that crook who stole my pocketbook!" "No dice, Comus," said the inspector. "Wipe off that makeup." "McComas?" said the woman loudly. "My name is Rafferty, and all these folks saw it. He was a fat man with a mustache." "Inspector," said Nikki Porter, making a surreptitious scientific test. "This is a female. Believe me." And so, indeed, it proved. All agreed that the mustachioed fat man had been Comus, creating a diversion in the desperate hope that the resulting confusion would give him an opportunity to steal the little dauphin.

"Stupid, stupid," muttered Ellery, gnawing his fingernails.

"Sure," grinned the inspector. "We've got him nibbling his tail, Ellery. This was his do-or-die pitch. He's through."

"Frankly," sniffed Nikki, "I'm a little disappointed."

"Worried," said Ellery, "would be the word for me."

INSPECTOR QUEEN WAS too case-hardened a sinner's nemesis to lower his guard at his most vulnerable moment. When the 5:30 bells bonged and the crowds began struggling toward the exits, he barked: "Men, stay at your posts. Keep watching that doll!" So all hands were on the *qui vive* even as the store emptied. The reserves kept hustling people out. Ellery, standing on an information booth, spotted bottlenecks and waved his arms.

At 5:50 P.M. the main floor was declared out of the battle zone. All stragglers had been herded out. The only persons visible were the refugees trapped by the closing bell on the upper floors, and these were pouring out of elevators and funneled by a solid line of detectives and accredited store personnel to the doors. By 6:05 they were a trickle; by 6:10 even the trickle had dried up. And the personnel itself began to disperse.

"No, men!" called Ellery sharply from his observation post. "Stay where you are till all the store employees are out!" The counter clerks had long since disappeared.

Sergeant Velie's plaintive voice called from the other side of the glass door. "I got to get home and decorate my tree. Maestro, make with the key."

Ellery jumped down and hurried over to release him. Detective Piggott jeered, "Going to play Santa to your kids tomorrow morning, Velie?" at which the sergeant managed even through his mask to project a four-letter word distinctly, forgetful of Miss Porter's presence, and stamped off toward the gentleman's relief station.

"Where you going, Velie?" asked the inspector, smiling.

"I got to get out of these x-and-dash Santy clothes somewheres, don't I?" came back the sergeant's mask-muffled tones, and he vanished in a thunderclap of his fellow-officers' laughter.

"Still worried, Mr. Queen?" chuckled the inspector.

"I don't understand it." Ellery shook his head. "Well, Mr. Bondling, there's your dauphin, untouched by human hands."

"Yes. Well!" Attorney Bondling wiped his forehead happily. "I don't profess to understand it, either, Mr. Queen. Unless it's simply another case of an inflated reputation . . ." He clutched the inspector suddenly. "Those men!" he whispered. *"Who are they?"*

"Relax, Mr. Bondling," said the inspector good-naturedly. "It's just the men to move the dolls back to the bank. Wait a minute, you men! Perhaps, Mr. Bondling, we'd better see the dauphin back to the vaults ourselves."

"Keep those fellows back," said Ellery to the head-quarters men, quietly, and he followed the inspector and Mr. Bondling into the enclosure. They pulled two of the counters apart at one corner and strolled over to the platform. The dauphin was winking at them in a friendly way. They stood looking at him.

"Cute little devil," said the inspector.

"Seems silly now," beamed Attorney Bondling. "Being so worried all day."

"Comus must have had *some* plan," mumbled Ellery.

"Sure," said the inspector. "That old man disguise. And that purse-snatching act."

"No, no, Dad. Something clever. He's always pulled something clever."

"Well, there's the diamond," said the lawyer comfortably. "He didn't."

"Disguise . . ." muttered Ellery. "It's always been a disguise. Santa Claus costume—he used that once—this morning in front of the bank. . . . Did we see a Santa Claus around here today?"

"Just Velie," said the inspector, grinning. "And I hardly think—"

"Wait a moment, please," said Attorney Bondling in a very odd voice.

He was staring at the Dauphin's Doll.

"Wait for what, Mr. Bondling?"

"What's the matter?" said Ellery, also in a very odd voice.

"But . . . not possible . . ." stammered Bondling. He snatched the doll from its black velvet repository. *"No!"* he howled. *"This isn't the dauphin! It's a fake—a copy!"*

Something happened in Mr. Queen's head—a little *click!* like the sound of a switch. And there was light.

"Some of you men!" he roared. *"After Santa Claus!"*

"After who, Ellery?" gasped Inspector Queen.

"Don't stand here! *Get him!"* screamed Ellery, dancing up and down. "The man I just let out of here! The Santa who made for the men's room!"

Detectives started running, wildly.

"But Ellery," said a small voice, and Nikki found that it was her own, "that was Sergeant Velie."

"It was *not* Velie, Nikki! When Velie ducked out just before two o'clock, *Comus waylaid him!* It was Comus who came back in Velie's Santa Claus rig, wearing Velie's whiskers and mask! *Comus has been on this platform all afternoon!"* He tore the dauphin from Attorney Bondling's grasp. "Copy . . . He did it, he did it!"

"But Mr. Queen," whispered Attorney Bondling, "his voice. He spoke to us . . . in Sergeant Velie's voice."

"Yes, Ellery," Nikki heard herself saying.

"I told you yesterday Comus is a great mimic, Nikki. Lieutanant Farber! Is Farber still here?"

The jewelry expert, who had been gaping from a distance, shook his head and shuffled into the enclosure.

"Lieutenant," said Ellery in a strangled voice. "Examine this diamond. . . . I mean, *is* it a diamond?"

Inspector Queen removed his hands from his face and said froggily, "Well, Gerry?"

Lieutenant Farber squinted once through his loupe. "The hell you say. It's strass—"

"It's what?" said the inspector piteously.

"Strass, Dick—lead glass—paste. Beautiful job of imitation—as nice as I've ever seen."

"Lead me to that Santa Claus," whispered Inspector Queen.

But Santa Claus was being led to him. Struggling in the

grip of a dozen detectives, his red coat ripped off, his red pants around his ankles, but his whiskery mask still on his face, came a large shouting man.

"But I tell you," he was roaring, "I'm Sergeant Tom Velie! Just take the mask off—that's all!"

"It's a pleasure," growled Detective Hagstrom, trying to break their prisoner's arm, "we're reservin' for the inspector."

"Hold him, boys," whispered the inspector. He struck like a cobra. His hand came away with Santa's face.

And there, indeed, was Sergeant Velie.

"Why, it's Velie," said the inspector wonderingly.

"I only told you that a thousand times," said the sergeant, folding his great hairy arms across his great hairy chest. "Now, who's the so-and-so who tried to bust my arm?" Then he said, "My pants!" and as Miss Porter turned delicately away, Detective Hagstrom humbly stooped and raised Sergeant Velie's pants.

"Never mind that," said a cold, remote voice.

It was the master, himself.

"Yeah?" said Sergeant Velie.

"Velie, weren't you attacked when you went to the men's room just before two?"

"Do I look like the attackable type?"

"You did go to lunch?—in person?"

"And a lousy lunch it was."

"It was *you* up here among the dolls all afternoon?"

"Nobody else, Maestro. Now, my friends, I want action. Fast patter. What's this all about? Before," said Sergeant Velie softly, "I lose my temper."

While divers headquarters orators delivered impromptu periods before the silent sergeant, Inspector Richard Queen spoke.

"Ellery. Son. How in the name of the second sin did he do it?"

"Pa," replied the master, "you got me."

DECK THE HALL with boughs of holly, but not if your name is Queen on the evening of a certain December twenty-fourth. If your name is Queen on that lamentable evening you are seated in the living room of a New York apartment uttering no falalas but staring miserably into a somber fire. And you have company. The guest list is short but select. It numbers two, a Miss Porter and a Sergeant Velie, and they are no comfort.

No, no ancient Yuletide carol is being trolled; only the silence sings.

Wail in your crypt, Cytherea Ypson; all was for nought; your little dauphin's treasure lies not in the empty coffers of the orphans but in the hot clutch of one who took his evil inspiration from a long-crumbled specialist in vanishments.

Fact: Lieutenant Geronimo Farber of police headquarters had examined the diamond in the genuine dauphin's crown a matter of seconds before it was conveyed to its sanctuary in the enclosure. Lieutenant Farber had pronounced the diamond a diamond, and not merely a diamond, but a diamond worth in his opinion over one hundred thousand dollars.

Fact: It was this genuine diamond and this genuine Dauphin's Doll which Ellery with his own hands had carried into the glass-enclosed fortress and deposited between the authenticated Sergeant Velie's verified feet.

Fact: All day—specifically, between the moment the dauphin had been deposited in his niche until the moment he was discovered to be a fraud; that is, during the total period in which a theft-and-substitution was even theoretically possible—no person whatsoever, male or female, adult or child, had set foot within the enclosure except Sergeant Thomas Velie, alias Santa Claus; and some dozens of persons with police training and specific instructions, not to mention the Queens themselves, Miss Porter, and Attorney Bondling, testified unqualifiedly that Sergeant Velie had not touched the doll, at any time, all day.

Fact: All those deputized to watch the doll swore that they had done so without lapse or hindrance the everlasting day; moreover, that at no time had anything touched the doll—human or mechanical—either from inside or outside the enclosure.

Fact: Despite all the foregoing, at the end of the day they had found the real dauphin gone and a worthless copy in its place.

"It's brilliantly, unthinkably clever," said Ellery at last. "A master illusion. For, of course, it *was* an illusion. . . ."

"Witchcraft," groaned the inspector.

"Mass mesmerism," suggested Nikki Porter.

"Mass bird gravel," growled the sergeant.

Two hours later Ellery spoke again.

"So Comus had a worthless copy of the dauphin all ready for the switch," he muttered. "It's a world famous dollie, been illustrated countless times, minutely described, photographed. . . . All ready for the switch, but how did he make it? How? How?"

"You said that," said the sergeant, "once or forty-two times."

"The bells are tolling," sighed Nikki, "but for whom? Not for us." And indeed, while they slumped there, Time, which Seneca named father of truth, had crossed the threshold of Christmas; and Nikki looked alarmed, for as that glorious song of old came upon the midnight clear, a great light spread from Ellery's eyes and beatified the whole contorted countenance, so that peace sat there, the peace that approximateth understanding; and he threw back that noble head and laughed with the merriment of an innocent child.

"Hey," said Sergeant Velie, staring.

"Son," began Inspector Queen, half-rising from his armchair; when the telephone rang.

"Beautiful!" roared Ellery. "Oh, exquisite! How did Comus make the switch, eh? Nikki—"

"From somewhere," said Nikki, handing him the telephone receiver, "a voice is calling, and if you ask me it's saying 'Comus.' Why not ask him?"

"Comus," whispered the inspector, shrinking.

"Comus," echoed the sergeant, baffled.

"Comus?" said Ellery heartily. "How nice. Hello there! Congratulations."

"Why, thank you," said the familiar deep and hollow voice. "I called to express my appreciation for a wonderful day's sport and to wish you the merriest kind of Yule tide."

"You anticipate a rather merry Christmas yourself, I take it."

"*Laeti triumphantes,*" said Comus jovially.

"And the orphans?"

"They have my best wishes. But I won't detain you, Ellery. If you'll look at the doormat outside your apartment door, you'll find, on it—in the spirit of the season—a little gift, with the compliments of Comus. Will you remember me to Inspector Queen and to Attorney Bondling?"

Ellery hung up, smiling.

On the doormat he found the true Dauphin's Doll, intact except for a contemptible detail. The jewel in the little golden crown was missing.

"IT WAS," said Ellery later, over pastrami sandwiches, "a fundamentally simple problem. All great illusions are. A valuable object is placed in full view in the heart of an impenetrable enclosure, it is watched hawkishly by dozens of thoroughly screened and reliable trained persons, it is never out of their view, it is not once touched by human hand or any other agency, and yet, at the expiration of the danger period, it is gone—exchanged for a worthless copy. Wonderful. Amazing. It defies the imagination. Actually, it's susceptible—like all magical hocus-pocus— to immediate solution if only one is able—as I was not— to ignore the wonder and stick to the fact. But then, the wonder is there for precisely that purpose: to stand in the way of the fact.

"What is the fact?" continued Ellery, helping himself to a dill pickle. "The fact is that between the time the doll was placed on the exhibit platform and the time the theft was discovered no one and no thing touched it. Therefore between the time the doll was placed on the platform and the time the theft was discovered *the dauphin could not have been stolen*. It follows, simply and inevitably, that the dauphin must have been stolen *outside that period*.

"Before the period began? No. I placed the authentic dauphin inside the enclosure with my own hands; at or about the beginning of the period, then, no hand but mine had touched the doll—not even, you'll recall, Lieutenant Farber's.

"Then the dauphin must have been stolen after the period closed."

Ellery brandished half the pickle. "And who," he demanded solemnly, "is the only one besides myself who handled that doll after the period closed and before Lieutenant Farber pronounced the diamond to be paste? *The only one?*"

The inspector and the sergeant exchanged puzzled glances, and Nikki looked blank.

"Why, Mr. Bondling," said Nikki, "and he doesn't count."

"He counts very much, Nikki," said Ellery, reaching

for the mustard, "because the facts say Bondling stole the dauphin at that time."

"Bondling!" The inspector paled.

"I don't get it," complained Sergeant Velie.

"Ellery, you must be wrong," said Nikki. "At the time Mr. Bondling grabbed the doll off the platform, the theft had already taken place. It was the worthless copy he picked up."

"That," said Ellery, reaching for another sandwich, "was the focal point of his illusion. How do we know it was the worthless copy he picked up? Why, he said so. Simple, eh? He said so, and like the dumb bunnies we were, we took his unsupported word as gospel."

"That's right!" mumbled his father. "We didn't actually examine the doll till quite a few seconds later."

"Exactly," said Ellery in a munchy voice. "There was a short period of beautiful confusion, as Bondling knew there would be. I yelled to the boys to follow and grab Santa Claus—I mean the sergeant, here. The detectives were momentarily demoralized. You, Dad, were stunned. Nikki looked as if the roof had fallen in. I essayed an excited explanation. Some detectives ran; others milled around. And while all this was happening—during those few moments when nobody was watching the genuine doll in Bondling's hand because everyone thought it was a fake—Bondling calmly slipped it into one of his greatcoat pockets and from the other produced the worthless copy which he'd been carrying there all day. When I did turn back to him, it was the copy I grabbed from his hand. And his illusion was complete.

"I know," said Ellery dryly, "it's rather on the let-down side. That's why illusionists guard their professional secrets so closely; knowledge is disenchantment. No doubt the incredulous amazement aroused in his periwigged London audience by Comus the French conjuror's dematerialization of his wife from the top of a table would have suffered the same fate if he'd revealed the trap door through which she had dropped. A good trick, like a good woman, is best in the dark. Sergeant, have another pastrami."

"Seems like funny chow to be eating early Christmas morning," said the sergeant, reaching. Then he stopped. Then he said, "Bondling," and shook his head.

"Now that we know it was Bondling," said the inspector, who had recovered a little, "it's a cinch to get that diamond back. He hasn't had time to dispose of it yet. I'll just give downtown a buzz—"

"Wait, Dad" said Ellery.

"Wait for what?"

"Whom are you going to sic the hounds on?"

"What?"

"You're going to call headquarters, get a warrant, and so on. Who's your man?'

The inspector felt his head. "Why . . . Bondling, didn't you say?"

"It might be wise," said Ellery, thoughtfully searching with his tongue for a pickle seed, "to specify his alias."

"Alias?" said Nikki. "Does he have one?"

"What alias, son?"

"Comus."

"*Comus!*"

"*Comus?*"

"Oh, come off it," said Nikki, pouring herself a shot of coffee, straight, for she was in training for the inspector's Christmas dinner. "How could Bondling be Comus when Bondling was with us all day?—and Comus kept making disguised appearances all over the place . . . that Santa who gave me the note in front of the bank—the old man who kidnapped Lance Morganstern—the fat man with the mustache who snatched Mrs. Rafferty's purse."

"Yeah," said the sergeant. "How?"

"These illusions die hard," said Ellery. "Wasn't it Comus who phoned a few minutes ago to rag me about the theft? Wasn't it Comus who said he'd left the stolen dauphin—minus the diamond—on our doorstep? Therefore Comus is Bondling.

"I told you Comus never does anything without a good reason," said Ellery. "Why did 'Comus' announce to 'Bondling' that he was *going* to steal the Dauphin's Doll? Bondling told us that—putting the finger on his *alter ego* —because he wanted us to believe he and Comus were separate individuals. He wanted us to watch for *Comus* and take *Bondling* for granted. In tactical execution of this strategy Bondling provided us with three 'Comus' appearances during the day—obviously confederates.

"Yes," said Ellery, "I think Dad, you'll find on backtracking that the great thief you've been trying to catch for five years has been a respectable estate attorney on

Park Row all the time, shedding his quiddities and his quillets at night in favor of the soft shoe and the dark lantern. And now he'll have to exchange them all for a number and a grilled door. Well, well, it couldn't have happened at a more appropriate season; there's an old English proverb that says the Devil makes his Christmas pie of lawyer's tongues. Nikki, pass the pastrami."

BY THE CHIMNEY WITH CARE

by Nick O'Donohoe

Nick O'Donohoe has worked as a surveyor, an English teacher and as an operator of a puppet show. He is presently working on his dissertation, in the Humanities Doctoral Program at Syracuse University. He plays the guitar and a poor game of poker and is teaching part-time at Virginia Polytechnic Institute. In addition to his Nathan Phillips-Roy Cartley series of short stories, he has completed two novels and is working on a third. He is very fond of his cat, who is sometimes fond of him.

It was the one day a week I could sleep late—so naturally the phone rang. I muttered, "Go away," and tried to sleep through it. Nobody would keep trying me forever.

But the phone kept ringing, and suddenly there was a furry black tail swishing back and forth in my face. I sat up and dumped the cat off my chest. "Thanks a bunch, Marlowe." He sneered. "You my answering service these days?" He stood on the bed, lashing his tail and waiting.

I gave in and picked up the phone. "Cartley and Phillips, home office. And Phillips speaking."

"Nathan." It was Cartley's voice, as rasping as I've ever heard it. "Nate, I've got my living room blocked off, and I want to keep the kids out. It's that time of the year, you know." He was trying to sound lighthearted; I've heard lighter pile-drivers.

I'm slow at that hour. "And you want help in the living room, right? *Ho-ho-ho!* But it's a whole week before—"

"Can't say, Nate, there's an extension phone," he broke in sharply.

163

A high-pitched giggle came on the line. "Hi, Uncle Roy! Are you talking to Nathan?"

I got the idea, finally. "Who is this? Amy? Paul?" After two outraged denials I had it easy. "Aw, I knew it was you, Howie. Listen, I'll be right over. Who said you could listen in on us?"

"I can be a detective, too."

I tried to sound injured. "Why are you bugging me, Howie? I haven't done anything wrong."

"Not yet." He was triumphantly confident. I was going to be a crook, and the kids would catch me. That always happened when they visited Uncle Roy before Christmas. I loved it.

I said goodbye and stumbled into the bathroom, where I nearly brushed my teeth with Ben-Gay. After that I drove over. By the time I hit the boulevard around Lake of the Isles I was awake enough to wonder why Roy had wanted me over right now.

At the front door I was surrounded; I knelt to hug Amy and Paul, then twisted my right arm forward just enough to shake hands with Howie. "Hi, Howie. Old enough to know better, yet?"

"Getting older," he said, trying to look world-weary and not doing badly—for a ten-year-old. "Have you been behaving yourself, Nathan?" he added.

I narrowed my eyes and curled my lip. "That's for me to know and you to find out." I wasn't sure what kind of a bad guy to be just yet. "Only person I'll talk to here is my accomplice." I stood up and called to Roy, "Merry Christmas, almost. We have plans to make in the living room?"

"Sure." I looked at him and suddenly knew we weren't going to wrap presents. He edged through the living-room door, blocking the view with his body; I did the same. A haze of cigarette smoke drifted out over our heads. As I came through, Roy glanced behind me nervously. I shut the door quickly, braced it with the doorstop and turned around.

I spun back around, hung my coat over the doorknob to block the keyhole, then walked quickly over and shut the front curtains. Roy sat down in one of the chairs.

"Good thinking," he said, and rubbed his face. "God, I haven't been able to think of a *thing*."

"Who is he?" I said. It was all I could think of to say.

"What do you mean, 'who is he?' " Roy said irritably. "Don't look at his chest; concentrate on his face."

It was hard. My eyes were drawn to the knife wound. He was up against the chimney, his knees folded under him, his body somehow suspended upright. The flesh on his face was sagging. It made him look weary beyond belief.

Then I pictured the same face, slouched forward in the back seat of a squad car. "Gam Gillis!"

"Right."

"What's he doing *here?* You don't even *have* a safe."

Roy gestured at the fireplace, below the body. "He's hung on the damper. Look at his jacket. The collar must be hooked in back, and all his weight's on it. When the collar button pops off, down he'll go." Cartley felt his pockets methodically, then drummed his fingers against one knee in frustration. "Nate, you got any cigarettes?"

"Sorry." For the first time in my life, I wished I smoked. Roy was a wreck. "Want me to go for some?"

"No, I want you to take the kids somewhere while the police are here."

"When are they coming?" He suddenly looked stricken.

"Jesus, Roy, you forgot to *call?*"

He wiped at his face, nodding. I picked up the phone and began dialing. "By the way, who do you think put Gillis here?"

"Who else? Petlovich."

"Oh," I said—but it was a big *"oh"*; Roy and I had gotten Gillis to turn state's evidence on Petlovich two years ago, over a jewelry theft we'd been checking out for an insurance company. "You think Petlovich left Gillis as a message. In other words—" I stopped. I didn't want any other words.

Just then the police answered. "Give me Lieutenant Pederson, please." While I waited, I asked Roy, "You gonna tell your wife?"

"Hell, no! Her mother sprained her ankle at just the right time. Maybe this'll be over before she's back."

"What about the kids—can you send them someplace?"

"Not a chance. My brother goes wilderness camping in California. The National Guard couldn't get hold of him." He felt his pockets again, automatically.

Just then the phone said, "Homicide. Pederson here."

"Good to hear you. This is Nathan Phillips. How's Minneapolis's second finest?"

He answered levelly, "Phillips, any time you give me your full name and say it's good to hear me, something's up. *What's* up?"

I must have been as rattled as Roy. "There's been a murder at Roy's house. James Gillis, an ex-con; you can look up his connection with us. Oh, and bring a pack of cigarettes?"

Roy called out "Camels," just as Pederson said, "Camels, right? Sure thing. Wait a minute, aren't Jack's kids visiting Roy now?"

"Yeah. Can you hurry?"

"You bet." He added too casually, "Did Roy do it?"

"I . . ." I turned to look at Roy. "Uh, Roy's okay," I said carefully. "No. No, of course not. You'll see." I hoped he would. "See you when you get here." I hung up.

"Thanks, Nate. Now let's go collect the kids." He stared at the fireplace. So had I, on and off. We were both watching the collar-button hole stretching.

"Waiting for the other shoe to drop," I said, "When the bough breaks—"

"Nathan, for Christ's *sake!*" He glared, and I kicked myself.

"Sorry." I edged out the door, and the kids jumped up. I said to them, "There wasn't anything in there at all. He just wanted a quiet place to yell at me for not taking you guys anywhere. So we're going sledding, right now."

They scrambled for their coats. Los Angeles kids don't get much chance for winter sports. Afterwards, I'd take them to my apartment for lunch, and call Roy from there.

Howie grinned and said, "You gonna crash sleds with opened my mouth and Cartley said, "Sure he will."

Howie grinned and said, "you gonna crash sleds with me?"

"Nathan will love that." It was the closest to a grin Cartley had managed all morning.

"Yeah," I said, pulling on my stocking cap, "Nathan loves bruises." We went.

Incidentally, Nathan got creamed.

The kids loved my apartment. I hadn't put a thing away in weeks. All kinds of fragile, fascinating oddities were lying about within reach. I said. "Don't break anything I haven't already broken," and went to the kitchen to heat soup and make sandwiches. While I was out there, I heard a giggling and the sound of a cat losing hold of the upholstery.

Before I could get to the door, Amy came into the kitchen, hugging Marlowe and holding him up by his armpits. Marlowe was hanging limp, purring frantically. He raised his pleading eyes to me. His claws, bless his heart, were in.

"Cats break, too, Amy." I took Marlowe out of her arms, putting an arm under his back legs. He let his claws out just enough to show he was unhappy. "He looks like he wants to go out." About as far out as Skylab. "Could you open the door?"

She ran over and reached up to the knob. When the door opened four inches Marlowe streaked out. Good enough. I could go down and let him all the way out later.

Paul peered around the kitchen door, then stepped in. "You done anything against the law yet, Nathan?"

"I'm not telling. What's in your hand?" He opened his fist. Clutched in it was a glass cat.

I took it from him, held it up to the light and polished it, then put it back on his palm and played with the tail to make the cat dance. "That's Marlowe's girl friend. A friend gave her to me and said Marlowe needed a steady girl friend."

Paul examined the statue. "How come she's clear?"

"My friend said Marlowe's girl friend should be hard to see, so his other girl friends wouldn't get jealous."

In came Howie, then, glancing quickly around the kitchen for signs of iniquity. His eyes lit triumphantly on the scotch bottle next to all the dirty dishes.

"So *that's* what you've been doing, Nathan." He pointed to the bottle, then to me, like the world's smallest prosecuting attorney. "You've been drinking alone!"

Amy scurried to my defense—sort of. She stood on tiptoe, hanging onto the counter-top and peering over it. "No, he hasn't," she said primly.

"How do you know, Blondie?" For a ten-year-old, Howie had a hell of a sneer. I quit being that tough at nine.

She smiled triumphantly. "Anyone can tell, smarty. There are *two* dirty glasses by the bottle, and *one* of them has lipstick on it."

"Nathan's got a gir-ul, Nathan's got a gir-ul." That was Paul. God, they were cute! Suddenly I wished Roy would hurry up.

I picked up Amy and swung her over the counter. You want to have your soup," I growled, "or shall I cook *you* up for the rest of us?"

She screamed and laughed, and I put her down. "Soup's ready," I announced. They all ran to the table, which Howie, to my surprise, had set. That's why he hadn't been in the kitchen earlier, uncovering my sins.

While I was in the kitchen making more sandwiches, there was a pounding on the door, and a deep, grim voice said deadpan, "Police."

Howie ran to the kitchen and looked at me wide-eyed; I said, "It's no use. Let them in, and I'll give myself up." Howie opened the front door dubiously, and Lieutenant Pederson walked in, grinning, Roy a step behind him.

After "Mr. Pederson" was re-introduced to the kids, and I'd served the sandwiches and the last of the soup, Pederson looked up and said innocently, "Things are kind of slow at the station. How would you like to tour it, and see the jail and the lab?"

They had their coats on before he had even pushed back from the table.

When Roy and I were alone I said, "Now that's above and beyond the call of duty. What gives?"

Roy looked much happier with life. "Jon didn't feel the police investigation would turn anything up very fast, so he offered to baby-sit for a couple of hours while we check out some possibiities."

"Great. Do we have any?"

"Possibilities? Not many. We can't question Petlovich till someone finds out where he is. His parole officer hasn't seen him in a while."

I raised an eyebrow. "Sounds dubious. How long till we can get ahold of him?"

"Maybe this afternoon. We'll be seeing Gillis's woman."

"Long-standing?"

"Same one as when he helped us send up Petlovich. Her name's Mary Jordan. Two shoplifting convictions and a bad-check charge, dropped later. Otherwise, she's clean—not hard to be cleaner than the men she hangs around with. She might know where Petlovich is."

"Fat chance." I said, pulling on my stocking cap. Cartley looked at me oddly.

"You're not going to shave?"

I shrugged. "We need to look tough. I always cut myself."

He shrugged back. Out we went.

Gillis's apartment was on the east side of 35W, not too far south of downtown. Farther down, in the plusher residential areas, along Minnehaha Creek, there were sound fences on either side of the highway, painted a tasteful, unobtrusive green. Up here, they wouldn't have put a fence up, and someone would have stolen the paint.

Roy and I climbed up two flights of bowing, scarred stairs to a splintered door. The hallway had visible piles of dirt in the corners and along the baseboards. It looked like any other walk-up, only grimier. The baseboards had shrunk away from the linoleum, and I didn't blame them.

Roy pounded on the door. We both had enough sense to stand aside. Inside there was a scuffling, and the volume on TV chortled appreciation.

Roy said with no patience, "Miss Jordan, we're investigators, Cartley and Phillips. We worked with Gam a couple of years back—"

The laughter was cut off and a couple of seconds later the door was jerked open. A black-rooted redhead with booze breath and smeared mascara looked at us. "Come on in. I'd make you some eggs, but I only got fresh ones."

Roy walked in, first looking through the crack between door and wall to see if anyone was waiting. I glanced out the window at the fire escape. Roy said, "I didn't expect you to love us, but I didn't expect you to be drunk in front of the TV today, either." He was red-faced.

As I came in, she walked over to the encrusted sink-and-stove in the room's corner, picked up a half-empty flat pint bottle, and stared at it argumentatively.

"Did you hear what he said?" she demanded of it, swaying. "He thinks I shouldn't drink you." Then she tipped it up and took a long pull. She giggled as she set it down. She had to be her own laugh-track now.

Cartley looked irritated. He opened his mouth, but I winked at him and he shut up as I said, "Don't listen to him, lady—drink up. Gillis wasn't worth staying dry for

—why waste an afternoon crying for a down-and-out stoolie with just enough brains to get killed?"

I ducked, but shouldn't have bothered. The glass went over me by three feet.

"Wait a—" Roy said and stopped as another glass flew by me, low and to the right. Two more tries, and there was nothing within her reach but the bottle. She hefted it, glared at me frustratedly, then took another drink.

Roy sounded like sweet reason itself. "Young Nate, here, came along with his own ideas, ma'am. I came to see if I could track down who killed Gillis."

She looked at him, startled, and wiped her mouth on the back of her hand. "Petlovich." If she had any doubts, they weren't in her voice. "Nobody else would have killed him. Who would have wanted to?"

"I would," I offered, keeping in character. "You would have, too, if he hadn't been your meal ticket."

She nearly did throw the bottle. "He ain't given me a dime, you lying bastard. I paid for this place and our food and—hell, he ain't even taken me out for dinner in two or three months." She stopped, probably realizing that he wouldn't, ever again.

Roy said quickly, "All I want is Petlovich's address, Mary. Nothing else. You want him to go up for it, don't you?"

She knotted her hands into spindly, white-knuckled fists. "You bet I do." She pointed at me suddenly. "And I'd send him up, too, if I could!" She ran into the apartment's tiny bathroom and slammed the door. It was loose in the frame; we could hear her weeping.

Roy said quietly, "Maybe it'd be better from here if you waited outside, Nate. Thanks for priming her."

"You're less than welcome." I meant it. "I'm tired of playing the bad guy."

On my way out I stopped and looked at a pair of polyester trousers with pulled threads poking out of them, draped over a chair. I glanced toward the bathroom door, then checked the trousers pockets.

No wallet—that had been on the body—but the right front pocket held his checkbook. I flipped idly but quickly through the stubs. For a man that lived off his woman, this guy had been living pretty high lately.

He had written three checks to good restaurants, one to a department store and one for a couple of hundred, marked simply "cash"—all dated within the last three months. He had the deposits recorded in the back. They had been made, one for each check, barely in time and barely enough to cover the amount.

I put the checkbook back. As I did, the bathroom doorknob turned. I gave a quick nod to Roy and edged out to the hall.

Through the door, I could hear him mutter and her snuffle and spit. I shuffled from one foot to the other, idly trying to guess what color the walls had been twenty years ago. I felt like taking a bath.

When Roy came out, he gave me an address in Saint Paul, and away we went. I told him about the checkbook.

"*Oho!*" he said. "So she was lying about the money."

"Or else she didn't know about it."

Roy looked dubious. "How much were those restaurant checks again?" I told him. "It's an odd amount, so you can bet he wasn't cashing a check. Could you eat your way through forty-five dollars and thirty-eight cents' worth of food at any of those places? Never mind—*you* probably could."

"Yeah, but I wouldn't—not alone. Or with a friend, either, unless I was in the money or thought I was going to be.'"

"'I know." He grabbed the armrest as I took a right turn. "She found that address pretty fast, too. Well, we're headed to see Petlovich, aren't we?" Roy was cheerful again. On the way to Saint Paul, he made three rotten jokes and yelled at my driving at every other turn. It wasn't fair. I had signaled at most of those turns, or meant to.

Saint Paul was a bust, a waste of time. We came up the stairs, we knocked from beside the door, we heard a scrambling in the room, we stood back. A slug ripped through the door; Roy let go of the knob, and we both flattened against the wall. After a minute of silence, Cartley threw the door open and we charged in, heads down and guns up.

There was nothing much in the room—a battered suitcase, a sack of groceries, a newspaper and some mail. The window was open, and the shade, jerked down, roller and all, hung half in the window and half out. I looked out. Ten feet below the window were the deep tracks where he had hit, and the footprints of a man sprinting away.

We turned back to the table. Cartley went for the mail and I checked the newspaper. He tossed the letters down in disgust. "Bills!"

"No Christmas cards? Funny, I thought he was on my list."

"I haven't gotten one from you either." Cartley stared at the mail again. "If Petlovich has money, he isn't paying off debts with it. I wonder why he waited so long to leave town. If the cops didn't come for him, a collection agency would."

"I don't know about his bills, but I know why he didn't blow town till now." I showed Roy the Minneapolis *Star*, afternoon edition. In the lower right-hand corner of the front page was a human-interest story about the body that had been found hung by the chimney in an unnamed Minneapolis home. The article said the police suspected one Willem Petlovich, former second-story man.

Roy stared at it woodenly. "That shouldn't have spooked him. He had to know he'd be a suspect."

"Maybe," I said. "But the paper ties him in explicitly. Maybe he figured he'd have a day or two before anyone knew where to look for him."

"He's that dumb?"

"He's got caught once. By you, even."

"By you, too. All right, quit the kidding. He got caught because he was ratted on." We holstered our guns and left.

On the way back, I asked, "Want to report the shooting to Pederson?"

"And catch hell for playing cops without badges or a warrant?" He sighed. "Guess we better. Jon won't like this. He didn't take care of the kids so we could go break laws."

"Yeah. Say, why don't you drop me off at home? I ought to feed Marlowe, and—"

"Sure. Right *after* we talk to Jon." He considered. "No. I'll wait for you while you feed him now. Nate, I'd really appreciate it if you'd sack out on the couch at my house tonight. Bring your gun."

It made sense. "Uh, yeah. Roy, while you talk to Jon, can I make a phone call?"

He grinned then. "Okay, coward. But after you talk to

that woman nobody's supposed to know about, you can come in and catch hell like a man."

I ran a stop sign, unintentionally for once. "Damn it, is everyone on my private life? I suppose the kids told you while I was in the kitchen."

He leaned back and hitched at his belt. "If you can't fool visitors, you couldn't fool your partner."

"Yeah?" It wasn't much of a crack, but it was all I had left.

The next morning I opened my eyes and found a pair of cool blue eyes, framed by blond bangs, not more than six inches from my face. I closed my eyes and tried to think. Wasn't the hair sandier?

Then I remembered where I was and that only made it more confusing. I opened my eyes again and, after a few tries, focussed on the face around the eyes. I pulled the blanket up over my chest, feeling embarrassed and then silly about it.

"Oh! H'lo, Amy." She was standing beside the sofa. "Sleep well?" She nodded.

I hadn't. This house had more creaking boards and rattling windows than the House of Usher. "Had breakfast yet?" She shook her head. "What's the matter, don't you talk in the morning?"

She straightened her flannel nightgown and folded her arms self-assuredly. "I'm waiting till the others get up," she said.

Great! I was guilty again. Ah, life as a hardened criminal! I went into the bathroom, brushed my teeth and changed my pajama bottoms for trousers.

I was throwing cold water on my face when I heard a whoop from Howie and a shriek from Paul. I tottered out and collided with Cartley, striding out in his bathrobe to collect the evidence and punish the wicked. He was boiling mad. He looked like a walking bathrobe with a ham roast in it.

In the living room, Amy was standing demurely by the front door while Paul tugged at it. She ran a hand over her blond hair to make sure she looked tidy and grown-up, then turned to Roy. "We caught Nathan. He's trying to keep us shut in the house, isn't he?"

Roy laughed, tried to unlock the door, then stopped laughing and threw his weight against it. It didn't budge.

I was in the kitchen before he hit it a second time.

I rammed the back door with my shoulder, on the dead run. It jarred my teeth, snapped my head back, but the door barely rattled. I tried again. I might as well have hit Mount Rushmore.

I ran back through the sitting room and snatched my gun from under the sofa pillow. I could hear Roy going through closets downstairs; I charged upstairs. I flipped through every wardrobe with my gun muzzle, poked under every bed, even looked in the shower stall and the clothes hamper. Amy and Paul, watching from the living room, must have loved it.

I met Roy back in the sitting room, at the foot of the stairs. I called out before I came down—when I saw his eyes I was glad I had. He was staring every which way and pacing. His gun shivered in his fist like a live mouse.

I said in my calmest deadpan, "Nobody home, Roy. You should make your visitors sign a guestbook. You get such a lot of them."

He relaxed. "Yeah," he said and coughed. "I'm beginning to think I should sublet this place."

"I—" I stopped as Howie came out of the kitchen and lounged against the doorway.

"Nice try, Nathan," he said, looking sideways at Amy and Paul. He was pale. "Pretty good crime, huh? Lock us in, then finish us off." He didn't look like he enjoyed playing anymore. "I wouldn't even have guessed, if I hadn't poked around the basement."

"Jesus!" I was closest. I ran to the kitchen and fumbled frantically with the basement doorknob. Roy was right behind me before I got it open.

It was in the corner near the hot-water heater. Not too surprising, since it was right in front of Roy's fuel-oil tank. It was small, shapeless and attached to a clock. Anybody over three who watched television could see it was a bomb.

It didn't look powerful. It didn't have to be, so long as it set off the fuel-oil tank. I picked up a broom and was shoving the bomb along the floor gingerly, away from the tank, as Paul and Amy slipped past Roy and danced around me, chanting, "We caught Nathan!"

Howie looked relieved. I suppose I looked pretty silly, doubled over and poking delicately from a broom's length away at a wad of clay, a battery and an alarm clock whose hands were nearly touching.

"Go back upstairs," I said. Softly. Roy said it louder. They giggled and shook their heads. We couldn't drag them all out. We might not have time, and if they kicked too hard—

I tossed the broom to Roy, saying, "Shove the bomb in the corner," in a conspiratorial tone. Then I snatched up Amy and continued, "While I kidnap the girl. *Ya* ha ha."

I tucked her under my arm and dashed up the stairs, with Amy laughing and struggling and Paul and Howie in hot pursuit. As I left I called out, "And set it off with your bowling ball!" I hoped he understood.

I only glanced at the front window. I'd never get the kids out in time if the boys caught up with me and tried to "arrest" me before I could break it open. I ran upstairs, to the kids' bedroom in back; I locked the door for a second while I threw open the window and climbed onto the roof, still carrying Amy. The boys burst in and followed, right on out the window.

We were right over the pile of snow at the end of the driveway. Far below me, through the window, I could hear the muffled grind of a bowling ball rolling slowly across the basement floor; the sound was nearly covered by the hasty slap of flat feet on the basement stairs.

I snarled, "You'll never take us alive," wrapped Amy in my arms and rolled off the roof to land on my back in the snow nine feet below.

The wind was knocked out of me, and I felt a sharp stabbing pain in my right side. Above me, the boys were hesitating at the roof's edge.

As Amy yelled, "Jump! It's easy," there was a loud boom from the basement, and the chime of broken glass on the other side of the house as Roy leaped through the front window. The boys jumped and sank in the snow almost to their waists.

I rolled Amy off me as Roy came running up, still in his bathrobe, bleeding from a small cut on his right hand. He felt my side where I was clutching it, said matter-of-factly, "Yep," and slipped his bathrobe off to put under me.

Then he stood there in his pajamas, looking foolish and cold. "I'll get you to a doctor. Thanks, Nate." He shuffled, and looked at the kids, dazed. Amy was still unruffled, but her eyes were shining. Howie and Paul were jumping up and down with excitement.

He looked back at me. "Do you feel all excited too, Nate?"

Talking hurt. It felt that I should slip the words out edgeways. "Gee, Uncle Roy, can we do that again?"

He chuckled, but his jaw jumped as he looked at the back door. I rolled my head cautiously and looked myself. There was a two-by-four across it. Screwed into the doorframe at either end; a U-bolt went around the door knob. If that bomb had ignited the fuel oil, we'd never have gotten out in time.

Suddenly Roy was as cool as I've ever seen him. I said, "Roy"—quietly—but he didn't hear me.

He added, even more quietly, "If it turns out that guy knew the kids were here, I'll make sure he doesn't see the inside of a courtroom myself."

He was shaking, and he wasn't cold, and even in his pajamas he didn't look silly at all.

The hospital bed had the usual sheets—snow-white, rigid with starch and smelling like the underside of a band-aid. There was a single Christmas-tree ornament hanging on the bedside lamp, and a cardboard Santa lay on the night stand looking round and two-dimensional. Cut-out letters on the mirror read, *Merry Christmas.*

Roy looked at his reflection, rubbing his chin—he hadn't shaved—and said, "You're supposed to take it easy, and this is the easiest I can get for you."

I scratched and winced; I could feel the pain all along my side. "My timing's rotten. Sorry, Roy. You won't even have the bandage on long. You cracked a rib, not broke it."

"If you're not gonna be cheerful, I'm not gonna talk." I leaned back and sulked while he left, whistling.

I settled back into the pillow, wishing I felt like taking it easy. There was a murderer loose who wanted to kill Cartley, one who wasn't losing any sleep over killing a few kids in the process. I was in the hospital for twenty-four hours and restricted for much longer. And my partner and best friend was thinking seriously about murder. I tried to take it easy, feeling cold-blooded.

Painful as it was, I shifted restlessly and tried to think. The bombing had been disturbingly amateurish. The bomb itself had been inefficient and the house-barricade childish. Even the first murder smacked of cheap detective shows. Only the break-in showed any professionalism; the first break-in had all the class of Gillis's and Petlovich's best effort.

Irrelevantly, I wondered what Gam and Mary did with those nights out on the town. It couldn't have been anything much; apparently Mary had enjoyed herself, or else wasn't talking. I pictured a tired thug and a bored woman, eating something Cordon bleu and taking turns reading each other their rights.

I was dozing when the phone rang. I could have ignored it, since Marlowe wasn't on duty, but I remembered where I was and what was going on before it stopped ringing.

"Yeah?"

"Boy!" It was Howie. "You sure took a long time to get to the phone."

"Don't whine. It's a big room. I was clear across it, dusting the grand piano. What's up, Howie?"

"Just wanted to tell you I figured out what you're doing, and why." He sounded half lighthearted, half scared —strained. I was reminded of Cartley's call the other morning.

I said, "What?" then had a thought. "No, I take it back. Howie, Amy and Paul aren't on the extension, are they?"

"No."

"But they're in the room behind you."

"Yes.'" On cue I heard them talking in the background, a long way from the phone.

"Howie," I said cautiously, "you're pretty sure that bomb this morning wasn't anything your uncle and I did, aren't you?"

He let out a quick sigh, then said, "Sure."

"Do the others know?"

"No way." He was very firm, almost military.

"Right. Well, we're not playing, and you know it, so what did you call about?"

He tried to sound. "I'll bet anything Uncle Roy has gone to see some woman that helps you."

"Why?"

" 'Cause he said he had to see a girl about a restaurant, just after he got a phone call. I thought you'd know about it," he added in real surprise. "I figured it was your girl helping you."

I was irritated. "Doesn't he know any other girls?"

Howie said self-righteously, "He's *married*. And if you've got more than one girl, I bet you're in trouble."

"Not if the first one never finds out—oh, wait. Of course. Sure." Funny how things fall together when you're not looking for them. "Howie, thanks for calling. What you just told me was important. But why did you call me? What made it important to you?"

His whisper was moist and breathy; he must have had the mouthpiece right against his lips. " 'Cause when Uncle Roy left he took two guns and all kinds of bullets, and I've never seen him do that before."

The sheets weren't just snowy—suddenly they felt like ice. I said, "I'll do something about it right now. Howie, nobody ever said you weren't on the ball, and nobody's ever going to."

"Thanks, Nathan," he said seriously, then hung up.

Right after the click I called Pederson. I was lucky enough to find him in.

"What do you want?" he groused. "Phillips, I thought if you took a rest, I'd have one.

"Fat chance. Are you doing anything?"

"Plenty."

"Drop it and pick me up at the hospital. Roy needs someone from Homicide."

"There are other cops besides me, you know." I could hear the *whuff* as he lit up one of his cigars and pulled at it. "Some of them are even Homicide."

"He needs a friend—two of them. He's in trouble, and some rookie with a gun won't get him out of it."

"Why not?"

"Because his own gun's getting him into it right now."

That was as close as I could come without committing myself.

It worked. There was a moment's silence, then Pederson said roughly, "I don't understand, and I'll be right over. Be downstairs and ready in ten minutes, even if it hurts."

Ten minutes later he was there. I was ready, and God, did it hurt! I gave him the address, and he drove faster than I'd have dared through downtown, even with a siren. We skidded onto Lake Street, wove through traffic till we shot under 35W, then screeched into a right turn we almost skidded out of. I filled him in the whole time, not stopping when I grabbed the dash for support.

He interrupted twice. "How do you know all this?"

"The restaurant bills. The man who kept a woman in that slum didn't show her three good nights on the town.".

He grunted, and we went on. A little later he said, "You know, Phillips, I wish you could have done without me. My badge is sticky; it doesn't pull off just because a friend's involved."

How do you answer that? "I know. I'm hoping we'll get there before anything too bad happens." He sped up then. I hadn't thought it possible.

We pulled in across the street from the building. Roy's car was nowhere in sight, but maybe he'd stowed it. Pederson headed for the front door, but I pulled at his arm and pointed. We ran to the fire escape and started climbing.

We hung back from the window at first. It was three inches open; we couldn't hear anything in the apartment. Finally, we looked in. Roy wasn't there. The only person there was Mary Jordan, a .44 held against her right leg, sitting in a chair and staring at the door.

All three of us tensed; we heard, dimly, footsteps in the hall. I had my gun out again. This time it might do me some good. The woman locked her fingers on her gun and raised it. I steadied my .38 on my left arm. This had to be perfect.

Pederson clamped onto my wrist. I pointed with the gun barrel towards the door, and he understood. He nodded, raised his gun and aimed faster than I could when I was already set, then fired. My own shot was barely behind his.

The shots were a foot apart, three inches from the top of the door. Mine was too far to the side; Pederson's must have gone right over Roy's head, if Roy was in front of the door. He was—we heard him drop to the floor; a second later Mary's gun jumped in her hand, nearly knocking her chair over backwards. The bullet went through the center of the door.

Then we dropped below the sill while she turned, spitting fury, and fired four shots out the window at us. One bullet hit the window frame; it ripped the board loose and powdered an already crumbling brick. Then the door burst open and the spitting sound got louder.

Pederson shoved up the broken window and vaulted over the sill, a virile fifty-odd. I hobbled after him, a doddering old gent of thirty-one. Cartley had her around the waist with one arm and had pinned her arms to her body with the other.

He had lifted her off the floor, turning his hip between her legs to spread them and keep her from kicking backwards. Pederson reached for the handcuffs. I reached for a chair, and sat in it, emptying her handbag on the table.

Inside were matchbooks, still unused, from all the restaurants Gillis had written checks to, plus a receipt—dated two days back—from the store where he had done his previous buying. I looked up.

"Playing detective, Mary? Did you find out who she was?"

She clammed up, then. Pederson looked at her with interest. "Aren't you even waiting to shut up till I read your rights? You *are* an amateur." That stung, but she stayed quiet.

Roy was looking back and forth. He tossed his gun on the table and said, looking tired, "All right, what is it I don't know?"

I gestured at Mary. "Only what she finally knew. I'm not the only one with an invisible lady friend."

"Lady friend?" Pederson stared at me. *"You?* You never even shave—" He shut his mouth as Roy began chuckling.

"I've had a busy day—I put off shaving." I turned to Mary. "One thing I can't put off, Mary—what's the name of the girl that aced you out?" I wanted her to make a scene and keep Pederson occupied.

"If I'd 'a known," Mary said, "the cops'd know by now."

Roy looked back at me helplessly, then suddenly understood. "The bills?"

I nodded. "If you hadn't been so worried, you'd have seen it, too. Gam must have been a real bastard, borrowing from Mary to take out some other woman. Mary found out, convinced him to break into your house—probably by saying you had evidence against him—" I glanced at her, but she wasn't reacting, so I went on—"and stabbed him after backing him up to the fireplace with her gun.

"He did the breaking in. That's why that was professional, but everything else—the bomb, the bolted doors, the red herring to Petlovich—was amateur. Deadly amateur, but amateur." Still no reaction—Pederson was looking at me strangely.

I tried my last shot. "He really wiped the floor with her before she got him, though. What a rotten, low-life—"

She tried to swing at me, ignoring Pederson, Roy and her own cuffed wrists. "You wouldn't dare talk that way if he was here!" she snapped.

Pederson grabbed her. I sidled over quietly, picked Roy's gun off the table and said politely to him, "Roy, I'd like to shake your hand. We made it."

Roy still had one hand in his coat. He looked at me narrowly, then grinned and stuck out his empty hand. His pocket hung limp. "Thanks for trying, Nate, but the other gun's in the glove compartment. I cooled down on the way over here. One of the kids tipped you off?"

"Yeah," I said, feeling silly. "That Howie is growing up fast; he and Amy make a hell of a team. She's sharper than he is, but he's trying to turn pro."

Roy glanced at Mary Jordon. She was sobbing in frustration as Pederson edged her towards the door. "Tell him not to try too hard, will you?"

THE PROBLEM OF THE CHRISTMAS STEEPLE

by Edward D. Hoch

A full-time writer since 1968, Ed Hoch is certainly one of the two or three most prolific fiction writers in the United States, with some six hundred stories in the mystery genre. He is best known for four series detectives: Rand, a British cipher expert; Nick Velvet, a most original thief; Simon Ark, a mystical detective; and Captain Leopold, perhaps the best-known of his creations. Mr. Hoch is a winner of the Mystery Writers of America's highest award, the Edgar.

"Like I was sayin' last time," Dr. Sam Hawthorne began, getting down the brandy from the top shelf, "the year 1925 was a bad one for murder and other violent crimes. And just about the worst one o' them all came on Christmas Day, when the year was almost over. Here, let me pour you a small—ah—libation before I start . . ."

It had been a quiet fall in Northmont since the kidnapping and recovery of little Tommy Belmont. In fact, about the biggest news around town was that the new Ford dealer over in Middle Creek would soon be selling dark green and maroon cars along with the traditional black ones.

"You see, Dr. Sam," my nurse April said, "pretty soon you won't be the only one round these parts with a bright yellow car."

"Dark green and maroon are a long way from yellow,"
I reminded her. Kidding me about my 1921 Pierce-Arrow
Runabout was one of her favorite sports. My first winter
in Northmont I'd put the Runabout up on blocks and
driven a horse and buggy on my calls, but now I was gettin' a bit more venturesome. As long as the roads were
clear I drove the car.

This day, which was just two weeks before Christmas,
April and I were drivin' out to visit a small gypsy encampment at the edge of town. The traditionally cold
New England winter hadn't yet settled in, and except for
the bareness of the tree limbs it might have been a pleasant September afternoon.

The gypsies were another matter, and there wasn't
much pleasant about their encampment. They'd arrived a
month earlier, drivin' a half-dozen horse-drawn wagons,
and pitched their tents on some unused meadowland at
the old Haskins farm. Minnie Haskins, widowed and into
her seventies, had given them permission to stay there,
but that didn't make Sheriff Lens and the townsfolks any
happier about it. On the few occasions when gypsies had
appeared at the general store to buy provisions, they'd
been treated in a right unfriendly manner.

I'd gone out to the encampment once before to examine a sick child, and I decided this day it was time for a
return visit. I knew there wasn't much chance of gettin'
paid, unless I was willin' to settle for a gypsy woman tell-
in' April's fortune, but still it was somethin' I felt bound
to do.

"Look, Dr. Sam!" April said as the gypsy wagons came
into view. "Isn't that Parson Wigger's buggy?"

"Sure looks like it." I wasn't really surprised to find
Parson Wigger visiting the gypsies. Ever since coming to
town last spring as pastor of the First New England
Church he'd been a controversial figure. He'd started by
reopening the old Baptist church in the center of town
and announcin' regular services there. He seemed like a
good man who led a simple life and looked for simple so-
lutions—which was why so many people disliked him.
New Englanders, contrary to some opinions, are not a
simple folk.

"Mornin', Dr. Sam," he called out as he saw us drive
up. He was standin' by one of the gypsy wagons, talkin'

to a couple of dark-haired children. "Mornin', April. What brings you two out here?"

"I treated a sick boy a while back. Thought I'd see how he's coming along." I took my bag from the car and started over. Already I recognized my patient, Tene, as one of the boys with the parson. "Hello, Tene, how you feeling?"

He was around eleven or twelve, and shy with non-gypsy *gadjo* like myself. "I'm okay," he said finally.

"This the boy was sick?" Parson Wigger asked.

I nodded. "A throat infection, but he seems to be over it."

At that moment Tene's father appeared around the side of the wagon. He was a dark brooding man with a black mustache and hair that touched the top of his ears, leaving small gold earrings exposed. Though Parson Wigger was the same size and both men looked to be in their mid-thirties, they could hardly have been more different. Except for an old arm injury which had left him with a weak right hand, Carranza Lowara was the picture of strength and virility. By contrast Wigger gave the impression of physical weakness. The parson's hair was already thinning in front, and he wore thick eyeglasses to correct his faulty vision.

"You are back, Doctor?" Tene's father asked.

"Yes, Carranza, I am back."

He nodded, then glanced at April. "This is your wife?"

"No, my nurse. April, I want you to meet Carranza Lowara. He is the leader of this gypsy band."

April took a step forward, wide-eyed, and shook his hand. "Pleased to meet you."

"I'm trying to help these people get settled for the winter," Parson Wigger explained. "These wagons are hardly good shelter for twenty people. And the two tents are not much better."

"We have lived through the winters before," Carranza Lowara said. He spoke English well, but with an accent I hadn't been able to place. I supposed it must be middle European.

"But not in New England." The parson turned to me and explained. "They came up from the south, as do most gypsies. I've encountered them before in my travels. Spain deported gypsies to Latin America hundreds of years ago, and they've been working their way north ever since."

"Is that true?" I asked Lowara. "Do you come from Latin America?"

"Long, long ago," he replied.

I happened to glance back at my car and saw a gypsy woman in a long spangled skirt and bare feet. She was examining my car intently. I'd seen her on my previous visit, and suspected she was Lowara's wife or woman. "Is she of your family?" I asked.

"Come here, Volga." The woman came over promptly, and I saw that she was younger than I'd first supposed. Not a child, certainly, but still in her twenties. She was handsomer than most gypsy women, with high cheekbones and slightly slanted eyes that hinted at a mixture of Oriental blood. I introduced her to April, and they went off together to visit the other wagons.

"She is my wife," Lowara explained.

"Tene's mother?"

"Yes."

"She seems so young."

"Gypsy women often marry young. It is a custom. You should come to a gypsy wedding sometime and see the groom carry off the bride by force. It is not like your Christian weddings, Parson."

"I imagine not," Parson Wigger replied dryly. "But I will come to a gypsy wedding only if you honor me with your presence at my church."

The gypsy shook his head. "Your townspeople do not like us."

"They might like you more if they saw you attending Christian services."

Lowara shrugged. "We have no religion. We would as soon go to your church as any other."

"Come, then, on Christmas Day. It's just two weeks away. Once you know the people and are friendly with them, you might even find an old barn to stay the winter."

"Would a barn be any warmer than our tents? I think not."

"Come anyway," the parson pleaded. "You won't regret it."

The gypsy nodded. "I will talk to the others. I think you will see us in two weeks."

Parson Wigger walked me back to my Runabout. "I think their appearance on Christmas morning will have a good effect on the townspeople. No one can hate a fellow Christian on Christmas."

"Some call them beggars and thieves. They say the women are good for nothing but telling fortunes."

"They are human beings with souls, like the rest of us," Parson Wigger reminded me.

"I agree. You only have to convince a few hundred of your fellow citizens." I didn't have to remind him that his own popularity in Northmont was not too high at that moment.

April came back from her tour of the wagons, and we drove away with a wave to Parson Wigger. "He's really tryin' to help those people," she said. "That Volga thinks highly of the parson."

"She's Lowara's wife. She must have been a child bride. I treated her son and never even knew she was the mother."

"There's an old woman in one wagon who tells fortunes," April said with a giggle.

"She tell yours?"

April nodded. "Said I was gettin' married soon."

"Good for you." April was some years older than me, in her mid-thirties, and not the most beautiful girl in town. I figured the old gypsy woman was a good judge of human nature.

On Christmas mornin' it was snowin' gently, and from a distance down the street Parson Wigger's church looked just the way they always do on greeting cards. I wasn't that much of a churchgoer myself, but I decided I should show up. Last Christmas I'd spent the entire day deliverin' a farm woman's baby, and an hour in church sure wouldn't be any harder than that.

Parson Wigger was out front, bundled against the cold and snow, greetin' the people as they arrived. I waved to him and stopped to chat with Eustace Carey, who ran one of Northmont's two general stores. "How are you, Doc? Merry Christmas to ye."

"Same to you, Eustace. We've got good weather for it —a white Christmas but not too white."

"Folks say the gypsies are comin' to the service. You heard anything about it?"

"No, but it is Christmas, after all. Nothin' wrong with them comin' to church."

Eustace Carey snorted. "What's wrong is them bein' here in the first place! I think they hexed old Minnie to get permission to camp on her land. These gypsy women can hex a person, you know."

I was about to reply when a murmur went up from the waiting churchgoers. A single crowded gypsy wagon pulled by a team of horses was comin' down the center of the street. "Looks like they're here," I remarked to Carey.

It was obvious then that Parson Wigger had been standin' in the snow for exactly this moment. He hurried out to the wagon and greeted Lowara and the others warmly. It seemed that all the gypsies had come, even the children, and after the parson shook hands with them, they filed into church.

"I don't like 'em," Carey said behind me. "They look funny, they smell funny, they got funny names."

"Oh, I don't know about that, Eustace."

We followed the gypsies into church and took our seats in one of the front pews. I glanced around for April, then remembered that she'd be at the Catholic church, on the other side of town.

After a few moments' wait Parson Wigger came out wearin' his traditional long black cassock and white surplice. He carried a Bible in one hand as he mounted the pulpit and then began to speak. "First of all, I want to wish each and every one of my parishioners—and I feel you are *all* my parishioners—the very merriest of Christmases and the happiest of New Years. I see 1926 as a year of promise, a year of building our spiritual lives."

I'd never been a great one for listening to sermons, and I found my eyes wandering to the double row of gypsies down front. If the sermon was boring them too, they were very good at masking their feelings. Sitting right behind them, and none too happy about it, was old Minnie Haskins, who'd given them permission to use her land.

Later, when Parson Wigger had concluded his sermon and prayer service and we'd sung the obligatory Christmas hymns, I sought out Minnie Haskins in the back of the church. Despite her years she was a spry little woman who moved about with remarkable agility. "Hello there, Dr. Sam," she greeted me. "Merry Christmas!"

"Merry Christmas to you, Minnie. How's the leg?"

"Fit as a fiddle!" She did a little kick to show me. "A

touch o' rheumatism can't keep me down!" Then she pulled me aside as the others were leaving and whispered, "What're all them gypsies doin' here, Doc? I'm in enough trouble with folks for lettin' them camp on my farm. Now they come to church!"

"It's Christmas, Minnie. I think they should be welcomed at church on Christmas Day."

"Well, lots o' folk are upset with Parson Wigger for invitin' them, I'll tell ye that!"

"I haven't heard any complaints yet except from Eustace Carey."

"Well, him an' others."

Carey joined us then, still grumbling. "Soon as I can get the parson alone I'm goin' to give him a piece o' my mind. Bad enough fillin' the church with gypsies, but then he takes 'em right down front."

"Where are they now?" I asked.

"Would you believe it? He's taken them up in the steeple to show them the view!"

I followed them out to the sidewalk, and we looked up through the fallin' snow at the towerin' church steeple. Though each of its four white sides had an open window for the belfry, no bell had rung there since its days as a Baptist church. The Baptists had taken their bell with them to a new church in Groveland, and Parson Wigger hadn't yet raised enough money to replace it.

As we watched, the gypsies began comin' out of the church and climbin' back onto their wagon. "They can't read or write, you know," Carey said. "No gypsies can."

"Probably because they haven't been taught," I replied. "A little schoolin' for the youngsters like Tene would help."

"Well," Carey said, "I'm still goin' to talk with the parson about this, soon's I can catch him alone."

I glanced around for Minnie, but she'd disappeared, swallowed up by the fallin' snow. We could barely see across the street now, as the fat white flakes tumbled and swirled in the breeze. I could feel them cold against my face, clingin' to my eyelashes, and I decided it was time to go home. Just then Volga Lowara came out of the church and climbed into the wagon. The driver snapped the reins and they started off.

"I'm going in to see the parson now," Carey said.

"Wait a minute," I suggested. I could have been wrong

but I didn't remember seeing Carranza leave the church. He might have stayed behind to talk with Parson Wigger.

"The heck with it," Carey decided at last, his hat and coat covered with fat white snowflakes. "I'm goin' home."

"I'll see you, Eustace. Wish the family a Merry Christmas." It was somethin' to say, avoidin' obvious mention of the fact that his wife hadn't accompanied him to Christmas services.

I decided there was no point in my waitin' around, either. As Carey disappeared into the snow I started in the oppositie direction, only to encounter Sheriff Lens. "Hello there, Dr. Sam. Comin' from church?"

"That I am. A snowy Christmas, isn't it?"

"The kids with new sleds'll like it. Seen Parson Wigger around?"

"He's in the church. What's up?"

"Funny thing. I'll tell you about it." But before he could say more the familiar figure of Parson Wigger appeared in the church doorway, still wearin' his long black cassock but without the white surplice. For just an instant a stray beam of light seemed to reflect off his thick glasses. "Parson Wigger!" the sheriff called out, startin' through the snow for the church steps.

Wigger turned back into the church, bumpin' against the door jamb. It was almost as if the sight of Sheriff Lens had suddenly terrified him. The sheriff and I reached the back of the church together, just in time to see Wigger's black cassock vanish up the stairs to the belfry.

"Damn!" Lens exploded. "He closed the door after him. Is he running away from us?"

I tried the belfry door, but it was bolted from the other side. "He'd hardly run up there to get away from us. There's no other way out."

"Lemme at that door!"

It was an old church, and a powerful yank by Sheriff Lens splintered the wood around the loose bolt. Another yank, and the door was open.

Lens led the way up the wooden steps. "We're comin' up, Parson," he called out.

There was no answer from above.

We reached the belfry and pushed open the trap door above our heads. The first thing I saw was Parson Wigger outstretched on the floor a few feet away. He was face up, and the jeweled hilt of a small gypsy dagger protruded from the center of his chest.

"My God!" Sheriff Lens gasped. "He's been murdered!"

From the trap door I could see the entire bare belfry and the snow swirling around us outside. It seemed there was not another living creature up there with us.

But then somethin' made me turn and look behind the open trap door.

Carranza Lowara was crouched there, an expression of sheer terror on his face.

"I did not kill him," he cried out. "You must believe me—*I did not kill him!*"

It was the damnedest locked-room mystery I ever did see, because how could you have a locked room that wasn't even a room—that was in fact open on all four sides? And how could you have a mystery when the obvious murderer was found right there with the weapon and the body?

And yet—

First off I'd better tell you a bit more about that belfry itself, because it was the first time I'd ever been up there, and some things about it weren't obvious from the ground. The big bell was gone, all right, though the wooden frame from which it had hung was still in place. There was also a round hole cut in the floor, maybe four inches in diameter, through which the heavy rope for ringing the bell had passed.

But the thing that surprised me most about Parson Wigger's belfry was the thin wire mesh fencing tacked up over all four open windows. It was like chicken wire, with gaps of a couple inches between the individual strands. Since it obviously wasn't meant to keep out flies it took me a moment to figure out its purpose.

"Birds," Sheriff Lens explained, noting my puzzlement. "He didn't want birds roosting up here."

I grunted. "You can't even see it from the street, the wire's so fine."

Wigger's body had been taken away, and the gypsy had been arrested, but we lingered on, starin' through the wire mesh at the street below. "The news has really spread," Lens observed. "Look at that crowd!"

"More than he had for services. Tells you somethin' about people, I guess."

"Think the gypsy did it, Doc?"

"Who else? He was alone up here with Wigger."

Sheriff Lens scratched his thinning hair. "But why kill him? God knows, Wigger was a friend o' theirs."

There was a sound from below, and Eustace Carey's head emerged through the open trap door. "I just heard about the parson," he said. "What happened?"

"He was showin' the gypsies the view from up here. They all came down except Lowara, an' I guess he musta hid in here. We saw Parson Wigger down by the front door, lookin' out at the gypsies gettin' ready to leave, and I wanted to talk to him. He seemed to run away from us, almost, an' bolted the steeple door after him. By the time Doc Sam and I got up here, he was dead, with the gypsy's knife in his chest."

"No one else was up here?"

"No one."

Carey walked over to the west side of the belfry, where the wind-driven snow covered the floor. "There are foot-prints here."

"He had a lot of gypsies up here lookin' at the view. Footprints don't mean a thing." Sheriff Lens walked over to the open trap door.

Suddenly I remembered something. "Sheriff, we both agree that Wigger looked as if he was running away from you. What was it you were so anxious to see him about?"

Sheriff Lens grunted. "Don't make no difference, now that he's dead," he replied, and started down the stairs.

The next mornin' at my office I was surprised to find April waitin' for me. It was a Saturday, and I'd told her she needn't come in. I'd stopped by mainly to pick up the mail and make sure no one had left a message for me. Most of my regular patients called me at home if they needed me on a weekend, but there was always the chance of an emergency.

But this time the emergency wasn't the sort I expected. "Dr. Sam, I've got that gypsy woman, Volga, in your of-fice. She came to me early this mornin' and she's just sick about her husband bein' arrested. Can't you talk to her?"

"I'll see what I can do."

Volga was waitin' inside, her face streaked with tears, her eyes full of despair. "Oh, Dr. Hawthorne, you must help him! I know he is innocent! He could not kill Parson Wigger like that—the parson was our friend."

"Calm down, now," I said, taking her hands. "We'll do what we can to help him."

"Will you go to the jail? Some say he will be lynched!"

"That can't happen here," I insisted. But my mind went back to an incident in Northmont history, after the Civil War, when a black man traveling with a gypsy woman had indeed been lynched. "Anyway, I'll go talk to him."

I left her in April's care and walked the three blocks through snowy streets to the town jail. Sheriff Lens was there with an unexpected visitor—Minnie Haskins.

"Hello, Minnie. Not a very pleasant Christmas for the town, is it?"

"It sure ain't, Dr. Sam."

"You visitin' the prisoner?"

"I'm tryin' to find out when they'll be off my land. I was out there to the caravan this mornin', and all they'd say was that Carranza was their leader. They couldn't go till Carranza told 'em to."

"I thought you give them permission to stay."

"Well, that was before they killed Parson Wigger," she replied, reflecting the view of the townspeople.

"I'd like to speak with the prisoner," I told Sheriff Lens.

"That's a bit irregular."

"Come on, Sheriff."

He made a face and got out the keys to the cell block. We found the gypsy sitting on the edge of his metal bunk, staring into space. He roused himself when he saw me, somehow sensing a friend. "Doctor, have you come to deliver me from this place?"

"Five minutes," Sheriff Lens said, locking me in the cell with Lowara.

"I've come, Carranza, because your wife Volga asked me to. But if I'm going to help you, I have to know everything that happened in the belfry yesterday."

"I told the truth. I did not kill Parson Wigger."

"What were you doing there? Why didn't you leave with Volga and the others?"

He brushed back the long raven hair that covered his

ears. "Is it for a *gadjo* like yourself to understand? I stayed behind because I felt a kinship for this man, this parson who had taken the *roms* unto himself. I wanted to speak with him in private."

"And what happened?"

"He went down after the others had left the belfry and stood in the doorway, looking after them. Then he came back upstairs, quite quickly. I heard him throw the bolt on the door below, as if he feared someone might follow him. When he came up through the trap door my back was turned. I never saw what did it. I only heard a slow gasp, as of a deep sigh, and turned in time to see him falling backward to the floor."

"You saw no one else?"

"There was no one to see."

"Could he have been stabbed earlier?" I asked. "Down in the church?"

"He could not have climbed those steps with the knife in him," Lowara said, shaking his head. "It would have killed him at once."

"What about the knife? You admit that jeweled dagger is yours?"

He shrugged. "It is mine. I wore it yesterday beneath my coat. But in the crowd after services I was jostled. The knife was taken from me."

"Without your realizing it? That's hard to believe."

"It is true, nevertheless."

"Why would anyone want to kill Parson Wigger?" I asked.

He smiled and opened his hands to me. "So a gypsy would be blamed for it," he said, as if that was the most logical reason in the world.

The snow stopped falling as I walked back to the church. In my pocket, neatly wrapped in newspaper, was the jeweled dagger that had killed Parson Wigger. The sheriff had given up any hope of finding fingerprints on the corded hilt with its imitation ruby, and had allowed me to borrow it to conduct an experiment.

It had occurred to me that the knife could have been thrown or propelled from some distance away, and that it might be slender enough to pass through the chicken-wire barricade. To test my theory I entered the unguarded church and climbed once more to the belfry in the steeple.

But I was wrong.

True, the knife could be worked through the wire with some difficulty, but coming at it straight ahead or even at an angle, the width of the crosspiece—the hilt guard— kept it from passing through. It simply could not have been thrown or propelled from outside.

Which left me with Carranza Lowara once more.

The only possible murderer.

Had he lied?

Remembering that moment when Sheriff Lens and I found him standin' over the body, rememberin' the terror written across his face, I somehow couldn't believe it.

I went back downstairs and walked around the pews, hopin' some flash of illumination would light up my mind. Finally I stuffed the dagger back in my coat pocket and went outside. It was as I took a short cut across the snow-covered side yard that somethin' caught my eye, as white as the snow and half buried in it.

I pulled it free and saw that it was a white surplice like the one Parson Wigger had worn during the Christmas service. There was a dark red stain on it, and a tear about an inch long.

I stood there holding it in my hand, and then turned to stare up at the steeple that towered above me.

"I reckon we gotta ship the gypsy over to the county seat," Sheriff Lens was saying when I returned to the jail and placed the dagger carefully back on his desk.

"Why's that, Sheriff?"

"Eustace Carey says there's talk o' lynchin'. I know damn well they won't do it, but I can't take no chances. It happened fifty years ago and it can happen again."

I sat down opposite him. "Sheriff, there's somethin' you've got to tell me. That man's life may depend on it. You sought out Parson Wigger on Christmas Day for some reason. It was somethin' that couldn't even wait till after the holiday."

Sheriff Lens looked uneasy. "I told you—it don't matter now."

"But don't you see it *does* matter—now more than ever?"

The sheriff got to his feet and moved to the window. Across the square we could see a small group of men watching the jail. That must have decided him. "Mebbe you're right, Doc. I'm too old to keep secrets, anyway. You see, the Hartford police sent through a report suggesting I question Parson Wigger. Seems he wasn't no real parson at all."

"What?"

"He'd been passin' himself off as a parson down Hartford way for two years, till somebody checked his background and they run him outta town. Some said he was runnin' a giant con game, while others thought he was more interested in the parish wives. Whatever the truth, his background was mighty shady."

"Why didn't you tell me this before?"

"Like I said, the man's dead now. Why blacken his character? He never did no harm in Northmont."

The door opened and Eustace Carey came bargin' in, followed by a half-dozen other local businessmen. "We want to talk, Sheriff. There's ugly words goin' around. Even if you keep that one safe, there might be an attempt to burn the gypsy wagons."

I knew then that I had to speak out. "Wait a minute," I said. "Settle down, and I'll tell you what really happened to Parson Wigger. He wasn't killed by the gypsy, and he wasn't killed by any invisible demon, unless you count the demon within himself."

"What do you mean by that?" Carey demanded.

I told them what I'd just learned from Sheriff Lens. "Don't you see? Don't you all see? The parson was standin' there in the doorway and he saw us comin' for him. It was the sight of the sheriff that frightened him, that told him the jig was up. Why else would he run into the church and up the belfry stairs, boltin' the door behind him? It was fear that drove him up there, fear of Sheriff Lens and the truth."

"But who killed him?"

"When he heard that bolt break, when he heard us on the stairs and realized his masquerade was about to be uncovered, he took the gypsy's dagger and plunged it into his own chest. There was never any invisible murderer or any impossible crime. Parson Wigger killed himself."

It took a lot more talkin' after that, of course, to convince them it was the only possible solution. You see, I had to get Carranza out of his cell and demonstrate that he couldn't have stabbed the parson with his right hand because of that old arm injury. Then I showed, from the angle of the wound, that it had to be done by a right-handed person—unless he'd stabbed himself.

"There was no one else up there," I argued. "If Carranza Lowara didn't kill him, he must have killed himself. It's as simple as that."

They released Lowara the next mornin', and Sheriff Lens drove him out to the gypsy encampment in the town's only police car. I watched them go, standin' in the doorway of my office, and April said, "Can't you close that door, Dr. Sam? Now that you've solved another case can't you let the poor man go home in peace?"

"I have something else that must be done, April," I told her. "See you later."

I got into the Runabout and drove out over the snow-rutted roads to Minnie Haskins' place. I didn't stop at the farmhouse but continued out around the back till I reached the gypsy encampment. When Volga saw the car she came runnin' across the snow to meet me.

"How can we ever thank you, Dr. Hawthorne? You have saved my husband from certain imprisonment and even death!"

"Go get him right now and I'll tell you how you can thank me."

I stood and waited by the car, venturing no closer to the wagons, where I could see little Tene playing in the snow. Presently Carranza joined me with Volga trailing him.

"I owe you my thanks," he said. "My freedom."

I was starin' out across the snowy fields. "I owe you somethin' too. You taught me something about the different types of deception—deception as it is practiced by the *gadjo* and by the *rom*."

As I spoke I reached out and yanked at his long black hair. It came away in my hand, and Volga gasped. He was almost bald without the wig, and seemed at least ten years older. I stripped the mustache from his upper lip too, and he made no effort to stop me.

"All right, Doctor," he said. "A little deception. Will you have me arrested again because I wear a wig and false mustache? Will you say after all that I killed Parson Wigger?"

I shook my head. "No, Carranza. This doesn't tell me

that you killed Wigger. But it does tell me that Volga killed him."

She gasped again, and fell back as if I'd struck her. "This man is a demon!" she told her husband. "How could he know?"

"Silence!" Carranza ordered. Then, turning to me, he asked, "Why do you say these things?"

"Well, I proved for myself that you didn't kill Wigger. But I didn't for a minute believe that such a man would kill himself simply because the sheriff wanted to talk to him. And yet he had run away from us. That was the key to it—the key to the crime and the key to the impossibility. I was lookin' around in the churchyard, and in a snowbank I found this." I drew the bloodstained surplice from under my coat.

"And what does that prove?"

"See the tear made by the knife goin' in? And the blood? Parson Wigger had to be wearin' this when he was stabbed. Yet Sheriff Lens and I saw him without it in the church doorway. Are we to believe he went up to the belfry, put on his surplice, stabbed himself, removed it somehow, stuck the knife back in his chest and died—all while we were breakin' in the door? Of course not!

"So what is the only other possibility? If the body in the belfry was Wigger's, then the person we saw in the doorway was *not* Wigger. He fled from us simply because if Sheriff Lens and I had gotten any closer we'd have known he was not Wigger."

Volga's face had drained of all color, and she stared silently as I spoke. "If not Wigger, then who? Well, the man in the cassock ran up into the belfry. We were right behind him and we found two persons up there—the dead Wigger and the live Lowara. If the man in the cassock was not Wigger—and I've shown he wasn't—then he had to be you, Carranza."

"A good guess."

"More than that. I'd noticed earlier you were both the same size. At a distance your main distinguishing feature was your black hair and mustache. But I remembered that day two weeks ago when I was out here and noticed your earrings under your short hair. When I visited your cell, your hair was long enough to cover your ears. It couldn't have grown that fast in two weeks, so I knew you were wearing wigs. If the hair was false, the mustache could be too—mere props to add to your gypsy image. A bit of deception for the *gadjo*."

"You have proved I was Wigger for a fleeting moment. You have not proved Volga killed him."

"Well, what did you accomplish by posing as Wigger? From a distance, with our vision blurred by the falling snow, the sheriff and I saw only a tall man in a black cassock, wearing Wigger's thick glasses. If we hadn't come after you we'd have gone away convinced that Wigger was still alive after Volga and the others had left the church. You did make two little slip-ups, though. When you turned away from us in the church doorway you bumped into the frame because you weren't used to his thick glasses. And yesterday in the cell you told me how Wigger had stood in the doorway—something you couldn't have seen if you'd really been in the belfry all that time, as you said."

"That does not implicate Volga!" the gypsy insisted.

"Obviously you weren't doing this to protect yourself, because it gave you no alibi. No one saw you leave the church. The only possible purpose of your brief impersonation was to shield another person—the real killer. Then I remembered that Volga was the last gypsy to leave the church. She'd been alone in there with Wigger, she was your wife, and she was the most likely person to be carrying your little dagger. Where? In your stocking top, Volga?"

She covered her face with her hands. "He—he tried to—"

"I know. Wigger wasn't a real parson, and he'd been in trouble before because of his interest in parish wives. He tried to attack you up there, didn't he? You were only a handsome gypsy woman to him. He knew you could never tell. You fought back, and your hand found the dagger you always carried. You stabbed him up there and killed him, and then you found Carranza in the church and told him what you'd done."

"It would have been a gypsy's word against a parson's reputation," Carranza said. "They would never believe her. I sent her back with the wagon and tried to make it look as if he was still alive."

I nodded. "You put on his cassock because at a distance the bloody rip in the cassock wouldn't show on the black cloth. But you couldn't wear the white surplice without the blood showing. You barely had time to get the cassack back on Wigger's body, stuff the surplice through the chicken wire, and push it out so it wouldn't be found in the belfry. You couldn't put that back on the body because you hadn't been wearing it downstairs."

Carranza Lowara sighed. "It was hard work with my weak hand. I got the cassock back on the body just as the lock gave way. Will you call the sheriff now?"

I watched his son playing with the other gypsies and wondered if I had the right to judge. Finally I said, "Pack up your wagons and be gone from here by nightfall. Never come near Northmont again."

"But—" Carranza began.

"Wigger was not a good man, but maybe he wasn't bad enough to deserve what he got. I don't know. I only know if you stay around here I might change my mind."

Volga came to me. "Now I owe you more than ever."

"Go. It's only a Christmas present I'm giving you. Go, before it fades like the melting snow."

And within an hour the wagons were on the road, heading south this time. Maybe they'd had enough of our New England winter.

"I never told anyone that story," Dr. Sam Hawthorne concluded. "It was the first time I took justice into my own hands, and I never knew if I did right or not. No, the gypsies didn't come back. I never saw them again."

He emptied the last of the brandy and stood up. "It was in the spring of 'twenty-six that a famous French criminal sought shelter in Northmont. He was called the Eel because of his fantastic escapes. But I'll save that story till next time. Another—ah—libation before you go?"

DEATH ON CHRISTMAS EVE

by Stanley Ellin

Stanley Ellin writes slowly. He averages one short story a year, reworking his plots and phrases until they are perfect. From the beginning they have been winners. His first seven short stories won prizes in the annual contests of Ellery Queen's Mystery Magazine. Three Edgars (two for best short story, one for best novel of the year) and Le Grand Prix de Littérature Policière continue the tradition. Both his shorter works and his novels have been adapted for television and films.

As a child I had been vastly impressed by the Boerum house. It was fairly new then, and glossy; a gigantic pile of Victorian rickrack, fretwork, and stained glass, flung together in such chaotic profusion that it was hard to encompass in one glance. Standing before it this early Christmas Eve, however, I could find no echo of that youthful impression. The gloss was long since gone; woodwork, glass, metal, all were merged to a dreary gray, and the shades behind the windows were drawn completely so that the house seemed to present a dozen blindly staring eyes to the passerby.

When I rapped my stick sharply on the door, Celia opened it.

"There is a doorbell right at hand," she said. She was still wearing the long out-moded and badly wrinkled black dress she must have dragged from her mother's trunk, and she looked, more than ever, the image of old Katrin in her later years: the scrawny body, the tightly compressed lips, the colorless hair drawn back hard enough to pull every wrinkle out of her forehead. She reminded me of a steel trap ready to snap down on anyone who touched her incautiously.

I said, "I am aware that the doorbell has been disconnected, Celia," and walked past her into the hallway. Without turning my head, I knew that she was glaring at me; then she sniffed once, hard and dry, and flung the door shut. Instantly we were in a murky dimness that made the smell of dry rot about me stick in my throat. I fumbled for the wall switch, but Celia said sharply, "No! This is not the time for lights."

I turned to the white blur of her face, which was all I could see of her. "Celia," I said, "spare me the dramatics."

"There has been a death in this house. You know that."

"I have good reason to," I said, "but your performance now does not impress me."

"She was my own brother's wife. She was very dear to me."

I took a step toward her in the murk and rested my stick on her shoulder. "Celia," I said, "as your family's lawyer, let me give you a word of advice. The inquest is over and done with, and you've been cleared. But nobody believed a word of your precious sentiments then, and nobody ever will. Keep that in mind, Celia."

She jerked away so sharply that the stick almost fell from my hand. "Is that what you have come to tell me?" she said.

I said, "I came because I knew your brother would want to see me today. And if you don't mind my saying so, I suggest that you keep to yourself while I talk to him. I don't want any scenes."

"Then keep away from him yourself!" she cried. "He was at the inquest. He saw them clear my name. In a little while he will forget the evil he thinks of me. Keep away from him so that he can forget."

She was at her infuriating worst, and to break the spell I started up the dark stairway, one hand warily on the balustrade. But I heard her follow eagerly behind, and in some eerie way it seemed as if she were not addressing me, but answering the groaning of the stairs under our feet.

"When he comes to me," she said, "I will forgive him.
At first I was not sure, but now I know. I prayed for
guidance, and I was told that life is too short for hatred.
So when he comes to me I will forgive him."

I reached the head of the stairway and almost went
sprawling. I swore in annoyance as I righted myself. "If
you're not going to use lights, Celia, you should, at least,
keep the way clear. Why don't you get that stuff out of
here?"

"Ah," she said, "those are all poor Jessie's belongings.
It hurts Charlie so to see anything of hers, I knew this
would be the best thing to do—to throw all her things
out."

Then a note of alarm entered her voice. "But you won't
tell Charlie, will you? You won't tell him?" she said, and
kept repeating it on a higher and higher note as I moved
away from her, so that when I entered Charlie's room and
closed the door behind me it almost sounded as if I had
left a bat chittering behind me.

As in the rest of the house, the shades in Charlie's room
were drawn to their full length. But a single bulb in the
chandelier overhead dazzled me momentarily, and I had
to look twice before I saw Charlie sprawled out on his bed
with an arm flung over his eyes. Then he slowly came to
his feet and peered at me.

"Well," he said at last, nodding toward the door, "she
didn't give you any light to come up, did she?"

"No," I said, "but I know the way."

"She's like a mole," he said. "Gets around better in the
dark than I do in the light. She'd rather have it that way
too. Otherwise she might look into a mirror and be scared
of what she sees there."

"Yes," I said, "she seems to be taking it very hard."

He laughed short and sharp as a sea-lion barking.
"That's because she's still got the fear in her. All you get
out of her now is how she loved Jessie, and how sorry she
is. Maybe she figures if she says it enough, people might
get to believe it. But give her a little time and she'll be the
same old Celia again."

I dropped my hat and stick on the bed and laid my
overcoat beside them. Then I drew out a cigar and waited
until he fumbled for a match and helped me to a light.
His hand shook so violently that he had hard going for a
moment and muttered angrily at himself. Then I slowly

exhaled a cloud of smoke toward the ceiling, and waited.

Charlie was Celia's junior by five years, but seeing him then it struck me that he looked a dozen years older. His hair was the same pale blond, almost colorless so that it was hard to tell if it was graying or not. But his cheeks wore a fine, silvery stubble, and there were huge blue-black pouches under his eyes. And where Celia was braced against a rigid and uncompromising backbone, Charlie sagged, standing or sitting, as if he were on the verge of falling forward. He stared at me and tugged uncertainly at the limp mustache that dropped past the corners of his mouth.

"You know what I wanted to see you about, don't you?" he said.

"I can imagine," I said, "but I'd rather have you tell me."

"I'll put it to you straight," he said. "It's Celia. I want to see her get what's coming to her. Not jail. I want the law to take her and kill her, and I want to be there to watch it."

A large ash dropped to the floor, and I ground it carefully into the rug with my foot. I said, "You were at the inquest, Charlie; you saw what happened. Celia's cleared, and unless additional evidence can be produced, she stays cleared."

"Evidence! My God, what more evidence does anyone need! They were arguing hammer and tongs at the top of the stairs. Celia just grabbed Jessie and threw her down to the bottom and killed her. That's murder, isn't it? Just the same as if she used a gun or poison or whatever she would have used if the stairs weren't handy?"

I sat down wearily in the old leather-bound armchair there and studied the new ash that was forming on my cigar. "Let me show it to you from the legal angle," I said, and the monotone of my voice must have made it sound like a well-memorized formula. "First, there were no witnesses."

"I heard Jessie scream and I heard her fall," he said doggedly, "and when I ran out and found her there, I heard Celia slam her door shut right then. She pushed Jessie and then scuttered like a rat to be out of the way."

"But you didn't see anything. And since Celia claims that she wasn't on the scene, there were no witnesses. In other words, Celia's story cancels out your story, and since you weren't an eyewitness you can't very well make a murder out of what might have been an accident."

He slowly shook his head.

"You don't believe that," he said. "You don't really believe that. Because if you do, you can get out now and never come near me again."

"It doesn't matter what I believe; I'm showing you the legal aspects of the case. What about motivation? What did Celia have to gain from Jessie's death? Certainly there's no money or property involved; she's as financially independent as you are."

Charlie sat down on the edge of his bed and leaned toward me with his hands resting on his knees. "No," he whispered, "there's no money or property in it."

I spread my arms helplessly. "You see?"

"But you know what it is," he said. "It's me. First, it was the old lady with her heart trouble any time I tried to call my soul my own. Then, when she died and I thought I was free, it was Celia. From the time I got up in the morning until I went to bed at night, it was Celia every step of the way. She never had a husband or a baby—but she had me!"

I said quietly, "She's your sister, Charlie. She loves you," and he laughed that same unpleasant, short laugh.

"She loves me like ivy loves a tree. When I think back now, I still can't see how she did it, but she would just look at me a certain way and all the strength would go out of me. And it was like that until I met Jessie . . . I remember the day I brought Jessie home, and told Celia we were married. She swallowed it, but that look was in her eyes the same as it must have been when she pushed Jessie down those stairs."

I said, "But you admitted at the inquest that you never saw her threaten Jessie or do anything to hurt her."

"Of course I never *saw!* But when Jessie would go around sick to her heart every day and not say a word, or cry in bed every night and not tell me why, I knew damn well what was going on. You know what Jessie was like. She wasn't so smart or pretty, but she was good-hearted as the day was long, and she was crazy about me. And when she started losing all that sparkle in her after only a month, I knew why. I talked to her and I talked to Celia, and both of them just shook their heads. All I could do was go around in circles, but when it happened, when I saw Jessie lying there, it didn't surprise me. Maybe that sounds queer, but it didn't surprise me at all."

"I don't think it surprised anyone who knows Celia," I said, "but you can't make a case out of that."

He beat his fist against his knee and rocked from side to side. "What can I do?" he said. "That's what I need you for—to tell me what to do. All my life I never got around to doing anything because of her. That's what she's banking on now—that I won't do anything, and that she'll get away with it. Then after a while, things'll settle down, and we'll be right back where we started from."

I said, "Charlie, you're getting yourself all worked up to no end."

He stood up and stared at the door, and then at me. "But I can do something," he whispered. "Do you know what?"

He waited with the bright expectancy of one who has asked a clever riddle that he knows will stump the listener. I stood up facing him, and shook my head slowly. "No," I said. "Whatever you're thinking, put it out of your mind."

"Don't mix me up," he said. "You know you can get away with murder if you're as smart as Celia. Don't you think I'm as smart as Celia?"

I caught his shoulders tightly. "For God's sake, Charlie," I said, "don't start talking like that."

He pulled out of my hands and went staggering back against the wall. His eyes were bright, and his teeth showed behind his drawn lips. "What should I do?" he cried. "Forget everything now that Jessie is dead and buried? Sit here until Celia gets tired of being afraid of me and kills me too?"

My years and girth had betrayed me in that little tussle with him, and I found myself short of dignity and breath. "I'll tell you one thing," I said. "You haven't been out of this house since the inquest. It's about time you got out, if only to walk the streets and look around you."

"And have everybody laugh at me as I go!"

"Try it," I said, "and see. Al Sharp said that some of your friends would be at his bar and grill tonight, and he'd like to see you there. That's my advice—for whatever it's worth."

"It's not worth anything," said Celia. The door had been opened, and she stood there rigid, her eyes narrowed against the light in the room. Charlie turned toward her, the muscles of his jaw knotting and unknotting.

"Celia," he said, "I told you never to come into this room!"

Her face remained impassive. "I'm not *in* it. I came to tell you that your dinner is ready."

He took a menacing step toward her. "Did you have your ear at that door long enough to hear everything I said? Or should I repeat it for you?"

"I heard an ungodly and filthy thing," she said quietly, "an invitation to drink and roister while this house is in mourning. I think I have every right to object to that."

He looked at her incredulously and had to struggle for words. "Celia," he said, "tell me you don't mean that! Only the blackest hypocrite alive or someone insane could say what you've just said, and mean it."

That struck a spark in her. "Insane!" she cried. *"You* dare use that word? Locked in your room, talking to yourself, thinking heaven knows what!" She turned to me suddenly. "You've talked to him. You ought to know. Is it possible that—"

"He is as sane as you, Celia," I said heavily.

"Then he should know that one doesn't drink in saloons at a time like this. How could you ask him to do it?"

She flung the question at me with such an air of malicious triumph that I completely forgot myself. "If you weren't preparing to throw out Jessie's belongings, Celia, I would take that question seriously!"

It was a reckless thing to say, and I had instant cause to regret it. Before I could move, Charlie was past me and had Celia's arms pinned in a paralyzing grip.

"Did you dare go into her room?" he raged, shaking her savagely. "Tell me!" And then, getting an immediate answer from the panic in her face, he dropped her arms as if they were red hot, and stood there sagging, with his head bowed.

Celia reached out a placating hand toward him. "Charlie," she whimpered, "don't you see? Having her things around bothers you. I only wanted to help you."

"Where are her things?"

"By the stairs, Charlie. Everything is there."

He started down the hallway, and with the sound of his uncertain footsteps moving away I could feel my heartbeat slowing down to its normal tempo. Celia turned to look at me, and there was such a raging hated in her face that I knew only a desperate need to get out of that house at once. I took my things from the bed and started past her, but she barred the door.

"Do you see what you've done?" she whispered hoarsely. "Now I will have to pack them all over again. It tires me, but I will have to pack them all over again— just because of you."

"That is entirely up to you, Celia," I said coldly.

"You," she said. "You old fool. It should have been you along with her when I—"

I dropped my stick sharply on her shoulder and could feel her wince under it. "As your lawyer, Celia," I said, "I advise you to exercise your tongue only during your sleep, when you can't be held accountable for what you say."

She said no more, but I made sure she stayed safely in front of me until I was out in the street again.

From the Boerum house to Al Sharp's Bar and Grill was only a few minutes' walk, and I made it in good time, grateful for the sting of the clear winter air in my face. Al was alone behind the bar, busily polishing glasses, and when he saw me enter he greeted me cheerfully. "Merry Christmas, counsellor," he said.

"Same to you," I said, and watched him place a comfortable-looking bottle and a pair of glasses on the bar.

"You're regular as the seasons, counsellor," said Al, pouring out two stiff ones. "I was expecting you along right about now."

We drank to each other, and Al leaned confidingly on the bar. "Just come from there?"

"Yes," I said.

"See Charlie?"

"And Celia," I said.

"Well," said Al, "that's nothing exceptional. I've seen her too when she comes by to do some shopping. Runs along with her head down and that black shawl over it like she was being chased by something. I guess she is, at that."

"I guess she is," I said.

"But Charlie, he's the one. Never see him around at all. Did you tell him I'd like to see him some time?"

"Yes," I said. "I told him."

"What did he say?"

"Nothing. Celia said it was wrong for him to come here while he was in mourning."

Al whistled softly and expressively, and twirled a forefinger at his forehead. "Tell me," he said, "do you think it's safe for them to be alone together like they are? I mean, the way things stand, and the way Charlie feels, there could be another case of trouble there."

"It looked like it for a while tonight," I said. "But it blew over."

"Until next time," said Al.

"I'll be there," I said.

Al looked at me and shook his head. "Nothing changes in that house," he said. "Nothing at all. That's why you can figure out all the answers in advance. That's how I knew you'd be standing here right about now talking to me about it."

I could still smell the dry rot of the house in my nostrils, and I knew it would take days before I could get it out of my clothes.

"This is one day I'd like to cut out of the calendar permanently," I said.

"And leave them alone to their troubles. It would serve them right."

"They're not alone," I said. "Jessie is with them. Jessie will always be with them until that house and everything in it is gone."

Al frowned. "It's the queerest thing that ever happened in this town, all right. The house all black, her running through the streets like something hunted, him lying there in that room with only the walls to look at, for—when was it Jessie took that fall, counsellor?"

By shifting my eyes a little I could see in the mirror behind Al the reflection of my own face: ruddy, deep jowled, a little incredulous.

"Twenty years ago," I heard myself saying. "Just twenty years ago tonight."

THE ADVENTURE OF THE UNIQUE DICKENSIANS

by August Derleth

If imitation is the sincerest form of flattery, the plethora of Holmesian pastiches produced since the 1880s might have been gratifying to Sir Arthur Conan Doyle, had not so many of them been so poor.

Among the best of the imitators of the Sacred Writings was August (William) Derleth, who was born in Sauk City, Wisconsin, and who, starting at the age of thirteen, produced a large and varied collection of literary products. Cofounder of Arkham House and Mycraft & Moran, publishers of supernatural and mystery books, he claimed that he was "the most versatile and voluminous writer in quality writing fields." Mystery fans, however, remember him for his creation of Solar Pons.

"This Christmas season," said Solar Pons from his place at the windows of our quarters at 7B, Praed Street, "holds the promise of being a merry one, after the quiet week just past. Flakes of snow are dancing in the air, and what I see below enchants me. Just step over here, Parker, and have a look."

I turned down the book I was reading and went over to stand beside him.

Outside, the snowflakes were large and soft, shrouding the streetlight, which had come on early in the winter dusk, and enclosing, like a vision from the past, the scene at the curb—a hansom cab, no less, drawn by a horse that looked almost as ancient as the vehicle, for it stood with a dejected air while its master got out of the cab, leaning on his stick.

"It has been years since I have seen a hansom cab," I said. "Ten, at least—if not more. And that must surely be its owner."

The man getting out of the cab could be seen but dimly, but he wore a coat of ankle length, fitting his thin frame almost like an outer skin, and an old beaver hat that added its height to his, and when he turned to look up at the number above our outer entrance, I saw that he wore a grizzled beard and square spectacles.

"Could he have the wrong address?" I wondered.

"I fervently hope not," said Pons. "The wrong century, perhaps, but not, I pray, the wrong address."

"No, he is coming in."

"Capital, capital!" cried Pons, rubbing his hands together and turning from the window to look expectantly toward the door.

We listened in silence as he applied below to Mrs. Johnson, our landlady, and then to his climbing the stairs, a little wheezily, but withal more like a young man than an old.

"But he clutches the rail," said Pons, as if he had read my thoughts. "Listen to his nails scrape the wall."

At the first touch of the old fellow's stick on the door, Pons strode forward to throw it open.

"Mr. Solar Pons?" asked our visitor in a thin, rather querulous voice.

"Pray come in, sir," said Pons.

"Before I do, I'll want to know how much it will cost," said our client.

"It costs nothing to come in," said Pons, his eyes dancing.

"Everything is so dear these days," complained the old fellow as he entered our quarters. "And money isn't easily come by. And too readily spent, sir, too readily spent."

I offered him a seat, and took his hat.

He wore, I saw now, the kind of black half-gloves customarily worn by clerks, that came over his wrists to his knuckles. Seeing me as for the first time, he pointed his cane at me and asked of Pons, "Who's he?"

"Dr. Parker is my companion."

He looked me up and down suspiciously, pushing his

thin lips out and sucking them in, his eyes narrowed. His skin was the color of parchment, and his clothes, like his hat, were green with age.

"But you have the advantage of us, sir," said Pons.

"My name is Ebenezer Snawley." Then he turned to me and stuck out an arm. "They're Pip's," he said, referring to the clerical cuffs, which I saw now they were. "No need for him to wear 'em. He's inside, and I'm out, and it would be a shameful waste to spend good money on gloves for the few times I go out in such weather." His eyes narrowed a trifle more. "Are you a medical man?"

I assured him that I was.

"Have a look at that, Doctor," he said, indicating a small growth on one finger.

I examined it and pronounced it the beginning of a wart.

"Ah, then it's of no danger to my health. I thank you. As you're not in your office, no doubt there'll be no fee."

"Doctor Parker is a poor man," said Pons.

"So am I, sir. So am I," said Snawley. "But I had to come to you," he added in an aggrieved voice. "The police only laugh at me. I applied to them to have the nuisance stopped."

"What is the nature of the nuisance?" asked Pons.

"Aha! you've not told me your fee for consultation," said Snawley.

"I am accustomed to setting my fee in accordance with the amount of work I must do," said Pons. "In some cases there is no fee at all."

"No fee? No fee at all?"

"We do on occasion manifest the spirit of Christmas," continued Pons.

"Christmas! Humbug!" protested our client.

"Do not say so," said Pons.

"Christmas is a time for well-meaning fools to go about bestowing useless gifts on other fools," our client went on testily.

"But you did not come to discuss the season," said Pons gently.

"You are right, sir. I thank you for reminding me. I came because of late I have been much troubled by some fellow who marches up and down before my house bawling street songs."

"Are they offensive songs?"

Our visitor shook his head irritably. "Any song is offensive if I do not wish to hear it."

"Scurrilous?"

"Street songs."

"Do you know their words?"

"Indeed, and I do, Mr. Pons. And I should. 'Crack 'em and try 'em, before you buy 'em eight-a-penny. All new walnuts. Crack 'em and try 'em, before you buy 'em. A shilling a-hundred. All new walnuts,'" he said in mimicry. "And such as 'Rope mat! Doormat! You really must buy one to save the mud and dust; think of the dirt brought from the street for the want of a mat to wipe your feet!' Indeed I do know them. They are old London street cries."

Pons's eyes now fairly glowed with pleasure. "Ah, he sells walnuts and rope mats."

"A ragbag of a fellow. Sometimes it is hats—three, four at a time on his head. Sometimes it is cress. Sometimes flowers. And ever and anon walnuts. I could not chew 'em even if I bought 'em—and there's small likelihood of that. Catch me wasting good money like that! Not likely."

"He has a right to the street," observed Pons.

"But Mr. Pons, sir, he limits himself to the street along my property. My house is on the corner, set back a trifle, with a bit of land around it—I like my privacy. He goes no farther than the edge of my property on the one side, then back around the corner to the line of my property on the other. It is all done to annoy me—or for some other reason—perhaps to get into the house and lay hands on my valuables."

"He could scarcely effect an entrance more noisily," said Pons, reflectively. "Perhaps he is only observing the Christmas season and wishes to favor you with its compliments."

"Humbug!" said Snawley in a loud voice, and with such a grimace that it seemed to me he could not have made it more effectively had he practiced it in front of a mirror.

"Is he young?"

"If any young fellow had a voice so cracked, I'd send him to a doctor." He shook his head vigorously. "He can't be less than middle-aged. No, sir. Not with a voice like that. He could sour the apples in a barrel with such a voice."

"How often does he come?"

"Why, sir, it is just about every night. I am plagued by his voice, by his very presence, and now he has taken to adding Christmas songs to his small repertoire, it is all the more trying. But chiefly I am plagued—I will confess it—by my curiosity about the reason for this attention he bestows upon me. I sent Pip—Pip is my clerk, retired, now, like myself, with his wife dead and his children all out in the world, even the youngest, who finally recovered his health—I sent Pip, I say, out to tell him to be off, and he but laughed at him, and gave him a walnut or two for himself, and sent one along for me! The impudence of the fellow!" His chin whiskers literally trembled with his indignation.

Pons had folded his arms across his chest, clasping his elbows with his lean fingers, holding in his mirth, which danced around his mouth and in his eyes. "But," he said, visibly controlling himself, "if you are a poor man, you can scarcely be in possession of valuables someone else might covet."

Plainly now our client was torn between the desire to maintain the face he had put upon himself, and to lift a little of it for us to see him a trifle more clearly; for he sat in dour silence.

"Unless," pursued Pons, "you have valuables of a more intangible nature. I suspect you are a collector."

Our visitor started violently. "Why do you say so?"

"I submit that coat you are wearing cannot be newer than 1890, the waistcoat likewise. Your cane is gold-headed; I have not seen such a cane about since 1910. Heavy, too. I suspect it is loaded. And what you have left outside is a period piece—obviously your own, since you drove it yourself. No one who had worn your clothing steadily since it was made could present it still in such good condition."

"You are as sharp as they say you are," said our client grudgingly. "It's true I'm a collector."

"Of books," said Pons.

"Books and such," assented Snawley. "Though how you can tell it I don't pretend to know."

"The smell of ink and paper make a special kind of mustiness, Mr. Snawley. You carry it. And, I take it, you are particularly fond of Dickens."

Snawley's jaw dropped; his mouth hung momentarily agape. "You amaze me," he said.

"Dr. Parker charges me with amazing him for the past year and a half, since he took up residence here," said Pons. "It will do you no harm. It has done him none."

"How, Mr. Pons, do you make out Dickens?"

"Those street songs you know so well are those of Dickens's day. Since you made a point of saying you should know them, it is certainly not far wide of the mark to suggest that you are a Dickensian."

A wintry smile briefly touched our client's lips, but he suppressed it quickly. "I see I have made no mistake in coming to you. It is really the obligation of the police, but they are forever about getting out of their obligations. It is the way of the new world, I fear. But I had heard of you, and I turned it over in mind several days, and I concluded that it would be less dear to call on you than to ask you to call on me. So I came forthwith."

"Nevertheless," said Pons, his eyes twinkling, "I fancy we shall have to have a look at that fellow who, you say, is making such a nuisance of himself."

Our client made a rapid calculation, as was evident by the concentration in his face. "Then you had better come back with me now," he said. "for if you come at any other time, the price of the conveyance will surely be added to the bill."

"That is surely agreeable with me," said Pons. "If it will do for Parker."

Snawley bridled with apprehension. "Does he come, too?"

"Indeed, he does."

"Will he be added to the fee?"

"No, Mr. Snawley."

"Well, then, I will just go below and wait for you to come down," said our client, coming to his feet and seizing his hat from the mantel, where I had put it next to Pons's unanswered letters, unfolded and affixed to the mantel by a dagger, a souvenir of one of his adventures.

Our client had hardly taken himself off before Pons's laughter burst forth.

When he relieved himself, he turned to me. "What do you make of that fellow, Parker?"

"I have never seen the like," I replied. "Parsimonious, suspicious, and, I suspect, not nearly as poor as he would have us believe."

"Capital! Capital! It is all too human for the rich to affect poverty and the poor to affect wealth. We may take it that Mr. Snawley is not poor. If he has a corner house and room enough for someone to walk from one end of the property, around the corner, to the other, we may assume that Mr. Snawley's 'bit of land,' as he puts it, is appreciably more than what the average individual would take for a 'bit.' "

He was getting into his greatcoat as he spoke, and I got into mine. As I reached for my bowler, he clapped his deerstalker to his head, and we were off down the stairs to where our equipage waited at the curb.

Snawley ushered me into the cab.

Behind me, Pons paused briefly to ask, "How long does this fellow stay on his beat?"

"Two, three hours a night. Rain, fog, or shine. And now, with Christmas almost upon us, he has brought along some bells to ring. It is maddening, sir, maddening," said our client explosively.

Pons got in, Snawley closed the door and mounted to the box, and we were off toward Edgware Road, and from there to Lambeth and Brixton and Dulwich, seeing always before us, from every clear vantage point, the dome of the Crystal Palace, and at every hand the color and gayety of the season. Yellow light streamed from the shops into the falling snow, tinsel and glass globes, aglow with red and green and other colors shone bright, decorations framed the shop windows, holly and mistletoe hung in sprays and bunches here and there. Coster's barrows offered fruit and vegetables, Christmas trees, fish and meat, books, cheap china, carpets. Street sellers stood here and there with trays hung from their necks, shouting their wares— Christmas novelties, balloons, tricks, bonbons, comic-papers, and praising the virtues of *Old Moore's Almanack*. At the poultry shops turkeys, geese, and game hung to entice the late shoppers, for it was the day before Christmas Eve, only a trifle more than two years after the ending of the great conflict, and all London celebrated its freedom from the austerities of wartime. The dancing snowflakes reflected the colors of the shops—sometimes red, sometimes yellow or pink or blue or even pale green —and made great halos around the streetlamps.

Snawley avoided crowded thoroughfares as much as possible, and drove with considerable skill; but wherever we went, people turned on the street to look at the hansom cab as it went by—whether they were children or strollers, policemen on their rounds or shoppers with fowl or puddings in their baskets—startled at sight of this apparition from the past.

II

Our destination proved to be Upper Norwood.

Ebenezer Snawley's home was an asymmetric Jacobean pile, dominated by a small tower, and with Elizabethan bay windows that faced the street. It rose in the midst of a small park that occupied the corner of a block and spread over a considerable portion of that block. A dim glow shone through the sidelights at the door; there was no other light inside. The entire neighborhood had an air of decayed gentility, but the falling snow and the gathering darkness sufficiently diminished the glow of the streetlamp so that it was not until we had descended from the cab, which had driven in along one side of the property, bound for a small coach house at the rear corner—directly opposite the street corner—and walked to the door of the house that it became evident how much the house, too, had decayed for want of adequate care, though it was of mid-Victorian origin, and not, therefore, an ancient building—little more than half a century old.

Leaving his steed to stand in the driveway, where the patient animal stood with its head lowered in resignation born of long experience, our client forged ahead of us to the entrance to his home, and there raised his cane and made such a clatter on the door as might have awakened the neighborhood, had it slept, at the same time raising his voice petulantly to shout, "Pip! Pip! Pip Scratch! Up and about!"

There was a scurrying beyond the door, the sound of a bar being lifted, a key in the lock, and the door swung open, to reveal there holding aloft a bracket of three candles a man of medium height, clad in tight broadcloth black breeches and black stockings, and a sort of green-black jacket from the sleeves of which lace cuffs depended. He wore buckled shoes on his feet. He was stooped and wore on his thin face an expression of dubiety and resignation that had been there for long enough to have become engraved upon his features. His watery blue eyes looked anxiously out until he recognized his master; then he stepped aside with alacrity and held the candles higher still, so as to light our way into the shadowed hall.

"No songs yet, Pip? Eh? Speak up."

"None, sir."

"Well, he will come, he will come," promised our client, striding past his man. "Lay a fire in the study, and we will sit by it and watch. Come along, gentlemen, come along. We shall have a fire by and by, to warm our bones—and perhaps a wee drop of sherry."

Pip Scratch stepped forward with a springy gait and thrust the light of the candles ahead, making the shadows to dance in the study whither our client led us. He put the bracket of candles up on the wall, and backed away before Snawley's command.

"Light up, Pip, light up." And to us, "Sit down, gentlemen." And to Pip Scratch's retreating back, "And a few drops of sherry. Bring—yes, yes, bring the Amontillado. It is as much as I can do for my guest."

The servant had now vanished into the darkness outside the study. I was now accustomed to the light, and saw that it was lined with books from floor to ceiling on three walls, excepting only that facing the street along which we had just come, for this wall consisted of the two Elizabethan bay windows we had seen from outside, each of them flanking the fireplace. Most of the shelves of books were encased; their glass doors reflected the flickering candles.

"He will be back in a moment or two," our client assured us.

Hard upon his words came Pip Scratch, carrying a seven-branched candelabrum and a salver on which was a bottle of Amontillado with scarcely enough sherry in it to more than half fill the three glasses beside it. He bore these things to an elegant table and put them down, then

scurried to the bracket on the wall for a candle with which
to light those in the candelabrum, and, having accomplished this in the dour silence with which his master now
regarded him, poured the sherry, which, true to my esti-
mate, came only to half way in each of the three glasses—
but this, clearly, was approved by Mr. Snawley, for his
expression softened a trifle. This done, Pip Scratch hurried
from the room.

"Drink up, gentlemen," said our client, with an air
rather of regret at seeing his good wine vanish. "Let us
drink to our success!"

"Whatever that may be," said Pons enigmatically, raising his glass.

Down went the sherry, a swallow at a time, rolled on
the tongue—and a fine sherry it proved to be, for all that
there was so little of it, and while we drank, Pip Scratch
came in again and laid the fire and scurried out once
more, and soon the dark study looked quite cheerful, with
flames growing and leaping higher and higher, and showing row after row of books, and a locked case with folders
and envelopes and boxes in it, a light bright enough so
that many of the titles of the books could be seen—and
most of them were by Dickens—various editions, first and
late, English and foreign, and associational items.

"And these are your valuables, I take it, Mr. Snawley,"
said Pons.

"I own the finest collection of Dickens in London," said
our client. After another sip of wine, he added, "In all
England." And after two more sips, "If I may say so, I
believe it to be the best in the world." Then his smile
faded abruptly, his face darkened, and he added, "There
is another collector who claims to have a better—but it is
a lie, sir, a dastardly lie, for he cannot substantiate his
claim."

"You have seen his collection?" asked Pons.

"Not I. Nor he mine."

"Do you know him?"

"No, nor wish to. He wrote me three times in as little as
ten days. I have one of his letters here."

He pulled open a drawer in the table, reached in, and
took out a sheet of plain paper with a few lines scrawled
upon it. He handed it to Pons, and I leaned over to read
it, too.

THE ADVENTURE OF THE UNIQUE DICKENSIANS 219

Mr. Ebenezer Snawley

Dear Sir,

I take my pen in hand for the third time to ask the liberty of viewing your collection of Dickens which, I am told, may be equal to my own. Pray set a date, and I will be happy to accommodate myself to it. I am sir, gratefully yours,

Micah Auber

"Dated two months ago, I see," said Pons.

"I have not answered him. I doubt I would have done so had he sent a stamp and envelope for that purpose. In his case, stamps are too dear."

He drank the last of his sherry, and at that moment Pip Scratch came in again, and stood there wordlessly pointing to the street.

"Aha!" cried our client. "The fellow is back. A pox on him! Pip, remove the light for the nonce. There is too much of it—it reflects on the panes. We shall have as good a look at him as we can."

Out went the light, leaving the study lit only by the flames on the hearth, which threw the glow away from the bay windows, toward which our client was now walking, Pons at his heels, and I behind.

"There he is!" cried Snawley. "The rascal! The scoundrel!"

We could hear him now, jingling his bells, and singing in a lusty voice which was not, indeed, very musical— quite the opposite. Singing was not what I would have called it; he was, rather, bawling lustily.

"Walnuts again!" cried our client in disgust.

We could see the fellow now—a short man, stout, who, when he came under the streetlamp, revealed himself to be as much of an individualist as Snawley, for he wore buskins and short trousers, and a coat that reached scarcely to his waist, and his head was crowned with an absurd hat on which a considerable amount of snow had already collected. He carried a basket, presumably for his walnuts.

Past the light he went, bawling about his walnuts, and around the corner.

"Now, you will see, gentlemen, he goes only to th~ ~ne

of my property, and then back. So it is for my benefit that he is about this buffoonery."

"Or his," said Pons.

"How do you say that?" asked Snawley, bending toward Pons so that his slightly curved hawk-like nose almost touched my companion.

"In all seriousness," said Pons. "It does not come from the sherry."

"It cannot be to his benefit," answered our client, "for I have not bought so much as a walnut. Nor shall I!"

Pons stood deep in thought, watching the streetsinger, fingering the lobe of his left ear, as was his custom when preoccupied. Now that all of us were silent, the voice came clear despite the muffling snow.

"He will keep that up for hours," cried our host, his dark face ruddy in the glow of the fire. "Am I to have no peace? The police will do nothing. Nothing! Do we not pay their salaries? Of course, we do. Am I to tolerate this botheration and sit helplessly by while that fellow out there bawls his wares?"

"You saw how he was dressed?" inquired Pons.

"He is not in fashion," replied Snawley, with a great deal of sniffing.

I suppressed my laughter, for the man in the street was no more out of the fashion than our client.

"I have seen enough of him for the time being," said Pons.

Snawley immediately turned and called out. "Pip! Pip! Bring the lights!"

And Pip Scratch, as if he had been waiting in the wings, immediately came hurrying into the room with the candelabrum he had taken out at his employer's command, set it down once more on the table, and departed.

"Mr. Snawley," said Pons as we sat down again near the table, Pons half turned so that he could still look out on occasion through the bay windows toward the street-lamp, "I take it you are constantly adding to your collection?"

"Very cautiously, sir—*ve-ry* cautiously. I have so much now I scarcely know where to house it. There is very little —*ve-ry* little I do not have. Why, I doubt that I add two or three items a year."

"What was your last acquisttion, Mr. Snawley?"

Once again our client's eyes narrowed suspiciously. "Why do you ask that, Mr. Pons?"

"Because I wish to know."

Snawley bent toward Pons and said in a voice that was unusually soft for him, almost as with affection, "It is the most precious of all the items in my collection. It is a manuscript in Dickens's hand!"

"May I see it?"

Our client got up, pulled out of his pocket a keyring, and walked toward the locked cabinet I had previously noticed. He unlocked it and took from it a box that appeared to be of ebony, inlaid with ivory, and brought it back to the table. He unlocked this, in turn, and took from it the manuscript in a folder. He laid it before Pons almost with reverence, and stood back to watch Pons with the particular pride of possession that invariably animates the collector.

Pons turned back the cover.

The manuscript was yellowed, as with age, but the paper was obviously of good quality. *Master Humphrey's Clock* was written at the top, and the signature of Charles Dickens meticulously below it, and below that, in the same script, began the text of the manuscript, which consisted of at least a dozen pages.

"Ah, it is a portion of *The Old Curiosity Shop* not used in the published versions of that book," said Pons.

"You know it, sir!" cried our client with evident delight.

"Indeed, I do. And I recognize the script."

"You do?" Snawley rubbed his hands together in his pleasure.

"Where did you acquire it?"

Snawley blinked at him. "It was offered to me by a gentleman who had fallen on evil days and needed the money—a trifle over a month and a half ago."

"Indeed," said Pons. "So you got it at a bargain?"

"I did, I did. The circumstances made it possible. He was desperate. He wanted five hundred pounds—a ridiculous figure."

"I see. You beat him down?"

"Business is business, Mr. Pons. I bought it at two hundred pounds."

Pons took one of the sheets and held it up against the candles.

"Take care, sir! Take care!" said our client nervously.

Pons lowered the sheet. "You have had it authenticated?"

"Authenticated? Sir, I am an authority on Dickens. Why should I pay some 'expert' a fee to disclose what I already know? This is Dickens's handwriting. I have letters of Dickens by which to authenticate it. Not an *i* is dotted otherwise but as Dickens dotted his *i's*, not a *t* is crossed otherwise. This is Dickens's script, word for word, letter for letter."

Offended, our client almost rudely picked up his treasure and restored it to box and cabinet. As he came back to his chair, he reminded Pons, "But you did not come here to see my collection. There is that fellow outside. How will you deal with him?"

"Ah, I propose to invite him to dinner," answered Pons. "No later than tomorrow night—Christmas Eve. Or, rather, shall we put it that you will invite him here for dinner at that time?"

Our client's jaw dropped. "You are surely joking," he said in a strangled voice.

"It is Christmas, Mr. Snawley. We shall show him some of the spirit of the season."

"I don't make merry myself at Christmas and I can't afford to make idle people merry," replied Snawley sourly. "Least of all that fellow out there. It is an ill-conceived and ill-timed jest."

"It is no jest, Mr. Snawley."

Pons's eyes danced in the candlelight.

"I will have none of it," said our client, coming to his feet as if to dismiss us.

"It is either that," said Pons inexorably, "or my fee."

"Name it, then! Name it—for I shall certainly not lay a board for that infernal rogue," cried our client raising his voice.

"Five hundred pounds," said Pons coldly.

"Five hundred pounds!" screamed Snawley.

Pons nodded, folded his arms across his chest, and looked as adamant as a rock.

Our client leaned and caught hold of the table as if he were about to fall. "Five hundred pounds!" he whispered. "It is robbery! Five hundred pounds!" He stood for a minute so, Pons unmoved the while, and presently a crafty expression came into his narrowed eyes. He began to work his lips out and in, as was his habit, and he turned his head to look directly at Pons. "You say," he said, still in a whisper, "it is either five hundred pounds or—a dinner . . ."

"For four. The three of us and that lusty bawler out there," said Pons.

"It *would* be less expensive," agreed our client, licking his lips.

"Considerably. Particularly since I myself will supply the goose," said Pons with the utmost *savior faire*.

"Done!" cried Snawley at once, as if he had suddenly got much the better of a bad bargain. "Done!" He drew back. "But since I have retained you, I leave it to you to invite him—for I will not!"

"Dinner at seven, Mr. Snawley?"

Our client nodded briskly. "As you like."

"I will send around the goose in the morning."

"There is no other fee, Mr. Pons! I have heard you aright? And you will dispose of that fellow out there?" He inclined his head toward the street.

"I daresay he will not trouble you after tomorrow night," said Pons.

"Then, since there is no further fee, you will not take it amiss if I do not drive you back? There is an underground nearby."

"We will take it, Mr. Snawley."

Snawley saw us to the door, the bracket of candles in his hand. At the threshold Pons paused.

"There must be nothing spared at dinner, Mr. Snawley," he said. "We'll want potatoes, dressing, vegetables, fruit, green salad, plum pudding—and a trifle more of that Amontillado."

Our client sighed with resignation. "It will be done, though I may rue it."

"Rue it you may," said Pons cheerfully. "Good night, sir. And the appropriate greetings of the season to you."

"Humbug! All humbug!" muttered our client, retreating into his house.

We went down the walk through the now much-thinned snowfall, and stood at its juncture with the street until the object of our client's ire came around again. He was a stocky man with a good paunch on him, cherry-red cheeks and a nose of darker red, and merry little eyes that looked out of two rolls of fat, as it were. Coming close, he affected not to see us, until Pons strode out into his path, silencing his bawling of walnuts.

"Good evening, Mr. Auber."

He started back, peering at Pons. "I don't know ye, sir," he said.

"But it *is* Mr. Auber, isn't it? Mr. Micah Auber?"

Auber nodded hesitantly.

"Mr. Ebenezer Snawley would like your company at dinner tomorrow night at seven."

For a long moment, mouth agape, Auber stared at him. "God bless my soul!" he said, finding his voice, "Did he know me, then?"

"No," said Pons, "but who else would be walking here affecting to be a hawker of such wares if not Michah Auber, on hand in case anything turned up?"

"God bless my soul!" said Auber again, fervently.

"You will meet us at the door, Mr. Auber, and go in with us," said Pons. "Good evening, sir."

"I will be there," said Auber.

"And leave off this bawling," said Pons over his shoulder.

We passed on down the street, and Auber, I saw, looking back, went scuttling off in the other direction, in silence.

We hurried on through the snow. The evening was mellow enough so that much of it underfoot had melted, and the falling flakes dissolved on our clothing. But Pons set the pace, and it as not until we were in the underground, on the way back to our quarters, that I had opportunity to speak.

"How did you know that fellow was Micah Auber?" I asked.

"Why, that is as elementary a deduction as it seems to me possible to make," replied Pons. "Consider—Snawley's valuables consist of his collection, which is primarily of Dickensians. Our client acquired his most recent treasure a trifle over six weeks ago. With a fortnight thereafter Micah Auber writes, asking to see his collection. Having had no reply, and assessing our client's character correctly by inquiry or observation—perhaps both—Auber has adopted this novel method of attracting his attention. His object is clearly to get inside that house and have a look at our client's collection."

"But surely this is all very roundabout," I cried.

"I fancy Snawley himself is rather roundabout—though not so roundabout as Auber. They are all a trifle mad, some more so than others. This pair is surely unique, even to the dress of the period!"

"How could Auber know that Snawley had acquired that manuscript?"

"I fancy it is for the reason that Snawley has laid claim to possession of the largest Dickens collection in London . . ."

"In the world," I put in.

"And because the manuscript was undoubtedly stolen from Auber's collection," finished Pons. "Hence Auber's persistence. We shall have a delightful dinner tomorrow evening, I fancy."

III

Pons spent some time next day looking through references and making a telephone call or two, but he was not long occupied at this, and went about looking forward to dinner that evening, and from time to time throughout the day hummed a few bars of a tune, something to which he was not much given, and which testified to the warmth of his anticipation.

We set out early, and reached Ebenezer Snawley's home at a quarter to seven, but Micah Auber had preceded us to the vicinity; for we had no sooner posted ourselves before Snawley's door than Auber made his appearance, bearing in upon us from among a little group of yew trees off to one side of the driveway, where he had undoubtedly been standing to wait upon our coming. He approached with a skip and a hop, and came up to us a little short of breath. Though he was dressed for dinner, it was possible to see by the light of the moon, which lacked but one day of being full, that his clothing was as ancient as our client's.

"Ah, good evening, Mr. Auber," Pons greeted him. "I am happy to observe that you are in time for what I trust will be a good dinner."

"I don't know as to how good it will be. Old Snawley's tight, mighty tight," said Auber.

Pons chuckled.

"But, I don't believe, sir, we've been properly introduced."

"We have not," said Pons. "My companion is Dr. Lyndon Parker, and I am Solar Pons."

Auber acknowledged both introductions with a sweeping bow, then brought himself up short. "Solar Pons, did ye say?" He savored the name, cocked an eye at Pons, and added, "I have a knowledge of London ye might say is extensive and peculiar. I've heard the name. Give me a moment—it'll come to me. Ah, yes, the detective. Well, well, we are well met, sir. I have a need for your services, indeed I do. I've had stolen from me a val'able manuscript—and I have reason to believe our host has it. A prize, sir, a prize. A rare prize."

"We shall see, Mr. Auber, we shall see," said Pons.

"I will pay a reasonable sum, sir, for its recovery—a reasonable sum."

Pons seized hold of the knocker and rapped it sharply against the door. Almost at once our client's voice rose.

"Pip! Pip! The door! The gentlemen are here."

We could hear Pip Scratch coming down the hall, and then the door was thrown open. The only concession Pip had made to the occasion was a bracket of seven candles instead of three.

"A Merry Christmas to you, Pip," said Pons.

"Thank you, sir. And to you, gentlemen," said Pip in a scarcely audible whisper, as if he feared his master might hear him say it.

"Come in! Come in! Let us have done with it," called our client from the study.

The table was laid in the study, and the wine glasses were filled to the brim. Snawley stood at its head, frockcoated, and wearing a broad black tie with a pin in it at the neck, though he was as grizzled as ever, and his eyes seemed to be even more narrowed as he looked past Pons toward Aubery with no attempt to conceal his distaste.

"Mr. Snawley," said Pons with a wave of his hand toward Auber, "let me introduce our lusty-voiced friend."

"A voice not meant for singing," put in our client.

"Mr. Auber," finished Pons.

Snawley started back as if he had been struck. "Micah Auber?" he cried.

"The same," said Auber, bowing, his bald head gleaming in the candlelight, and all in the same movement producing a monocle on a thing black cord, which he raised to one eye and looked through at our client, who was still so thunderstuck that he was incapable of speech. "Ye do me the honor to ask me to dine."

All Snawley could think to say in this contretemps was, "To save five hundred pounds!"

"As good a reason as any," said Auber urbanely.

At this juncture Pip Scratch made his appearance, bearing a large platter on which rested the goose Pons had had sent over that morning, all steaming and brown and done to a turn. He lowered it to the table and set about at once to carve it, while our host, recovering himself, though with as sour an expression as he could put upon his face, waved us to our seats.

Pons seized his glass of Amontillado and raised it aloft. "Let us drink to the success of your various enterprises!"

"Done," said Auber.

"And to a Merry Christmas!" continued Pons.

"Humbug!" cried Snawley.

"I would not say so, Mr. Snawley," said Auber. "Christmas is a very useful occasion."

"Useful?" echoed our client. "And for whom, pray?"

"Why, for us all," answered Auber with spirit. "It is a season for forebearance, perseverance, and usefulness."

"Humbug!" said Snawley again. "If I had my way, I should have every Christmas merrymaker boiled in his own pudding!"

"Ye need a bit more sherry, Mr. Snawley. Come, man, this dinner cannot have cost ye that much!"

So it went through that Christmas Eve dinner, with the two collectors exchanging hard words, and then less hard words, and then softer words, mellowed by the wine for which Pons kept calling. The goose was disposed of in large part, and the dressing, and the potatoes, the carrots, the fruit, the green salad—all in good time, and slowly— and finally came the plum pudding, brought flaming to the table; while the hours went by, eight o'clock struck, then nine—and it was ten before we sat there at coffee and brandy, and by this time both Snawley and Auber were mellow, and Pip Scratch, who had cleared the table of all but the coffee cups and liqueur glasses, had come in to sit down away a little from the table, but yet a party to what went on there.

And it was then that Auber, calculating that the time

was right for it, turned to our client and said, "And now, if ye've no mind, I'd like a look at your collection of Dickens, Mr. Snawley."

"I daresay you would," said Snawley. "I have the largest such in the world."

"It is you who says it."

"I wait to hear you say it, too!"

Auber smiled and half closed his eyes. "If it is all that matters to ye, I will agree to it."

"Hear! Hear!" cried Snawley, and got a little unsteadily to his feet and went over to his shelves, followed like a shadow by the faithful Pip, and with Auber's eyes on him as if he feared that Snawley and his collection might escape him after all.

Snawley unlocked his cabinet and handed Pip a book or two, and carried another himself. They brought them to the table, and Snawley took one after the other of them and laid them down lovingly. They were inscribed copies of *David Copperfield, Edwin Drood,* and *The Pickwick Papers.* After Auber had fittingly admired and exclaimed over them, our client went back for more, and returned this time with copies of *The Monthly Magazine* containing *Sketches by Boz,* with interlineations in Dickens's hand.

Pip kept the fire going on the hearth, and between this task and dancing attendance upon his master, he was continually occupied, going back and forth, to and fro, with the firelight flickering on his bony face and hands, and the candle flames leaping up and dying away to fill the room with grotesque shadows, as the four of us bent over one treasure after another, and the clock crept around from ten to eleven, and moved upon midnight. A parade of books and papers moved from the cabinet to the table and back to the cabinet again—letters in Dickens's hand, letters to Dickens from his publishers, old drawings by Cruikshank and 'Phiz' of Dicken's characters—Oliver Twist, Fagin, Jonas Chuzzlewit, Mr. Bumble, Little Amy Dorrit, Uriah Heep, Caroline Jellyby, Seth Pecksniff, Sam Weller, Samuel Pickwick, and many another—so that it was late when at last Snawley came to his recently acquired treasure, and brought this too to the table.

"And this, Mr. Auber, is the crown jewel, you might say, of my collection," he said.

He made to turn back the cover, but Auber suddenly put forth a hand and held the cover down. Snawley started back a little, but did not take his own hands from his prized manuscript.

"Let me tell ye what it is, Mr. Snawley," said Auber. "It is a manuscript in Dickens's hand—a part of that greater work known as *Master Humphrey's 'Clock*, and specifically that portion of it which became *The Old Curiosity Shop*. But this portion of it was deleted from the book. It is a manuscript of fourteen and a half pages, with Dickens's signature beneath the title on the first page."

Snawley regarded him with wide, alarmed eyes. "How can you know this, Mr. Auber?"

"Because it was stolen from me two months ago."

A cry of rage escaped Snawley. He pulled the precious manuscript away from Auber's restraining hand.

"It is mine!" he cried. "I bought it!"

"For how much?"

"Two hundred pounds."

"The precise sum I paid for it a year ago."

"You shall not have it," cried Snawley.

"I mean to have it," said Auber, springing up.

Pons, too, came to his feet. "Pray, gentlemen, one moment. You will allow, I think, that I should have a few words in this matter. Permit me to have that manuscript for a few minutes, Mr. Snawley."

"On condition it comes back to my hand, sir!"

"That is a condition easy for me to grant, but one the fulfilment of which you may not so readily demand."

"This fellow speaks in riddles," said Snawley testily, as he handed the manuscript to Pons.

Pons took it, opened the cover, and picked up the first page of the manuscript, that with the signature of Dickens on it. He handed it back to Snawley.

"Pray hold it up to the light and describe the watermark, Mr. Snawley."

Our client held it before the candles. After studying it for a few moments he said hesitantly, "Why, I believe it is a rose on a stem, sir."

"Is that all, Mr. Snawley?"

"No, no, I see now there are three letters, very small, at the base of the stem—KTC."

Pons held out his hand for the page, and took up another. This one he handed to Auber. "Examine it, Mr. Auber."

Auber in turn held it up to the candles. "Yes, we've made no mistake, Mr. Snawley. It is a rose, delicately done—a fine rose. And the letters are clear—KTC, all run together."

"That is the watermark of Kennaway, Teape & Company, in Aldgate," said Pons.

"I know of them," said Snawley. "A highly reputable firm."

"They were established in 1871," continued Pons. "Mr. Dickens died on June 8, 1870."

For a moment of frozen horror for the collectors there was not a sound.

"It cannot be!" cried our client then.

"Ye cannot mean it!" echoed Auber.

"The watermark cannot lie, gentlemen," said Pons dryly, "but alas! the script can."

"I bought it in good faith," said Auber, aghast.

"And had it stolen in good faith," said Pons, chuckling.

"I bought it from a reputable dealer," said Auber.

"From the shop of Jason Brompton, in Edgware Road," said Pons. "But not from him—rather from his assistant."

Auber gazed at Pons in astonishment. "How did ye know?"

"Because there is only one forger in London with the skill and patience to have wrought this manuscript," said Pons. "His name is Dennis Golders."

"I will charge him!" cried Auber.

"Ah, I fear that cannot be done. Mr. Golders left Brompton's last January, and is now in His Majesty's service. I shall see, nevertheless, what I can do in the matter, but do not count on my success."

Snawley fell back into his chair.

Auber did likewise.

Pip Scratch came quietly forward and poured them both a little sherry.

Midnight struck.

"It is Christmas day, gentlemen," said Pons. "It is time to leave you. Now you have had a sad blow in common, perhaps you may find something to give you mutual pleasure in all these shelves! Even collectors must take the fraudulent with the genuine."

Snawley raised his head. "You are right, Mr. Pons. Pip! Pip!" he shouted, as if Pip Scratch were not standing behind him. "Put on your coat and bring out the cab. Drive the gentlemen home!"

Our client and his visitor accompanied us to the door and saw us into the hansom cab Pip Scratch had brought down the driveway from the coach house.

"Merry Christmas, gentlemen!" cried Pons, leaning out.

"It burns my lips," said Snawley with a wry smile. "But I will say it."

He wished us both a Merry Christmas, and then, arm in arm, the two collectors turned and went a trifle unsteadily back into the house.

"This has been a rare Christmas, Parker, a rare Christmas, indeed," mused Pons, as we rode toward our quarters through the dark London streets in our client's hansom cab.

"I doubt we'll ever see its like again," I agreed.

"Do not deny us hope, Parker," replied Pons. He cocked his head in my direction and looked at me quizzically. "Did I not see you eyeing the clock with some apprehension in the course of the past half hour?"

"You did, indeed," I admitted. "I feared—I had the conviction, indeed I did—that the three of them would vanish at the stroke of midnight!"

BLIND MAN'S HOOD

by John Dickson Carr

*Well known for his "locked-room" mysteries, John Dick-
son Carr was a master practitioner of the true detective
story, and played fair with the reader. Under his own
name and a pseudonym, Carter Dickson, he produced a
long list of short stories, mysteries and historical novels,
several of which were made into movies and radio plays.
Although most of his works were set in England, Carr was
born in Uniontown, Pennsylvania, the son of a criminal
lawyer. The best of his works weave a marvelous sense of
time and place into their fabric.*

Although one snowflake had already sifted past the lights,
the great doors of the house stood open. It seemed less a
snowflake than a shadow; for a bitter wind whipped after
it, and the doors creaked. Inside, Rodney and Muriel
Hunter could see a dingy, narrow hall paved in dull red
tiles, with a Jacobean staircase at the rear. (At that time,
of course, there was no dead woman lying inside.)

To find such a place in the loneliest part of the Weald
of Kent—a seventeenth-century country house whose
floors had grown humped and its beams scrubbed by the
years—was what they had expected. Even to find electricity was not surprising. But Rodney Hunter thought he
had seldom seen so many lights in one house, and Muriel
had been equally startled by the display. "Clearlawns"
lived up to its name. It stood in the midst of a slope of flat
grass, now wiry white with frost, and there was no tree
or shrub within twenty yards of it. Those lights contrasted

232

with a certain inhospitable and damp air about the house as though the owner were compelled to keep them burning all the time.

"But why is the front door *open?*" insisted Muriel.

In the driveway, the engine of their car coughed and died. The house was now a secret blackness of gables, emitting light at every chink, and silhouetting the stalks of the wisteria vines which climbed it. On either side of the front door were little-paned windows, whose curtains had not been drawn. Towards their left they could see into a low dining room, with table and sideboard set for a cold supper; towards their right was a darkish library moving with the reflections of a bright fire.

The sight of the fire warmed Rodney Hunter, but it made him feel guilty. They were very late. At five o'clock, without fail, he had promised Jack Bannister, they would be at "Clearlawns" to inaugurate the Christmas party.

Engine trouble in leaving London was one thing; idling at a country pub along the way, drinking hot ale and listening to the wireless sing carols until a sort of Dickensian jollity stole into you, was something else. But both he and Muriel were young; they were very fond of each other and of things in general; and they had worked themselves into a glow of Christmas, which—as they stood before the creaking doors of "Clearlawns"—grew oddly cool.

There was no real reason, Rodney thought, to feel disquiet. He hoisted their luggage, including a big box of presents for Jack and Molly's children, out of the rear of the car. That his footsteps should sound loud on the gravel was only natural. He put his head into the doorway and whistled. Then he began to bang the knocker. Its sound seemed to seek out every corner of the house and then come back like a questing dog; but there was no response.

"I'll tell you something else," he said. "There's nobody in the house."

Muriel ran up the three steps to stand beside him. She had drawn her fur coat close around her, and her face was bright with cold.

"But that's impossible!" she said. "I mean, even if they're out, the servants—! Molly told me she keeps a cook and two maids. Are you sure we've got the right place?"

"Yes. The name's on the gate, and there's no other house within a mile."

With the same impulse they craned their necks to look through the windows of the dining room, on the left. Cold fowl on the sideboard, a great bowl of chestnuts; and, now they could see it, another good fire, before which stood a chair with a piece of knitting put aside on it. Rodney tried the knocker again, vigorously, but the sound was all wrong. It was as though they were even more lonely in that core of light, with the east wind rushing across the Weald, and the door creaking again.

"I suppose we'd better go in," said Rodney. He added, with a lack of Christmas spirit: "Here, this is a devil of a trick! What do you think has happened? I'll swear that fire has been made up in the last fifteen minutes."

He stepped into the hall and set down the bags. As he was turning to close the door, Muriel put her hand on his arm.

"I say, Rod. Do you think you'd better close it?"

"Why not?"

"I—I don't know."

"The place is getting chilly enough as it is," he pointed out, unwilling to admit that the same thought had occurred to him. He closed both doors and shot their bar into place; and, at the same moment, a girl came out of the door to the library, on the right.

She was such a pleasant-faced girl that they both felt a sense of relief. Why she had not answered the knocking had ceased to be a question; she filled a void. She was pretty, not more than twenty-one or -two, and had an air of primness which made Rodney Hunter vaguely associate her with a governess or a secretary, though Jack Bannister had never mentioned any such person. She was plump, but with a curiously narrow waist; and she wore brown. Her brown hair was neatly parted, and her brown eyes—long eyes, which might have given a hint of secrecy or curious smiles if they had not been so placid—looked concerned. In one hand she carried what looked like a small white bag of linen or cotton. And she spoke with a dignity which did not match her years.

"I am most terribly sorry," she told them. "I *thought* I heard someone, but I was so busy that I could not be sure. Will you forgive me?"

She smiled. Hunter's private view was that his knocking had been loud enough to wake the dead; but he murmured conventional things. As though conscious of some faint incongruity about the white bag in her hand, she held it up.

"For Blind Man's Bluff," she explained. "They do cheat so, I'm afraid, and not only the children. If one uses an ordinary handkerchief tied round the eyes, they always manage to get a corner loose. But if you take this, and you put it fully over a person's head, and you tie it round the neck"—a sudden gruesome image occurred to Rodney Hunter—"then it works so much better, don't you think?" Her eyes seemed to turn inward, and to grow absent. "But I must not keep you talking here. You are—?"

"My name is Hunter. This is my wife. I'm afraid we've arrived late, but I understood Mr. Bannister was expecting—"

"He did not tell you?" asked the girl in brown.

"Tell me what?"

"Everyone here, including the servants, is always out of the house at this hour on this particular date. It is the custom; I believe it has been the custom for more than sixty years. There is some sort of special church service."

Rodney Hunter's imagination had been devising all sorts of fantastic explanations, the first of them being that this demure lady had murdered the members of the household and was engaged in disposing of the bodies. What put this nonsensical notion into his head he could not tell, unless it was his own profession of detective-story writing. But he felt relieved to hear a commonplace explanation. Then the woman spoke again.

"Of course, it is a pretext, really. The rector, that dear man, invented it all those years ago to save embarrassment. What happened here had nothing to do with the murder, since the dates were so different; and I suppose most people have forgotten now why the tenants *do* prefer to stay away during seven and eight o'clock on Christmas Eve. I doubt if Mrs. Bannister even knows the real reason, though I should imagine Mr. Bannister must know it. But what happens here cannot be very pleasant, and it wouldn't do to have the children see it—would it?"

Muriel spoke with such sudden directness that her husband knew she was afraid. "Who are you?" Muriel said. "And what on earth are you talking about?"

"I am quite sane, really," their hostess assured them, with a smile that was half-cheery and half-coy, "I dare say it must be all very confusing to you, poor dear. But I am forgetting my duties. Please come in and sit down before the fire, and let me offer you something to drink."

She took them into the library on the right, going ahead with a walk that was like a bounce, and looking over her shoulder out of those long eyes. The library was a long, low room with beams. The windows towards the road were uncurtained; but those in the side wall, where a faded red-brick fireplace stood, were bay windows with draperies closed across them. As their hostess put them before the fire, Hunter could have sworn he saw one of the draperies move.

"You need not worry about it," she assured him, following his glance towards the bay. "Even if you looked in there, you might not see anything now. I believe some gentleman did try it once, a long time ago. He stayed in the house for a wager. But when he pulled the curtain back, he did not see anything in the bay—at least, anything quite. He felt some hair, and it moved. That is why they have so many lights nowadays."

Muriel had sat down on a sofa and was lighting a cigarette, to the rather prim disapproval of their hostess, Hunter thought.

"May we have a hot drink?" Muriel asked crisply. "And then, if you don't mind, we might walk over and meet the Bannisters coming from church."

"Oh, please don't do that!" cried the other. She had been standing by the fireplace, her hands folded and turned outwards. Now she ran across to sit down beside Muriel; and the swiftness of her movement, no less than the touch of her hand on Muriel's arm, made the latter draw back.

Hunter was now completely convinced that their hostess was out of her head. Why she held such fascination for him, though, he could not understand. In her eagerness to keep them there, the girl had come upon a new idea. On a table behind the sofa, bookends held a row of modern novels. Conspicuously displayed—probably due to Molly Bannister's tact—were two of Rodney Hunter's detective stories. The girl put a finger on them.

"May I ask if you wrote these?"

He admitted it.

"Then," she said with sudden composure, "it would probably interest you to hear about the murder. It was a most perplexing business, you know; the police could make nothing of it, and no one ever has been able to solve it." An arresting eye fixed on his. "It happened out in the hall there. A poor woman was killed where there was no one to kill her, and no one could have done it. But she was murdered."

Hunter started to get up from his chair; then he changed his mind and sat down again. "Go on," he said.

"You must forgive me if I am a little uncertain about dates," she urged. "I think it was in the early eighteen-seventies, and I am sure it was in early February—because of the snow. It was a bad winter then; the farmers' livestock all died. My people have been bred up in the district for years, and I know that. The house here was much as it is now, except that there was none of this lighting (only paraffin lamps, poor girl!); and you were obliged to pump up what water you wanted; and people read the newspaper quite through, and discussed it for days.

"The people were a little different to look at, too. I am sure I do not understand why we think beards are so strange nowadays; they seem to think that men who had beards never had any emotions. But even young men wore them then, and looked handsome enough. There was a newly married couple living in this house at the time: at least, they had been married only the summer before. They were named Edward and Jane Waycross, and it was considered a good match everywhere.

"Edward Waycross did not have a beard, but he had bushy side-whiskers which he kept curled. He was not a handsome man, either, being somewhat dry and hard-favored; but he was a religious man, and a good man, and an excellent man of business, they say: a manufacturer of agricultural implements at Hawkhurst. He had determined that Jane Anders (as she was) would make him a good wife, and I dare say she did. The girl had several suitors. Although Mr. Waycross was the best match, I know it surprised people a little when she accepted him, because she was thought to have been fond of another man—a more striking man, whom many of the young girls were after. This was Jeremy Wilkes, who came of a very good family but was considered wicked. He was no younger than Mr. Waycross, but he had a great black beard, and wore white waistcoats with gold chains, and drove a gig. Of course, there had been gossip, but that was because Jane Anders was considered pretty."

Their hostess had been sitting back against the sofa, quietly folding the little white bag with one hand, and speaking in a prim voice. Now she did something which turned her hearers cold.

You have probably seen the same thing done many times. She had been touching her cheek lightly with the fingers of the other hand. In doing so, she touched the flesh at the corner under her lower eyelid, and accidently drew down the corner of that eyelid—which should have exposed the red part of the inner lid at the corner of the eye. It was not red. It was of a sickly pale color.

"In the course of his business dealings," she went on, Mr. Waycross had often to go to London, and usually he was obliged to remain overnight. But Jane Waycross was not afraid to remain alone in the house. She had a good servant, a staunch old woman, and a good dog. Even so, Mr. Waycross commended her for her courage."

The girl smiled. "On the night I wish to tell you of, in February, Mr. Waycross was absent. Unfortunately, too, the old servant was absent; she had been called away as a midwife to attend her cousin, and Jane Waycross had allowed her to go. This was known in the village, since all such affairs are well known, and some uneasiness was felt—this house being isolated, as you know. But she was not afraid.

"It was a very cold night, with a heavy fall of snow which had stopped about nine o'clock. You must know, beyond doubt, that poor Jane Waycross was alive after it had stopped snowing. It must have been nearly half-past nine when a Mr. Moody—a very good and sober man who lived in Hawkhurst—was driving home along the road past this house. As you know, it stands in the middle of a great bare stretch of lawn; and you can see the house clearly from the road. Mr. Moody saw poor Jane at the window of one of the upstairs bedrooms, with a candle in her hand, closing the shutters. But he was not the only witness who saw her alive.

"On that same evening, Mr. Wilkes (the handsome gentleman I spoke to you of a moment ago) had been at a tavern in the village of Five Ashes with Dr. Sutton, the local doctor, and a racing gentleman named Pawley. At about half-past eleven they started to drive home in Mr.

Wilkes's gig to Cross-in-Hand. I am afraid they had been drinking, but they were all in their sober senses. The landlord of the tavern remembered the time because he had stood in the doorway to watch the gig, which had fine yellow wheels, go spanking away as though there were no snow; and Mr. Wilkes in one of the new round hats with a curly brim.

"There was a bright moon. 'And no danger,' Dr. Sutton always said afterwards; 'shadows of trees and fences as clear as though a silhouette-cutter had made 'em for sixpence.' But when they were passing this house Mr. Wilkes pulled up sharp. There was a bright light in the window of one of the downstairs rooms—this room, in fact. They sat out there looking round the hood of the gig and wondering.

"Mr. Wilkes spoke: 'I don't like this,' he said. 'You know, gentlemen, that Waycross is still in London; and the lady in question is in the habit of retiring early. I am going up there to find out if anything is wrong.'

"With that he jumped out of the gig, his black beard jutting out and his breath smoking. He said: 'And if it is a burglar, then, by Something, gentlemen'—I will not repeat the word he used—'by Something, gentlemen, I'll settle him.' He walked through the gate and up to the house—they could follow every step he made—and looked into the windows of this room here. Presently he returned, looking relieved (they could see him by the light of the gig lamps), but wiping the moisture off his forehead.

" 'It is all right,' he said to them; 'Waycross has come home. But by Something, gentlemen, he is growing thinner these days, or it is shadows.'

"Then he told them what he had seen. If you look through the front windows—there—you can look sideways and see out through the doorway into the main hall. He said he had seen Mrs. Waycross standing in the hall with her back to the staircase, wearing a blue dressing gown over her nightgown, and her hair down round her shoulders. Standing in front of her, with his back to Mr. Wilkes, was a tallish, thin man like Mr. Waycross, with a long greatcoat and a tall hat like Mr. Waycross's. *She* was carrying either a candle or a lamp; and he remembered how the tall hat seemed to wag back and forth, as though the man were talking to her or putting out his hands towards her. For he said he could not see the woman's face.

"Of course, it was not Mr. Waycross; but how were they to know that?

"At about seven o'clock next morning, Mrs. Randall, the old servant, returned. (A fine boy had been born to her cousin the night before.) Mrs. Randall came home through the white dawn and the white snow, and found the house all locked up. She could get no answer to her knocking. Being a woman of great resolution, she eventually broke a window and got in. But when she saw what was in the front hall, she went out screaming for help.

"Poor Jane was past help. I know I should not speak of these things; but I must. She was lying on her face in the hall. From the waist down her body was much charred and—unclothed, you know, because fire had burnt away most of the nightgown and the dressing gown. The tiles of the hall were soaked with blood and paraffin oil, the oil having come from a broken lamp with a thick blue-silk shade which was lying a little distance away. Near it was a china candlestick with a candle. This fire had also charred a part of the paneling of the wall, and a part of the staircase. Fortunately, the floor is of brick tiles, and there had not been much paraffin left in the lamp, or the house would have been set afire.

"But she had not died from burns alone. Her throat had been cut with a deep slash from some very sharp blade. But she had been alive for a while to feel both things, for she had crawled forward on her hands while she was burning. It was a cruel death, a horrible death for a soft person like that."

There was a pause. The expression on the face of the narrator, the plump girl in the brown dress, altered slightly. So did the expression of her eyes. She was sitting beside Muriel, and moved a little closer.

"Of course, the police came. I do not understand such things, I am afraid, but they found that the house had not been robbed. They also noticed the odd thing I have mentioned, that there was both a lamp *and* a candle in a candlestick; there were no other lamps or candles downstairs except the lamps waiting to be filled next morning in the back kitchen. But the police thought she would not have come downstairs carrying both the lamp *and* the candle as well.

"She must have brought the lamp, because that was broken. When the murderer took hold of her, they thought, she had dropped the lamp, and it went out; the paraffin spilled, but did not catch fire. Then this man in the tall hat, to finish his work after he had cut her throat, went upstairs, and got a candle, and set fire to the spilled oil. I am stupid at these things, but even I should have guessed that this must mean someone familiar with the house. Also, if she came downstairs, it must have been to let someone in at the front door; and that could not have been a burglar.

"You may be sure all the gossips were like police from the start, even when the police hemm'd and haw'd, because they knew Mrs. Waycross must have opened the door to a man who was not her husband. And immediately they found an indication of this, in the mess that the fire and blood had made in the hall. Some distance away from poor Jane's body there was a medicine bottle such as druggists use. I think it had been broken in two pieces; and on one intact piece they found sticking some fragments of a letter that had not been quite burned. It was in a man's handwriting, not her husband's, and they made out enough of it to understand. It was full of—expressions of love, you know, and it made an appointment to meet her there on that night."

Rodney Hunter, as the girl paused, felt impelled to ask a question.

"Did they know whose handwriting it was?"

"It was Jeremy Wilkes's," replied the other simply. "Though they never proved that, never more than slightly suspected it, and the circumstances did not bear it out. In fact, a knife stained with blood was actually found in Mr. Wilkes's possession. But the police never brought it to anything, poor souls. For, you see, not Mr. Wilkes—or anyone else in the world—could possibly have done the murder."

"I don't understand that," said Hunter, rather sharply.

"Forgive me if I am stupid about telling things," urged their hostess in a tone of apology. She seemed to be listening to the chimney growl under a cold sky, and listening with hard, placid eyes. "But even the village gossips could tell that. When Mrs. Randall came here to the house on that morning, both the front and the back doors were locked and securely bolted on the inside. All the windows were locked on the inside. If you will look at the fastenings in this dear place, you will know what that means.

"But, bless you, that was the least of it! I told you about the snow. The snowfall had stopped at nine o'clock in the evening, hours and hours before Mrs. Waycross was murdered. When the police came, there were only two separate sets of footprints in the great unmarked half acre of snow round the house. One set belonged to Mr. Wilkes, who had come up and looked in through the window the night before. The other belonged to Mrs. Randall. The police could follow and explain both sets of tracks; but there were no other tracks at all, and no one was hiding in the house.

"Of course, it was absurd to suspect Mr. Wilkes. It was not only that he told a perfectly straight story about the man in the tall hat; but both Dr. Sutton and Mr. Pawley, who drove back with him from Five Ashes, were there to swear he could not have done it. You understand, he came no closer to the house than the windows of this room. They could watch every step he made in the moonlight, and they did. Afterwards he drove home with Dr. Sutton and slept there; or, I should say, they continued their terrible drinking until daylight. It is true that they found in his possession a knife with blood on it, but he explained that he had used the knife to gut a rabbit.

"It was the same with poor Mrs. Randall, who had been up all night about her midwife's duties, though naturally it was even more absurd to think of *her*. But there were no other footprints at all, either coming to or going from the house, in all that stretch of snow; and all the ways in or out were locked on the inside."

It was Muriel who spoke then, in a voice that tried to be crisp, but wavered in spite of her. "Are you telling us that all this is true?" she demanded.

"I am teasing you a little, my dear," said the other. "But really and truly, it all did happen. Perhaps I will show you in a moment."

"I suppose it was really the husband who did it?" asked Muriel in a bored tone.

"Poor Mr. Waycross!" said their hostess tenderly. "He spent the night in a temperance hotel near Charing Cross Station, as he always did, and, of course, he never left it.

When he learned about his wife's duplicity"—again Hunter thought she was going to pull down a corner of her eyelid—"it nearly drove him out of his mind, poor fellow. I think he gave up agricultural machinery and took to preaching, but I am not sure. I know he left the district soon afterwards, and before he left he insisted on burning the mattress of their bed. It was a dreadful scandal."

"But in that case," insisted Hunter, "who did kill her? And, if there were no footprints and all the doors were locked, how did the murderer come or go? Finally, if all this happened in February, what does it have to do with people being out of the house on Christmas Eve?"

"Ah, that is the real story. That is what I meant to tell you."

She grew very subdued.

"It must have been very interesting to watch the people alter and grow older, or find queer paths, in the years afterwards. For, of course, nothing did happen as yet. The police presently gave it all up; for decency's sake it was allowed to rest. There was a new pump built in the market square; and the news of the Prince of Wales's going to India in 'seventy-five to talk about; and presently a new family came to live at 'Clearlawns' and began to raise their children. The trees and the rains in summer were just the same, you know. It must have been seven or eight years before anything happened, for Jane Waycross was very patient.

"Several of the people had died in the meantime. Mrs. Randall had, in a fit of quinsy; and so had Dr. Sutton, but that was a great mercy, because he fell by the way when he was going out to perform an amputation with too much of the drink in him. But Mr. Pawley had prospered—and, above all, so had Mr. Wilkes. He had become an even finer figure of a man, they tell me, as he drew near middle age. When he married he gave up all his loose habits. Yes, he married; it was the Tinsley heiress, Miss Linshaw, whom he had been courting at the time of the murder; and I have heard that poor Jane Waycross, even after *she* was married to Mr. Waycross, used to bite her pillow at night because she was so horribly jealous of Miss Linshaw.

"Mr. Wilkes had always been tall, and now he was finely stout. He always wore frock coats. Though he had lost most of his hair, his beard was full and curly; he had twinkling black eyes, and twinkling ruddy cheeks, and a bluff voice. All the children ran to him. They say he broke as many feminine hearts as before. At any wholesome entertainment he was always the first to lead the cotillion or applaud the fiddler, and I do not know what hostesses would have done without him.

"On Christmas Eve, then—remember, I am not sure of the date—the Fentons gave a Christmas party. The Fentons were the very nice family who had taken this house afterwards, you know. There was to be no dancing, but all the old games. Naturally, Mr. Wilkes was the first of all to be invited, and the first to accept; for everything was all smoothed away by time, like the wrinkles in last year's counterpane; and what's past *is* past, or so they say. They had decorated the house with holly and mistletoe, and guests began to arrive as early as two in the afternoon.

"I had all this from Mr. Fenton's aunt (one of the Warwickshire Abbotts) who was actually staying here at the time. In spite of such a festal season, the preparations had not been going at all well that day, though such preparations usually did. Miss Abbott complained that there was a nasty earthy smell in the house. It was a dark and raw day, and the chimneys did not seem to draw as well as they should. What is more, Mrs. Fenton cut her finger when she was carving the cold fowl, because she said one of the children had been hiding behind the window curtains in here, and peeping out at her; she was very angry. But Mr. Fenton, who was going about the house in his carpet slippers before the arrival of the guests, called her 'Mother' and said that it was Christmas.

"It is certainly true that they forgot all about this when the fun of the games began. Such squealings you never heard!—or so I am told. Foremost of all at Bobbing for Apples or Nuts in May was Mr. Jeremy Wilkes. He stood, gravely paternal, in the midst of everything, with his ugly wife beside him, and stroked his beard. He saluted each of the ladies on the cheek under the mistletoe; there was also some scampering to salute him; and, though he *did* remain for longer than was necessary behind the window curtains with the younger Miss Twigelow, his wife only smiled. There was only one unpleasant incident, soon forgotten. Towards dusk a great gusty wind began to come up, with the chimneys smoking worse than usual. It being nearly dark, Mr. Fenton said it was time to fetch in the Snapdragon Bowl and watch it flame. You know the game? It is a great bowl of lighted spirit, and you must thrust in your hand and pluck out a raisin from the bottom without scorching your fingers. Mr. Fenton carried it in on a tray in the half darkness; it was flickering with that bluish flame you have seen on Christmas puddings. Miss Abbott said that once, in carrying it, he started and turned round. She said that for a second she thought there was a face looking over his shoulder, and it wasn't a nice face.

"Later in the evening, when the children were sleepy and there was tissue paper scattered all over the house, the grown-ups began their games in earnest. Someone suggested Blind Man's Bluff. They were mostly using the hall and this room here, as having more space than the dining room. Various members of the party were blindfolded with the men's handkerchiefs, but there was a dreadful amount of cheating. Mr. Fenton grew quite annoyed about it, because the ladies almost always caught Mr. Wilkes when they could; Mr. Wilkes was laughing and perspiring heartily, and his great cravat with the silver pin had almost come loose.

"To make it certain nobody could cheat, Mr. Fenton, got a little white linen bag—like this one. It was the pillowcase off the baby's cot, really; and he said nobody could look through it if it were tied over the head.

"I should explain that they had been having some trouble with the lamp in this room. Mr. Fenton said: 'Confound it, Mother, what is wrong with that lamp? Turn up the wick, will you?' It was really quite a good lamp, from Spence and Minstead's, and should not have burned so dull as it did. In the confusion, while Mrs. Fenton was trying to make the light better, and he was looking over his shoulder at her, Mr. Fenton had been rather absently fastening the bag on the head of the last person caught. He has said since that he did not notice who it was. No one else noticed, either, the light being so dim and there being such a large number of people. It seemed to be a girl in a broad bluish kind of dress, standing over near the door.

"Perhaps you know how people act when they have just been blindfolded in this game. First they usually stand very still, as though they were smelling or sensing in which direction to go. Sometimes they make a sudden jump, or sometimes they begin to shuffle gently forward. Everyone noticed what an air of *purpose* there seemed to be about this person whose face was covered; she went forward very slowly, and seemed to crouch down a bit.

"It began to move towards Mr. Wilkes in very short but quick little jerks, the white bag bobbing on its face. At this time Mr. Wilkes was sitting at the end of the table, laughing, with his face pink above the beard, and a glass of our Kentish cider in his hand. I want you to imagine this room as being very dim, and much more cluttered, what with all the tassels they had on the furniture then; and the high-piled hair of the ladies, too. The hooded person got to the edge of the table. It began to edge along towards Mr. Wilkes's chair; and then it jumped.

"Mr. Wilkes got up and skipped (yes, skipped) out of its way, laughing. It waited quietly, after which it went, in the same slow way, towards him again. It nearly got him again, by the edge of the potted plant. All this time it did not say anything, you understand, although everyone was applauding it and crying encouraging advice. It kept its head down. Miss Abbott says she began to notice an unpleasant faint smell of burnt cloth or something worse, which turned her half ill. By the time the hooded person came stooping clear across the room, as certainly as though it could see him, Mr. Wilkes was not laughing any longer.

"In the corner by one bookcase, he said out loud: 'I'm tired of this silly, rotten game; go away, do you hear?' Nobody there had ever heard him speak like that, in such a loud, wild way, but they laughed and thought it must be the Kentish cider. 'Go away!" cried Mr. Wilkes again, and began to strike at it with his fist. All this time, Miss Abbott says, she had observed his face gradually changing. He dodged again, very pleasant and nimble for such a big man, but with the perspiration running down his face. Back across the room he went again, with it following him; and he cried out something that most naturally shocked them all inexpressibly.

"He screamed out: 'For God's sake, Fenton, take it off me!'

"And for the last time the thing jumped.

"They were over near the curtains of that bay window, which were drawn, as they are now. Miss Twigelow, who was nearest, says that Mr. Wilkes could not have seen anything, because the white bag was still drawn over the woman's head. The only thing she noticed was that at the lower part of the bag, where the face must have been there was a curious kind of discoloration, a stain of some sort, which had not been there before: something seemed to be seeping through. Mr. Wilkes fell back between the curtains, with the hooded person after him, and screamed again. There was a kind of thrashing noise in or behind the curtains; then they fell straight again, and everything grew quiet.

"Now, our Kentish cider is very strong, and for a moment Mr. Fenton did not know what to think. He tried to laugh at it, but the laugh did not sound well. Then he went over to the curtains, calling out gruffly to them to come out of there and not play the fool. But after he had looked inside the curtains, he turned round very sharply and asked the rector to get the ladies out of the room. This was done, but Miss Abbott often said that she had one quick peep inside. Though the bay windows were locked on the inside, Mr. Wilkes was now alone on the window seat. She could see his beard sticking up, and the blood. He was dead, of course. But, since he had murdered Jane Waycross, I sincerely think that he deserved to die."

For several seconds the two listeners did not move. She had all too successfully conjured up this room in the late 'seventies, whose stuffiness still seemed to pervade it now.

"But look here!" protested Hunter, when he could fight down an inclination to get out of the room quickly. "You say he killed her after all? And yet you told us he had an absolute alibi. You said he never went closer to the house than the windows. . . ."

"No more he did, my dear," said the other.

"He was courting the Linshaw heiress at the time," she resumed; "and Miss Linshaw was a very proper young lady, who would have been horrified if she had heard about him and Jane Waycross. She would have broken off the match, naturally. But poor Jane Waycross meant her to hear. She was much in love with Mr. Wilkes, and she

was going to tell the whole matter publicly: Mr. Wilkes
had been trying to persuade her not to do so."

"But—"

"Oh, don't you see what happened?" cried the other
in a pettish tone. "It is so dreadfully simple. I am not
clever at these things, but I should have seen it in a moment, even if I did not already know. I told you everything so that you should be able to guess.

"When Mr. Wilkes and Dr. Sutton and Mr. Pawley
drove past here in the gig that night, they saw a bright
light burning in the windows of this room. I told you that.
But the police never wondered, as anyone should, what
caused that light. Jane Waycross never came into this
room, as you know; she was out in the hall, carrying either
a lamp or a candle. But that lamp in the thick blue-silk
shade, held out there in the hall, would not have caused
a bright light to shine through this room and illuminate it.
Neither would a tiny candle; it is absurd. And I told you
there were no other lamps in the house except some
empty ones waiting to be filled in the back kitchen. There
is only one thing they could have seen. They saw the great
blaze of the paraffin oil round Jane Waycross's body.

"Didn't I tell you it was dreadfully simple? Poor Jane
was upstairs waiting for her lover. From the upstairs window she saw Mr. Wilkes's gig, with the fine yellow
wheels, drive along the road in the moonlight, and she
did not know there were other men in it; she thought he
was alone. She came downstairs—

"It is an awful thing that the police did not think more
about that broken medicine bottle lying in the hall, the
large bottle that was broken in just two long pieces. She
must have had a use for it; and, of course, she had. You
knew that the oil in the lamp was almost exhausted, although there was a great blaze round the body. When
poor Jane came downstairs, she was carrying the unlighted lamp in one hand; in the other hand she was carrying a lighted candle and an old medicine bottle
containing paraffin oil. When she got downstairs, she
meant to fill the lamp from the medicine bottle, and then
light it with the candle.

"But she was too eager to get downstairs, I am afraid.
When she was more than halfway down, hurrying, that
long nightgown tripped her. She pitched forward down
the stairs on her face. The medicine bottle broke on the

tiles under her, and poured a lake of paraffin round her body. Of course, the lighted candle set the paraffin blazing when it fell; but that was not all. One intact side of that broken bottle, long and sharp and cleaner than any blade, cut her throat when she fell on the smashed bottle. She was not quite stunned by the fall. When she felt herself burning, and the blood almost as hot, she tried to save herself. She tried to crawl forward on her hands, forward into the hall, away from the blood and oil and fire.

"That was what Mr. Wilkes really saw when he looked in the window.

"You see, he had been unable to get rid of the two fuddled friends, who insisted on clinging to him and drinking with him. He had been obliged to drive them home. If he could not go to 'Clearlawns' now, he wondered how at least he could leave a message; and the light in the window gave him an excuse.

"He saw pretty Jane propped up on her hands in the hall, looking out at him beseechingly while the blue flame ran up and turned yellow. You might have thought he would have pitied, for she loved him very much. Her wound was not really a deep wound. If he had broken into the house at that moment, he might have saved her life. But he preferred to let her die, because now she would make no public scandal and spoil his chances with the rich Miss Linshaw. That was why he returned to his friends and told a lie about a murderer in a tall hat. It is why, in heaven's truth, he murdered her himself. But when he returned to his friends, I do not wonder that they saw him mopping his forehead. You know now how Jane Waycross came back for him, presently."

There was another heavy silence.

The girl got to her feet, with a sort of bouncing motion which was as suggestive as it was vaguely familiar. It was as though she were about to run. She stood there, a trifle crouched, in her prim brown dress, so oddly narrow at the waist after an old-fashioned pattern; and in the play of light on her face Rodney Hunter fancied that its prettiness was only a shell.

"The same thing happened afterwards, on some Christmas Eves," she explained. "They played Blind Man's Bluff over again. That is why people who live here do not care to risk it nowadays. It happens at a quarter past seven—"

Hunter stared at the curtains. "But it was a quarter past seven when we got here!" he said. "It must now be—"

"Oh, yes," said the girl, and her eyes brimmed over. "You see, I told you you had nothing to fear; it was all over then. But that is not why I thank you. I begged you to stay, and you did. You have listened to me, as no one else would. And now I have told it at last, and now I think both of us can sleep."

Not a fold stirred or altered in the dark curtains that closed the window bay; yet, as though a blurred lens had come into focus, they now seemed innocent and devoid of harm. You could have put a Christmas tree there. Rodney Hunter, with Muriel following his gaze, walked across and threw back the curtains. He saw a quiet window seat covered with chintz, and the rising moon beyond the window. When he turned round, the girl in the old-fashioned dress was not there. But the front doors were open again, for he could feel a current of air blowing through the house.

With his arm round Muriel, who was white-faced, he went out into the hall. They did not look long at the scorched and beaded stains at the foot of the paneling, for even the scars of fire seemed gentle now. Instead, they stood in the doorway looking out, while the house threw its great blaze of light across the frosty Weald. It was a welcoming light. Over the rise of a hill, black dots trudging in the frost showed that Jack Bannister's party was returning; and they could hear the sound of voices carrying far. They heard one of the party carelessly singing a Christmas carol for glory and joy, and the laughter of childen coming home.

THE THIRTEENTH DAY
OF CHRISTMAS

by Isaac Asimov

Isaac Asimov is perhaps best known in the mystery field for his Black Widowers *stories. He has to date compiled three volumes of these mystery puzzles:* Tales of the Black Widowers, More Tales of the Black Widowers *and* Casebook of the Black Widowers. *He has also to his credit two full-length mystery novels:* A Whiff of Death *and (my favorite)* Murder at the A.B.A.

This was one year when we were glad Christmas Day was over.

It had been a grim Christmas Eve, and I was just as glad I don't stay awake listening for sleigh bells any more. After all, I'm about ready to get out of junior high. —But then, I kind of stayed awake listening for bombs.

We stayed up till midnight of Christmas *Day,* though, up till the last minute of it, Mom and I. Then Dad called and said, "Okay, it's over. Nothing's happened. I'll be home as soon as I can."

Mom and I danced around for a while as though Santa Claus had just come, and then, after about an hour, Dad came home and I went to bed and slept fine.

You see, it's special in our house. Dad's a detective on the force, and these days, with terrorists and bombings, it can get pretty hairy. So when, on December twentieth, warnings reached headquarters that there would be a Christmas Day bombing at the Soviet offices in the United Nations, it had to be taken seriously.

The entire force was put on the alert and the F.B.I. came in too. The Soviets had their own security, I guess, but none of it satisfied Dad.

The day before Christmas he said, "If someone is crazy enough to want to plant a bomb and if he's not too worried about getting caught afterwards, he's likely to be able to do it no matter what precautions we take."

Mom said, "I suppose there's no way of knowing who it is."

Dad shook his head. "Letters from newspapers pasted on paper. No fingerprints; only smudges. Common stuff we can't trace, and he said it would be the only warning, so we won't get anything else to work on. What can we do?"

Mom said, "Well, it must be someone who doesn't like the Russians, I guess."

Dad said, "That doesn't narrow it much. Of course, the Soviets say it's a Zionist threat, and we've got to keep an eye on the Jewish Defense League."

I said, "Gee, Dad, that doesn't make much sense. The Jewish people wouldn't pick Christmas Day to do it, would they? It doesn't mean anything to them, and it doesn't mean anything to the Soviet Union, either. They're officially atheist."

Dad said, "You can't reason that out to the Russians. Now, why don't you turn in, because tomorrow may be a bad day all round, Christmas or not."

Then he left, and he was out all Christmas Day, and it was pretty rotten. We didn't even open any presents, just sat listening to the radio, which was tuned to an all-day news station.

Then at midnight, when Dad called and said nothing had happened, we breathed again, but I still forgot to open my presents.

That didn't come till the morning of the twenty-sixth. We made *that* day Christmas. Dad had a day off, and Mom baked the turkey a day late. It wasn't till after dinner that we talked about it again.

Mom said, "I suppose the person, whoever it was, couldn't find any way of planting the bomb once the Department drew the security strings tight."

Dad smiled, as though he appreciated Mom's loyalty. He said, "I don't think you can make security that tight, but what's the difference? There was no bomb. Maybe it was a bluff. After all, it did disrupt the city a bit and it gave the Soviet people at the United Nations some sleepless nights, I bet. That might have been almost as good for the bomber as letting the bomb go off."

I said, "If he couldn't do it on Christmas Day, maybe he'll do it another time. Maybe he just said Christmas to get everyone keyed up, and then, after they relax, he'll—"

Dad gave me one of his little pushes on the side of my head. "You're a cheerful one, Larry. No, I don't think so. Real bombers value the sense of power. When they say something is going to happen at a certain time, it's got to be that time or it's no fun for them."

I was still suspicious, but the days passed and there was no bombing, and the Department gradually got back to normal. The F.B.I. left, and even the Soviet people seemed to forget about it, according to Dad.

On January second the Christmas-New Year's vacation was over and I went back to school, and we started rehearsing our Christmas pageant. We didn't call it that, of course, because we're not supposed to have religious celebrations at school, what with the separation of church and state. We just made an elaborate show out of the song, "The Twelve Days of Christmas," which doesn't have any religion to it—just presents.

There were twelve of us kids, each one singing a particular line every time it came up and then coming in all together on the "partridge in a pear tree." I was number five, singing "Five gold rings" because I was still a boy soprano and I could hit that high note pretty nicely, if I do say so myself.

Some kids didn't know why Christmas had twelve days, but I explained that on the twelfth day after Christmas, which was January sixth, the Three Wise Men arrived with gifts for the Christ child. Naturally, it was on January sixth that we put on the show in the auditorium, with as many parents there as wanted to come.

Dad got a few hours off and was sitting in the audience with Mom. I could see him getting set to hear his son's clear high note for the last time because next year my voice changes or I know the reason why.

Did you ever get an idea in the middle of a stage show and have to continue, no matter what?

We were only on the second day, with its "two turtledoves," when I thought, "Oh, my, it's the *thirteenth* day of Christmas." The whole world was shaking around me and I couldn't do a thing but stay on the stage and sing about five gold rings.

I didn't think they'd ever get to those "twelve drummers drumming." It was like having itching powder on instead of underwear—I couldn't stand still. Then, when the last note was out, while they were still applauding, I broke away, went jumping down the steps from the platform and up the aisle, calling, "Dad!"

He looked startled, but I grabbed him, and I think I was babbling so fast that he could hardly understand.

I said, "Dad, Christmas isn't the same day everywhere. It could be one of the Soviet's own people. They're officially atheist, but maybe one of them is religious and he wants to place the bomb for that reason. Only he would be a member of the *Russian* Orthodox Church. They don't go by our calendar."

"What?" said Dad, looking as though he didn't understand a word I was saying.

"It's *so*, Dad. I read about it. The Russian Orthodox Church is still on the Julian Calendar, which the West gave up for the Gregorian Calendar centuries ago. The Julian Calendar is thirteen days behind ours. The Russian Orthodox Christmas is on *their* December twenty-fifth, which is *our* January seventh. It's *tomorrow*."

He didn't believe me, just like that. He looked it up in the almanac, then he called up someone in the Department who was Russian Orthodox.

He was able to get the Department moving again. They talked to the Soviets, and once the Soviets stopped talking about Zionists and looked at themselves, they got the man. I don't know what they did with him, but there was no bombing on the thirteenth day of Christmas, either.

The Department wanted to give me a new bicycle for Christmas, but I turned it down. I told them I was just doing my duty.

COLLECTIONS OF TALES FROM THE MASTERS OF MYSTERY, HORROR AND SUSPENSE

Edited by Carol-Lynn Rössel Waugh, Martin Harry Greenberg and Isaac Asimov

Each volume boasts a list of celebrated authors such as Isaac Asimov, Ray Bradbury, Ron Goulart, Ellery Queen, Dorothy Sayers, Rex Stout and Julian Symons, with an introduction by Isaac Asimov.

MURDER ON THE MENU   86918-7/$3.50
This gourmet selection offers a fabulous feast of sixteen deliciously wicked tales, sure to please the palate of everyone with a taste for mystery, menace and murder.

SHOW BUSINESS IS MURDER   81554-0/$2.75
Get the best seat in the house for the most entertaining detective fiction from Hollywood to Broadway. The curtain's going up on murders that ought to be in pictures, and crimes that take center stage for excitement.

THIRTEEN HORRORS OF HALLOWEEN   84814-7/$2.95
Here are a devil's dozen ghoulish delights, filled with bewitching tales of murder and the macabre.

THE BIG APPLE MYSTERIES   80150-7/$2.75
An anthology of thirteen detective stories set in the vibrant, electric—and sometimes dangerous—city of New York.

THE TWELVE CRIMES OF CHRISTMAS   78931-0/$2.50
When twelve masters get into the holiday spirit, it's time to trim the tree, deck the halls...and bury the bodies. Here are a dozen baffling tales of murder and mischief committed during the so-called merry season.

AVON Paperbacks